Cinnamon Toast and the End of the World

Born in Nova Scotia, Janet E. Cameron moved to Ireland in 2005 after she met her husband, an Irish journalist, while travelling in Japan. She has completed a Master of Philosophy in Creative Writing at Trinity College, Dublin and has been short-listed for the Fish Short Story Prize (2008) and the Fish Short Memoir Prize (2012). She has also published an adaptation of *A Midsummer Night's Dream* for younger ESL (English as a Second Language) learners (2010, Black Cat Publishing, Genoa). She now teaches part-time at Dublin Business School. *Cinnamon Toast and the End of the World* is her first novel.

www.asimplejan.com
@ASimpleJan

CINNAMON TOAST AND THE END OF THE WORLD

A Novel

Janet E. Cameron

HACHETTE
BOOKS
IRELAND

First published in 2013 by Hachette Books Ireland

Copyright © Janet E. Cameron 2013

A CIP catalogue record for this title is available from the British Library.

ISBN 978 1444 74396 8

Typeset in AGaramond, Gabriola and Gill Sans Condensed by Bookends Publishing Services. Printed and bound by CPI Group (UK) Ltd, Croydon, CR0 4YY.

Hachette Books Ireland policy is to use papers that are natural, renewable and recyclable products and made from wood grown in sustainable forests. The logging and manufacturing processes are expected to conform to the environmental regulations of the country of origin.

Hachette Books Ireland
8 Castlecourt Centre
Castleknock
Dublin 15, Ireland

A division of Hachette UK Ltd.
338 Euston Road
London NW1 3BH

www.hachette.ie

To John and Nettie – with love and thanks

Cinnamon Toast

'It's not the end of the world.'

That's what people will tell you. That's what people will tell you when they want to say, 'Your problems are stupid, your reaction to them is laughable, and I would like you to go away now.'

'Oh, Stephen, for God's sake, it's not the end of the world,' my mother will say, over and over, in tones of sympathy or distraction. Or sometimes plain impatience.

So of course if she's ever running around looking for her keys and cursing, I'll always tell her, 'It's not the end of the world, Mom.' And if she's really been pissing me off, I'll scoop the keys up from wherever she's left them and stick them in my coat pocket. Then I'll settle back to watch with a sympathetic expression while she tears the house apart looking. Lost keys? Not the end of the world.

I'm not an asshole to my mother all the time, by the way. It's just sort of a hobby. There's really not a lot to do in my town.

Anyway, what I'm trying to say is, 'not the end of the world' is utter bullshit. Sometimes it really is the end of the world. Sure, everything's continuing the same as it ever did, but there's been a shift. Suddenly you don't know what the rules are. People will do things that leave you baffled. Or maybe you'll surprise yourself, start acting like a person you don't recognise. And you have to live in it now, this new world. You can't ever go back.

The end of the world doesn't have to be floods and fires and screaming and Nostradamus and the Mayans hanging around looking smug. It can be, say, two o'clock in the morning in the TV room in the basement with the light from the screen freezing all the cigarette smoke into shapes like ectoplasm. My best friend Mark leans forward to light another cigarette and – boom – the world ends.

Do you ever get these mental images – impulses, whatever – of things you wouldn't ever do in real life? Like, suppose you're sitting at your desk watching the shyest girl in the whole school (Rachel Clements!) giving some kind of speech, and then she forgets what to say next – not because she didn't prepare or anything, just because she's scared. So, you're dying of sympathy for her and clenching and unclenching your fist in nervous tension, watching this poor girl up there sweating and stammering away. But at the same time another part of your brain is looking at the pink rubber eraser on your desk and thinking, *Throw it at her*. And you can see yourself doing it, bouncing that thing right off her forehead. Boing!

Okay, maybe it's just me who thinks this way. But the point is, I'd never do these things. These mental blips. Who knows where they come from or how to stop them? And if you don't, is it the end of the world?

Anyway, it was two in the morning on Saturday night in April, and me and Mark were drinking cans that had gone all warm from sitting in our backpacks, because it's not like we could walk right up and stick them in the fridge in front of my mom, right? And smoking. Smoking my mother's brand, so if she ever finds them, I can blame it on her. Once I spent a whole afternoon with a big pile of used butts and one of

Mom's lipsticks, marking each one with her colour. The idea was she'd find them and think she'd gone on some kind of crazed smoking bender and blacked out.

Didn't work. I started feeling guilty and just threw them in the trash.

So me and Mark were in the basement, tired and stupid, laughing at the infomercials on TV, buzzing from the beer and working our way through that red pack of Du Maurier Lights like it was some kind of assignment. These are my favourite times, but it's kind of hard to explain why. If you're up that late, you're probably alone or with somebody you've always known, I guess. Or maybe it's because there's no light changing, so it's as if you're in this little corner of the world that's safe from time. That hour of night has always felt perfect to me. Perfect to be doing the same old shit or doing nothing at all.

Mark's been my best friend forever, since my parents moved here when I was eight. We fell into routines that lasted years. Saturday nights we'd go to my place and watch TV till we passed out wrapped in old sleeping bags on the two disintegrating couches in the basement. I'd take the green one with the mildew stains and he'd take the orange one the neighbours didn't want. Sundays we'd wander the streets of our little town – usually high on cheap home-grown weed – and we'd end up at his place and eat stuff spooned out of cans until I had to go back and do my homework. And Mark's homework too, he's not great at school.

Neither of us ever planned this, of course. It's not like we'd say, 'Hey, it's three o'clock, we better hurry or we'll miss getting chased out of the parking lot behind Sunset Manor by that old guy with the Sherlock Holmes hat and his fat yellow half-blind dog who can barely bark anymore.' But for years, if you wanted to find us at three o'clock on a Sunday afternoon, that's where we'd be. It happened without us making any kind of arrangement, like birds going south for the winter know how to fly in a V.

I never even thought about whether we liked each other. I mean, how do you feel about oxygen?

That Saturday night, Mark lit another cigarette. His hand was cupped around the flame to shelter it – long habit from mostly smoking outside – and there was a flicker of warm light on his face. Everything else was frozen in the flat white beam of the television screen, like we were on the surface of the moon.

It reminded me of going camping with my father that one time, when I was a little kid, just before he left. We'd built a fire together. Yellow and orange flames nodding and weaving, embers floating up. You could hear the ocean a long way off. The dark sky opened out into trails and clusters of galaxies over our heads, and every once in a while a spark would give a satisfied cracking pop, as if this were a live thing in front of us stretching itself with contentment. The two of us there, with our tiny hearthglow at the edge of the world. Safe from time. I couldn't talk. I was too happy. I didn't want to ruin it. There was always something that could ruin it.

A quiver of that feeling came back, watching Mark's face, quick firelight against the bleached glare of the TV. A campfire on the moon. Don't say anything. Don't ruin it.

I was hanging off the couch looking at him through the smoke, the ghost-in-a-bottle smoke.

And that's when I kissed him.

Except of course I didn't. It was just something that happened in my head, like seeing myself throwing erasers at Rachel Clements. One of those strange little impulses. But so vivid and real. I could almost feel it, our teeth knocking together because I wouldn't know what I was doing at first, the way our faces would look all weird being so close. He'd taste like stale beer and Du Maurier Lights and so would I.

Nothing happened. Nobody moved. The TV continued to broadcast images of a miraculous food processor into my house. Mark kept making sarcastic comments about it. The few streetlamps outside were still probably beaming cones of misty light against the dark, and my mother was more than likely sleeping peacefully upstairs. Pretty quiet for the end of the world.

Mark leaned against the sofa, taking an easy swig off the beer, letting white smoke drift from his lips. In the TV kitchen, people with big teeth and lacquered hair hovered around the food processor like they were at a party waiting for a chance to talk to it. More blades and attachments kept getting added to the offering, fanned on a white counter before us. All for this amazing low price.

'Stephen? You asleep?'

Kind of a stupid thing for Mark to say because I was sitting up with my eyes open. I glanced at him quick, smoke curled around his fingers like mist at the foot of a mountain. It hurt to breathe.

The sleeping bag was draped across my shoulders. I pulled it tighter and hauled myself to my feet.

'I gotta go. Gotta go to the can.'

I shambled up to my room alone. The laces of the sleeping bag trailed on the floor after me.

My room was a cold place. I'd moved all my stuff in here when I was twelve, thinking I wasn't a kid anymore and it was time to start over. This used to be the guest room. It still felt like one. There was nothing on the white walls but a calendar from the Royal Bank. For years I had a bikini girl on a beach pinned up by the window, the first thing you'd see as you opened my door. She fell down a few months ago and I never bothered putting her up again.

I lay on the bed with my clothes on, knees pulled into my chest like I thought I could make myself into a dot that would get smaller and then disappear.

I'd kissed exactly one person before, a girl at a party a couple of years ago. We were both drunk – there wasn't a lot of motor control involved. I remember she'd been eating ketchup chips. It was nothing like the scene I'd just imagined.

An image out of nowhere. Completely random. No idea where it came from. Oh, right. Total bullshit. When I did things like imagine throwing erasers at Rachel Clements, I'd be surprised at myself. I would not feel half sick because I wanted it so much.

And if I'm honest …

It wasn't the first time I'd had these thoughts. Not the first time, not even the thousandth. Ever since I was a kid, I'd had this stuff in my head. Ever since I was eleven or twelve I'd been telling it to go away, waiting to wake up and have it gone.

So what was different about tonight?

It was the light on Mark's face. It was the extra hours of day now that it was spring. It was having less than three months of high school left. It was the TV and the smoke and the stale, flat taste of beer and my mother asleep upstairs and what I'd just said, and what he'd just said, and the food processor on the screen, turning the resources of the earth into pureed mush. It was everything.

I kissed him. He kissed me back. We came up for air and sat with our foreheads resting together, breathing into the silence, hands moving over each other's faces. A few seconds of perfect certainty. The end. Roll the credits.

I swore and punched myself in the head.

He'd kill me.

Mark hated fags, queers, anything to do with that. How did I think he'd react if I sidled up and planted one on him? I'd end my days with my head split open on that concrete floor in front of the TV. Nice mess of blood and brains and failure for someone to mop up in the morning.

The stain would never go away. It would be like those children's stories where you follow the adventures of a statue or a tin soldier, and at the end they get thrown in the fire with the trash. After the burning, there's always something that remains. A heart, a little silver key. I imagined my mother would try to sell the house, have some real estate agent walking people too quickly through the basement, trying to explain it away: the shape of my love splattered onto the floor.

Love. Is that what I'm calling it?

Remember when I said I'd never thought about whether me and Mark actually liked each other? When I said it was the same as oxygen, that you inhale it without even knowing it's there?

Bullshit again.

I knew I liked oxygen. In fact there was a good chance I loved it. And it occurred to me that it would be nice to be able to breathe. Nice to be able to breathe without somebody thinking I was doing something disgusting just to spite them.

The window was a square of darkness, then it was full of cautious grey light that quietly shifted into blue. I heard a rush of water in the sink downstairs, chirps of cupboard doors opening and closing. My mother. A smart little clack as she loaded the tape player on the counter

7

with her favourite Sunday-morning tune: the Velvet Underground with 'Sunday Morning'.

I sat on the edge of my bed and blinked into the light. I'd been sitting there for hours. When I finally got up, it felt like I'd forgotten how to walk.

Mark was at the kitchen table with my mother, wearing my father's old suit jacket and eating cinnamon toast.

Cinnamon toast is my mother's thing. Her background is Russian, so really we should be having, I don't know, brown bread and pickles or porridge made of old copies of *Pravda* or whatever they eat over there. It was all these British children's books she'd grown up with. I read the same ones when I was a kid. Taught herself how to make cinnamon toast after she read about the Famous Five or some other band of English schoolkids preparing it on a campfire for one of their endless little picnics.

Cinnamon toast. She told me she'd loved the sound of the words. 'Didn't know what it was,' she said, 'but I knew I had to have it.'

So there was Mark, chowing down on Enid Blyton food, in my father's jacket with the leather patches on the elbows, big seventies lapels. The physical fact of him was making me uncomfortable. He was shoving toast in his face – a mess of crumbs sprinkled over the table and a light glaze of butter coating his chin. I leaned against the counter with my elbows grazing the sink. Mom left the kitchen to check something in the wash.

Sun on his hair, big hands curled around a blue-striped mug with chipped edges. His shadow was cut out on a square of sunlight on the table behind him, with the shadow of the floating steam rising, and watery lines of heat from the cup's surface. Mark looked up at me and I turned away.

'Hey, what happened last night?'

'What do you mean?' I pretended to rub my eyes.

'You just took off. Had to get rid of all the butts and cans myself and I didn't know what to do with them, so …' He held up his backpack, which was swollen with garbage. Our Sunday morning ritual of getting rid of the evidence from Saturday. I had a hundred places around the house to stash it all. But today I'd left him to deal with that alone.

'Fell asleep upstairs. Sorry.' I stared into the yellow and green linoleum at my feet. I'd never had to work at having a conversation with Mark before.

'You'll be late,' I said.

He glanced at our clock, a plastic daisy on the wall.

'Shit. You're right. Ten minutes.' Mark stood up, slung his backpack over his shoulder and stuck a piece of cinnamon toast in his mouth. He mumbled something about returning the jacket and was out the door in seconds.

Striding down the driveway munching on a piece of toast, with the sun falling on the shoulders of my father's coat. Off to church. Mark's belief in God tended to waver in and out depending on how he felt about himself and life in general. But he never missed a service at St Andrew's Presbyterian. 'It's forty minutes out of the week where you're concentrating on *not* being a selfish dickhead,' he'd told me once. 'Everything else is mostly pushing in the other direction.'

I realised my mother was standing beside me. Weird how she'd always seemed so tall when I was a little kid, and now she was barely up to my shoulder. At this rate I'll be able to carry her around in a shoebox by the time she's seventy. Well, I'll save on old people's homes, anyway.

'So, Mom. Is this some freaky hormonal thing, dressing teenage boys up like your ex-husband?'

She laughed and wrapped her hands around a mug of tea for warmth. My mother is fair-haired and light, fine-boned. It would be nice if I looked more like her, but I'm dark and angular like my father, all bumping elbows and jutting knees. You'd want to fold me up and stack me in a corner. Mom was in flannel pyjamas, with her hair down her back in light brown waves and a bathrobe I remembered from early childhood. It'd been turquoise back then. I wasn't sure what colour I'd call it now.

'He didn't have time to go home and change for church,' she said.

'He should just keep it. It's not like I'm going to wear it.'

'Doesn't really fit you, does it? You don't have the shoulders.' She ambled over to the tape player and rewound the cassette.

'So … what were you guys talking about when I came in?' I said.

Mom tweaked opened a cupboard door, gazed into it for a moment and then seemed to forget why she was there. I had to ask her again.

'Oh,' she said. 'Mark? The usual. Cooking. He wants to make supper for his little sister tomorrow.'

The sounds of 'Sunday Morning' started to fill the kitchen once more, innocent musicbox notes of the intro, then Lou Reed's drifting drugged-up voice talking about wasted years and a restless feeling by his side, telling us to watch out. The world was behind us.

We moved around each other. The room should have felt bigger with Mark gone, but I was still acting like he was there, sitting invisibly at the table with a plate of crumbs in front of him. After a while, Mom decided she'd had enough cinnamon toast and it was time to go off and do something else. Left me alone with this empty feeling whirling around inside.

I felt drained, lifeless. I was sure that everything was ruined. I'd never feel the same way around Mark. It would never be easy and comfortable between us again.

I was right, as it turned out.

Now, you tell me that's not the end of the world.

Part 1
The past is right behind you

Chapter 1

So tired I felt like something freeze-dried, brine shrimp in an envelope sold off to children as Sea Monkeys. Mark would be in church by now, talking to God. He'd be expecting us to meet up afterwards – it was almost time for the next phase of our hectic weekend schedule, the part where we'd get stoned and then wander around town annoying old people. The guy in the Sherlock Holmes hat was waiting with his wheezy dog outside Sunset Manor. Just another Sunday.

I stared into the sink, hypnotised by the shapes of mugs and dishes rolling against each other. Then I pushed them aside, stuck my head under the tap, and turned on the cold water. It flowed over my neck and face, soaked my hair. Cold and perfect. I shuddered. At times when I am a bit overwhelmed, I find that this is a very, very good thing to do. My skull sank to rest on an empty tea mug and the water kept coming.

Then it stopped. My mother was gazing down at me.

'Are you okay, honey?'

'I'm fine.'

'Your head's in the sink.'

'It is?' I started to laugh. Mom lifted her reading glasses so she could rub her eyes. I stared up at her like a landed fish.

'Stephen. You can tell me anything, you know.'

'Fine. Go away.'

'Oh, for God's sake.'

'You just said I could tell you anything.'

She twisted the tap and the water rushed down at me again.

'Don't drown, you little so-and-so.'

After a minute, I turned off the tap, stretched out blindly and grabbed the end of a roll of paper towels so I wouldn't get soaked when I stood up. The daisy clock was still ticking forward. I padded into the sewing room and apologised to my mother for being a jerk. She told me I was dripping on her and I should find something constructive to do.

So I sneaked out back for a cigarette.

I had to step carefully – in April our yard was mostly mud and flat yellowish grass, plus whatever had been stuck in the snow banks all winter coming out to get to know us again. There were sheets hanging on the line. Good. It would keep me out of view of the house. The sun was bouncing off them, flapping walls of white light. I had a seat on the big block of wood we use for chopping up logs. It was cold, but I like to be a little bit cold.

Sun on my face. And the wind such a calm, patient thing moving through the tree branches. You could imagine touching it, like a horse's back.

This is where I lived. Riverside, Nova Scotia (population 1,816). The kind of place where all those movies about small-town America seem to get filmed. You know the kind I'm talking about. The camera rambles down the street and you see people chirping greetings and friendly chitchat at each other, waving from their houses, old people raking leaves, with a soundtrack of quick, bouncy notes on the strings. For a horror movie just run the same scene but add a slow, tense cello.

I was falling asleep behind this maze of sheets with a lit cigarette in my hand.

So, was my life comedy or horror? I'd prefer a horror movie. At least you know what you're dealing with there. Something low-budget and tacky. Bad costumes, bad special effects. *It Came from the Commune.*

The commune. That was where I grew up, before we came to Riverside. Wasn't really a commune, though, just a place we lived. Down a dirt road on the side of the north mountain off the bay, me and my parents and about twenty others in ramshackle houses a few minutes' walk from each other. There were a couple of cleared pastures and abandoned farms – otherwise it was all trees. My family lived in a dome made up of triangles of wood stuck together. The windows were triangles too, like eyes in a pumpkin on Halloween. The electricity only worked sometimes. No TV, of course. My father hated it.

It was quiet there. I remember it was always quiet. You could hear the sea. You could hear somebody walking down the road a hundred feet away or the horses swishing their tails or the goats nannering to each other. At night, the stars were huge and if it was a full moon everything was lit up like day.

The last time I went down to see the old place, the roof had fallen in, and the triangle eyes just stared.

In the field behind the old Higgins farm, the grass used to be taller than your head. If you were seven years old, that is. I remember this one afternoon in late summer. I was crouching there with the high, green sheaths all around me, watching a grasshopper and trying to keep very still. School was over for the day. It was August, but I had school in the summer and any time Mom wasn't busy with her job in the Valley. We'd sit on the floor by the woodstove with books and scribblers and rolls of newsprint to draw on, working our way through the Nova Scotia Elementary School curriculum, just the two of us. My father was the one who was supposed to be doing this because he was brilliant and all, and he only had to be at the university two days a week. But the whole thing bored him.

The wind had riffled the tall grass, tossed the Black-eyed Susans with their funny domed centres. The grasshopper was watching me. I held my breath. Then I lunged and cupped my hand over the bug, slid my other hand under, tearing up bits of grass. I could feel him jumping around in the space I'd made with my hands.

I ran to show my best friend Dylan and almost tripped over her, lying quiet and straight five feet away. The little girl from down the road. I'd known her since I could talk. Her mom was always dressing her in sparkly head scarves and she was wearing one that day, and a long flowered blue skirt over red sneakers. Dylan said we should go to her place and get a jar so it could be the grasshopper's house. We could name him Pigeon, she said. Very dumb. Rocket was his real name.

We were always together like that. If Dylan was going somewhere and she wanted me to follow, she'd wave her empty hand and I'd come running up and take it.

When we got to the edge of the field, I realised Rocket was gone – no point in going to Dylan's house now. We changed direction and went down to the brook, where we lay with our faces on the water blowing bubbles and chewing on peppermint leaves. Dylan remembered there were baby goats at her neighbours' farm so we took off in that direction, but then we saw a group of the big girls having an argument with Dylan's sister Summer and we had to stop. It looked like Summer was going to get a pounding and that would be very, very good to see. (The 'big girls' were really only about twelve or thirteen, but to us at seven they were practically gods. And like gods, you had your favourites and the ones you'd curse with shaking fists. Dylan and I had already spent a good part of our lives cursing Summer.)

They were all in a patch of woods at the edge of the pasture. Summer was scowling, with her back to a rock covered in patches of papery yellow lichen.

'Well, you've seen horses doing it, right?'

'Yeah, but it's different for people.' A dark wispy girl named Andromeda was facing her down. The other girls watched.

'You're so stupid,' said Summer, and she twisted her head scarf tighter. Andromeda spat her gum into the grass.

'Come on, Summer. I saw my dad's. It doesn't look like that at all.'

'It gets hard when they want to do it with a girl. It changes.'

Everybody laughed. Summer looked like she'd been cheated of something. She noticed me and Dylan at the edge of the group.

'Oh, you think it's funny?' she said. 'I can prove it. Stephen, c'mere.'

'Whoa-no!' I took off at a run. Summer tackled me, pinned me to the ground. I thrashed and Dylan kicked at her, and the other girls seemed confused about which of us they should be helping. Dylan bit her sister on the arm. She screamed and let me go. The two of us went pelting down the dirt road together.

Behind my old house there was a maple with a tyre swing and we clambered into the tree's branches and waited for the big girls. We decided to chew up leaves and spit them into their hair, did a couple for practice and watched them plop onto the ground. Dark fizzy frogs dripping slime. I asked Dylan if we should tell on her sister.

She took a leathery wad of maple out of her mouth. 'Nah. I don't think Summer was really gonna do anything to your wiener, Stephen. She just wanted to win.'

I had to agree. Usually stuff like this never happened. The worst about being practically the only boy was getting married so many times when the girls played at weddings, but even that wasn't too bad. You just had to stand there bored out of your mind and say yes every time somebody asked you a question.

We stayed in the tree for a while. The sun dappled our hands and I watched an inchworm rearing up on a twig in front of me. We spat a few more leaf bombs onto the ground. Then there was music coming from my house.

'Oh, neato!' said Dylan. We had to go in.

The dome of my house was a circle wrapping itself around us. We had rugs on the walls. We had a couch and a table and a record player, a swing hanging from the ceiling. There was plastic over the triangle windows instead of glass – it made everything seem fuzzy, like the people in the field outside were something you were dreaming. That day the whole place smelled like vegetable soup.

My mom was in jeans and one of my father's T-shirts, her hair coiled on top of her head and a pencil stuck in there to hold it. Dylan leaped onto a chair behind her so she could take that pencil out. I was convinced my mother was the prettiest person on the mountain, with her neat little face and narrow cat's eyes. She'd leave for work at her office job in the Valley in high boots and swirly skirts and thin tight sweaters and I was very proud of her.

Mom laughed as the pencil went sliding out of her hair. Dylan was bouncing on the chair. 'Dance with me, Maryna!'

'Well, all right.' A little smile, my mother was almost blushing. She took both Dylan's warm pink hands in hers and they swayed and bobbed to the song on the record player – 'S.O.S.', Dylan's favourite.

Then the screen door banged and my father was home, in his corduroy jacket with the patches on the elbows, a sheaf of folders under his arm.

'Well,' he said, 'this is quite the ruckus. Quite the ruckus you're cooking up here.' But he was smiling, in that absent way he had. He walked in through the noise, hit a switch on the record player and the needle reared up and settled back on its little stand. I jumped onto the table so I'd be tall enough to kiss him hello. There was only a small space under his eye where you could do this; his beard was getting out of control again.

'Hey, buddy-bear.' My father rested his hand on my head for a moment.

'Hi, Stanley.' We put our foreheads together so it looked like he only had one big eye and I laughed.

I remember my father in those days as someone tall and twisty, long arms and legs and bright brown eyes, with wiry dark hair he'd gather in a ponytail or carry in a cloud around his head. His friends called him Spider. He insisted I call him Stanley or Stan. No father names. He wanted everybody to be on an equal footing in this family, he always told me. 'Like friends.'

'Not on the table, honey,' my mother said. Stan picked me up under my armpits and lowered me to the floor, then pushed a chair to one side so he could wrap his arms around Mom as she stood at the counter cutting slices of brown bread.

'You had a shower,' she said, breathing him in.

'Course. Used the gym at school. Not like the rest of you savages out here.'

We didn't have a shower in our house. We had to use the one at Dylan's every few days, or else we'd just sponge ourselves off over a tub of water heated on the woodstove. There was no flush toilet in the dome either: just a board with a couple of holes in a tiny wooden shed out back – take a deep breath before you go in and hold it!

Stanley was talking about his classes, how well they were going. 'Kids are all terrified of me. Should do something to make it worse, eh? Put slow-burning fuses in my beard.'

'Like Blackbeard,' I said. We'd been reading about pirates together and I thought he'd be pleased I'd remembered. He glanced back, asked me what Blackbeard's real name was.

'Edward Teach?'

Stan nodded at me slowly. I felt my shoulders start to relax.

Dylan went home and we ate soup at the table that Mom had wiped clean of my footprints. When it was dark, Stanley took out his guitar. I sang with him. 'Satellite of Love' was our favourite because I liked the part about 'Monday, Tuesday, Wednesday and Thursday'. He was smoking marijuana. I knew what it was, of course, even as a kid. He'd told me over and over that it was just for relaxing and only for adults. He didn't need to say this because I hated it so much: the smell, and what it did to his eyes and voice. He'd been really nice to us that night, though, so I didn't run off like I usually did when he brought out those thin white papers and plastic bags.

In bed that night I listened to my mother wash the dishes and waited for the moment when she'd throw the used-up water from the basin into the sink and it sounded like it was going to fall on my head. I always loved that. Sound bounced around strangely in our circle house. I could hear my mother humming, and the clear plastic on the triangle window of my little room puffing out and breathing in with the wind, like a sail on a ship. My bed was built into the side of the house. Nothing could move it. I fell asleep.

The next day was my birthday.

Eight felt older than seven. Something about those two circles sitting solidly on top of each other. A good number. My parents took me and Dylan off the mountain to see *Star Wars* for my birthday treat. The Death Star blew up and the whole audience went crazy. My father jumped to his feet and cheered. After the movie, I ran up and down the streets with Dylan, and we spied on the people in the stores and pretended to be Luke in his X-wing fighter. We made a promise to have a day just like this for her birthday too, and every year after that until we were old.

But by the end of the week, Dylan was gone.

Her parents had been planning to move away for a while. Nobody had told the kids because they didn't want us to spend weeks moping and crying and carrying on. I moped and cried and carried on anyway. I'd known Dylan for as long as I'd been able to form memories. How could she be leaving, just because her mom and dad felt like living somewhere else?

The day of the move came. I was almost offended by how normal it all was. Saying goodbye forever turned out to be like preparing for any long car ride – loading and reloading, doors not closing right, people forgetting things and having to go to the bathroom at the last minute. Mom and I watched their rattling grey truck pull onto the dirt road, Dylan waving out the back window at me until they were out of sight.

I thought I'd feel better the next day. I didn't.

Poking through their empty house, up and down the dirt road by myself – I felt hollow. But I didn't have time to dwell on it.

We were next.

Chapter 2

No sound except the sheets on the line snapping in the wind, or a tangle of birds somewhere over my head. Half-asleep, sitting on this wooden block with a cigarette between my fingers burned down to the filter.

Back to the house. Maybe I could force myself to study.

I plodded into the living room, where the whole Grade Twelve curriculum was spread out over two card tables for me like a wedding buffet. The command centre of my super-villain headquarters. Most kids saw high school as a place for having fun and being with your friends, and the stuff you were asked to do in classes was like rent – you paid it so you'd be allowed to continue to stay there, and to keep the authorities off your back. I'd fallen into a different trap. They got me early on with those gold stars. Gold stars on white paper when I was a kid. I was addicted. Especially later when they became invisible.

Now I had three months left to collect the last few.

I couldn't go upstairs and study in my bedroom, of course. There'd be too much temptation to revert to my natural state of existence: whacking off, falling asleep, and reading books I'd already read. I was capable of amusing myself in small enclosed spaces for indefinite periods of time. I would have made a pretty good hamster.

Anyway.

Still had no idea what I was going to say to Mark when he got back from church. I flipped through the pages of my math textbook, collapsed into my chair and spun myself around until I was nauseated.

'Hey, Mom!'

She answered me from upstairs. Yes? What did I want?

'Hey, Mom! My whole life is fucked.'

'You don't have to swear.' I heard a door pull firmly shut.

Was it always? Fucked, I mean. I thought back again to when I was a kid. I'd just turned eight, lost my best friend and moved to Riverside, to this house. And that was when the trouble really started.

Being a child always felt like a trick to me, some kind of scam. Looking back, I can't even picture myself as a little kid. I think of a *Peanuts* line drawing instead – something with wide bracketed eyes and a big round head, that goggled up at people and was bewildered, easily fooled, always a bit scared. Waiting for the four panels and the punchline to be over so I could stop being part of someone else's joke.

Mom and I had held hands as we walked to school together in the damp morning air. I was about to start Grade Three at Riverside Regional Elementary. This would be very good for me, she'd said. There'd be lots of other children. All kinds of friends.

She was right about the children. I'd never seen so many in one place. The playground went on forever, with kids climbing complicated metal structures, swooping on towering swing sets, the chains creaking and groaning. Everybody seemed like they were in a contest to see who could be the loudest. I guess that's how you proved you were having fun.

But friends? No. None of these kids wanted to be friends with me. I didn't blame them. I kept doing everything wrong.

First of all, we were late, Mom and me, huddled in the doorway while the class was standing for 'O Canada'. I was still holding her hand, which was another mistake, and when the teacher reminded my mother that I was starting classes five weeks into the school year, Mom just smiled and said that it didn't matter. I didn't need any review, in fact I was at least two years ahead of these other kids and really should be starting Grade Five. I could feel a whispery rumbling noise behind me, everybody starting to shuffle and talk.

I looked wrong too. The other kids were cool – the girls pretty as teacups in little dresses and coloured tights, the boys all T-shirts and jeans and jean jackets, like a page from the Sears catalogue. (Except one, slouching at the back of the class in a big army-coloured coat, definitely not part of this group.) Nobody was wearing a scratchy sweater with a pattern of Christmas trees on the front. Or green corduroys that rolled up and belled weirdly around the ankles. Nobody had a book-bag their mother had sewn for them, blue with a red felt S. Nobody but me.

Later, I was working at my desk when I got bored and forgot where I was for a second and started singing. Everyone laughed. The teacher told me to apologise because I'd disrupted the class. When I wrote the date in my scribbler (October 15, 1977) the letters looked wobbly and weird, as if something had got inside me and was changing everything that came out. I could not seem to stop making these terrible mistakes.

So I understood why nobody was in much of a hurry to be my friend. Mom said it was just a bad first day. But every day after that was pretty much the same.

A group of girls would come up to me at recess or lunch, stand around in a semi-circle and ask questions in bored, flat voices, like they were taking a census. Blowing bubbles with their gum, taking it out of their mouths to look at, putting it back again.

'Heard your parents aren't even married. That true?'

'Why do you wear those clothes?'

'If your parents aren't married, how do you know your father's really your father? Your father could be anybody, right?'

'Your mom buys your clothes at Frenchy's, doesn't she? They sell dead people's stuff there.'

'Why can't you throw a ball?'

'Why do you always know the answer in class but you act like such a retard when anybody tries to talk to you?'

'Do you have mental problems? My mom says kids whose parents aren't married have mental problems.'

I asked my parents about some of the stuff the girls had been saying.

'Married?' Mom seemed worried. 'Well, we were planning on it. Sometime this year. You know, it would be better from a legal standpoint, better for you. We were talking about this, right, Stanley?'

My father sighed like he was blowing a bug off his arm. He was leaning on the kitchen counter, staring down at the funny pages of the newspaper.

'We were thinking about having some kind of wedding at the end of December.' She was folding and unfolding her hands. 'Or February, maybe? Stan?'

He flicked aside a newsprint page full of coloured squares. I didn't want to be in that room anymore.

Every day I'd ask my mother when we could go home. Must have driven her crazy. 'But we already *are* home,' she'd tell me, smiling. I'd look at her as if she was hiding something.

October 1977 became November. November turned into December. The ground froze and crunched under us and we wore the tops of our snowsuits to school. I learned how to deal with the girls. It took a while, but eventually I trained myself so I could just switch a channel in my head and stop listening.

The boys were different.

Lunchtime was safe because I could fasten myself to the teacher on yard duty and nobody would go near me. Recess was safe too. Bathrooms were safe if I was quick. But there was still the walk home from school.

From a distance you might think I was really popular, a crowd of guys buzzing around me, some on bikes and some walking, even a few big kids from Grade Six.

'Hey, Spaz.'

'Hey, Retard.'

'Hey, Faggot.'

'He looked! He knows his name!'

'Are you a faggot, Stephen?'

My fault. Shouldn't have turned my head. Usually I'd make my face go dead and keep my eyes on the end of the road. Stanley had taught me to do that.

'Ignore them,' he'd said. 'Just ignore them.'

The rest of my parents' advice was stupid.

'Laugh it off,' my mother told me. 'They'll respect you if you can laugh at yourself.'

'Next time they insult you, agree with them,' said Stan.

'I read somewhere that when people call you names, they're really talking about themselves. Maybe try telling these kids that.'

'Show them it doesn't bother you.'

I never told my parents half of what was really going on.

'Your father's a freak. Your mother's a big slut, and you're a little retard.'

'Oh, he's getting mad!'

'I know! I'm scared! I'm really scared! Help, you guys!'

Kevin Dickson, pretending to cower behind Phil Doyle. But I hadn't even looked at him.

'Are you retarded? Are you retarded, Stephen?'

'Duh. Duh. Duh.'

Just keep walking, I told myself.

If you ran, it was like admitting the truth: that this was much worse than it looked, and could turn horrible at any minute. And if you admitted the truth yourself, everybody else stopped pretending too. Then worse than bad names would happen.

Like this.

'Let's make him eat dog shit.'

I didn't get very far. They got me by the arms. Two of them. Another boy grabbed my hair and held my head back, and somebody else pried open my mouth and kept it open while I screamed.

Even then I was thinking, *They're never going to do this*. But Randy McTavish really did find a piece of it on the ground that was frozen enough to pick up, and he brought it up close to my face, and I could see it there in his red-mittened hand, and everybody was laughing, and I thought, *Oh, yes they are*.

Something hopeless happened in my head then. I went limp. Stopped screaming, stopped struggling. Gave up. I gave up.

They didn't seem interested after that.

'We weren't really gonna do it.'

'Aw, look at the little girl crying.' Some of them were making sobbing noises at me.

'Gonna tell your mommy?'

Then Randy McTavish threw the shit at my head and they all walked off to find something else to do.

That happened almost every day. Not the dog shit, but the other stuff. Yeah, just about every day.

I retraced my steps, picking up my books where they'd been tossed around the sidewalk. And my action figures: C-3P0 and the sand-person, crushed into a mud puddle close to the school. (I wouldn't have cared about the sand-person except Dylan had given it to me. She said it was actually a girl named Sandy who was married to C-3P0, which I thought was dumb, but I still wanted to keep it.)

Then I went home and had a big fight with my mother.

'Why do I have to keep going back there?' I stomped around the house, slamming doors and kicking at the walls. 'Why can't we just read the books at home like we did before?'

My mother followed me. My father hung around watching and leaning over the banister by the stairs.

'Well, Maryna?' Stan said. 'What do you want to tell him?'

'But you're enrolled,' she said. 'And I'm on full-time now. I can't just—'

'I miss Dylan. Everybody hates me here.'

'Oh, honey, I'm sure nobody hates you.'

My mother looked as if she'd been forced backwards, her legs against the lower steps, Stanley on one side of her and me on the other. She was trying to say something about how if I was patient and waited for everybody to get to know me, that I'd grow to really enjoy school and would make friends I'd have my whole life long and …

My father stood with his back turned, arms folded, laughing and shaking his head. I couldn't listen to another second, so I told them about the dog shit.

'There,' said Stanley. 'You see what kind of people these are?'

She sank down and put her head in her hands.

'You wanted him to have a normal life, Maryna. You wanted to move down here so he'd have a normal life. Are you happy now?'

'I didn't know this would happen!' She was crying, in her Mom way, tears but no sounds. 'Stephen, come here, sweetheart.'

She tried to pull me into a hug. I wanted to go to her, but I couldn't. Not with him standing over me. He had to see that I was on his side. She'd forgive me. She'd always be there. I didn't know if he would, and that was scary.

So I pushed away from her. 'Leave me alone! I hate you. You're the one who wanted to move here. This is all your fault!' It was like I was reciting lines that Stanley had written for me to say.

'Come on, buddy,' he said, looking at Mom over my head. 'Let's get C-3Po cleaned off.' My father and I shuffled off to the kitchen together, his hand grazing the back of my head. Two against one. I was being rewarded.

○

I remember being nervous all through classes the next day. I'd noticed those boys liked to make things worse as they went along, every time a little more serious, like this was a story moving towards a really great ending. The final bell rang and I was close to shaking.

But the boys who usually followed me were gone. I didn't see them in the coat room as I pulled my brown and orange snowsuit top from its swinging hanger. I didn't see them in the crowd of kids surging towards the doors. In the playground no one said a word to me. Was this luck or some danger I couldn't see? I decided to get home fast.

Then somebody was striding in my direction, big army-coloured coat like armour bulking him up. It was the scary kid, the blond boy who sat at the back of the class and didn't talk to anybody. Mark McAllister. Everybody was afraid of this guy, and nobody really knew him, always off on the sides or standing around the edges. There were rumours that if you gave him money, he'd beat people up for you.

But he'd never done anything to me, so when he came closer I smiled and said, 'Hi'.

The boy stood in front of me and glowered and didn't answer. Then he told me Phil Doyle gave him fifty cents to beat me up. I could see Phil over his shoulder, in a corner of the playground with the usual group, watching and grinning.

The blond boy's empty cuffs jutted out from his jacket. His hands were somewhere in those sleeves, probably bunched into fists. I thought about running. Or should I stay here and drop into a turtle shape and try to block him? I realised nothing had happened yet, so I asked if he was really going to do it.

He took a step backwards, shrugged.

'I don't really like Phil Doyle,' he said.

Then he turned away and started off across the playground, lost in that enormous coat. The boys in their huddle were whispering together. He glanced at me over his shoulder.

'You're coming, right?'

I was too stunned to answer. I just ran after him. We spent the fifty cents on Pop Rocks.

In the morning, Mark McAllister showed up at my place to walk to school with me, like it was the most natural thing in the world.

'That your boyfriend?' Kevin Dickson sneered at Mark when we were on our way home.

'Why? You jealous?' he shot back. When Mark insulted someone, it felt real. You got the idea he knew what Kevin was thinking and was disgusted by it.

But the fighting was the real reason people were scared of Mark. Most kids would just kick or smack at each other blindly with nothing much connecting. Mark took being violent seriously. He'd humiliate people. Make guys two or three years older than him cry in front of their friends. Nobody wanted that. So even with a crowd of kids there, not one of them would take him on.

You didn't mess with Mark. And soon that meant you didn't mess with me either. We developed this animal kingdom partnership thing. I helped him with schoolwork, which he wasn't great at, and he helped me with everything else. Life, I guess. I wasn't much good at that.

'You're acting like you're scared all the time,' he told me. 'You can be scared if you want, but don't *act* scared. It just makes people want to get you.'

'Okay.'

'And when the teacher gives you a book, don't tell her you already read it. That's snotty.'

'I didn't want to get in trouble,' I said. 'In case I had the wrong book.'

'You won't get in trouble for that,' Mark said slowly.

'Okay.'

'And that thing you did yesterday ...'

'I'm sorry.'

'When you were trying to hold my hand or something.'

'Sorry, sorry.'

'You never, ever do that again, okay?'

That was an accident. I was suddenly scared of something and I'd grabbed on to Mark's hand without thinking. It was the sort of thing I still did with my parents. Mark shook me off like I'd spat on him, and I'd apologised over and over and promised never to do it again.

One day, he came to school with a dark purple bruise under his eye.

'What happened? Did you fall down?' I reached up and traced the outline of the mark. I was being very careful not to hurt him, but he still knocked my hand away.

'Don't touch people, Stephen. It's weird.'

I said I was sorry, again. Still learning the rules. Mark leaned over and whispered in my ear. 'It was my dad.'

I thought about Mark's father, how much bigger he was than Mark. 'But that's not fair.'

'I know. You're not allowed to tell anybody.'

I kept my mouth shut. You didn't spill your friend's secrets. That was one rule I already knew.

I was fascinated by him. Very pale, a few freckles sprinkled over his nose. His eyes were blue, but not like Dylan's. They were lighter – made me think of the sky when it seemed the most far away. He was like that himself, sharp-edged like the little white airplanes that left trails across the blue and far away, even if he was right in front of you. I could spend all day just looking.

But why did Mark decide to be friends with me in the first place? I never found out, not for almost ten years.

'Stephen, think back. Did I seem like a popular kid to you?'

'Well, you were cool, anyway. Even in Grade Three.'

He'd laughed. This was just a week ago. A Sunday, the last before the world ended. We were in his dad's old workshop, mildly stoned off somebody's home-grown stash Mark had bought cheap. His father had been gone for years and he'd never used the room much anyway.

Mark was drawing faces in the sawdust on the workbench as we both leaned against it.

'Okay,' he said. 'You want to know why I started hanging around with you? This is embarrassing, but remember I was just a kid.'

He'd glanced out the narrow, cobwebby window in the corner. 'I knew you wouldn't refuse. To be my friend, I mean. I just had to stop people beating you up and you were pretty much guaranteed to want to hang out with me. And I knew you wouldn't say anything to the other kids. About me, my house, my mother. You wouldn't go around telling a bunch of secrets. Who would you tell them to, right? You were always on your own. Nobody liked you.' He shrugged. 'Sorry, but that's how I thought back then. Like I said, I was a kid.'

So, I got it, finally. Made me feel sorry for Mark the child, being so desperate. And I wasn't insulted or anything. I was glad Mark had decided to keep owing Phil Doyle fifty cents, whatever the reason.

Chapter 3

I didn't have any brothers or sisters. I had Mark and I had Lana, my
other best friend ever since I was fourteen.

It was Saturday afternoon, a week after the world ended, and I was
over at her place killing time before my babysitting job at the Healeys',
both of us cross-legged on her purple bedspread surrounded by pictures
torn from catalogues and magazines. She was making some kind of
collage, an album cover for an imaginary band. Mark was in Arnottville
with his girlfriend. I'd been avoiding him.

Last week when church was over, he'd dropped my father's jacket
over my shoulders as I lay slumped across the card table in my living
room, and I'd opened my eyes and nearly told him everything. But
I didn't. Instead I forced myself through the afternoon, smiling and
laughing, turning everything into a joke, all very painful and fake.
Mark knew something was wrong, but he didn't come out and say it. I
got the feeling he was waiting for me to tell him in my own time.

I moved back and felt Lana's bedsprings twang and adjust themselves around me. There was something wedged under my knee – a round plastic container in a muted shade of orange. Weird. I'd seen an object just like this, in my mother's purse once, when I'd been rooting around looking for smokes. The thing popped open like a seashell as I was examining it and I found myself staring into a ring of prim white tablets.

'Don't take one unless you want to grow boobs,' Lana said merrily. 'They're birth control pills!'

I froze for a pulse beat of cold horror.

Okay, I knew Mom went on dates. Occasionally. I even remembered the first one, a couple of years after Stanley left. I was eleven. 'Stephen, I'm going out to meet a *new friend*,' she'd told me, in the kitchen where the babysitter couldn't hear. 'But I won't introduce you until I'm sure it's something serious. And that goes for any other *new friend* I might make. Do you understand?'

I understood. There'd been no introductions so far.

I'd got a whiff of Mom's love life last year when I'd overheard her on the phone complaining about someone. 'But I didn't *know* he was married!' she'd said. And more. A lot more. I'd slammed my door and put a tape on, so she'd remember I was home.

Birth control pills. This meant my mother and the married guy had probably ... oh, God.

Lana chuckled to herself and angled two curving paper zucchinis over a photo of Reagan so they appeared to be bursting out of the old man's nose. She was in her usual get-up: black clothes that looked as if they weighed an awful lot, thick make-up ringing her eyes in raccoon shades, with her cheeks rice-white and her hair short and dark and twisted into spikes. The closest thing we had to punk in this town. Lana was from Toronto, so maybe she felt like she had to be an ambassador for urban life. She was also kind of solid and round. Plump, you might say. I wouldn't call her fat. Everyone else did, though.

'Great, Lana. So you're doing it now?'

'Not yet.' She shot a flirty glance towards the photograph staring numbly from her bedside table: a pale kid with thick glasses and black hair, clusters of pimples blooming on his cheekbones. Adam, the boyfriend in Halifax. Lana had told me many times that this picture had been taken before he was cool, and now the guy was an absolute rock star. They'd met in a record store when she was Christmas shopping in the city and every few weekends she'd spend hours on a bus going to see him.

'I don't know about this guy, Lana. If he's making you go on the pill …'

'Relax. It was my idea. Remember the schlong malfunction?'

Of course I did. A few months ago the two of them had been on the point of having sex at the boyfriend's place while his parents were out on a grocery run. But nothing was working for him down there and I guess he'd freaked out and said some pretty nasty things. She'd cried, telling me about it. I knew I was going to have to beat this guy up at some point. Or put in a decent attempt.

Lana looked down at her fingernails, short, ragged and flecked with black rinds of nail polish. 'Well, look,' she said. 'He told me later it was all subconscious fear, right? Because he doesn't want to get me pregnant. Now it's gonna be easy for him.'

She flicked over a page of the Sears catalogue in front of her. The men's underwear section. Sick little trap-door jolt, seeing these images here. I watched as she attacked them with a pair of scissors.

●

I went straight to the Healeys' from Lana's house. Supper waited in Tupperware containers on the kitchen counter and my six-year-old friend Kyle was in the backyard, scaling a bank of lumpy crystalline snow. I dropped my winter coat over a chair. Everything out there was still melting, drip by drip, disintegrating in beads that caught the light.

A square hardback book had been set on the table, next to a bowl piled with oranges and plums. *Chess for Children*. Jesus, this thing again. There was a copy in our house somewhere. Unless I'd burned it.

'What do you think – is he old enough?' I nearly jumped. Mrs Healey was standing in the doorway.

'I know Kyle couldn't get through the whole thing on his own yet,' she said. 'But if someone read it *to* him …' An encouraging smile.

'Sure. No problem.'

'You can change to a story or something if he doesn't like it. But maybe he will. Could even turn out to be a prodigy, huh?' She paced into the kitchen, smoothed a cloth across the spotless counter.

We watched Kyle through the window as he filled a red plastic beach bucket with soot-tinged, leftover snow. I noticed he was using a fork. Mrs Healey sighed. The stained-glass animals suspended on the pane in front of us rattled in sympathy.

After she'd left, I propped myself against the stove and started flipping through *Chess for Children*. The same cartoon figures smiled up at me, page after page of them. *Pawns are brave soldiers. Knights are clever. This game is fun!*

That's the thing about a book. You can leave it for years but it'll still be there, every detail perfect, waiting for you to come back.

It was the only game Stanley and I ever played together, and I hated it. He'd taught me the rules when I was eight. I was all excited. I thought it would be fun. It wasn't.

'Think it through, Stephen,' my father would say. 'Take your time and think it through.'

So I'd rock back and forth and look at my hands and pretend to be considering the board. Then I'd do the first thing that came into my head. And I'd lose, which always made me feel squashed and frustrated.

'But I took your horse!'

'I know. I sacrificed it.' Grinning at me.

Even losing at chess lacked a satisfying ending. Nobody ever captured the king. The point was to trap him, freeze him so that any move would be impossible. So he wouldn't get killed and he wouldn't be a prisoner. Instead he'd be stuck, looking out the palace window and realising it was all over, forever.

Later I started to understand the whole idea behind defensive strategy, and that was even worse. I couldn't make a move without anticipating how it would be punished. If I do this, he'll do that. And then this and then that. Stanley would get bored waiting for me to move and wander off. When he was out of the room, I'd cheat.

Would things have turned out differently if I'd been smarter? Better at games?

○

My parents got married in February 1978. Stanley was in jeans and his white sweater from Peru. Mom wore a pink, fluttery dress with a flower pattern, too light for the cold. We drove to another town and they signed some papers in a courthouse. Then we got back in the car and drove home. Stanley headed straight for his little study and the door banged shut behind him. My mother and I went to the kitchen together. She'd decided to make a cake.

'What's a lucky colour?' she said.

'Orange.'

A little smile, her eyes crinkling. 'Really?'

I figured orange was a good bet because it was two colours at once. One of them might be lucky. My mother dropped yellow food colouring from a tiny glass bottle into the icing while I stirred and it turned buttery and bright. Then it was a soft sunrise orange that deepened to a pumpkin shade as splashes of red fell.

'I like it,' Mom said.

This was a special occasion, so we had supper in the dining room. Stanley's ugly mood clung to everything like an extra layer of sooty air. When my mother left to get the cake, he turned and smiled at me, as if he thought I was funny.

'Well, congratulations, buddy. You're not a bastard anymore. How does it feel?'

I said I was sorry. I wasn't sure what else to do.

My mother came back into the room, without the cake. Then she was standing behind Stanley's chair and laying a hand on his shoulder.

'Don't,' she said. Her voice was low and firm and quiet.

My father sighed deeply. After a moment, he placed his hand over hers and leaned back, head against the pink flower pattern of her dress. He shut his eyes.

'Maryna.' Stanley's thin mouth was lost in that bramble of beard. 'Did we really need to do this?'

'It's done. Now don't humiliate our son.'

I put one foot on the floor. They didn't seem to notice. Mom's fingers grazed the soft dark hair just above his ear.

'Let's go for a drive,' she said.

'What's the point?'

'A walk, then.'

He agreed to go for a walk. I thought it was funny, the three of us just leaving the house for no good reason – like we'd come back to find Goldilocks asleep in one of our beds. We zipped up our winter coats and shoved our feet into boots, walked in the dark until we were huddled on a bench in a long empty park that led to the river. A thin curve of moon hung over our heads. Stanley put his arms around us both. The surfaces of our coats shifted and slid against each other, made pockets of air between us. So bundled up it would take a long time to feel anything if we fell.

When we got home, we ate square slabs of cake with orange icing. I hoped it really was a lucky colour.

Stanley spent more and more time in his study. Then one day he left. It was April, a little more than a year after the wedding, and the snow was just starting to melt. I asked Mom where he'd gone and she told me she didn't know.

Every time I picked up our mail at the post office I got nervous, thinking I might see my name on an envelope in Stanley's handwriting. But nothing like that ever appeared in the bundles of bills and magazines I brought home for Mom. After a couple of years, I stopped expecting it. Sometimes I wondered if he was dead.

When I was twelve, everybody in my year moved up to the high school.

The place was huge, bigger than a mall, and full of people who looked more like adults than children. Riverside didn't have the population for a Junior High and a Senior High. Instead we had six years in the same building – a boundless vista of boredom with no end in sight but graduation. Graduation in 1987. I was sure the farm kids would be bussed to school in rocket ships by then.

Such a strange time, those first few years at the high school. I was always hyper and buzzing with too much energy, or else I'd be exhausted, barely able to lift my head. And sometime in Grade Eight or Nine, it was like I woke up and I was taller than my mother. It felt crazy and sudden, like everything else that was going on then, scary, saddening and out of control.

Poor Mom. Spending all day typing other people's letters in an office two towns away, then back home for supper and TV with me. Very occasionally there'd be a night out with a *new friend*, but nobody she liked enough to introduce. I don't even remember seeing her with real friends much. And I wasn't great company.

Sometimes I'd be in my room, doing my Saturday-morning impression of an abandoned corpse, and I'd look up to see her sitting on the edge of my bed – shuffling through my cassettes, creaking open the little plastic cases and unfolding the lyric sheets.

'Love is a Stranger,' she read out once, in a puzzled monotone. 'Okay. So this one's about love in a car waiting to kidnap you, I guess. Well, that's interesting. But kind of sad, don't you think?'

'Mom, why are you even here? I'm trying to sleep.'

'It's two-thirty in the afternoon. And …' A few uneven thumps as she knocked her heels against a box under my bed. 'I'm a little bored. Wanted some company, I guess. Can I borrow this tape?'

It was times like those that I wanted to hug her, but I didn't.

All this upset would have been fine, more or less – if it hadn't been for school.

Thanks to Mark, I stopped getting beaten up, but that didn't make me what you'd call popular. It was like there was still new-kid stink clinging to me, even after other new kids had appeared, taken root and turned into star athletes and class presidents. I stayed outside it all. I wasn't sure why.

Maybe it had something to do with gym class. That was where I seemed to go wrong the most. Our high-school gym was the size of a city block. I looked out over it the first day in Grade Seven and felt this hopeless thudding inside. So many more opportunities to get kicked or elbowed or slammed up against the wall or stepped on or sworn at, while out doing one's best for one's team. And I was right. Screwing up would not only get the other kids screaming at me – the teacher would be in there as well. Mr Richardson. He seemed to enjoy yelling at twelve-year-olds. I gave him lots of opportunities to enjoy himself.

This was also around the time being in the changing rooms with the other guys was really starting to freak me out.

Anyway.

The best day I had in Junior High was about halfway through Grade Eight. I was thirteen. I remember walking into the gym in my usual state of low dread, taking in the familiar rising stink that came off the place – rancid gym clothes and stale sweat, nausea and failure and fear. Here we go. Basketball, the one I hated most. I took a deep breath and started marching towards the locker rooms with everyone else.

Then out of nowhere – a revelation. I was never sure what brought it on. Like a message from an angel, clarity descended from a cold, perfect place.

You don't have to do this.

My God. It was true.

Nobody had a gun to my head. I was just a kid being asked to do something by a teacher. And I could say no.

I settled on a bench at the front of the gym and took out my math homework. Mr Richardson asked me what I was doing there, and I replied in a bland neutral tone that I had that bug going around and couldn't play today. He made a mark on his clipboard and walked off. It was that easy.

I kept this up for weeks, on the sidelines doing homework for other classes or reading. Spaceships and aliens, swords and sorcery. I read *The Hitchhiker's Guide to the Galaxy* so many times I practically had it memorised. I was also writing a really terrible science fiction novel about people on another planet who had to keep taking this drug called Quargux or they'd all turn into gelatinous goo. When the plot got too slow, my characters would just shoot at each other with ray guns for no particular reason. Usually this happened in restaurants, because I figured when they weren't fighting or dying, they'd be eating.

I actually spent hours thinking about this stuff.

And sex, of course, like everybody else. I thought about people doing it all the time. I wasn't exactly sure how I felt about it all, though I enjoyed dropping three-word sex scenes into my novel. It was a good way to end a chapter. If there was a guy and a girl in the scene, I'd write: 'Then they fucked.' Or if there were more than two people involved, I might go for four words: 'Then they all fucked.'

Some of the kids in my class were doing it for real by the time we got to Grade Eight. Even at thirteen. Mark was – or at least that's what he told me. It made me feel a bit squirmy and weird, knowing this about him.

Anyway, so there I'd be, hunched over on a bench in Grade Eight gym class, all this stuff cluttering up in my head. Reading, doing homework, writing bits of my terrible novel, lost to the world. Then – whack! A ball would go slamming into the side of my face. And I'd think, *Bad spot. I better move.* But that ball would find me wherever I went. It was the usual guys, most of the time.

Then one morning I looked up from my book to see Mark firing a basketball right at me. Really hard too. My head jolted sideways and the bridge of my nose got clipped by the spine of the paperback I was reading (*The Lathe of Heaven*, third time). He looked at me with no expression at all, as if the bench in front of him was empty.

I didn't bring this up until we were walking home from school together, like always.

'So … what did you do that for?' No need to explain what I meant. He knew.

He didn't answer. We'd stayed like that for a few tense minutes, Mark pushing on ahead, me taking in the back of him: heavy khaki backpack, bulky winter coat, shoulders hunched forward, hands in fists.

'Mark?' My voice was a little kid's squeak. 'Why did you—'

He turned around. 'Cause you're a fucking embarrassment, that's why. Everybody thinks so. I'm sick of it.'

I stared at my friend, creeping cold panic taking hold.

Then he told me the guys were all mad because I wouldn't play sports, and I was floating with relief. But at the same time I started getting enraged because this made no sense at all.

'That's stupid!' I'd shifted my backpack, whacked myself in the shoulder blade. 'I thought they'd all be happy I wasn't playing. Why would they want me out there?'

'They don't. But they don't like seeing you *not* playing either. It's like you think you're too good for us.'

'Too good? I suck. Everybody knows that. What is wrong with these people?' I was wildly gesturing at nothing as we moved along the cracking sidewalk. February. Snow for months, then rain. The ground was half-formed slush. The air was cold and wet, heavy and almost unbearable.

'It's not just that. You walk around with a snotty look on your face all the time. People think you're full of yourself.'

I didn't know what to say to this. He went on. 'You're always getting good marks in everything.'

'Yeah, sorry about that.'

'And you don't talk to people.'

'Nobody fucking talks to *me*!'

He glanced up at the sky. Did not seem to enjoy giving me this information. 'Well, don't forget your dad acted kind of snobby when he lived here. Maybe that's another reason.'

Mark shouldn't have brought up Stanley. This was against the rules. I stumbled on, kicking at things and glowering.

Then I exploded again. 'Snotty! Fuck! And what exactly am I supposed to be so snotty about? We live in the shit part of town. We don't have any money. Everything I own is second-hand. Everything I fucking own is mine because somebody else didn't want it. I don't even have a father. I mean, we don't know where he is. Nobody knows where he is …'

I was throwing a fit about having no money. This was not allowed. Mom didn't make a lot at her job, and we couldn't find Stanley, so there were at least three years back then when things were bad for money, really bad.

I marched along in silence with my head down.

'I want to kill him.'

'I know.'

'I want to kill him with power tools.'

'I can get you a drill if you want.' Mark reached over and hit me a glancing blow on the shoulder. 'Look, I shouldn't have chucked that thing at your head.'

'It hurt.'

'Yeah, I threw it kind of hard. But, you …' He seemed to give up on what he was saying. Then he kicked a flattened beer can in our path clear to the end of the street and tried again. 'But you keep doing these stupid things. All these stupid things to make everybody hate you. And they shouldn't. They really shouldn't.' Mark took hold of my arm and turned me around to face him. 'Stephen. You have to do something about all this. Okay?'

It was obvious I had to do something about it. Mark wouldn't have told me that otherwise. So I stopped sitting on the sidelines during gym class. I spent the time wandering around the rest of the school instead, looking for a quiet place to read – and later for a quiet place to read and smoke. I failed gym, of course, but I was fine with that.

The Stanley problem solved itself. We found him, just a few weeks after the basketball incident. Or he let himself be found. All of a sudden he was in Montreal getting married, so of course he needed a divorce from my mother. There were lawyers' letters sent back and forth, child support and alimony arranged. We didn't worry about money as much after that.

I never spoke to my father or got so much as a postcard while all this was going on. I suspected Mom was on the phone with him, but I didn't know how to bring up the subject. When I was little, I told her everything. Then later there was so much I had to keep to myself.

It started with me trying to wipe the stuck-up expression off my face, like Mark said. First of all, I'd tried to figure out if he was right.

I looked at myself in the toaster in our kitchen and concentrated on my usual school thoughts. What was on my mind, making my way through a crowd of my fellow students as they herded past me?

Inbreeds. Morons. Backwoods assholes. Go fuck yourselves, all of you.

Yeah, that was a fairly snotty look, all right.

I tried another expression. Something blank and agreeably vacant. I'd try to stick with that one.

Then there was problem number two: I didn't talk to people much. Well, that wasn't going to change, considering people didn't talk to me. How could I turn this into something I wouldn't get hated for?

Maybe if I acted like I was shy. Nobody hated shy people.

It was easy. You look at the floor a lot. Smile vaguely and shuffle around when people try to talk to you. Don't put up your hand in class. Don't make eye contact. If you get the urge to say something, don't.

This seemed to work. People were nicer for a while, or at least less hostile. Maybe it was a good idea, this shy thing.

No, actually, it was a horrible idea. In fact it was probably the worst idea I'd ever had. Because after a few months I realised I really was shy. And once I was in it, I couldn't escape. I'd go to talk and find my face was made of cement. Nothing would come out. On winter days, I'd feel myself turning grey at the edges and fading into the walls.

Was this defensive strategy? It was paralysing. And it went on for years.

So there you go. Started off standing up for myself and walking out of gym class, and finished by warping my personality completely to keep them all happy. This game was hard and dangerous and confusing, and it seemed like everybody had a copy of the rule sheet except me.

Fun. So much unbelievable fun.

Chapter 4

I checked our mailbox at the post office after school. The vestibule with its rows of tiny grey doors and numbered keyholes, like a morgue for elves. There were a few bills, Mom's new copy of *Chatelaine*. And a letter addressed to me. It was from a college in Halifax. I tore it open.

'Dear Mr Shulevitz ... We are pleased to offer you a place ... full scholarship ... inform us of your intentions to accept or refuse ...'

I read the letter twice in the post office. I read it outside on the sidewalk. The walk home turned into a run.

When Mom got in from work I shoved the envelope at her without saying a word.

'Well!' she said, after she'd given my letter a quick up and down. 'That's really nice.' Still wrapped in her coat with the furry hood, too warm for April.

'Mom, it's a full scholarship.'

'This'll take care of your tuition, yes. But—'

'Great programme too. Sort of an overview of western culture. Basically you get to read everything in a year – starts with the ancient world and goes on until the twentieth century. You know. All the philosophers. The really important literary stuff. Like Dante. And … Virgil. And …'

I realised I was lurching from side to side and waving my arms as I talked, practically dancing for her attention.

'So when are you going to hear from Acadia?' Mom stepped out of her boots and left them listing and empty on the black rubber mat.

Acadia was farther up the Valley, maybe forty minutes away. They had a very good agricultural studies programme. I'd applied there, but I hadn't really meant it.

I told her I didn't know anything yet.

'Actually, this is kind of a coincidence.' Mom seemed suddenly taller. 'Because I'm waiting for a letter from Acadia myself.'

Of course. She'd been talking about going back to school for years. My mother didn't want to be a secretary forever. Her plan was to study psychology and then train as a counsellor or a therapist. The kind of person you could trust to make sense of your problems.

'I guess you inspired me,' she said. 'Oh, it'll be wonderful, won't it, honey?' And she talked and talked, about how we could drive to our classes together in the mornings, go shopping for textbooks, have lunch in the cafeteria. 'But don't worry,' she said. 'I realise you won't want to be sitting at a table with your old mom. I could just, you know, see you there. With your new friends. Such a relief not to have to worry. And it'll be perfect for you. Right? No need to leave home. We'll save a fortune.'

Mom was smiling and waiting for my reaction. I told her all this was a lot to think about. Then I ran off to my room.

Upstairs, I lifted the vinyl cover from my typewriter and rolled in a blank sheet of paper. The machine gave off a low hum of expectation, followed by light cricket taps as I hit one key and then another.

'Please inform us of your intentions,' the letter from Halifax had said.

'I gratefully accept.'

But I realised I'd have to make another copy. I'd screwed up – typed the wrong first name over my address. The college didn't know about a guy named Stephen from Riverside. They were waiting to hear from Stepan Vladimir Shulevitz, who was me.

That was my official name, the one on my birth certificate. So weird seeing it in print. Even my last name looked kind of whiskery and weed-like compared to what you'd find here in town.

Everybody in our town had names that made them sound like country singers or hobbits, I always thought. Cindy Meriwether. Jimmy Whynott. Or you'd get all these Scottish and Irish families – people with ancestors who'd set themselves down like tree roots digging into the soil. This was New Scotland. They belonged here.

And then there was me and my mother.

Shulevitz. Solovyov.

We lived in the same house and didn't even match. She never took my father's name. I was the one who was expected to keep it. The name was Jewish, but that meant nothing to me. Stanley had rejected it all when he decided to run off and be a stupid hippy, and then he'd rejected us too.

I wasn't always that nice to my mother, growing up. But she'd usually turn it around and claim that she was the one who was failing me. After Stanley left, she used to get completely stressed worrying about my cultural development, always coming back from the library in Digby loaded down with books on Judaism and Israel. I'd leave them on the kitchen counter until they were overdue. I told her I didn't want any culture. And if I did, why couldn't it be from her side?

'Well, that doesn't seem fair,' she'd said. 'It's not your father's fault I'm here and he's not.'

I'd stared at her. My mother blushed and pretended to be interested in the newspaper spread over the kitchen table where she was sitting. She'd asked me a couple of clues for the crossword, but the words weren't that difficult.

This was a few months before Lana moved to town – it must have been the fall of 1983, around October. I was fourteen. Mom and I had just finished lunch and there was this weird no-time feeling in the house. Normally I'd be hanging around with Mark. But this was his first Saturday on the job at Home Hardware. The minister at his church had arranged it for him and he was very proud of himself. Outside, the sky was low and cloudy. The leaves were bright and the trunks of the maples were dark.

I could see the top of my mother's head as I leaned against the counter by the sink. She'd dyed her hair over the summer and now there was this expanding circle of light brown and grey growing out against the blonde, like something you'd see on a monk. I used to imagine everybody in town was following its progress and discussing it.

I judged her pretty harshly in those days. But I couldn't control how she made me feel – so helpless and frustrated. The way she'd run for the garbage truck with the trash, in big flapping sweatpants and a pair of my sneakers under her chewed-up old housecoat. She'd rub at a stain on her shirt in public, even if it was right over her boob, or carry reading glasses propped on her forehead all day like a second set of eyes. Her tone of voice when one of the kids in town insulted her. 'Excuse me?'

Polite, confused, friendly. I always wished I could inject myself with something that would keep me from noticing it all.

Culture. We'd been talking about culture that Saturday afternoon. I told my mother I was actually interested in her side of the family, those Russians back in Toronto. Was there anything special she remembered? She'd stared into space for a minute.

'Russian culture, Mom.'

'Oh, I know. But it's only my father who was Russian. Mama was Ukrainian.'

'Didn't think there was a difference.' On the maps they'd give us to label in school there was just an enormous land mass stretching across Asia and Europe. Put the letters USSR on it and you were done.

But my mother was laughing. 'If she could hear you! Mama's parents stopped speaking to her after she fell in love with my father. Did you know that? They said they'd rather she were dead than married to a Russian.'

Mom went quiet.

I'd never met these people. I remembered her being away for a funeral when I was five and again when I was six. The second time she'd come home loaded down with boxes, mainly books in Cyrillic. Stanley had waited until she was at work and then threw most of them out.

She'd never cried for her parents in front of me. I was always kind of scared she would, and I didn't have a clue how I'd go about comforting her. When I was little, the thought of my mother as an orphan used to send me into corners weeping with my arms over my head. She'd been the one telling me everything was okay.

Rain started to splatter against the window glass. I looked down at my sneakers with their flat muddy laces, kept my mouth shut and waited for her thoughts to move on.

Then Mom taught me the only Ukrainian phrase she could remember just then: *tse kinets' svitu*, which means 'it's the end of the world'.

'You say it when everybody's running around acting crazy,' she said. 'I heard this one a lot when I was a kid. A lot!'

She repeated the phrase for me until I got it right, or close enough. I liked the feel of the words. This was different from the lines of smudgy French we used to copy into our workbooks at school. *Tse kinets' svitu.* I said it to her. She said it back to me.

A few hours later, it was dark and we were side by side at the sink doing the dishes from supper. The kitchen was very quiet. Just the drip of the washcloth, slow hollow clunks as cups and plates moved against each other, the floor giving off little creaks under my mother's feet. I got a fresh towel from the drawer, asked if there was any more Ukrainian she could teach me.

'Oh, honey. It's complicated. See, I was never interested in that stuff when I was a kid. It was something my parents did – mainly when they didn't want me to know what they were saying. It embarrassed me, if you want the truth.' She ran the tap over a bright metal pot dripping with soap suds. 'I just wanted to be like everybody else.'

○

October 1983 drifted into November. Trees reached up with their leafless branches that seemed to ache. We had a test in Grade Nine Social Studies and there were a couple of questions about the Union of Soviet Socialist Republics, where the rest of my mother's people were skulking around, aiming missiles at our heads, plotting to turn Riverside into radioactive sludge. I filled in the blanks quickly, sat with my head bowed over the paper, trying to stay awake. But there was one part I'd left unanswered. Near the top of the page, next to the date.

My name. I took my time, pressing hard on my stubby pencil as I dragged it around the loops of the letters: 'Stephen Shulevitz'. All around me the sound of people scratching away, erasers sawing through paper, a girl swearing under her breath.

I looked at the name for a while. Then underneath it, in light letters I could rub out when I had to, I wrote a different one.

'Stephen Solovyov.' Her last name. It felt right, like the last jigsaw piece snapping into place. 'Shulevitz' was just proof there was something missing in our house. And my father couldn't give a fuck about me. So what was I going to do, carry his name around my whole life, maybe pass it on to my kids? I was hers, not his.

I could change it. Why not? Maybe even get people to call me Stepan. I started to feel like a different person, staring into the paper saying it in my head.

Mark coughed and I angled my test towards him so he could copy it. I rubbed my eraser over 'Stephen Solovyov' until it was gone.

After school that day, me and Mark headed off for the usual place, the drop-off over the river, to smoke some weed he'd bought off his cousin.

I was nervous. This was only the second time I got high, and I'd hated it so much when we'd done this over the summer on my fourteenth birthday. To start off with, I was fairly resentful back then because smoking dope was one thing I'd always promised myself I was never going to do. And I'd been certain I'd keep that promise – right up until Mark had put the joint in my hand. Poisonous-looking snarl of a thing bundled into white paper, trailing smoke from both ends. I'd held it to my mouth and breathed it in.

It stung my throat and my eyes, made my tongue go swollen and dry. I'd felt hot in the wrong places, and hungry and scared. And stupid – sitting there drooling and fascinated by a strip of birch bark I'd peeled off the trunk of a tree, how soft it was and the tiny changes you could see in the colour from one layer to the next. Mark had sat back laughing and told me I was, like, so fucked up.

All I'd been able to think about was my father. The way he used to sit for hours wrapped in heavy smoke, eyes red and drowned, breaking into helpless giggles over stuff that wasn't funny. I'd looked at my hands then and half expected to see his, scratching at the tree bark with their spidery fingers.

As soon as I got home, I'd showered the smell off me. For days I was too ashamed to look my mother in the eye.

But this time would be different. I wasn't going to turn into Stanley. Not now, not ever. I told Mark my idea. The new name.

'Solovyov.' Mark rolled the word around like he had eggs in his mouth. He was wedged between the roots of a sugar maple with the river behind him. The trees were stripped branches with a few flares of yellow leaves. They'd be gone soon. Mark started to laugh, his whole body crumpling downwards.

'What?' My voice was thick and gluey. 'Does it sound stupid? Too many Os?' I was a couple feet away from him, leaning back on the heels of my hands. The ground under me was hard and my fingers were numb.

'No, it's okay,' Mark said. 'Change it, man. Go ahead.'

I felt lighter. Mark was grinning at me, blond and blue-eyed, one of the natives. His face was red from the weed. It was like he was full of live coals. I wondered what it would be like to have infrared vision, if the heat from his body would make a new colour against the cold air.

'Hey. Be Solovyov now. Then later you make it shorter.' There was obviously a joke in there somewhere, but I just stared at him blankly. 'Stephen Solo,' he said.

'Holy shit! Stephen Solo! Stephen Fucking Solo! I have to do it!' My hands were gripping his upper arms and I was shaking him.

This was weird, for us. We were never what you'd call physical together. Other guys were. You'd see them rolling around like puppies, joking and acting like they were beating the hell out of each other, insults as nicknames. I couldn't do that stuff.

When he was feeling hyper, Mark would do pretend-fighting at me anyway: punches that whooshed past my ear, Bruce Lee kicks that stopped a millimetre from my gut. Or he might get all huggy, usually when he was wasted. I'd stand still and wait for it to be over, hold myself apart.

But right then, my face was stretched in a big messy grin and I could feel his bones through the blocky fabric of his army surplus jacket as I shook him. Mark just went with it, his head rolling. I started to find this really funny. Then he brought one hand up against my chest and pushed me backwards.

'C'mon, get off me, you homo.'

I sat staring at the pale yellow grass threading through my fingers, blinking and trying to think of what I could do to apologise.

'Jeez, Stephen. I didn't mean it,' Mark said. 'Gotta take everything so serious.' He dragged himself towards me. 'Fucking Solovyov.' Mark nudged my shoulder with his head. I fell over. No bones. He smiled down at me with that red face – like a cartoon sun, like God. I started to laugh and didn't stop for a while.

'I have to change it,' I said. 'I have to.'

My mother's reaction to the idea had confused the hell out of me. I thought she'd be happy I'd chosen her side. She wasn't.

'You're too young to be making that kind of decision. You know it and I know it.'

This was a problem. To change my name legally, I needed her permission. Otherwise I'd have to wait five years until I was nineteen, and by then 'Shulevitz' would be stuck to me like concrete.

I went nuts. Wouldn't leave her alone. I typed multi-page letters about why I was right and she was wrong and mailed them to her at work. I'd stand on the stairs in front of her with my arm across the banister arguing my case until she got so exasperated that she seemed about to push me over the railing. I knew I was being an asshole, even back then. But, I'd reasoned, all she had to do was sign a stupid paper. Two seconds of her life. Why couldn't she do this for me?

One night I went too far.

It was eleven o'clock. I had her cornered in the kitchen. She sank into a spindly wooden chair and stared out into nothing.

'Oh, God, Stephen, would you go to your room? Would you just go to your room and leave me alone?'

'You can't make me.'

My mother hid her face in her folded arms, head on the table with its plastic red check cloth dotted with frozen bits of candle wax.

'I'm still here,' I said. 'Just because you can't see me doesn't mean I'm not here.'

'I know you're still there! I know, I know, I know!'

She stood up. Her chair went tumbling to the floor. The car keys were piled next to our salt and pepper shakers which were shaped like staring yellow and green owls. I got the keys first. I knew what she was going to do. In those days, whenever Mom got especially frustrated and crazy, usually because of me, she went for a drive. The engine starting up was like the door slamming, like Mom yelling the last word over her shoulder.

'Give me those,' she said.

'No.'

Mom tried to pry open my hand. Her strong fingers with their long nails pushed and gouged. I shoved my arm behind my back and the next thing I knew, we were grappling for this jingling metal ring like a brother and sister squabbling over the controls for a video game.

She ordered me to give her the keys again. I refused. Couldn't let her go. This crazy panic flapping around my head like bat's wings. If she left now, she'd be gone forever. I knew it.

'You're a brat!' she said. 'I raised a brat. Now I'm stuck in this awful town. In this bug-eaten house. With this *brat*!'

'Tough shit.'

'How *dare* you use that kind of language with me, mister.'

'Tough shit, Maryna.'

'Don't call me that. I'm your mother!'

She got hold of my right hand and forced my fingers open. I'd switched the keys to my left. I held the ring over her head. She actually jumped for them. I felt sick, horrified.

But I laughed. 'Have to do better than that, Maryna.' His voice.

She slapped me. I bit my tongue as my jaw jolted from the shock.

We stared at each other, breathing hard. Mom had tears in her eyes. So did I.

'You hit like a girl,' I said.

I threw the car keys on the floor.

On the front steps in the dark, I sat with my head in my hands. I could hear her behind me in the kitchen, clatter of the keys as she gathered them up, her footsteps, then the door creaking at the other end of the house. Frost was sheathing the dead grass in white and making the pavement sparkle. I watched the car and waited for her to come around from the back. I really wanted a cigarette. There were some hidden in the bookcase down in the basement, but I couldn't leave my post to get them.

After a while, I realised how quiet it was and I knew I was alone. She wasn't coming for the car. She'd probably sneaked off through the backyard in the darkness as I stood guard over her escape route. She was walking. Running. I'd made my mother run away from home.

It was cold on the steps and the house was warm, but I couldn't go back in. I had to find her.

Hedges bristled by the sidewalks, all twigs and no leaves. I paced past the grocery store. The bakery. The bank. It was spooky – all these bright houses with the colours leached out, dimmed to shadow. A raccoon was tearing apart the trash outside the pizza delivery place that had just opened.

I started to run. I jogged down Main Street. There was the town hall, with its red bricks and clock face, its 'Town of Riverside' spelled out in solid metal letters. Deserted. I'd try the park next.

But wait. I looked closer. There was a little figure huddled on the steps under the clock. She was smoking. I came nearer and she didn't move or look at me. I lowered myself onto the cold steps, keeping the distance of two invisible people between us. In the daytime, this was where the tough kids hung out. The town looked different from this angle.

'Please don't fight with me anymore,' my mother said.

I let out a long breath – dragon vapour in the dark. Hadn't bothered with a jacket and my teeth were starting to knock together.

'Okay.'

'Thank you.'

We stayed where we were. A plastic ghost from Halloween drooped in a tree by the Saunders' place. Its big night was over. Now it was garbage. Nothing good was ever going to happen to it again.

'*Tse kinets' svitu*,' I said.

She stubbed her cigarette against the concrete step, flicked the butt onto the sidewalk, lit another one. 'You're telling me.'

'Don't know any more, huh?'

'I don't want to be a foreigner, Stephen.'

'I am. I mean, I feel like one.'

My mother turned to me, her eyes crinkled in confusion. 'Why would you say a thing like that?'

Should have realised how stupid it sounded. I stretched out my legs and bounced my knees. 'I feel like an alien half the time. Waiting for the mother ship to bring me back to my home planet.' I smiled at her, kind of goofy.

'Maybe you should take me with you.' She smiled too. She tried, anyway. I couldn't shake the idea that we were actually afraid of each other.

The hard, straight corners of the steps dug into my back and made me feel like I was some kind of reptile, sore from growing protective ridges along my spine. I wanted to offer her something. An apology or a confession.

'Mom, I smoked up. I smoked, you know, marijuana.'

She was staring at me again. I pretended she wasn't.

'Oh, Stephen. Already?' My mother shook her head, like she was looking at a licence application that she couldn't bring herself to rubber-stamp. 'No, no. Fourteen's way too young. Your brain's still developing. And your body. You should really wait until you're in college.'

'Sure, Mom. Okay.' I said it fast to shut her up. I don't know what I'd been expecting – maybe for her to come down hard, forbid me to smoke weed or I'd get no allowance and would end up grounded for a year. It's possible that's what I wanted, deep down – border checks and barbed wire, guard towers watching over me. At least you know where you are that way.

'Just like Stanley. Right?' I was knocking my heels against the steps.

She sighed. The hair on her forehead drifted up and then settled back down over her eyebrows. 'I guess Stan wasn't much of a role model, huh? Always toking up in front of you. But at least it's better than drinking. Or *this*.' She held up her cigarette with its curl of smoke and glared at me. 'I never want to see you with one of these, ever. Understood?'

I nodded.

'Listen to me, the voice of authority.' My mother closed her eyes. 'I can't believe I hit you.'

That shrill scene in the kitchen came crashing back at me – the colours too sudden and bright, the sounds too harsh, making me queasy with shame.

'That's my father, you know,' she said. 'My father coming out in me.'

It was so rare that she'd mention him. 'What was he like?'

I had family all over the country I'd never met and never would. Some were dead, like my Russian and Ukrainian grandparents. Most were mad at my mother and father for getting together in the first place. And there were other factors. Family battles. Unforgivable acts. Wars that had been slogging on for years before I was born.

'My father.' Exhaustion weighed down her voice. 'He was an abusive drunk from Perm. There's your culture. If you want it.'

63

I sank into the steps, felt concrete against my neck. It was a clear night and the cold made the stars seem closer.

'Mom?'

'Yeah?'

'Why doesn't he want to see me?' I kept my eyes focused on the sky.

'Why does who?' She looked at me vaguely, then sat up a bit straighter. 'Oh.'

'I mean, did he ever say anything to you? About me?'

'No. Honey, no. He … probably feels guilty.'

'I could tell him it's okay.' My voice got stuck. Something was squeezing my throat and pressing down on my eyes. I sat and didn't move and waited for it to leave.

Then there was soft pressure closing around my arm, holding me steady. My mother's hand. She was afraid to hug me, I realised. She thought I'd push her away. I stayed very still, concentrated on breathing.

After I was calmer, I hauled myself to my feet, took her hand and waited while she shook the creaks out, unfolded herself and stood up, her weight yanking on my arm like our clothesline with its groaning wheel. We were quiet as we walked home. A few windows were lit with yellow, or white shivering light from a TV set. Everything else was dark.

I checked my letter over one more time. It was late now. We'd both forgotten about supper.

There was a thin horizon of light under my mother's door. I knocked and she told me to come in. She was propping herself up in bed and wearing one of those gel masks that are supposed to stop you from getting eye wrinkles. A little prone superhero in a flannel nightie, squinting as I shuffled over the pink carpet towards her. From her night table, a lamp with a stained-glass shade threw angled squares of green and red over the room.

'Mom.' I held out the letter I'd written to the college in Halifax, my wrist and knuckles going emerald in the coloured light. 'Can you just read this for me? Check for spelling and stuff?'

She pushed the mask to her forehead and unfolded her reading glasses – two sets of eyes now, both peering at my letter.

I watched the numbers on her clock radio flip their shutters from 10:59 to 11:00. My mother put down the paper with my typing on it, stared into a dusty corner of her room where an electric fan sat waiting for summer.

'So this is it, then. You're leaving.'

'Yes,' I said. I really was.

Chapter 5

Lana had a letter of her own. 'University of Toronto,' she said. 'Beat that. I'll start with History. Should come in handy for when I take over the entire world.'

We were halfway up the north mountain, looking over the valley – the perfect backdrop for a speech like that. Walking here had been Lana's idea. She was on a weight-loss programme she'd worked out herself so she could look sexy for the prom, and for Captain Hormones in Halifax. This was the first day.

And the last. Because when we got to the foot of the mountain, gravity really kicked in, and after about an hour of heaving and sweating and suffering Lana announced that she wasn't taking another frigging step.

'Never doing this again.' She collapsed against the guard rail that separated cars and hikers from an inconvenient death tumbling into the valley. 'I mean, is this guy really worth it?'

'No.'

'Who asked you, Stephen?'

She was laughing and stretching up an arm to wipe the sweat off her face. I caught her elbow just in time. With all that make-up she'd look like a kid's smudged finger-painting, I told her. I was perched on the next guard rail post, waiting for my own breathing to steady. Maybe four years of smoking hadn't been such a smart idea after all.

This was when we got talking about university. I watched her going on about Toronto and how great it was going to be – the clubs, the coffee shops, the people – smiling as if she could see it all in front of her. And I was surprised to feel a little tug of something like anger. She was so damn happy to be leaving. Leaving Riverside. Leaving the Maritimes. Leaving me.

'I don't know why you didn't apply to U of T yourself, Stephen,' she was saying. 'You would've got in easy. Then we could be together.' A sudden blush under that thick make-up. 'All of us, I mean. Adam's going too.'

'Jeez. Is that why you chose it?'

'Course not. By the time I get to Toronto, I won't need *him*. I'll have a whole harem of my own.' She was grinning at me. 'You can join if you want, but there's a membership fee.'

The valley was a checkerboard patchwork below us: light new yellow-green of hardwoods coming into bloom, darker drifts of spruces, brown fields freshly ploughed. From this distance, it looked almost misty, like you'd expect to see castles with banners and turrets below instead of the usual bark-coloured Legoland houses.

'Aren't you gonna miss this place at all?' I said.

She rolled her eyes. 'I'll buy a postcard.'

I smiled, but my expression felt like my mother's watching me from across the breakfast table. What was I going to do without this girl?

Lana Kovalenko had moved to Riverside from Toronto in the middle of Grade Nine, when I was fourteen. I liked her right away. We'd met at her parents' house-warming party, the night my mom had that drunken meltdown and started spilling family secrets.

I remember it was January. Sunday afternoon. One of the first days of 1984, the last day of Christmas vacation before school started again. I felt kind of resentful for being dragged off to this thing – I was still really shy at that point.

Mom hauled me up out of the corner where I'd been sitting with my Walkman, ignoring everybody, and we joined the group clumping together in the living room. Mr Kovalenko started talking to my mother – phrases from a language I couldn't make out. She looked at him like she was trying to do math in her head.

'Sorry, Andrij. I'm not great with Ukrainian. Worse with Russian too, really. Just a few words here and there.'

'And your son doesn't speak it at all, huh?'

'No, Stephen's Canadian, I guess.' Mom dipped her head.

'You are? Ew!' It was somebody at my elbow. A girl, my age. She was all in black, her hair gelled up and her eyes dark, little gold hoops and studs running along the edges of her ears. The same roundish dumpling shape as her parents, but still. You didn't see girls like that in Riverside.

'Lana's … well, she's fluent,' said Mr Kovalenko. 'The grammar, though. My God! We sent her to Saturday school, but she never seemed to absorb much.'

'That's cause I was always high,' Lana whispered in my ear, and I'd laughed. She'd had to stand on tiptoes to reach me. I was at least a head taller than her.

My mother was starting to smile. 'Oh, Andrij, they like each other!'

'Come on,' Lana said. 'My room. You can tell me about this hillbilly redneck school for retards my parents are forcing me to attend.' She yelled out over her shoulder at her dad, as if it were an afterthought, 'Hey, *Tato*! I'm gonna take this fresh meat up to my room now, okay?'

My mother gave a shocked little laugh, and Mr Kovalenko told her that his daughter had an unusual sense of humour.

'Keep your door open, Svetka,' he said.

The Kovanlenkos' place was all creaking staircases and little angular rooms – like our house, like so many of these old Riverside buildings. Lana took us on a quick detour to the kitchen so we could grab a couple of beers. I hid them in the sleeves of my shirt. I guess it was a bit too big for me.

I was wearing the Riverside guys' uniform. All the boys here wore the same thing year round: jeans, T-shirt, another shirt with sleeves (usually plaid) and boots that looked like they were made by a tractor company, with the laces undone. Every few months, your mother would drag you off to get your hair cut by some old creep who'd learned how to barber in the army. I looked just like everybody else. I was always careful about that.

But I have to say, I was starting to feel like some kind of farm boy dork next to this Toronto girl.

Her room was crowded with boxes, most of her stuff still packed up from the move. I helped her put posters on the wall: pictures of bands they didn't play on the radio in Riverside. The Cure. Siouxsie and the Banshees. The Violent Femmes.

'Your father's nice,' I said. 'What did you call him? Taco?'

Lana laughed, dropped a corner of the poster she was holding and nearly lost the whole thing. 'It's *Tato*!' she said. 'Ukrainian. Means

"Dad"! Don't you do the ethnic thing at home? Your mother never calls you Stepanchik?'

'Fuck, no! Are you kidding?'

'I think it sounds nice. What are you anyway? Like, what do you consider yourself? You can be Ukrainian if you want. Your mom's half or we wouldn't have you in the house. Or 'Shulevitz' is Jewish, isn't it? Polish Jewish? That's okay too. But don't be Russian. They're bastards.'

Who could keep track of all this? Most families around here had spent the last five generations in Riverside.

Later it was my turn to go get more beer. I got lost coming back from the kitchen, which was a funny L-shape with too many doors leading off everywhere. But I figured it out, took my two bottles and scooted past the living room where all the adults were gathered. Nobody saw me. Perfect. But I saw them. And then I had to go back and look.

My mother, standing on her own, clutching her wine glass in her fist. She seemed to get taller and shorter as she hovered near this one chair, unsure of whether she should be standing up or sitting down. Somebody bumped into her and she apologised.

Then she was gathered into a conversation with a group of people, and I just about died watching. That vague spooked look, breaking off in the middle of a sentence, not sure what anybody wanted her to say next. Looking down, looking awkward, smiling as if to say sorry, waiting for all this to go away.

I stayed by the door, weighed down with stubby bottles in my sleeves. Everybody was chatting so easily, laughing, enjoying each other's company.

Say something, Mom. Come on.

I couldn't look at this anymore. Turned my back and climbed the stairs with more beer for Lana.

Lana was still sticking posters up over her blue striped wallpaper, playing her tapes of cool bands I'd never heard of and talking for a very, very long time about the Ukrainian Famine of 1933, probably because it proved Russians were evil and so I shouldn't be one.

'They came and took the grain away in trucks! A third of the population of Ukraine gone; I mean, how come nobody ever talks about this?' Lana lunged for the volume knob on her tape player. 'Oh, my God, this is the best song ever! He pushes his daughter down a well and then hangs himself. You'll love it.'

At about four in the afternoon, the light started to fade. Out the windows you could see that sulky bruise colour on the horizon, trees making a dark lattice against the sky. We were downstairs searching for unattended packs of cigarettes so we could sneak a few. I risked another quick look at the living room.

Okay, so now Mom was talking. Good.

She was the only one talking. Not so good.

My mother's face was red, her voice higher than usual and cracking in places. She was making vague gestures with her empty wine glass.

'Well, no, Papa wasn't anti-Semitic exactly – he just didn't like Jews much and, wow, he just hated Stanley! I made it worse, of course, running off and not finishing school, and then there was the baby. You know, when I had the baby out of wedlock and they both said they never wanted to see me again, and I was young, so I believed them …'

Jesus Christ. Was she drunk? I realised that Lana was standing beside me.

'The baby?' she said. 'Is that you?'

'Let's get out of here.' We headed back upstairs and stayed there.

I was sitting on the floor fooling around with her guitar, which we'd just unpacked. Lana was lying on her bed, hanging upside-down off the edge.

'Come on, tell me about these Riverside country boys.'

I shrugged. 'Everybody's boring.'

'So you're the only interesting boy.'

I grinned into the neck of the guitar. 'Basically.' Then I felt a bit disloyal. 'Oh, except for my friend Mark.'

'Is he good-looking?'

Everything stopped. I got this nervous, panicky sensation. Something very close to fear.

It was a simple question. Yes, or no.

A simple question, about something I wasn't allowed to think about. Except here she was, asking me to think about it.

'Well, he's …' I took a second, forced my voice into the shape of something normal. 'I mean, you know Mark. He's …'

He's beautiful.

I'd felt my face going red, a shocked feeling in the pit of my stomach. Beautiful. Was this Mark I was thinking about? Same old Mark McAllister, spitting phlegm on the side of the road on the way to school? Yes.

I kept my head down and picked at the strings on the guitar. Come on. Snap out of it.

'He's … he's really hideous-looking actually,' I said. 'No eyes and no nose. Got in a fight with a dog when he was a baby. And instead of ears he's got these big bone growth things, look kind of like antlers …' I was starting to make myself laugh, went on and on, talking about how Mark drooled so much we had to take it away in buckets, and that he could only say the word 'loofah', and he had this one hairy eyebrow that kind of moved around all over his face depending on what mood he was in and … Lana finally had to throw a pillow in my direction to shut me up. Whatever dangerous moment had just come to me, it was over.

'You are so weird,' she said.

I smiled at her. 'Yeah, I know.'

She'd smiled back, very slowly. 'I like weird.'

Just then Lana's dad called us for supper and we ignored him.

We went downstairs later and grabbed some food from the kitchen, looked in the fridge for more beer, but it was gone.

'Vodka,' said Lana. 'I know where there's vodka.'

There was a white door in the wall beside the fridge. She opened it, walked us into this tiny room full of shelves, about half stocked with cans and jars, bags of apples and potatoes, twisty lengths of garlic. I followed her. The ceiling sloped a bit: we were under the stairs. A collection of clunky-looking bottles full of clear liquid sat on the back shelf. Lana picked up the tallest and took a drink out of it.

'This one's nice. It tastes like star anise.'

I tried it. Choked. Lana laughed, but it didn't sound like a mean laugh. She took the bottle out of my hands, and when she set it back on the shelf, she still had her fingers linked through mine. We looked at each other for a second.

'Lana, you're, like, the coolest girl ever.'

Her voice was as soft as air. 'C'mere.'

I imagined she'd taste like star anise. Whatever that was.

But before anything could happen there were noises in the kitchen. We froze. It was our mothers. Right next to us, on the other side of the wall. I peered out a crack in the larder door but couldn't see them. Instead I was looking at another doorway across from me, open to a room full of half-packed boxes and house plants.

Mom's voice sounded weak, gravelly. She was apologising over and over, asking about the kids, were we still upstairs.

'He can't see me like this,' she said. 'And has anyone actually been up there to check on them? What if they're having sex? I mean, she could get pregnant and they'll have to leave school and get married and they'll ruin their lives …'

Lana collapsed into my shoulder, soundlessly laughing.

'I trust my daughter.'

Lana whispered, 'Big mistake.' I made myself smile but couldn't laugh. I thought it was a nice thing for Mrs Kovalenko to say.

My mother was still talking. 'God, why did I say all those awful things about Stan back there? Stephen could have walked by any second. I promised myself a long time ago I'd never do that. He's only going to hear about the positives from me. The good memories.'

Mrs Kovalenko murmured something about that being a nice healthy attitude.

Mom had started laughing, but I wasn't sure why. Then she told Lana's mother what I'd suspected all along, that she'd been talking with my father on the phone for years. For years, and he'd never once asked to speak to me.

'So where's my positive there?' she went on. 'What should I say, "Wow, this is great, huh? He's really giving you your space!"'

Painful to hear, I guess. But she was wrong. There was one time, about a month earlier. Mom hadn't been home. The phone rang and I'd picked it up. It was him.

I'd known the voice right away, but I couldn't make out what he was saying. There was a lot of noise. Loud music, people talking. Then he came in more clearly. Maybe he'd been holding the receiver the wrong way.

'This is Stan Shulevitz. I want to talk to my son.'

'It's me.'

'No, I want to talk to Stephen.'

I'd looked out the window. He sounded high.

My father had made an impatient noise. 'Who are you, the babysitter? Just put him on the phone. You know, little Stepan Vladimir. Maryna's boy. Stephen Shulevitz.'

'It's me! Stanley, where are you?'

The line had gone quiet for a few seconds. 'No, this is all wrong,' he'd said. 'My son's a child. He's only …' More noise from the background or maybe Stanley was just getting quieter. 'Wait, how old did you say you were?'

Before I could answer, the receiver went clunk against something. I'd kept talking, louder and louder, trying to get him back on the line. Then I was standing there babbling to a dial tone.

And that was it.

Mrs Kovalenko murmured something about 'giving him too much power over you'.

'But, Larissa, you don't know what it was like,' my mother said. 'He was gone, and there was this little person asking me every day, "Where's Stanley? When's he coming back? Mom, can we call him? Can we go visit?" I even gave Stephen a fake address once so he could write Stan a letter. I've still got that letter somewhere. I never opened it.'

I didn't realise I'd been quite so pathetic. Jesus Christ, was this woman ever going to stop talking?

Lana and I were sitting side by side on the floor at this point. It was easier to whisper to each other if we were about the same height. We could hear Mrs Kovalenko at the sink by the back door, probably getting my mother a glass of water. After that, there was nothing for a while except those almost soundless Mom sobs. Lana whispered in my ear that we had to get out of there and I nodded yes. Then my mother started up again. Nothing on earth would stop her.

'It just doesn't seem fair,' she said. 'He hurt me, he hurt my child, and nothing happens to him. He's got this great new life now, a new family. And he was so insistent at the beginning that I, you know, terminate the pregnancy …'

'Oh, fuck.' I said it out loud, breathed it.

Lana reached her arm around my shoulders, told me in a half-voice that everything was okay.

Didn't know that was your ambition for me all along, Stan. Or I would have been the best damn splash on the floor a father could have asked for.

I couldn't help thinking that if Mark were here, he'd despise me for the things my mother was saying. I wasn't sure why, but I was pretty certain he would.

If Mark were here. The image took hold suddenly, like a hand closing over my throat. If Mark were here with me instead of her, instead of Lana. If it had been him under this sloping ceiling, passing me a bottle of vodka to drink. Star anise. Shoved up against the wall, shelves pressing into my back, fumbling with buttons and zippers, half dying. Hands full, mouth full. Of him.

Jesus Christ. I was losing my mind.

How could I be thinking this now? Sitting here getting all excited about something so sick and so weird, Lana with her arm around me not suspecting a thing. When I'd just found out my father had wanted me dead before I was even born. This made no sense. I made no sense.

'And now out of nowhere, after all that, Stanley says he wants to see him …'

Everything stopped. When I could breathe again, I realised I was clutching Lana's hand like a frightened eight-year-old.

'Tells me to put Stephen on a plane and just send him off to Montreal this summer. I guess the new wife wants to meet him. And he's got sisters now, two little babies. I haven't said anything yet. I don't know how.'

Lana was mouthing at me, 'Did you know?'

I couldn't answer.

'Time to shut this down,' she said in my ear. Right. We pulled ourselves to our feet. Bits of 'The Maryna Show' were still filtering through the door, Mom talking about how she had no boyfriend and no real friends and that her job was a big zero. She had one thing in her life, she said, and guess what that was?

Block it out. Stay focused. Lana picked up a potato from the bag by the door, and I did the same. No idea what she had in mind, but it felt good to have a potato.

'It can't be healthy for him,' my mother was going on, 'I mean, no father, and then there's this crazy woman hovering around all the time. And you know what people say.'

I think I sensed what was coming next. Don't, Mom. Not out loud in front of everybody. Lana nudged the door. It had a slight squeak in the hinges, but the two women didn't notice.

'… I'm just so terrified he'll grow up to be a homosexual and it'll be all my fault.'

Oh, God. I gripped the doorframe, couldn't look at anything, couldn't see anything. For a split second, I imagined Lana telling this story in school, everybody gathered round.

But she was rolling her eyes at me, shaking her head. Disgusted with my mother. Lana wasn't going to laugh at this. The girl was on my side.

Mrs Kovalenko was giggling away. 'Come on, Maryna, you know it doesn't work like that. Anyway, weren't you just saying he's going to marry Svetlana?'

'Oh, wouldn't that be *nice?*'

Then Lana heaved her potato into the opposite room where it made a very satisfying crash: sounded like a whole bunch of house plants falling over. I lobbed mine and saw it go thunk against the wall.

But it worked. We heard a chair squeak along the floor, Lana's mother mumbling to herself that she'd better see what on earth that was, my mother toddling after her. When we peeped past the larder door, the kitchen was deserted. We disappeared out the back and stayed there for a minute, watching our breath hitting the winter dark. Lana had to stand on my tractor boots because she didn't have shoes on. I put my arms around Lana to steady her, but it didn't feel like romance anymore.

'I'm so sorry, Stepanchik.'

'It's okay.' The nickname actually did sound nice the way she said it.

She slipped a bit, pulled herself closer to me, mumbling into my T-shirt. 'I never should've heard that stuff.'

'Me neither.' Hand on her shoulder.

'Your dad sounds like a total bastard.'

'I'll let you know when I see him this summer.'

Lana drew back, looked up at me.

'You're going?'

I nodded.

'Wish I could come along. I'd kick his ass for you.'

My fingers on the back of her head, her stiff, gelled-up hair, her pretty eyes.

I felt so lonely.

We heard someone knocking on the back window. Turned around to see my mother and Mrs Kovalenko, their faces framed in the glass, waving at us and smiling.

So we shuffled inside, and I told my mother it was time to go home.

My mom was weaving a bit on the walk back. Part of me felt like pushing her into a snow bank. She'd humiliated me. But then I'd watched her getting drunk and stupid and embarrassing herself and I'd done nothing. Nothing to save her. The heel of Mom's boot slipped. I took her arm and she didn't fall. We stayed like that, walking.

'So, Mom,' I said. Then had to stop myself. *So, Mom, what? Was all that stuff true? Did Stanley change his mind about me after I was born? What are my sisters' names?* But saying this was impossible. I couldn't admit I'd been there listening.

'Mom,' I said again. Silence. I finished lamely, 'You didn't seem too happy back there.'

'Got that right.' She looked like she was concentrating very hard on putting one foot in front of the other. 'Living in this little town. It's like I've forgotten how to talk to people. Either I don't say anything, or I start blabbering on and can't stop.'

'That was after you drank all that wine, huh?'

Mom gave me her you-little-brat look. 'Yes, Stephen,' she said, 'that was after I drank all that wine. But it's not okay to drink just because you're in a socially uncomfortable situation. You understand that, right?' I told her, yes, of course I did.

'Excruciating,' she went on. 'Just like being back in high school. When I was so shy.'

'You were?' I tried to act casual. 'How'd you get out of it?'

She didn't say anything for a moment. The sky was dark and cloudy, a soft purplish colour. Probably getting ready to snow again.

'Well, I suppose I should tell you the truth. Same way I did tonight. Going to parties. Getting drunk. Getting stoned. Making a complete ass of myself.' She fished her pack of cigarettes out of her purse, opened it. 'A bad example for you. I'm a bad example. Of course that's how I met your father, at one of those parties …'

'Yeah, that worked out great.'

My mother had hardly heard me, off in some romantic daydream. 'God, Stanley was adorable. Just the smartest, funniest, sweetest boy. So many ideas. Talking to him was like waking up. I couldn't believe he wanted me.'

We walked past houses full of warm yellow light, snow on the roofs, everything bordered with glowing dots of red and green and blue from Christmas. Then we were back home. Mom threw her coat and purse on the floor and announced that she was going to bed.

'That was awful!' she called out over her shoulder. 'So embarrassing!' She started lurching upstairs, holding on to the banister. 'Let us never speak of this again, huh, Stan?'

I froze like I'd been shot, but she hadn't noticed anything.

After she went to bed I stayed sitting at the kitchen table, still woozy from the beer, trying to figure out what had happened.

One thing I did know. What I'd been thinking in the larder. What I'd been thinking about Mark. I had to deal with that right away.

I was a bit nervous because it had been a few months since I'd done this, since I'd had to. I'd thought things were getting better.

Third drawer down, next to the fridge. A box of wooden matches under a casserole dish. I took out a match. Lit it, held my little finger against the flame. Same place as last time because you didn't want to have too many marks, draw too much attention. The match burned out. I lit another one, kept it going. Until I started to sweat, felt like

80

throwing up. Until I was sure I wouldn't dare think anything like that again.

This is what I did, what I'd been doing for the past few years. To stop myself from ruining my life.

I'd stick a Band-Aid on it. The next day in class if I was having the same kind of thoughts I'd dig my thumb in there, go half crazy from pain for a second. But it would help to kill this feeling, keep it away from me, let it leave.

Such an idiot. It never left. It was mine. It was me.

The next morning I made my mother coffee instead of tea. She was sick from drinking so much. I was sick too, but I had to hide it. We sat at the kitchen table together. Mom mumbled something about me babysitting for the Healeys. I said sure. Then it was time to go to school.

And so we got set back on our little clockwork paths and went ticking on with our day, my mother and me. Continued with everything, as if we were normal people. People who remembered nothing.

Chapter 6

Okay, I guess there's a lot I left out of this. In fact there's a good chance you could accuse me of being full of it again. And maybe you'd be right.

For one thing, the world didn't end in my TV room this April because I realised I was attracted to Mark. You've probably figured that out by now. It ended, all right. But the reasons were bigger, more complicated. That other stuff – the guilty thoughts, the parts of me I was always trying to block. They'd been with me for a long time. Even before the party at the Kovalenkos'.

Let's go back to Grade Eight. The year before I met Lana. I was thirteen, plodding home from school with Mark in February. I was mad at him because he'd thrown that basketball at my head when I sat on the sidelines during gym class. He was mad at me – I was sure – because I was an embarrassing spaz and I was holding him back.

The same afternoon I was talking about before. But I didn't exactly tell the whole truth the first time this came up. Not about what happened after we got back to my place.

The air was heavy and wet. Mark had kicked a flattened beer can all the way down the sidewalk. We'd trudge forwards another hundred feet and when we met up with it again, he'd give it another kick. I shoved my hands in the pockets of my winter coat. It was cold, but mittens were for little kids and gloves were for wimps.

Mark was still telling me about how everything I was doing at school was wrong and I was pissing people off, even if I didn't know it. It made me ashamed and crazy with rage. Like sitting in a room full of strangers with your mom showing everybody your naked baby pictures.

'So if you think I'm such a loser, then why do you hang around with me?'

'What kind of stupid question is that?'

Heading for my house now. We were both sick of each other and I just wanted Mark to go home. But if he did, we'd be admitting this was a real fight. A quarrel, a tiff. A couple of girls.

On the corner of my street, he took a pack of Player's from his coat pocket and lit up.

'Jesus Christ!' I said. 'Put that away!' I stood hovering, trying to block him from view of these tall wooden houses, every window a potential watcher edging the curtains apart to see us better.

'What is your problem? There's nobody around.'

I couldn't believe how stupid he was being. Of course there were people around, I told him. Just because you can't see anybody on the street doesn't mean you're not being watched. How did he think gossip spread so fast in this town?

'Fuck's sake,' Mark growled, but he scraped the live end of the cigarette against a tree and the dregs drifted down into the snow. He twisted the tip, slotted it back into the pack.

I wasn't allowed to smoke. My mother was very clear about this.

She lit up a million times a day, but every time she did, there'd be this intense look in my direction. Then she'd start, on and on, about how she never wanted to see me with a cigarette in my hand, that it was her one rule, how it was a life-long, debilitating addiction and the surest way to break her heart.

We'd gone around to the back of my house and ended up at the rusty swing set by the shed. It was okay to sit on the swings, if you made it clear you weren't playing, just hanging out. The sound when you nudged yourself along was like something prehistoric talking to you about its aches and pains.

Mark sat with one hand wrapped around the rusty chain links of the swing, his face tilted upwards, daydreaming. I forgot I was mad at him for a second. Then I remembered, leaned back on my swing and scooped a handful of snow off the ground. I slapped it into a dense ball and chucked it hard at the back of his head.

Mark spluttered – shocked and furious, like he couldn't figure out who'd done this to him. He started to laugh. 'You fucker!'

He got me back worse. Then we were running around the yard. The snow was wet, excellent packing – you could make something more like an ice cannonball of destruction than the puffy round globes you'd see kids throwing at each other in the movies. I got him at close range a couple of times, was pelted half to death in return. Finally he had me in a headlock mashing icy crystals into my face and I had to give up. He stood there radiating smugness, then took out his pack of smokes again.

'Jeez, Mark, would you put that shit away? You're gonna kill yourself.' I stopped. Sounded just like my mother. He was looking at me like he wanted to say the same thing. I dug my fingers into the back of my neck.

'Give me one of those, will you?' I said.

'You actually want to smoke?'

'Yeah.' I met his eyes. A bargain.

He shrugged and held the pack towards me. It was blue and white, with a scowling bearded sailor in a circle looking up at us. Maybe he was the boy from the Cracker Jack box grown up. My mouth was dry. Ice on my neck melted into trails of cold water mixing with the sweat on my back. There was a wooden fence around the yard, but that wouldn't hide anything. Not from the neighbours at their high, upstairs windows.

'Not here,' I said. 'In the house.' My voice dropped almost to a whisper. Mark seemed like he was about to laugh, but he didn't say anything. We walked in silence, suddenly serious, up the steps to the back door. I let us in with my key. Mark pulled the door shut behind us and I heard it click.

'The basement.' I was still talking like I was in a spy movie. We left crescents of dirty snow water on the floor in the living room. I pushed open the basement door, hinges squeaking in a long thin whine like a question. Then I stopped. It would be safer if I used my mother's brand – I had this idea she'd be able to smell the traces from something different. Mark loped down to the basement and I told him I'd be there in a second, went upstairs and found the carton of cigarettes Mom kept in the bottom drawer of the dresser in her room, next to a tangle of gauzy scarves and her letters from Stanley.

I'd read them all, of course. Some of the early ones were pretty embarrassing. In the last few he just seemed tired. 'Maybe it would be better for all of us if you let him forget me,' he'd written. 'Kids bounce back fairly easily, don't they?'

Not the right time to be thinking about this. I took out a red rectangular pack of smokes from the carton, a thin light brick. Okay. Back to the basement.

We were alone in the house and we had a secret. He was waiting for me. We were about to do something that wasn't allowed.

Down the stairs and through the living room. I was forcing myself to walk slowly. Nervous. Excited.

Too excited. At the top of the basement steps, I had to sit for a minute and count backwards from a hundred in French.

I was used to this. For the past couple of years, I'd been turning into some kind of whack-off machine, and I figured this was a side effect – fending off stray boners, usually at the most embarrassing times possible. I found ways to deal with it. Nobody had caught me yet.

I continued to count backwards. When I got to *quarante-cinq*, it was safe to go down there. The air in the basement was already thick with smoke shapes.

'Mark, what the fuck are you doing? Open a window!' He grumbled that I was being, like, totally bossy, but he did what I wanted.

Mark had shucked off his winter coat and thrown it on one of the couches. He was wearing long sleeves, fake denim hanging open over a white T-shirt that looked a little too small for him. He stretched and pushed at the window frame. The T-shirt rode up.

Underneath he looked soft, like something unshelled. But you could see muscles moving under his skin. A few light-brown hairs curled up from the waistband of his jeans.

I could feel my face going hot, and my ears. I looked away, but it was too late.

There was cold air melting into the room. Mark leaned against the wall and stuck a cigarette in the side of his mouth, tried to inhale and exhale without touching it, like somebody on TV. The smoke kept drifting into his eyes and making him laugh. I watched his mouth moving, his lips. I opened the pack of cigarettes and eased off the square of silver paper. Looked at the shiny fragment held between my fingers like I'd forgotten where it came from.

That little glimpse. Where he'd looked so vulnerable, so much his secret self.

How would it feel to touch?

My own stomach kind of fell away. Just for a second I pictured it. Standing behind Mark, resting my head between his shoulder blades, my arms around him. The heat from his body warming my face, the feel of his skin. How his breathing might change if he liked what I was doing.

Oh, God. He was looking at me full on.

'Man, are you okay?'

I nodded.

'You sure we need the window open? You still got your ...'

There was no way I was taking this coat off. I concentrated on the stupid cigarettes. My fingers felt thick and clumsy. We'd just been running around like children out there in the yard.

Okay. Calm the fuck down. This was just another body. Like the rest. In the locker rooms at school. On TV. Pictures. All those underwear and swimsuit ads from the Sears catalogue, that thick heavy book with the slippery pages that we'd collect from the ordering counter in town every four months. Mom would throw away the old ones and I'd rescue them from the garbage and stash them in my room. Hidden better than her cigarette cartons and love letters.

But those were pictures. Real people were different. Harder to control my thoughts, my reactions. It made me feel so helpless. Like when I'd be trying to do my homework and I'd go drifting off into stupid daydreams thinking about my English teacher – Mr Randall, just out of college. He'd hand out poems on paper warm from the photocopy machine, try to explain to us why he loved them. Actually said the word 'love' out loud, to a wall of blank hostility and slouching stares.

I stuck the cigarette in my mouth, lit it, inhaled deeply.

It was horrible. Hot and poisonous, the kind of heat you'd get from an infected sore. But I didn't start coughing. I was proud of myself for that. And I made an effort to draw the smoke into my lungs, not to wimp out and keep it in my mouth where it couldn't contaminate me.

I thought I was doing pretty well there, but when I looked up Mark was laughing.

'You're holding that thing like a queer, man.'

I felt like somebody'd banged a book over the top of my head.

'No, I'm not!' I looked at the cigarette doubtfully. 'I'm not.'

He was still laughing, leaning back with his head on the fake wood panelling under the window. 'You are. Even your mom doesn't hold a smoke like that.' I don't know what my face was doing. Mark stopped, seemed sorry for me all of a sudden. 'Hey. It's not a big deal. Just hold it different.'

I imitated him carefully: his posture, fingers, hands, how he inhaled and breathed out. It's what I did whenever I wasn't sure of anything. Copying Mark. I was good at it.

'See, that's better,' he said.

'Okay.' I didn't want to get to the end of the cigarette because it would mean I'd probably have to smoke another one. I wished Mark would leave. He was talking about our History teacher Mrs Blakely and how ugly she was, with her wide mouth and flat, baggy body. I interrupted before he could go into detail.

'Mark?' Wasn't sure how to say this, or if I should. 'How do you know if somebody is … one. You know.'

'Is what? Oh, a homo?' Mark grinned. 'If his name's Chris Randall. Then you know.'

I forced a laugh. *Sorry, Mr Randall.*

Mark went on to say no, Randall probably wasn't one. He was just some loser who'd never got laid in his life. You could tell a fag pretty easy, he said. You can tell by looking. Didn't I know this stuff? Didn't I watch TV? They acted real weird and talked weird. Like a girl, but disgusting. And they'd try to touch you.

'Did you ever see one?'

'No. Thank God. Cause if I did ...' He had plans. Mark got carried away, even went into a little imitation: what this person would do and say and sound like as he was getting killed.

I felt sick and slow – my stomach, my head. Everything was crowding in and I needed to be alone. I wanted to tell Mark to shut up and go. Stop bugging me with his body and his presence and his words.

Instead I started making suggestions for him. Intestines. All the stuff you could do with the guy's intestines. Where to shove the stick of dynamite before you lit it. Time was slowing and grinding down, like a pencil sharpener with its handle pushing in circles, and the air was too thick to breathe. Everything I said sounded like somebody else talking. *Please go home, Mark.*

He did, eventually.

The house was empty. Mom wouldn't be back for another hour. I couldn't get the taste of cigarettes out of my mouth. And the smell. I opened all the windows in the basement but it was still there. Probably in my clothes and hair too. Upstairs to the bathroom. Not the little cold one off my bedroom – we should have called that the whack-off room – the big one we both used for baths and showers.

Pulled the shower curtain back, that high clattering ring.

I don't know how much time passed. I was picking at the edges of our crumbling bath mat, dry sides of the tub on either side of me, all my clothes on, brown plastic shower curtain blocking off the rest of the house. I wanted to cry but nothing would come. Not even my voice. Everything was stuck inside me boiling away to nothing.

The worst insult on the playground. You'd almost rather be dead.

I bit down hard on the muscled base of my thumb. I couldn't feel it.

That stupid little daydream. Resting myself against Mark's back. It would have been okay if I'd just imagined something dirty, something hostile. I wasn't proud of those thoughts – but I wasn't afraid of them either. And somehow they didn't touch me. I wasn't in them, any of the little porno movies I played out in my mind when I was alone, these perfect men together who wouldn't kiss or look each other in the eye.

Mark. My cheek against his warm shoulder, his neck. His skin under my fingertips. And then what? What was I so afraid of?

He'd turn around and kiss me.

I shivered.

That was it. I wanted him to kiss me, wanted us to kiss with open mouths and tongues touching, like you'd see on TV. Like you'd see guys and girls doing on TV.

A hundred times worse than thinking about fucking him. A million times worse.

Then there was Mr Randall. How I'd walk the halls at school silently saying his name. *Christopher. Chris.* When assignments came back, I'd be crazy with suspense to see what he'd written ('Sensitive and insightful.' 'V. good analysis!'), and later I might trace over his comments with a pen, memorising the shape of the letters, picturing him alone in his house reading something I'd written.

It was ridiculous. I tried to laugh. Nothing. No tears or even a sound. While this pressure built. Thick, white smoke rolling around inside me, touching everything with cancer. I never should have had that cigarette.

I felt like turning on the shower and getting soaked in my clothes. But that would be stupid.

I went downstairs to the kitchen instead and sat slouched at the table. There was bread in a white paper bag on a brown board scraped clean, the knife to cut it for toast left on its side against the owl salt and pepper shakers. I rolled the knife along the table, watched it thunking like a square wheel over the red and white checks on the plastic cloth.

Wouldn't the guys at school just love this? The ones who'd still trip me in the halls when Mark wasn't around. Their eyes lighting up. Ha ha ha. We always knew it. And now Mark would be one of them.

I gave myself a little cut on the side of my finger.

What would Stanley say? I still thought about Stanley a lot. Every day. Imagined his reactions to everything – me, Mom, Mark, books I was reading. But that's all it was. Imagination. Me talking to me.

Blood started to dribble out of the cut I'd made. It didn't feel like anything. Distant and numb, packed in Styrofoam.

My mother, stuck in this town with me like I was her jailor. I'd screwed up her whole life, being born. I shouldn't be here.

There was something in the core of me that was wrong. And it was possible that all this stuff about men had nothing to do with it. My soul kicking sand in my face, trying to cover up what was really going on. Whatever it was. I tried to imagine myself having a normal, happy life. Chatting with people easily, not worried if I was saying the right thing or standing right or if they liked me. The only person I could feel that comfortable with was Mark.

Mark. Oh, God.

There was a box of matches next to a squat round candle on a plate. We liked candles. Mom and me. Made everything smaller, less lonely. I shook a match out of the box and struck it. A good smell. Satisfying.

I hardly realised what I was doing next.

I was surprised to hear my own voice. I was yelling. Then I cried for a while. The pain was bigger than I was, and I guess that was a relief. I took big, deep, shuddering breaths, blew my nose, shook my head. It was like something had left me. The whole side of my hand was throbbing beside the red burst blister on my little finger. I'd have to put a Band-Aid on it before Mom saw.

But first I had bigger things to decide.

I moved to the counter, looked at my reflection in our toaster. Like I said before, I went through my usual school thoughts and watched what happened to my face. Snotty. Mark was right.

Then I thought about Mr Randall.

Jesus Christ. It was right there, for anyone to see.

That's when I had my brilliant idea. Keep your head down. Act shy. Defensive strategy. Like steel doors slamming shut one after the other.

I hated chess. I hated sports. I hated games. But it looked like I was stuck in one – and one I wouldn't win. But if I could get to the finish line alive, that might be enough. I'd have to do this alone, of course.

That part wasn't going to be a problem. I knew how to be alone.

Chapter 7

Every year was the same.

November would come and the first dusting of snow on the mountain. December was all buzzy nerves from tests and exams, followed by the loneliness of watching TV Christmas with my mom. By February, I was already sick of the snow, the way it piled in pyramids, chewed up and spat out by the plough, melting in sullen puddles off our boots. April would arrive with its thaws and the warm peat smell of the woods, and then June opened into that long light that made you feel like you were going to live forever. July and August were our birthday months. I'd spend them lying around reading or hanging out with Mark or Lana. Green-gold fields stretched off and away; the sun filled the river with light. Everything looked better when there was no school.

September. A breath of cold and a few trees strangled into flame colours to remind me that the easy times were over. Each year I'd be ready to begin again with a new stack of blank notebooks, trying to get away from the person I'd been the year before. Then October:

bright leaves, dark nights, coats and sweaters tumbling from the top shelf of the closet. Grey November blowing in. First snowfall on the mountain.

I was thirteen, and then I was fourteen and then seventeen. Years like nothing.

After Lana moved to town, it was as if she'd always been there. I spent a lot of time at the Kovalenkos' that winter as 1984 began, watching videos on the big soft people-eating couch in the TV room where I'd usually end up falling asleep on Lana's shoulder, especially if the movie was no good. Once I heard her father chuckle from his recliner and mutter something in Ukrainian. Lana threw a pillow at him and alarmed the dog.

'He said I'm gonna marry the boy next door,' Lana told me later. 'He's an idiot.'

But we didn't live next door. Lana's place was in the nice part of town. Every house had a satellite dish and the front porches were stuffed with hanging tubs of flowers.

In the summer of 1984, seven months after Lana's house-warming party, I went to see Stanley. I went to see my father, but he wasn't there. There was a stranger in his place – a man in a suit and tie, with short hair that was already starting to march back from the crown of his head, his wild beard scaled down to a little scrub and a handlebar moustache. Smiling at me politely and shaking my hand in the airport, like somebody famous who was trying to be nice to a fan. We were close to the same height – this was about a month before my fifteenth birthday.

I spent a week at the Shulevitz home in Montreal, mostly hanging out with Stan's wife Sheila and helping her take care of the little babies, my sisters. If I saw my father, I tried to be somewhere else, and I was pretty sure he was playing the same game. Sheila threw us together a couple of times. She'd heard Stanley mention something about teaching me to play chess as a kid, so one night she set us up with the board at the dining room table and made herself scarce.

Silence hung between us like humidity. My father hunched over the chess board, his eyes fixed on the pieces in front of him. I slouched, sat up straighter, slouched again. I stretched my legs under the table, bumped his foot with my sneaker and apologised. He mumbled that it was okay.

I moved pawns when I couldn't think of anything else to do. They stumbled forwards onto buried landmines and died. I watched as my other pieces got mowed down and eaten. My horses and my castles. My thin bishops with their gilled mouths gaping downwards in shock. My queen shuffled dejectedly around the board, afraid of bothering anyone. My king was easily surrounded and paralysed – surprised by Stanley's troops with his feet in a tub of water and a towel around his head. I couldn't protect him.

I toppled the piece over, tiny fat cross on its sleek black head.
'You win.'
'I win,' he said joylessly. 'Want to play again?'
'Okay, sure.'

We passed an hour like that and then he said something about needing to get some work done. My father stood up, clapped a hand on my shoulder and squeezed it. I sat at the table for a long time. The castle walls crumbled and I was alone.

At the end of the week we said goodbye. His wife told me that this had been a lot of fun, that we should do it again next year. And so we did. Next year and the year after and on and on. A week in a great city with a nice young family and a guy who used to be my father.

At home I started skipping gym and reading grown-up books, got addicted to cigarettes. Grade Nine turned into Grade Ten.

I decided to quit being shy. Lana helped. I told her I had a problem talking to people, so she started bringing me along whenever she was out with a group of her friends. If I got too quiet, Lana would step on my foot under the table, and I'd force myself to say something.

I quit the other stuff too. The burning. The voodoo stupidity. I put the matches back by the casserole dish, slid the drawer shut and didn't open it again. The fingers on my left hand were all scarred up near the palms. I never let anyone see them.

In the spring, I skipped a lot of classes. It wasn't my idea.

This was around the first few months of 1985. Mark's dad had been gone for a while at that point, and his mother had boyfriends over a lot. Some of them seemed to be living there. Mark hated them all, thought the whole situation was bad for his little sister. Eventually he'd had to tell his mom not to bring men to the house anymore. They'd fought about it for weeks. He was only fifteen.

So I could understand why he was too restless to sit at a desk all day at school that year. We'd go down by the railway tracks instead, stand around throwing bottles at other bottles, sometimes have a few beers or smoke some low-quality weed. But I never went near anything stronger than hash.

Except once.

Patty Marsh's party. By then I was a few months shy of sixteen – old enough to get really fucked up, or so I'd thought. Everybody else who'd taken whatever the hell I had was strolling around the backyard gazing up at the stars. I was somewhere whimpering and clutching an aluminum garbage can. It was decorated with a picture of two little girls in old-time bonnets and inside there were clusters of tissues and something off Patty's hairbrush that looked like a big sticky tumbleweed and kept popping into weird staccato movements – faster and faster the longer I looked at it, like it was boiling.

Mark stuck something plastic in my mouth. There was a taste of searing mint.

'Leave puke on your teeth and pretty soon you won't have any.' He pried one of my arms off the trash can, tried to get me to take hold of this toothbrush that was jutting out of my face like a thermometer.

'Come on, man. I'm not gonna brush your fucking teeth for you.'

The toothpaste drool on my chin felt corrosive. I was sitting on the side of a pink bathtub staring up at Mark. There was a message on the trash can, scrolled in fancy handwriting under the little girls' feet: 'While days are warm and skies are blue, spend lots of time just being you.'

'I'm gonna die, Mark. I'm gonna die. I'm really sorry.'

'No, you're not. I told you. You're not allowed dying unless I say so.'

I argued with him for a while. I'd be dead any minute. I was so sure. I moved the toothbrush around my mouth and pictured my teeth breaking off and falling into my throat and then I couldn't breathe.

Mark laid a hand on my back. Little shivers went all through me and I felt myself starting to calm down. 'You're okay, Stephen,' he said carefully. 'Everything's gonna be okay. You believe me?'

I nodded.

He got the garbage can away from me somehow. We walked home through wet grass and backyards and I followed his voice in the dark. I couldn't see because I couldn't open my eyes – the stars were too overwhelming. I just felt the pressure of his arms around me as I was dragged along, pictured a lobster claw closed across my shoulders, twin furrows from my feet skidding through the grass.

The last thing I heard was Mark on the phone with my mother, telling her that I was with him, and that I was safe. When I opened my eyes the next morning, he was asleep on the floor beside the couch in his living room. I was on the couch.

'You went nuts when I tried to leave,' he explained to me later. 'So I didn't.'

○

Outside Riverside the world was churning out new horrors. Mom was getting sentimental because this old-time actor she'd always liked had cancer, and then it turned out not to be cancer at all – it was a new disease just for homos. They showed before and after pictures of him on the news a lot. In one frame he was a good-looking older guy in a tux under soft-focused light. In the second he looked stringy and tortured, and his eyes were insane. At school everybody made jokes about it. By October he was dead.

○

Grade Eleven. I got my driver's licence, after spending hours in the car practising with my mother. Poor Mom. The way she'd brace herself in the passenger seat, rigid and white-faced, shouting commands at me in a cracking voice. Sometimes I'd take my hands off the wheel completely and grin at her while she freaked out.

So I was sixteen and could legally drive. This was pretty incredible.

Mom wouldn't let me get a car of my own: she thought I'd drive drunk and end up killing myself. Besides, she said, we couldn't afford it. Mark had a car, though. A real piece of shit, but it had a tape deck so he could assault the neighbourhood with his crappy metal-head music at four in the morning. And, yeah, we drove drunk all the time.

We were deep into 1986. The superpowers were still stockpiling weapons and aiming them at each other, but Sting wrote a song about it, so that was okay. I'd sing the song at Mom to bug her because it was about Russians.

'Pop songs about nuclear war,' she said, disgusted. 'As if you poor kids didn't have enough troubles.'

Normal people started getting AIDS and then all of us were glad to be living in a nice safe place like Riverside. Nothing to worry about except herpes, crabs and gonorrhoea. Also substance abuse, child abuse, arson, teenage pregnancy, morons in Satan cults, suicide by firearms and the occasional episode of cow-fucking.

In the spring, Mark met a girl named Stacey in Arnottville, and they got serious fast.

I tried to see the appeal. She was blonde and had big tits – two qualities he admired. And blue eyes, which I believe he liked. Watery blue eyes. Hair the texture of fibreglass. A voice that seemed to droop into the back of her throat. Looked people up and down and kept whatever conclusions she'd drawn to herself. She looked me up and down sometimes. And dismissed me: Mark's annoying little sidekick, something left over from childhood.

Was he careful and serious, I wondered, when he kissed her?

I spent quite a bit of time with Stacey that summer, after Mark got thrown into Juvenile Detention for assault. Hard to believe that was only last year. The assault was really just a fight that got out of control outside a Valentine's Day dance at the Arnottville Legion Hall. They'd made Mark serve the three weeks in June and July so he wouldn't miss classes, which had totally pissed him off.

One afternoon me and Stacey were both waiting for him in the visitors' area at Juvie, and all these guys were coming up to me and calling me 'Mini-McAllister'. I asked Mark about this. He said he'd told everybody I was his younger brother.

'You just don't look like the kind of friend I'd have,' he said. 'Everybody in Riverside's used to it, but not these guys.'

'So!' I was in the car with Stacey going home. 'Guess I don't seem tough, huh?'

She glanced sideways, one hand on the steering wheel. 'No.'

'Think I should get a tattoo?'

We drove past a field of corn, sun turning the long folded leaves to dusty gold. Stacey lit a cigarette. I waited for her to offer me one. She didn't. I picked the pack up off the dashboard and took one anyway.

'Depends,' she said after a while. 'Tattoo of what?'

'The Jolly Green Giant.' I started laughing. 'I'd get the Jolly Green Giant on my arm. Would that be tough?'

'No.'

Safe to say I didn't like Stacey.

Then it was the end of July. Mark's birthday. He was out of Juvie and just turning seventeen, so there was a lot of drinking. And he got totally obnoxious.

'Hey! Hey ladies! This is my little brother. He's a virgin!'

'Jesus Christ, Mark, shut up!'

He could barely stand. We'd all just been thrown out of another Legion Hall dance in Arnottville, and Mark was reeling around the parking lot yelling at girls, while me and Stacey tried to keep him from falling on his face. You could hear music from the Legion, fuzzy and muffled like something underwater – that song I never liked about patio lanterns.

'Thought you didn't have a brother,' said a girl with a sticky lion's mane of hair frozen around her face.

Mark got me in a headlock and started rubbing his knuckles against my skull. 'You interested, Pam? Want to be his first?' He was choking me. 'Be gentle now.' Mark's voice was a dull slur. 'You be gentle with this one.'

'Fuck off.' All I could see were Mark's shoes and the pavement. Stacey and the other girl were laughing. 'Fuck off, fuck off, fuck off. Mark, fuck right off!'

'Aw, c'mon, don't say that.' Shifting his feet and rocking us. 'I love you, man. I totally do.'

He let me go and I was shaking my head, blinking. Mark turned to yell at more strangers walking by. 'This is my little brother! He's fucking helpless without me!'

Near the end of August, it was my turn. Seventeen years old. I told everybody I didn't want to celebrate – I wasn't much for birthdays – but Mom made a cake and Lana put together a stack of mix tapes and Mark took me out to this bar off the highway on the road to Arnottville. They didn't ID very often, otherwise there'd be no reason to be there.

We drank a lot of watered-down beer, listened to some terrible music and tried to pretend we were good at pool. None of the girls would talk to us because it was obvious we were high-school kids. And at the end of the night, Mark was out in the parking lot kicking the shit out of somebody. This time it was a sleazy-looking guy of about thirty-five, in a leather jacket and baseball cap. The hat had writing on it, stark capital letters. 'If girls are made of sugar and spice then why do they taste like tuna?'

The hat was on the ground. So was the guy who owned it. And a length of wood that had been propping open the screen to the back door, until Mark had wrenched it away so he could slam it into the side of the guy's head. Float like a butterfly, sting like a bee, whack with a two-by-four. That was Mark's style of hand-to-hand.

He was cursing and spitting. 'You cheap – stupid – piece – of shit!' Punctuating each word with a kick – to the guy's stomach, his throat, his ribs. I watched until I couldn't take it anymore.

I clutched at his arm and tried to drag him away. 'Stop it. Mark, stop it! You're gonna kill him! I don't want you to kill anybody.'

He let me have it – an elbow to the guts. I doubled over, almost threw up. But we had to get out of there before the guy's friends showed. Mark grabbed my arm and dragged me along after him. I followed with cramped steps and we ended up at a picnic table behind the Tasty Freeze across the highway from the bar, rustling cornfields on both sides of us, gravel making the ground roll away under our feet.

Mark was obviously still in the fight. He kicked at a rusty trash barrel with garbage foaming over the top. It was anchored to the side of the building by a chain, so it shuddered but didn't fall. He lunged at me, grabbed the neck of my T-shirt and yelled into my face.

'You fucking girl! I wasn't gonna kill him. And if I did, he deserves it!' Gave me a shove that threw me back a few steps.

'I … I didn't want you to get in trouble.'

He kicked the trash can again. Dented it.

'Fuck you, Stephen! Don't you know who that was?'

One of his mom's old boyfriends, he told me. Made sense, how quickly he'd set Mark off back at the bar.

'Hey, look, it's Maggie's little boy,' the guy had said, grinning and looking around at his friends, who were also in baseball caps and leather jackets. 'Mag-gie Mc-Al-lis-ter.' Savouring the name. A couple of the others had laughed.

'The fucker. The *fucker*,' Mark said. 'Used to sit there at the kitchen table, trip me up every time I went past …' Mark started pacing. He seemed to deflate the longer he walked. At first he was a man, a person who could have killed somebody. And then he was a kid like me. Tired and a long way from home.

Mark sat on the picnic table. He closed his eyes. I became aware of the sound of crickets in the cold night air. That creaky noise vibrating like the beat of a clock's second hand.

'This dickhead doing hot knives on the stove in front of my sister. Like he lived there. Him and not me. You remember?'

I remembered 'Tastes Like Tuna' then. Mark was right. The guy had moved right in and made himself at home, drinking in the middle of the day and watching TV with the curtains closed. Then one night Mark had shown up at our place around two in the morning because his mother had told him to leave. There'd been a fight between him and this guy, and Mark had lost.

'Should have killed him back there,' he said. 'Let the fucker die.'

I sat beside him on the table, dug into my pockets and handed Mark a lint-covered ball of Kleenex for his knuckles. When he pressed the white into the back of his hand, I saw dark spots emerge like ghost eyes. I stayed quiet. Some kind of bug town was building up around this one light in the back of the Tasty Freeze. Insects with legs like bundles of eyelashes. Little fluffs of moths. Crawly buzzing things.

'It was my house. I let him push me around like some stupid kid. I let her kick me out.' His eyes closed again and his hands were clenched together. 'God, I am so fucking worthless …'

'Aw, Mark. Don't.' I put my arm around him.

Then I was on the ground, all my weight on one elbow. Mark had pushed me off the picnic table. He was yelling at me.

'What is wrong with you? You queer or something?'

I turned my back, told him in a sulky growl to fuck off. Then I paced over sliding gravel, blinking and bending my arm to see if it still worked.

'I'm sorry,' he said.

I ignored him.

'Stephen, I'm *sorry*. C'mere.'

The lights were still on at the bar across the way. I listened to the stupid crickets, thought about walking into the corn rows and falling asleep there. Or heading off down the highway alone. Better than going anywhere with him.

'Get *over* here!' Mark was slapping the surface of the picnic table. I called him an asshole and a psycho. We stared at each other in the dark. Then I plodded over and took a seat on the table, at the farthest corner from him. Mark slid himself close. He grabbed my arm and draped it over his shoulders, like a dog angling its head under your hand when it wants a pat. His back started to tremble.

I reached my other arm around him, held on tight.

He told me everything. He couldn't seem to stop. He said he was sorry he'd pushed me, that he was stupid, that he didn't understand himself. How he'd almost hit Stacey a couple of weeks before when he was drunk, and he was terrified he might hit his little sister Krystal someday.

'If that ever happens, I'll kill myself.' One hand was clasping my arm, still tight across his chest. 'Maybe I'll do it anyway. I don't know what I'm good at. I don't know what I'm good *for*. I don't even know if I still believe in God.' He squeezed my forearm harder. It hurt. 'And look how I acted with you tonight. It's your birthday, man. It's your fucking birthday.'

'Come on. You know I don't give a shit.' I relaxed my hold and moved away by inches. He pressed his hand to his eyes, bloody tissue like a parade float flower still stuck to his knuckles.

'Never should've called you that,' he said. 'You're the only one who doesn't judge me. Except Krystal, and I can't exactly be a real person for her.' Mark took out his cigarettes and offered the pack to me. I took one, slapped my pockets but couldn't find my lighter. He struck a match and held it out.

His face in the brief firelight was so beautiful it shocked me.

'You don't judge me and you don't lie,' he was saying. 'You know how rare that is?'

'I lie all the time.' My voice died away on the last word.

'Not to me. You don't lie to me.'

I couldn't meet his eyes. I noticed a baseball cap on the ground by the table. Telling us about girls tasting like tuna. Mark must have carried it over, like a trophy. Or maybe I had, just to have something to cling to out of nerves. He saw it and gave a choked little laugh, settled the hat on my head at an awkward angle.

'Happy birthday. Looks fucking debonair.'

We had to go back to the bar to get Mark's wheels, went straight to the parking lot.

The guy Mark had beat up was long gone. But a couple of girls were there leaning against his car and the stupid hat turned out to be a conversation starter. Mark convinced them to go for a drive. We ended up somewhere on a dirt road surrounded by woods.

Mark and his girl started making out right away. So much for Stacey. I left the car with my girl and we went for a walk down the road in the moonlight. It smelled like there was a farm nearby. I couldn't register anything about the person I was with other than she was really short and had bushy brown hair and an acne problem and I thought her name started with T. I asked her lots of questions because I didn't want to talk about myself. Then she stopped and turned to face me.

'You want to go check out the woods? Might be somewhere we can lay down.'

I stared back at her stupidly. Then I stammered that it was a nice idea, but we didn't know each other that well. 'See, I never actually did it before,' I said. I realised my voice had gotten softer and I was looking at the ground. Slipping into my old shy act. It came in handy sometimes. 'I think it would be great to be friends first. Or if I'm lucky, it'll be with somebody I love.' I glanced up to see how the girl was taking this.

She was smiling like Christmas. 'Oh, that is so *sweet*! How come I never met you before?'

I risked a look back down the road. 'You think they're done? It's kind of cold out here.' We took a few steps closer to the car. They weren't done.

The months rolled away – I didn't even feel them go. A new school year, the last one. Everything gearing up for college and goodbye. Then it was April 1987. That night in the basement in front of the TV with the smoke shapes thick around our heads. And the world ended.

But why? Because I'd thought about kissing Mark? I'd imagined a lot worse over the years. That ache I'd first felt taking root when I was thirteen, unwrapping a pack of cigarettes and watching him push open my window to let the cold air inside. It was part of me.

So why had it hurt so much, that night? Why was it impossible to go back now?

It wasn't sex. That's not what had scared me. It was love. Love and stupid hope. But something else as well, standing behind it all, setting everything in motion.

I knew when the summer faded I'd be gone. And I realised then that there was something I had to do. The ghost shows up in Act One and gives you a mission. And if you're a man, you'll cut the soliloquies and do it.

Tell him. Tell him everything.

I couldn't leave Riverside without a goodbye for Mark, a real one. It would be unfair to both of us. He had to know.

Or … was I so sure that it would really be goodbye? What if he understood?

Or better.

Stupid, demented hope. Leave me alone. I'd pray if I knew how. For patience, for more time. For self-control – just enough so that I wouldn't make a complete disaster out of this.

Impossible things.

Chapter 8

I didn't understand time. It could freeze like cement in an hourglass. It would be Wednesday and I couldn't imagine it would ever be Friday. It would be February and I knew it would never be June. And then one day I was on my way to the hardware store where my best friend worked and hoping I wouldn't run into him there, with my college acceptance letter in my backpack and less than three months of high school left for both of us. It had all gone by like one afternoon.

The sidewalks were still grainy from sand trailed across the ice all winter, though it was almost May and the snow was long gone. I pushed my way into the shop, welcomed by the hollow clunk of cow bells on a string. Riverside's Home Hardware had the chain store logo, but the aisles were close together and packed with junk, wooden floors grey and worn. This was the place to get your lawn statues of the seven dwarves mooning each other, or those vulture-sized wooden butterflies people would clip to the sides of their houses for reasons I could never understand.

I was here because I'd run into some trouble clearing out the old hiding places in my room, getting ready for the big move to Halifax. Some of these spots were incredibly hard to get to – I'd made them back when I was twelve or thirteen, just a little guy with arms like dried pasta. Anyway, I'd had kind of a violent accident involving the wall in the back of my closet and now I needed plaster and paint. A lot of it.

There was a voice at my elbow. 'Sir? Can I help you with anything?' I flinched. Mark. He was in his red Home Hardware polo shirt, the uniform he had to wear here.

'Hey, college boy.' Mark was smiling, the kind of tense, fake smile he'd put on if he really wanted to punch somebody. I asked him what was up with this 'college boy' stuff.

'Your mom gave me the big news,' he said. 'When I went to your place and you weren't around.'

I could see why he was mad. I'd never told him about the acceptance letter. And he really had shown up at my house a few nights earlier, just to hang out. But when Mom called from the kitchen, I'd stayed quiet in my room. *I'm not home*, I told them silently. I heard my mother offer Mark some tea, and then they were chatting and laughing together for what seemed like hours while I'd waited – trapped, hugging my knees on my bed, stranded and motionless.

'Oh, that,' I said. 'Didn't think it was such a big deal. I mean, it's only Halifax.'

'Right. Your mom said you carry that college letter around with you.'

'I do not.'

'Let's see it.' Mark made a sudden lunge for my backpack. I dodged his arm, told him to quit it.

He laughed. 'Come on, man. I know you got it on you.'

He came at me again. I jolted backwards and behind us a free-standing rack loaded with house numbers tinkled and shuddered. Mark glanced up the aisle, probably checking to see if his boss was around.

I forced a smile of my own. All a big joke, folks, nothing strained or hostile going on here. We're friends. I opened my pack, found the letter, handed it over. Mark scowled down at the paper as if this were his draft notice I'd been hoarding away.

'Stepan Vladimir, eh? Happy for you,' he said blankly.

Then a tiny, hunched old lady wanted to talk to Mark about some hooks she'd bought for her kitchen. I skulked off to the back of the store as he explained that they were really only for wooden surfaces and even then she'd have to be careful of how much weight they'd hold.

'So why would you sell these things?' She stared up at Mark fiercely.

Don't watch. Paint and plaster. Find it and get out. I could still hear Mark's voice, and if I craned over the aisles I could see him. His shoulders were stooped, the back of his neck bent downwards – he was talking to his boss now, and she was almost as small as the old lady. No, the customer couldn't have a refund, his boss was telling him. The hooks were damaged. It was too late.

Jesus Christ. They cost thirty cents a piece. This is what he did all day?

Just quit for the afternoon, Mark. Walk out. Let's both go somewhere where we can try to be normal again. Get high in our little clearing by the river, nothing on our minds except school and dumb movies and no-name ripple chips.

How had everything changed so fast?

I wasn't going to find what I wanted. The colours were all wrong. Instead I picked out the closest substitutes, paid at the cash and then headed straight for the door, cowbells waiting to ring me out. Yes, I had to tell him. But not here. Not today.

Couldn't leave the store. Someone was gripping my arm. Mark again. I turned and we were facing each other.

'Listen, man. I wasn't being sarcastic back there,' he said. 'I really am happy for you, Stephen. Totally. And … I always knew you'd do it.' Mark smacked me on the back, a little pat. More like he was consoling than congratulating me.

'Okay,' I said.

Mark shook his head. 'Friggin' nutcase.'

'Thanks.' My voice felt creaky. 'Asshole.'

He must have seen a flicker of apology in my eyes because he smiled. I smiled back.

That's what you do, when you're in love.

Part 2
After the world ended

Chapter 9

Whitney Houston was screaming on my clock radio, cutting right through a dream. She wanted to dance with somebody. To feel the heat with somebody. The word 'heat' was a high cutesy squeak. The song charged on with marching band confidence. She'd find somebody to dance with, this girl.

I hit the off button several hundred times.

Then I stared at the ceiling and listened to the rain on the roof, trying to figure out this dream, still half in it. It was a weird one. I was making out with Mark on a bed, on this bed. And he kept telling me that he hated me, that everybody hated me, even God. This was disconcerting, because otherwise he'd seemed like he was really into it, but he wouldn't stop saying this stuff, right in my ear, over and over until I was pleading with him to stop.

There'd been a violent thunderstorm during the night and it was raining again. It would probably rain for days. A month had gone by since the end of the world, and now it was May.

I still hadn't told him anything.

Breakfast in the kitchen. Lots of low, dark clouds, so we had to turn on the lights. Mom flicked some pepper at her hard-boiled egg. The top fell off the owl-shaped shaker and the egg got buried in greyish powder. The owl's decapitated head glared up at us. I tried to look innocent.

'I should make you eat this, you know. It's what you deserve.' My mother got up from the table and dumped her plate into the sink.

'I'll be gone in a few months anyway.'

'Don't remind me!' She turned around and kissed the top of my head.

'Mom, quit it.'

Mark came by then, like always. Usually if there was any breakfast still around, he'd eat it and talk to my mother about cooking. Today he fished Mom's pepper-covered hard-boiled egg out of the sink and ate that.

I listened to them and didn't say much of anything. I'd decided the only way to get through what was left of the school year with Mark was to make myself go dead where he was concerned. So I'd stare at something just over his head, to the side of him, out the window. Trying to leave a blank in the world where he used to be.

School was a blur. Flickering fluorescent lights, rows of lockers with their vents that seemed to breathe out foulness. People shoving each other, greeting each other, watching each other. 'How weary, stale, flat and unprofitable seem to me all the uses of this world.' English class. Poor old Hamlet. Everybody in the play kept going on about how much they loved and admired him, but nobody seemed to actually listen to a word he said. No wonder the guy was always talking to himself.

Canadian History. The smell of damp clothes, melting gel and mousse running down the backs of necks, windows fogging from the warmth of wet humans squished into their chairs. We waded through the articles of the Manitoba Act. Apathetic little doodles collected in the margins of my binder, some very irritated-looking monsters and aliens with trees growing out of their heads.

'So boring,' said Lana. 'Canada needs a higher body count.'

I slapped at my face to stay awake.

Final bell. The sky was concrete. Trunks of the trees were dark, apple and cherry blossoms looking toothless and bedraggled, petals stuck to the ground like confetti. Mark and I walked home to my place through the downpour. Mom wouldn't be home for a couple of hours, so we decided to smoke up and watch *The Toxic Avenger*. Weed was usually just a Sunday thing for me. But as we got closer to the end of school, I found myself bending a lot of my old rules. And there was something cosy about the idea – the two of us in here getting stupid together while the rain hammered down. We made our way to the basement. Mark pushed open the door to the laundry room.

'I'm gonna use the dryer, okay?'

He started taking off his clothes.

I turned around. Climbed the stairs two and three at a time, calling out over my shoulder, 'Gotta do something! Just remembered. I'll be …'

Kept going, straight out the front door.

Don't look back. Don't think about it.

I was striding through town with the rain bucketing down on me, twisting through various shades of squirmy despair. *Jesus, Mark. Stripping off right there in my house like the first scene of some cheap porno.* But he'd done this before, wrapped himself in a sleeping bag and waited for his stuff to get dry. Well, why not? Nothing I owned would fit him. And we were both fellas, right? We were both dudes. Man.

Mist was rising from the river, mist on the side of the mountain. Nobody around but me.

I ended up in a wide, featureless park by the water's edge. We'd assemble there for fireworks every year on the first of July – otherwise I had no idea why it existed. I kept pacing forwards. Past the tiny tourist centre, where during the summer a high-school kid on government pay would wait for American retired couples to wander in asking for directions to other towns. Past a park bench – same place I'd sat with my parents in the snow, the day they got married. To the river.

Gradually I became aware of a dark shape hulking by the edge of the water. Almost looked like an animal. I got closer. It was. A cow with its mouth open in a frozen scream, drowned and washed up on the riverbank, stiff legs like branches jutting towards the sky. *Oh, great. So this is my life now.* Standing in the pissing rain staring at a dead cow. Next thing you know, I'll be writing poetry about it.

I turned my back on the wreck of the animal and sat by the riverbank, soaking up mud and feeling water drip down my neck. I didn't want to be here, with this horrible thing as my only companion. I wanted to be home. Safe and dry. Getting stoned and watching *The Toxic Avenger* with my friend, with Mark.

Peeling off his wet clothes in the laundry room, the shocked, red, goose-pimpled look of his skin. If you touched his cold back, your hand would leave an impression that looked like a hand, just for a second.

Nobody but the cow could hear me. So I said it, staring into the river.

'I love you.'

The surface of the water was pebbled and pockmarked from the rain. That dream. Mark whispering that he hated me, and so did God. I pictured this Almighty, leaning in over the earth for a look at all the amusing little people and their problems. I'd come into view and he'd go, 'Oh, for crying out loud, not *that* kid again!' Give the globe a spin and turn away, disgusted.

I tipped back my head. Drops of water dive-bombed out of a white sky. It wasn't ever going to stop.

Back through town. Lana was outside her house. Looking so sweet I almost wanted to cry, in a yellow raincoat and hat like you see on kindergarten children or old-time fishermen. She made her way over to the picket fence where I was standing, the soft rounded shape of her. Scissors and lengths of green were clutched in her pale hands; she'd been cutting peppermint by the side of the house.

'What's going on? You're soaked.'

I felt metal under my chin. Lana was trying to lift my head with the handle of the scissors, make me look at her.

'Stephen? Are you okay?'

I didn't answer. She broke off a sprig of peppermint and put it in my mouth. Such a sharp, clean taste. Chewing on a bunch of leaves kind of reminded me of the cow, though.

'Thanks.'

'Listen, do you want to come in? You can have supper with us. My parents won't mind.'

I took Lana's hands and kissed them, kissed both of them, like somebody in a Russian novel. Then I turned and walked away, splashing through the shallow murky puddles on the sidewalk.

'Hey, wait,' she said. 'Where are you going?'

'I don't know. Gotta go home. Shoot myself. Or something.'

She looked stricken and I was sorry I'd said anything.

'You're kidding, right?'

'Yeah. Just kidding.'

The windows of my house were lit. I came in through the back. In the kitchen, the counters were covered with food and there were pots bubbling away on every burner. It smelled nice, like home should smell. Mom was tearing up lettuce for a salad. Mark was at the stove. A frying pan popped and spat at him.

Then they were both staring at me, this soggy weirdo standing in the doorway like a drowned ghost.

'God, Stephen! Where on earth have you been?' my mother said. 'And look at you. You're dripping.'

'Yeah, what the fuck, man? Oh, sorry, Mrs S.'

'That's okay, Mark. At least *you* apologise for it.' She was talking to him but looking at me. They were both looking at me, waiting.

'Went out to buy something,' I said. It occurred to me that I was empty-handed. 'Forgot my wallet.'

My tractor boots were water-logged. I listened to the lid on a pot bumping up and down as it boiled over, like a person forgetting what they were going to say.

'Mark made spaghetti sauce,' my mother announced.

'I totally did! Like, not out of a jar or anything. You shoulda seen it. I was chopping up onions and garlic and … and all this stuff …'

Whoa. He was really high. But my mother didn't seem to notice.

'Isn't that great?' said Mom. 'Now, I don't know why you're not interested in cooking, Stephen. You'll be in your own place soon enough.'

'Don't remind me.'

My mother sent me upstairs to change. Dinner turned out to be a bit of a party. Mom put candles on the kitchen table. I kept getting up to turn on the overhead light and she kept turning it off again. It wasn't that I didn't like candles. I did. You put a candle on and you're in a different place. That warm light forgives everything. It's the way you'd hope God sees the world.

It was just that I didn't want to be looking at either of them that way.

But Mom won. The kitchen became this cosy, dark cave. Mark's and Mom's faces were all I could see, and I loved them both so much. It was torture.

Mark went to flick some pepper on his food and the top of the owl shaker fell off. A pile of grey powder splattered his dinner. He started laughing, head bowed almost to the table and hands linked at the back of his neck.

My mother cracked up in giggles.

'Oh, no! I meant that for Stephen. Just a little prank. I'm so sorry, Mark. Let me get you another plate.'

But I'd already slid Mark's plate with the pepper on it over to me, given him mine in exchange.

'It's okay. It's what I deserve.'

I suppose I'd meant this as a joke. They glanced at each other.

'Stephen, sweetheart,' said my mother. 'I'm the one who was messing around with the pepper. You didn't do anything.'

An exploded coalmine on a hill of red glop. I was going to continue to face down this spaghetti until they both forgot about what I'd said, and the strangeness of it.

'Mark, I'm going to put the rest of this sauce in a jar for you,' my mother said. 'You can take it home.'

'Aw, that'd be awesome, Mrs S.'

'So now I'm going to, you know, look for a Mason jar.' She said this in an almost theatrical tone and stepped out of the room.

Mark leaned close. 'Think she knows? That I'm kind of ...' He grinned, dipped his head. His eyes were red and swimming.

'She doesn't have a clue.'

'Smoked the whole thing myself. When I could see you weren't coming back.'

I started making patterns with the mess on my plate. The noise of the clock was small and relentless.

'Stephen?'

'Yeah?'

'Stephen, what the fuck is going on?'

He wasn't smiling anymore.

'Told you. I went out to buy something. I forgot my wallet.'

'No, I mean the past month or so.'

Something about this was all wrong. The way my mother had left, so suddenly and strangely. Oh, fuck.

'My mom asked you to talk to me, didn't she?'

'No …' Mark was suddenly interested in his fork. Then he let out a long, slow sigh. 'Okay, yes. But don't get mad at her. She's worried. Comes home every day and you got your head in the sink and you won't tell her what's wrong.'

'Nothing's wrong. Nothing's different. Put that in your report.'

'Now, don't get all …,' he said. 'I wasn't gonna tell her anything. She didn't ask me to. She just wanted me to get you talking.' He let the fork fall back to his plate. It speckled the plastic tablecloth with red. 'I mean, fuck's sake, Stephen. We both knew you were up there hiding from us that night I came by. You remember? And why'd you act like going to college was some big secret? Happy people don't do that shit. It's obvious you got some problem and you don't want to tell anybody about it.'

I looked him in the eye then, for maybe the first time in weeks. Then I looked away. At the daisy clock, the glass window in darkness reflecting this little pool of light on the table.

'You ever feel like God hates you?'

Mark gaped at me. It was as if I'd punched him. 'Are you serious? That is, like, the worst thing I ever heard.'

'Sorry.'

'God doesn't hate anybody, Stephen. God isn't ... capable of hate. You're His creation. He'd do anything to help you.' The chair groaned against the floor as he pushed himself backwards. Mark dug the heels of his hands into his eyes, like a child miming sleepiness. 'Hey, that sounded really dumb, huh? I am so stoned.'

'It's okay.'

'Can't believe you'd say something that fucked up.'

I started playing with the little yellow drop of flame. Mark moved the candle away.

'Look, are you on something?' he said. 'You don't seem like you're on something, but ...'

I sat up a bit straighter. 'Okay, McAllister.' Sounded ridiculous. 'Mark. If I ...' I coughed. I didn't know how he was reacting to this, because I couldn't look at him. I tried again. 'If I tell you something, do you promise you won't ...'

My mother came back, brandishing a Mason jar. 'I knew it!' she said. 'I knew I had one of these somewhere.'

Thank you, Mom. I couldn't believe how close that was. How stupid I'd just been. Blurting it out like a moron, nothing prepared. The wrong time.

Mom glopped the rest of Mark's sauce into the jar, glass catching the candlelight as it filled with red. She washed the sloppy bits off the edges and presented it to him. He turned it over and over in his hands.

'Hey, I totally made this stuff!'

He went home when the rain stopped. We cleaned up. I didn't say anything unless I had to. Then I went up to my room and tried to read. I couldn't.

I turned over and set the clock radio for another morning. Wondered what awful song would wake me up, and from what nightmare, and into what coma dream.

There would be days of this. Months. Years.

It was probably about this time that I started making that stupid list of ways and means to die.

Chapter 10

I could hear songbirds and crows, a tractor starting up somewhere, Mr Fitzwilliam opening the gas station across the way and humming to himself. It sounded like a hymn. The water picked up light from the morning sun and the day began.

I should have been happy.

I was in the little clearing overlooking the river where Mark and I always went, but I was by myself this time. It was seven o'clock in the morning. The past couple weeks or so, I hadn't been able to sleep. It would take forever for my brain to switch off at night and then as soon as there was light, I'd be wide awake again. All day I'd be blinking a lot, feeling like there was an invisible weight pressing around my skull, brain turning to gravel in my head.

Mid-May. Only a month to go before finals. This wasn't really important considering I'd already been accepted to university, but caring about exams was a tough habit to break. So I had all my textbooks with me and was writing out summaries of the chapters I needed. My notebook was open to a blank page.

My pen was on the paper. I didn't write anything.

I tried to focus on something good. The programme I'd be starting at college. That cool, intimidating stuff on the reading list. Plato and Dante, Nietzsche and Dostoyevsky. And I'd be living on my own. A different life, a better one.

But I couldn't picture it. Something had happened over the past few weeks, and the future didn't exist anymore. My new place, my new friends, my classes. Nothing. A blank. Meeting other guys like me. Total blank. When it came to that, all I could think of were images on TV, characters from jokes the kids would tell in the cafeteria at school. Cartoons.

I stared at the page in my notebook, eyeballs dried out and wooden from lack of sleep. Should have been. Happy. Such a moron of a word, those two stupid syllables slapping up against each other. So it should be easy to achieve, right? Why did I have to feel like this instead?

Why was I so sure I'd never see September?

This ache knocking around the back of my head – like when you're about to say goodbye to somebody, something, maybe forever.

Goodbye was the general mood around school. Graduation was a precipice we were edging towards, and the Grade Twelves were getting clingy and huggy and sentimental. Writing in each other's yearbooks, getting together for marathon bonding sessions. Even the prom seemed like it was going to be one enormous farewell party.

Just yesterday, we were in a group of fifteen or twenty at Cindy Harrison's house watching videos, as many *Friday the Thirteenth* chapters as we could stand. People were drifting off to sleep one by one, pushing a big bowl of popcorn around, relaxing into their chairs like their bones were unlocking themselves.

Jeff Webb's girlfriend had fallen asleep on him as they lay sprawled on the couch. I could see her wake up, run her fingers up the side of his neck and through his hair. She was so sure of him. Jeff said, 'Hey, weirdo. You loving the movie, huh?' And they kissed and smiled. A whole room full of people around them and they didn't care.

I was on the floor a few feet away from the TV, arms around my knees like a totem pole carving, trying to focus on this stupid movie. Mark was stretched out half asleep on a throw pillow beside me. On the glass screen, Jason Voorhees made his way through the woods with his hockey mask and his hiker's stride, looking for more thirty-year-old teenagers to plop a machete into. Mark's breathing was slow and steady, his eyes closing for a few seconds at a time before he'd blink himself awake.

And all I'd wanted was to get thrown through the glass of the TV set and feel a machete sink into my head. Thank you, Jason.

Although *Friday the Thirteenth, Part 7: The Mercy Killings* wouldn't make too much money. I pictured a dark wood full of disappointed people, all sinking to the forest floor without complaint as the shambling psycho walked among them with his chainsaw. A day at the office for him. Maybe a few of the murdered would give Jason the thumbs-up sign as they drifted to the ground.

Suicide by Jason. I'd have to file that one away with the rest of them. The ways and means. Razors, pills, hanging, guns, jumping in the river, rigging up a car to feed me carbon monoxide. I'd been through the pros and cons. I wasn't sure how or when it would happen. Really hoped I'd be dead before people started finding out about all this weird sex stuff. Because if they knew this about me, I was sure they were going to assume that it was *the reason*. Everybody milling around my mother's house in black, eating little triangle sandwiches with the crusts cut off. 'Oh, of course. That's why. Well, how unfortunate.'

I didn't want to be dismissed so easily. There were a hundred different reasons. Or there was no reason at all. There was just big, fat, fucking fate sitting on my head.

Too much time had gone by. The light was different already. I had to have breakfast with Mom, meet Mark and head off to school with him. Start another day.

On our way to school, I tried to fill in the silence.

Hey! Only a month to go and we're finished.

Man, I will not miss this place at all.

Wow! I have nothing to say but I'm going to keep blabbering on forever anyway.

We were halfway to Riverside Regional High School and about a block away from Riverside Regional Elementary.

Then Mark mumbled something about English class and it all fell apart because I realised I'd forgotten to do his homework.

Forgot Mark's homework, for the first time. The first time in almost ten years.

Mark and schoolwork were never a good mix. It's not that he's stupid. He just has some kind of block. A bit like me and sports. I used to lend him books I liked and he'd lie about reading them. It was sad to know we couldn't share this stuff.

I got hyper and panicky, started apologising.

'Hey, calm down,' said Mark. 'It's no big deal.'

'But, I should've remembered ...'

'Well, jeez, if you're that worried, we'll just copy it out now.'

Mark took hold of my backpack and lifted it off me like he was shelling a turtle.

'Whoa, Stephen. This is fucking heavy. What do you need all this shit for?'

He opened the pack, started shuffling books and papers around. Handling everything, looking at everything, taking stuff out and laying it on the sidewalk. He found a flattened pack of cigarettes in the bottom of the bag, shook one out of the little squashed box and stuck it in his mouth.

'Look, just leave it alone,' I said. The *Hamlet* short answers were in my Chemistry textbook where I'd left them: my answers and Mark's blank sheet folded together. The remedial kids had the same homework as the rest of us. The teachers just expected less.

Mark balanced the textbook on his knee and tried to write, but it wasn't working. He swore. Then he smacked the book onto the nearest flat surface, which was my back, and started to copy the answers onto his paper.

I moved away. He lodged the book between my shoulders again.

'What is your problem?' he said.

'I don't want us to be late.'

Mark was having trouble holding the textbook and my answers at the same time. He moved up close, fingers on the back of my neck. Blew a stream of smoke past my ear.

'Wait,' I said, 'I can copy it out faster than you can. I can do your handwriting too. Nobody will know.'

Mark ignored this. That pencil crawled along, letter after stubborn letter. He spat something on the sidewalk.

'I can even make it sound like something you'd write.'

The book slid off me.

'Fuck's that supposed to mean?'

'Just – you wouldn't use some of these words.'

He slammed the book onto my back again, kept scratching away. I winced and wished I was at the bottom of the river.

'Hey, what's this word? I can't read your writing.'

'How do I know what word you're looking at?'

He read, in that thick tortured voice he used whenever he had to read anything out loud. I hated the sound of it. It brought Mark down, and brought whatever he was reading down too, and they'd meet in a space that was all blunt edges and hostility and confusion. When it was his turn in class, the teachers used to let him struggle through a half a sentence and then say, 'All right, Mark, thank you.' And if he mixed up 'b' and 'd', which he sometimes did, everybody would laugh. He'd sit with his face going deep red, looking like he wanted to murder someone.

'This quote. Shows. That. Hamlet. Ass ... sumes his. Dead—'

'His death.' Still on question one.

'Assumes his death. Is in – something. Can't read this. Your letters are all, like ...'

This might have been bearable if I was wearing a winter coat or maybe a dozen sweaters. But I just had this one stupid T-shirt that was about a hundred years old and I could feel his weight and his breathing, could practically feel the ridges of his fingerprints on me.

'Inexorable,' I said. 'He assumes his death is inexorable. That's the question about the "divinity that shapes our ends", right?'

'I don't know. I didn't read the questions. Spell that.'

'I – N – X ...' I couldn't concentrate. 'No, that's not right.'

'What's after X?'

'I said it's not right, for fuck's sake!'

'Jeez, take it easy.' Mark leaned in closer. 'So it's not X. What is it?'

Change the channel. Think about something serious, something gross. The Holocaust. Gangrene. Old people doing it. People with gangrene and leprosy having sex with old people in the lobby of a

Holocaust museum, bits of everybody jiggling and falling off while tourists walk in and out crying and wailing.

'I – N – E ...' Desperately trying to think straight, spell one retarded little word. I couldn't. Not with him breathing in my ear. 'I – R – Fuck! Just fucking write "fate"!'

'How do you spell ...?'

'Oh, Jesus Christ!' I lunged away from him. The book went smack on the ground. The papers fell whirling around us.

'Goddammit,' I said. 'Can't you leave me the fuck alone? Every time I turn around you're in my face. And nobody's gonna think you wrote that yourself. You wouldn't say "inexorable". You wouldn't say it and you wouldn't write it. You don't know what it means!'

He stood and stared at me. Everything I'd said started echoing back. I listened to the creaking of the swings at the elementary school just down the street, children laughing and calling to each other. Mark turned around and marched back the way we'd come.

I ran after him, telling him I was sorry, hanging from his arm like a little kid. He lashed out with an elbow to my ribs that sent me reeling.

'Don't fucking touch me. Think I don't know what's going on here?'

Oh, God. I stood perfectly still, waited for it.

'So you're going to college. Guess you think that makes you something special.'

'It's not that!'

'It's because you're an arrogant piece of shit. You always thought you were better than the rest of us.' He turned his back, started away again. 'Fuck you.'

I tried to make him face me. He put his hands on my shoulders and shoved, and I stumbled backwards. There were knots of children bobbing down the street all around us. Must have been nearly time for the first bell.

When Mark spoke, his voice was level and calm. 'Stop following me around. I don't want to talk to you. Not now, not ever.' He looked me up and down. 'Fucking Jew bastard.' He left. I didn't try to stop him.

This was serious. Mark didn't give a shit about Jews one way or another. He wanted me to know he'd drawn some kind of line between us. He thought it was my number-one insult. It wasn't – it hadn't been for years – but he didn't know this.

I picked up the textbook and papers and shoved them into my backpack, then found myself sinking to the kerb. Children were passing by, debating with each other about whether I was sick or crazy or on drugs or all three. Somewhere behind me a voice was saying, 'Gonna be another beautiful day, eh? Good laundry weather.' Another voice was agreeing.

A very small hand touched my shoulder. 'Stephen? Are you okay?'

It was Kyle Healey.

'I'm fine, Kyle. I got a headache, that's all.'

'I don't have any aspirins. But I have some gum. Do you want it?'

I said sure, and he found a cube of green Hubba Bubba in the pocket of his cords, squashed and lint covered, with the wrapper half off. I thanked him and told him I'd have it later.

It occurred to me that he was alone. 'You're not walking with your friends?'

'My friends don't like me.'

'That's too bad.'

'Maybe they'll like me tomorrow.' He started walking away, waving over his shoulder. 'Bye, Stephen! Don't have a headache, okay? You shouldn't.'

'I won't.'

I watched Kyle making his way towards the school, keeping an obedient three paces behind a group of boys who kept turning around and telling him to go away.

My backpack was on the sidewalk. I hauled it towards me and took out the cigarettes. There was a bit of money in there and I got that too. The rest I just left. Schoolbooks. Notes. What did I need this shit for?

I looked down the street where Mark had gone. Then I turned and headed off in the opposite direction.

Chapter 11

The sign was round and solid, set into a concrete base. It reminded me of a tombstone. On one side was written: 'Welcome to Riverside – population 1,816. We're the friendly town.' On the other side: 'You are leaving Riverside. Come back again soon.' I'd reached the town limits. It never took long.

Wind rippled the grass and the sun beat down on the back of my neck. A few rust-coloured cows were staring heavily. I played around with the sign – stepping forwards and backwards, from one side to the other. Welcome! You are leaving! Welcome!

I decided to keep walking until I knew what to do.

Back to town, pacing those quiet streets. I was so stuck in my own head that I almost didn't hear my name. It was Lana, on the front steps of her house. Drying her hair in the sun, applying another coat of black to her toenails.

Nice to see my friend with no make-up on for once, a sweet-faced girl in jeans and her father's white shirt. When I asked Lana why she wasn't in school, she just said she couldn't be bothered on such a beautiful day.

'You okay, Stephen?'

I tried to tell her about the fight with Mark, but couldn't make myself say his name.

And I didn't mention it again, not until we'd got really stoned off some very strong hash her cousin had brought down from Toronto.

'Watch out,' Lana told me. 'This is not that lame crap you and Mark buy off Craig Morrel. Think he cleans that shit out of his lawnmower.'

'You think I'm a wimp.'

'No, but—'

'You do. You think I'm some kind of girl.' We were on the kitchen floor with our backs against the table where my mother had sat and drunkenly told her troubles to Lana's mother three years before. Lana had made a pipe out of an empty V8 bottle. It was like drinking smoke. And she was right. I wasn't used to anything too strong. After a while my heart started thudding, my eyeballs dried out and I began to be aware of my teeth. I couldn't stop thinking about them, visualising them, running my tongue all over my mouth and counting them. I figured they'd leave me alone if I ate something, so I went to the fridge, got a container of cherry-vanilla, found a spoon and started digging.

'Oh, do help yourself, Stephen.' Lana watched me tunnel my way through the vat of ice-cream with a tormented look on her face. Then we were both in there with our spoons working together.

'Fuck this diet,' she said. 'I could be eighty pounds and everybody would still call me fat. You know why?'

'People in this town are mentally lazy,' I said, droning. This was very good ice-cream. I stared at the fridge door, fascinated by all the notes the Kovalenkos had left there for each other. Advice, reminders, queries. A

lot of it seemed to involve socks. Mr Kovalenko signed everything with
Xs and Os for kisses and hugs.

Lana's dog let herself in at the back, standing on her hind legs and
coming down against the latch until the door gave up and opened. A
huge furry St Bernard named Florence, made up mostly of hair and
eyes and drool. You'd see splashes and puddles of it on the floor as she
made her stately progress through the kitchen.

'Exactly!' Lana said. 'Mentally lazy. They just stick an adjective onto
you and it's there for life. So unfair. I mean, why does everybody call
you "that Jewish kid"? You never do anything Jewish.'

'No, you're right there. No training, no culture. I'm feral.'

I got up and started banging through the cupboards, looking for
microwave popcorn. Stephen, the feral half-Jew. I said it to myself a
few times, then figured out it scanned the same as 'Rudolf the Red-
Nosed Reindeer', so of course I had to make up a song around it. I went
through several verses before I found some popcorn and threw a bag in
the microwave, while Lana kept trying to interrupt me with, 'What I'm
trying to say is ...'

'What I'm trying to say is, people in this town are stupid,' Lana
finished, finally. 'In fact, I think you and me are the only smart people
here.'

I didn't want to play this game. In the microwave a flat envelope of
popcorn kernels revolved on a glass plate.

'Mark hates me,' I said. A few sullen pops from inside the bag. 'He
was the only normal part of my life and I fucked it up. Forever.'

'Aw.' Lana threw an arm around my waist, head resting against my
shoulder. 'Too bad you guys are fighting. Still, I've never been able to
understand that whole male bonding thing. I mean, no offence, but
you're talking about him like he's your boyfriend.'

I broke away from her and glared out the window, at the trees with their spongy, green blossoms and tiny wet leaves. I'd already forgotten the words to my new song. Lana was still talking.

'Maybe you two should just fuck each other and get it over with.'

There was a series of controlled explosions from the microwave. I thought about the popcorn kernels, lying silent in their bag. 'When are we going to be planted?' they might be thinking. 'I can't wait to stretch my roots into the soil, and to feel the sun on my leaves! Oh, boy!' Then the heat forcing them out of their sleek brown shells into stiff little mushroom clouds. Some of us are born to be eaten.

○

Late afternoon rolled around and we found ourselves in the basement. I was curled up on the floor by the radiator sulking over my hand – bashed to death by a flying eight-ball in a game of contact pool. (That's when you run around the pool table trying to whack the balls into the pockets with your hands. And if you end up with wooden projectiles flying into somebody's face, or crushing the bones of a finger when you're zooming those things around, so much the better.)

We were mesmerised by this one song Lana had on a mix tape her boyfriend Adam from the city had made for her, kept rewinding it and playing it over and over: The Smiths, 'Reel Around the Fountain'. Side by side with our backs to the cold radiator bawling out the words for what seemed like hours.

'God, Lana. Why can't I live in this song?'

'In England they play this stuff on the radio,' she said. 'What do we get here? The *St Elmo's Fire* song. 'Man in Motion', every hour on the hour.'

'We'll have to move to England then.' A strange little silence. 'Everybody's gonna hate us over there.' I was apparently still talking. 'We don't have the right accents. They'll spit on us. We'll be wringing it out of our hair every night when we come home.'

'Sounds about right.' Lana seemed to be having some kind of staring contest with the dog. 'But we'll go anyway. We'll sit in our little flat together and we'll cry. And listen to this music.'

'Okay.'

I deserved it. All the phlegm the English could muster. Mark. That look on his face by the elementary school, before he'd turned away. He hated me.

My thoughts seemed unnaturally loud and I was afraid I'd actually been talking instead of thinking. Lana was oblivious. She'd turned her face to the light, leaning back with her eyes closed, singing the prettiest part of the song in a clear, high voice. Something about dreaming about you and falling out of bed twice, a mountain and a butterfly.

'Lana, I don't think I'm ever going to be happy. Is that normal?'

She looked thoughtful for a moment, but all she said was 'Trampoline', and headed out the back door at a run. Florence the St Bernard went woofing after her.

The Kovalenkos' trampoline was a famous and wonderful thing. One step and you were sky-bound. The best was when Lana's parents had a party, and you'd get all these neighbourhood adults sailing through the air with their hair flying around them – big, shaggy angels appearing over the Kovalenkos' hedges for a few seconds and then vanishing. It's impossible to stay angst-ridden on one of these things. Try it. All that bouncing and anti-gravity really does force you into happiness, even if it feels a little insane.

But you have to be careful: if you're doing this with more than one person, make sure you're taking off at the same time. Do not have one of you sitting there laughing and taking a break while the other comes crashing down on them by accident.

I saw my knee connect with Lana's head. I freaked.

She was holding her hand over her eye and groaning. 'Fuck's sake, Stephen!'

Momentum continued to bounce us along. I had this sudden paranoid thought that when she took her hand away she'd be all bloody and hideous and maybe the actual eyeball would be rolling around on the trampoline somewhere.

I pried Lana's hand from her face. She looked fine. The surface under us calmed and stilled. I leaned in and kissed her on the eyelid, just lightly, and told her I was sorry. Like something my mother would do when I was a kid, to stop me from getting hysterical over some little scrape.

My hand was on her cheek, holding her steady. She put her own hand over mine. So different without that make-up. A smattering of freckles, dark circles from a restless night, a scar she'd got banging her head on a table corner when she was five. All the stuff she kept painted over, coming out like flowers after the snow had melted. She looked younger than me, a little sister.

Lana kissed me on the lips, very softly. I edged away. She pulled me closer and kissed me again. There was pressure on my shoulders and I felt myself sinking. Then my head was knocking against the frame of the trampoline and she was above me, on top of me, and we were still kissing, her tongue moving in my mouth. I started to sweat. My arms were rigid by my sides. I wondered if she could tell I wasn't really kissing back.

The sun burned into my eyes. Half a tub of cherry-vanilla. Three bags of microwave popcorn. About a hundred marshmallows. All churning around my stomach in a mass, making itself known. We continued to bounce lazily. Lana was unbuttoning buttons and moving my hand up inside her shirt. Her father's shirt. How far was this going to go? If I told her to stop, she'd be hurt. Maybe she'd think it had something to do with her weight. What kind of life was this, where I had to be so cruel to my friends?

She shifted and I got an elbow in the gut. The trampoline sent us swaying like a ship at sea, a ship in a storm with the sailors hanging off the deck being sick into the waves.

Lana stopped, rolled off me. 'Hey. Is everything …?'

I didn't think. I just squirmed out from under her as fast as I could, slid off the trampoline and hit the ground. Ow. Had to get away from this sun, this carnivorous, blue sky. I crawled under the trampoline and sat clutching one of the metal poles. I could see Lana's shape weighing down the black circle above me.

'Stephen? What's wrong?'

For some reason, I could not open my mouth.

'Okay,' said Lana, 'once for yes and two for no. Is it the drugs? Was it too much?' I figured out what she meant and poked the Lana shape above me, once for yes. Well, that part was true, even if it was more like a detail.

'See, I told you to take it easy.'

The backyard was quiet. Birds twittered blankly. Bugs droned. A truck drove by with 'Man in Motion' blaring out the windows.

'Listen, we're just having fun here, right?' Her voice was shaky. 'I'm not … you know, expecting you to be my boyfriend. I can see how that would be embarrassing.'

I reached up and nudged her twice, very hard because I wanted there to be absolutely no doubt about this. She laughed, and the shape above me seemed to relax.

'So what is it? Being outside? Too much sun? Do you want to go to my room?'

I nudged her twice again, more gently this time. The dog approached as I sat scrunched up and cowering under the trampoline. I put my arms around Florence, buried my face in her soft majestic fur.

'Look, I just want to understand,' Lana said. 'Is it something to do with sex, like do you have some kind of problem being, uh, intimate?'

I held the dog tighter.

Lana's head appeared, upside-down on the edge of the black circle. 'Stephen, are you crying?'

'No.' My voice surprised me, thick and throaty, filtered through dog hair.

She slipped off and sat beside me on the ground, at the outer edge of the trampoline. I had Lana on one side of me and Florence the dog on the other.

'Tell me what's wrong.'

I squeezed my eyes shut and thought about how much I wanted to be away from there.

'Please. I can't guess any more, Stephen.'

My chest felt like it was compacting into itself and my throat was huge, face burning up.

And then I said it.

'I'm in love with Mark.'

The sentence hung there, as if it was printed on a cartoon word balloon. I braced myself for whatever Lana was going to do next.

She laughed. I wasn't expecting that. I sat feeling like the bottom had fallen out of the universe and I'd be falling forever.

But seconds later she was apologising. 'I thought you were joking!

You're always making stuff like that up.' Lana kissed my forehead, my eyes, my ears. 'I wasn't laughing at you. I promise I wasn't.'

Then Lana surprised me again. She started to cry. I held on to her. Florence got bored with us and went off to smell things.

'It's these stupid pills,' Lana said, swiping at her eyes with her fist. 'You know. The birth control pills – they get me all emotional for no reason. I'm happy, Stephen. Honest. I'm so glad you could trust me ...' She broke down again, her body trembling against mine.

We lay back under the trampoline in the cool grass with our arms around each other. It was nice under there. Like being a little kid hiding out in a tent in the backyard imagining nobody can find you. The grass pressed against us and left patterns creased into our skin. We were on our sides. She asked me how long I'd been attracted to guys. I told her probably forever.

'Even when you came to my house? That first time? When your Mom got drunk?' There was a little hitch to her breathing and I was afraid she'd start to cry again.

I ran my hand along her back. 'You were so nice to me that day. It really turned everything around. That this cool girl from Toronto wanted to be my friend.'

'You mean the fat girl with the dippy name.'

'Don't say that. You're beautiful, Svetlana.'

She asked me more questions, and I told her everything I could. Mark and Stephen, the whole sordid tale. Except it wasn't really sordid at all. I hadn't done anything yet, with or to anybody. So why was I putting myself through the torments of hell over this?

I stretched out on my back, so relaxed I felt like I might dissolve into the earth. 'Lana, you're the only one who knows. And I'm not telling anybody else, not in this town. So please don't—'

'Of course I won't.'

We were quiet for a while, tracing shapes on the black circle above us, leaning into each other with our heads touching.

'He won't love you back,' she said.

'I know.'

'Might even hurt you. I mean physically.'

'No, don't worry about that, Lana.'

But as soon as I'd said it, I wasn't sure.

'Stephen. You have to be careful. I'm not worried about most people here. After all, this place is boring, but it's not *Deliverance*. I'd watch myself around Mark, though.'

I told her again that Mark would never hurt me, not on purpose, that he thought of me as a kid brother. She moved onto her side again so she could look me in the eye.

'So how do you imagine Mark's going to react if people start calling him gay because of you?'

'But why would anybody think Mark was ...' Funny how I still couldn't bring myself to say the word. 'I mean, that's just stupid.'

'People here *are* stupid. You've been spending all your time together since you were practically babies. I'm telling you, everybody will say you're a couple.'

'A couple.' I tried to find this funny, told her if it were true, I wouldn't be here now.

'You'd be off somewhere blowing him. Yeah, I know.'

I sat up, bounced my head on the underside of the trampoline. 'Jesus, Lana, could you not talk like that?'

'Make you think about it?' She was grinning.

'Shut up. Yes.'

'Slut.'

I started laughing then and couldn't stop, sinking to the ground and clutching Lana's shoulders, my nose pressed into her neck.

It should have been a warm, normal moment, but I was already starting to feel twitchy and paranoid. This thing that had been safely sealed inside my head for so long was a piece of news now – it was currency. Lana could keep it in her sock drawer for twenty years or she could go out and give it to somebody else, exchange it, spend it. How could I be sure this wasn't going to get back to Mark?

The answer came, like the calm voice of God, like the sound of everything clicking into place. *You want to make sure nobody else tells Mark? Tell him yourself. Do it now.*

Yes. Do it now while I'm resolved. Do it now while I'm still a bit stoned. Do it now because I have to.

'I gotta go.' I crawled out from under the trampoline and headed for the back gate. Lana peeped out from its circular shadow, blinking in the late-afternoon light.

'Stephen? You're not going to do anything stupid, are you?'

I jumped over Lana's gate and was back where I'd started, a bit surprised to find the same streets, the same houses, just as I'd left them that morning.

So: back to walking. But this time I had a destination.

Chapter 12

Okay. Here we go. One foot in front of the other. Don't be scared. There was no time to be scared. I had a destination. Mark's place. Mark's place with Mark in it.

Marching along past these prim, wooden houses, built a hundred years before and slowly dying inside from rot, lining the streets to see me off like I was on parade. I'd be there in a few minutes. What was I going to say exactly? Maybe I shouldn't plan anything after all. Just let it come out.

Terrifying.

I wanted a tune to keep me going. I wanted bagpipes, a battle march, maybe one of Mark's Presbyterian hymns.

All I could come up with was the theme from *Benny Hill*.

Well, it had an okay tempo.

Late-afternoon light was touching everything with gold, shadows just starting to get long. Maybe at first he'd think I was joking. He'd laugh. I wouldn't. There'd be awkward silence. Then shock. He'd be horrified, looking at me like I was something gross. What next? Would he punch me?

Or worse. He might turn quiet. Politely ask me to leave. Then never talk to me again. I couldn't imagine life without Mark in it.

This town was too small. I was there already. Outside his house. I gazed up at the building with its frowning windows, and realised I was still humming *Benny Hill*. Like giggling before the throne of judgement.

Quit being an idiot. Get in there. Side door. It was never locked.

The door drifted open when I touched it, like a sigh. I knew that house as if it were my own. It would probably be the last time I was there.

I took the stairs slowly, and then I was in the living room with its deep-red shag carpet. The kitchen was six steps up from there. Funny the way the house was put together, the kitchen a half-floor above anything else. From the next room, you could see the people in there framed in the doorway, lit up and hanging in midair like figures on an icon. I sank to the floor beside the couch, huddling out of sight of the kitchen, paralysed. Mark was up there. I could see him and I could hear him, slow and thoughtful, moving from the fridge to the sink to the stove to the counter. The kitchen was filling up with steam. Everything was quiet. Just the low rumbling sound of boiling water in a pot. And somebody singing.

It was Mark. Had I ever heard him sing before? The tune was something solid and measured, rising gradually like his voice was climbing wide, stone steps. A hymn.

Sun slanted through the windows in the living room, dust motes caught the light in beams that looked solid to the touch. The water was bubbling and popping in liquid chuckles. Mark's voice paced through his song, fading out and repeating words when something in the kitchen needed his attention. The stove made little clicks as if reassuring itself that all was in order.

One quiet, perfect moment before I tell him. Hold on to it. Hold on.

I tried putting the words of the hymn together. Something about strength and resolve, fighting giants, being a pilgrim. Valour, being valiant. Courage, courage, courage.

Someone was whispering at me. 'Stephen, why are you hiding behind the couch?'

It was Krystal, Mark's little sister. Nine years old and thin like a blade of grass – very blonde, very blue-eyed, almost translucent. The kind of person you'd expect to see working the reception desk in heaven.

'Good question, Kris,' I whispered back.

Krystal shrugged, left the room and came back dragging a vacuum cleaner half her size. She was probably just in from dance class – still in her white ballet outfit, hair scraped away from her face and gathered in a tight coil near the top of her head. Who'd done that for her? Not her mother. Maggie McAllister wasn't the type. It must have been Mark. Mark brushing his little sister's hair and fixing it with pins so she'd look nice for her teacher and the other girls. It broke my heart.

I couldn't stand it anymore, took the damn vacuum away from her and tried to do the job myself. Then Krystal had to spend the next few minutes running around righting lamps and tables and catching objects while I fought this monster with its big square shrieking head, as it sank its teeth into the carpet and attempted to gobble up extension cords and the edges of curtains. I looked up at the kitchen. Mark was drying a plate, gazing scornfully down at me. He said something I couldn't hear above the roar of the machine and Krystal answered, 'I don't *know* what he's doing here!'

I suppose I should have been watching the vacuum cleaner instead, because I felt it thunk against something abruptly. Then I had to dive and catch the TV, which had toppled like a gravestone from its little stand.

Krystal shut off the machine. 'Stephen, please stop.'

The TV sputtered out a rerun of *Taxi* as soon as we plugged it back in. I wanted to sit there and watch it with Krystal. But I had a mission.

Six steps up. I couldn't make myself go into that kitchen. I stood holding on to the doorframe. Mark emptied a pot full of boiling water and hollow white noodles into a colander in the sink.

'Mark, I ...'

He ignored me and shook the water from the pasta, steam in a cloud around him. Vapour ascended out the window and dissolved into the air. '*Taxi*'s on.'

'So what's it mean?'

I felt like we'd been fast-forwarded a few minutes and I'd missed something. He asked me again.

'Inexorable. What's it mean?'

Oh, right. I'd almost forgotten about that fight this morning. 'It's ... something you can't control. That's been decided for you. You know – fate.'

'Doesn't seem too difficult.' The tap squeaked and Mark watched the pots and pans filling with water. 'Not worth acting like a complete ass—' He glanced down at Krystal in the living room. 'Not worth acting like a complete dummy over, was it?'

'I'm really sorry.' Still couldn't get him to look at me. 'I didn't mean any of it. All that stuff I said. Maybe I'm going nuts.'

I watched him take two plates down from the cupboard.

'Maybe.' A timer rang.

'Or it could be I'm freaked out over leaving Riverside.'

Mark made some kind of dismissive noise.

'Yeah, okay,' I said, 'but all my friends are here. You know, there's Lana. And you. Until, like, recently. Today, I mean.'

'Until recently.' There was a sudden blast of heat as Mark took a sizzling chicken out of the oven and set it on the stove top. 'Jeez, listen to you.' He dropped the dishtowel he'd been using to shield his hands. Then he reached out and ran his knuckles over my head. 'Look, we were both acting like total ... dummies. I shouldn't have called you that thing.' He lowered his voice to a whisper. 'You know. Jew bastard.'

'Well, it's sort of true. Even the bastard part. They weren't married till I was eight.'

'C'mon. You know I didn't mean it.' He got another plate out of the cupboard.

'There's, um, something else.'

Feet on the ledge of a fifty-storey building. One step into empty space.

'Yeah?' The chicken wobbled under the force of his carving knife.

Right. This is what you came here to do. So do it.

My hands were gripping each other. I found myself bending my thumb backwards until it hurt.

I couldn't. Couldn't make myself say the words. Mark continued to attack the chicken. I wanted a cigarette in the worst way, but we were not allowed to smoke in front of Krystal. I glanced down at her – completely absorbed in the TV. How much of this could she hear? I decided it was the least of my worries.

'Not doing a very good job ...,' Mark said. The bird was in pieces.

'I'm kind of scared.'

He turned to face me. The carving knife was still clutched in one hand. 'Why would you be scared?' He looked at me more closely. 'Whoa, man, you are totally … messed up.'

'Can you get rid of that knife?'

He set it on the stove. 'Okay. I'm not armed. What do you want to tell me?'

I was squirming, one hand on the back of my neck like I was getting ready to drag myself into a police car. Here we go. Voices from the TV downstairs, a studio audience laughing. Applause. Ending credits.

I brought my head up to meet his eyes, ducked down again.

'I can't.'

He was laughing. 'Jesus, Stephen—'

'You're gonna beat me up.' I felt pressure building, like when you're about to cry. *Oh, fuck, no. Get under control.*

'What?'

'You are. You're gonna, like, punch me in the face and stuff. You'll totally hate me …' My voice died to a rusty squeak.

'Stephen, come on. You're my little brother, man. I wouldn't do that. You know I wouldn't.' He looked sad. I was making him sad. I was upsetting everybody.

Mark had hold of my shoulders. 'Hey. Sorry if I was acting all scary this morning. I know I lose my temper sometimes. Stacey tells me that too. Guess I don't like getting reminded that I'm kind of, you know' – he looked out the window – 'stupid.'

'You're not!' I said, but you could barely hear it. I broke away from him and leaned with my forehead against the wall, struggling to get control. Mark went back to the sink and started drying dishes.

It seemed like this went on for a long time, but I could hear from the TV downstairs that it was only the span of a commercial break. A chorus was encouraging everyone: 'Get a little closer! Don't be shy! Get a little closer! With Arrid Extra Dry!'

'Stephen, listen to me,' Mark said, when it seemed like I'd recovered somewhat. 'You're not gonna say anything to make me hate you. Unless you're about to tell me you've been doing my mom.'

That made me laugh. 'No, Mark, I'm not doing your mom.'

'Well, good, cause if you married her, you'd be my dad. Don't think I'm ready for that.'

'Where is she anyway?'

'Meeting.' She was on a date. It was code he used for talking in front of Krystal. 'Look, you are seriously freaking me out.'

'I … I've been … *studying*. All afternoon. At Lana's place. She's got some really great … *books* from Toronto.' This was also code. Really dumb code. But we couldn't start going on about drugs with the little girl there.

'Yeah, looks like you've been hitting the books pretty hard. Have to get Lana to lend us some. You and me, huh?'

'Those books would melt your brain.'

'I can see that.' He noticed me staring off over his shoulder at the dishes piled under the tap. 'Hey, do you want the sink?'

I nodded and he moved the pots and pans out of the way, shoved my head under the tap and turned on the cold water. Perfect. Cold and perfect.

Krystal came hopping up the stairs. I heard her saying something about 'Stephen … in the sink again' and Mark telling her not to worry. Then I just concentrated on the water pouring down on me.

After a while, I reached up and turned off the tap, grabbed a dishtowel and used it to stop most of the drip from my hair. Mark and Krystal were downstairs setting places at three little fold-up tables in front of the couch. Steam rose from plates of food as Mark set them down. 'Don't burn your hands,' he told her.

Oh, God. It was me and Maryna. Alone in the house together without Stanley, waiting for him to come back. Two people and an invisible third.

Mark told me once that he felt like he had to stay in Riverside until Krystal graduated because he didn't trust his mother to take care of her. So he'd be stuck here, like my mother was stuck here because of me. He'd turn his part-time job at Home Hardware into full-time. Working all week at the store, coming back to this house every day. Who would he even talk to? Krystal?

Supper was ready. I sat on the couch between them. We were watching an old *Star Trek* rerun – the episode where they all get space madness for a day and Sulu chases everybody around with a sword. It was Krystal's choice. She had a thing for Captain Kirk. Not William Shatner. Captain Kirk. In his yellow and gold uniform, 1967.

'I'm going to marry him,' she told us with a secret smile.

'Aw, Kris,' I said. 'Thought you were gonna marry me.' Our little joke.

'I can marry both of you. Captain Kirk is very busy in space. Me and you and Mark can live here together. We can keep the house nice and wait for him to come home.'

I told her the whole living arrangement sounded great. Looked down at my plate. Empty already. I was still a bit stoned and I'd had nothing to eat all day but the junk food at Lana's. I got up and filled my plate in the kitchen, and then I did it again a few minutes later.

I stood by the stove staring into the living room below. Krystal was cross-legged and serious on the couch, with Mark sprawled beside her. What would he think when he looked back on it all, after I told him?

What was he going to remember – hanging out with his best friend Stephen or spending years next to some creepy little perv who was probably eyeing him up the whole time? I was going to ruin everything, present and past. So I could be honest.

Well, if you love somebody, why would you want to do that to him?

'Hey, save some for my mom!' Mark said. Too late. She should have thought of that before she went off to this 'meeting' of hers, left her children alone with someone like me.

Then it hit. Tired. Shuffling zombie tired. I could barely keep my eyes open, everything pressing down on me. But this wasn't a bad feeling. Meant I'd be able to sleep – finally. I'd had maybe six hours over the past week, but now there was no negotiating with it. I knew that at this point I could thunk down on the floor and be blessedly without thoughts of any kind for the whole night and longer.

I stumbled back to the couch, pushed Mark and Krystal out of the way and crashed down with my feet hanging off the edge, my head squished into the cushions, breathing in lint and the ghosts of lost change.

'Guess I should call your mother and tell her you're staying.' I could hear Mark from the sofa arm nearest my head. Those familiar *Star Trek* noises were filling the living room – the music cues, the voices, the strangely maternal hums and clicks of the machines. I was almost asleep.

'Hey. You should sing,' I said. 'That hymn. How to be valiant or something.'

'Oh, fu— frig. You were listening to that?'

Krystal shushed us. Mark moved closer, his head inches from mine.

'How come you like that stuff?' I said.

'I dunno.' He was trying to keep his voice down so Krystal didn't miss a word of her show. 'It feels ... permanent. It was there before I ever came along. It'll be there after I'm gone.' He shifted his weight, balancing. 'No, that sounds retarded. I'm not explaining this very well.'

'I love you.' I mumbled it into the side of the couch. Everything was shutting down, one control panel at a time. My eyes were closed. No idea what I was saying anymore.

'Hey, that's ... great, man.'

'Stephen's a big silly.' Krystal was talking from somewhere close to my feet.

'I think Stephen's been studying pretty hard today.'

I drifted off, glimmering beeps and whirs from the TV dropping slowly into the background, fading into the dark reaches of space.

When I opened my eyes again, it was morning. Krystal was smiling into my face, like she had some wonderful secret. I glanced at my watch and saw that I was almost late for the first bell at school.

Then Mark was shoving my feet off the couch so he could sit down. He handed me a yellow plate with a Pop-Tart on it. Strawberry. It took me a minute to figure out that he was wearing his red Home Hardware shirt.

'Aw, don't wear the red shirt.' I bit into the sugary rectangle in my hand. 'They're always the first to get killed.'

'Gotta wear it for work.' The corner of his mouth twitched when he looked at me.

I didn't get it. Had I been asleep for half the week? 'Is it Saturday?'

'Thursday. I'm not going to school today. No point.' He leaned back against the couch. 'I think I'm finished with school. Only about a month to go anyway.'

'Yeah, but Mark …'

'Don't worry. I'll show up sometimes. I'll do the exams too. Got a feeling they'll put me through anyway. Nobody wants me around another year.'

'Just don't like to see you giving up.'

He smiled. 'C'mon, get out of here. You're gonna be late.'

I was almost at the end of the McAllisters' driveway when I heard Mark yelling after me to stop. He was laughing. 'You can't go out there like that, man. Wait, wait, wait.'

I stopped, turned to face him. 'I'll be late.'

'Yeah, but …' He put one hand on my shoulder, reached up towards my face. What was this? Space madness?

Then he was picking through my hair and something was scratching and pulling at me. Barrettes. Pink plastic barrettes with bunny rabbits on them. That's what Krystal had been so damn happy about, grinning into my face first thing this morning.

'I promised Krystal I wouldn't tell you,' Mark was saying. 'But, fuck.'

'Thanks.'

'Wait a minute, there's one more …' He tilted my head, pulled at the hair near the back of my neck. 'Hey, remember yesterday you were all fucked up and you wanted to give me this big news or something?'

The barrette snapped open and he drew it away from me. Green with a yellow happy face smirking at the world.

'I don't really remember. I was pretty stoned.'

'Yeah, you totally were. Gotta get us some of that shit, eh? Ask Lana.'

I said I'd try, mumbled goodbye and started off for school, glancing back at Mark as he stood in the driveway and held up his hand. Then he smiled to himself like he'd decided this looked dumb, went back into the house.

I found my backpack where I'd left it the day before. It was soggy from rain and there was a slug crawling up one strap, but otherwise it was fine. Well, why not? Who'd steal a Canadian History textbook?

I was halfway to Riverside Regional High School and about a block away from Riverside Regional Elementary – exactly where I'd had that fight with Mark. Even wearing the same clothes. Everything was just the same.

Except nothing was.

True, Mark still didn't know, and I'd protect him for as long as I could. But Lana did. All of a sudden there was one person I didn't have any secrets from. I found I was actually looking forward to school, to seeing Lana and talking to her.

I shouldered my pack, turned towards the high school. Boldly going.

Chapter 13

I curled my fingers into a stiff tangle somewhere on the neck of the guitar, swiped at the strings with my other hand. My favourite Smiths song, sounding a bit mutilated. 'I Want the One I Can't Have'.

We were at Lana's place, in the living room, pretending to study. My back was against the couch and Lana was stretched across it, clapping sarcastically whenever I hit a buzzingly awful note. She'd given me the guitar the day after I'd had that meltdown under the trampoline, said it was her dad's but he hadn't played in years.

'We're going to be rock stars,' she'd informed me.

'Can I be Morrissey?'

'No. I'm Morrissey. I'm not sure who you are.'

So we were in a band – two acoustic guitars played by two people who couldn't sing very well. It was called The Wretched Noise, after an early review by Lana's mother.

Only a couple of weeks had gone by since that insane day of drugs and ice-cream and confessions and *Star Trek*, but it seemed like I was living a whole different existence. I hung around with Lana constantly. I didn't see much of Mark, not since he'd unofficially dropped out. I guess things had been going wrong for us ever since I started acting like such a self-absorbed weirdo around him back in April. Then when we quit walking to school together, something snapped. It broke our routine. After that, it was like I had to arrange to see Mark, as if we were relatives checking in for visits. And the real distance settled in.

There were times he'd still show up at school, like he said, but he was usually with the boys from his remedial classes. Randy McTavish, Kevin Dickson. Same people who'd tried to feed me dog shit back in Grade Three. He was different when he was with these guys. If I passed them in the halls, he'd grunt a 'hi' at me and keep going.

There were deep ridges pushed into my fingertips in the shape of guitar strings. I started picking out a tune instead of strumming – Mark's hymn about being valiant. I was obsessed with that song. Bizarre thing for a mostly atheist feral half-Jew to get fixated on, but you can't help what you're attracted to, I guess.

Then Lana wanted to talk about my new and exciting lifestyle. Again.

'We're going to have to get you laid, Stephen,' she said. 'Doesn't seem fair for you to be going through all this angst without so much as a lousy hand job to show for it.'

I collapsed over the guitar. 'Why do you talk like that?'

'Problem is, you're the only gay guy I know.'

I played this one chord really loud, put the guitar down.

'Don't call me that.'

'Well, it's true, isn't it?'

I didn't answer, went back to 'I Want the One I Can't Have', trying to force these plonking chords into the tune I had in my head. Awful.

Wretched noise. Behind me Lana was going on and on about how I should accept myself and my identity, and blah, blah, boring pointless blah. Until I couldn't stand it anymore.

'Would you shut up? I'm so sick of this.'

She looked puzzled, cross-legged on the couch in her bare feet. 'I thought it would be a relief for you to share it with somebody.'

'Okay, but does it have to be all we ever talk about?'

To be fair, that wasn't entirely true. She also liked gloating about her plans for Toronto, which usually left me feeling grumpy and abandoned. And the prom seemed to pop its gopher head into our conversations a fair amount – analysed in soul-numbing detail. Oh, it was all so stupid, she'd tell me. God, just asinine. But wait'll you hear what Adam's going to wear ... I'd be half-listening in a cross-eyed stupor, demented with boredom. Safe to say I was sitting this one out. Mark wasn't going either – he was already taking Stacey to her prom at Arnottville Regional and one was enough. Or that's what he'd told me, weeks ago.

Frightening, how I could already sense him fading into the past. It broke my heart, but in slow, day-to-day thuds. Like getting kicked to death by an extremely lazy horse.

Meanwhile, Adam the Halifax boyfriend was actually due in town for a pre-prom visit and Lana had started a countdown – the days, the hours, the minutes until he showed his face at her door. Oh, boy. I couldn't fucking wait.

Lana was fixing me with a pitying stare. 'You've never actually met one, have you? I mean, another one.'

'Your dad.'

'Oh, fuck off.'

'Totally coming on to me yesterday.'

'I'm serious.'

I sat pushing my fingers into my eyes.

'You know what? I don't want this. Any of it. It's a bad deal.' I stretched out on the floor face down, found a throw pillow and held it over my head.

Lana dropped off the edge of the couch. Then she turned me over and started tickling me. I hate this. Because you're laughing, but it's a reflex and it's almost painful. Meanwhile the other person thinks they've somehow tricked you into being happy. I tried to get her back. We rolled all over the carpet.

Her father's face appeared in the doorway. 'Guys …'

I realised I was pinning his daughter to the floor, sat up in a hurry. 'Mr Kovalenko, we weren't …'

Lana was laughing. She propped herself against me and started talking to her dad in Ukrainian. I heard '*Tato*' and 'Stepan', and then something in her voice made me pick up a cushion and smack it into the back of her head.

'You were about to tell him,' I said after Mr Kovalenko had left.

'Well, I don't want my dad thinking I'm some kind of—'

'You can't tell anybody, Lana.'

'But—'

'Nobody. I will never talk to you again, do you get me? Never.'

'Jeez. Angry young homo.'

'Do not *fucking* call me that!'

'When I was little, I didn't want to be a girl, if that's any consolation,' she said later, after we'd declared a shaky truce. We were lying beside each other on the carpet, Lana's forehead bumping against my ribs.

'It isn't. And what's that supposed to mean anyway?'

'Oh, you know. One minute you're a kid, running around doing kid stuff. Then suddenly you have to act completely different. Be all nicey-

nicey. Care about losing weight, wear shoes you can't actually walk in. That kind of thing. I thought it was a bad deal too.'

It struck me that she hadn't actually done any of this, except for maybe the shoes. 'So what are you saying – you wanted to be a boy?'

'I think I wanted to be a person.'

That made me laugh. It was such a silly thing to say, such a simple thing to wish for. Then I stopped. I took a deep breath and let it out again, lying on Lana's floor looking up at the ceiling.

'Yeah, that'd be cool.'

⊙

A person. I thought it meant more than just being a wingless biped without feathers. Maybe I was thinking about being an adult. A man.

Ten o'clock May sunshine bounced off the chromed edges of the tables and made a glare on the front of the Coke machine. I was in the school cafeteria with Lana and a cluster of Grade Twelves, killing time between classes. Across the table from me, a gorgeous jock idiot named Doug Sutton was having a difficult time trying to finish this joke about a couple of fags who wanted to be parents – kept losing track of the details and starting again. I wasn't really listening. The guy was dumber than a pile of raw meat. After what seemed like an hour, the punchline finally heaved into view, something involving a baby with a pacifier up its ass, and I did my usual laugh noise.

I always laughed at that stuff. What else was I going to do? The jokes were so dumb, so gross. Playground dumb and gross. If there was dialogue, the guys telling them would put on this bizarre screechy voice as the homo, sounded kind of like Mickey Mouse with his dick in a wringer.

Then Lana's friend Eleanor MacBride sat up straight and said something that shocked us all.

'That's not funny, Douglas. It's just stupid. My uncle's gay.' Giving Doug this eagled-eyed stare of righteousness.

We all got very uncomfortable. I went through a weird rollercoaster loop of reactions. Gratitude: Thanks, Eleanor. Irritation: Thanks for what? Admitting this person exists? Jeez. And where had this girl been for the eight million other stupid jokes that would have been just as insulting to poor old Uncle Gayboy MacBride? Then mad at myself: Why was it Eleanor who finally said something?

'I don't mind them,' Patty Marsh said into the squeamish silence. Somebody had left a lighter on the table and she was flicking at it with her long nails and watching it spin in circles. 'I mean, they got a right to exist. I just don't see why they have to rub your nose in it all the time.'

'Rub your nose in it, huh? Sounds real kinky, Patty.'

I regretted it right away. Not the words so much as the tone. I sounded angry.

Everybody stared. I decided the only thing to do was keep talking. So I smiled, leaning back with my arm around Lana.

'Cheer up, guys. You can still make Jew jokes. Really. No skin off my lampshade.'

'We don't make Jew jokes.' Doug was looking confused, staring hypnotised into Lana's pushed-up cleavage. 'We never make Jew jokes.'

'So none of you ever called me Stupid Jew-le-vitz in Grade Four?'

'You did? Guys!' Lana sounded appalled and strangely delighted.

Our class president Evan McDonald stretched. 'Actually, my dad was really mad at me when he heard we were calling you that. Made me apologise.' He shifted. 'Well, really I just lied and told him I did. Sorry, Stephen.'

'That's ... okay.'

'I'm sorry too,' said Patty.

They all apologised. It went around the table like an especially slow and solemn game of hot potato. I'd only wanted to change the subject.

Then the bell rang, which meant it was time for French. Except it wasn't, because our classes were cancelled so they could take the Grade Twelves to the AV room and show us the AIDS movie. A video about HIV, to be exact. There'd been a letter sent to all the parents about this. I'd been dreading it. There was no way I wanted to sit in a room with these people and watch this stuff. But that's what I did.

It was an American-produced film, very slick. A halfway popular actress narrating. Started with a quick montage of ways you couldn't get HIV, set to a bouncy beat – toilet seats featured prominently, and so did make-up, drinking fountains, and multiple shots of people hugging and kissing. They showed two girls locking lips for a second and some guy in the front row went, 'Yeah!' And then …

Oh. Well, holy fuck.

Two guys kissing each other. On the mouth. Two high-school kids.

It couldn't have lasted more than a second. But the whole place went nuts – everybody moaning about how gross it was, so gross, the most disgusting thing they'd ever seen, and on and on forever.

'Okay, settle down!' My old friend Mr Richardson, the gym class sadist.

'I gotta get out of here,' I said into Lana's ear.

'I know.'

We decided to skip Biology and go to the Tasty Freeze to get a chocolate dip cone. As we left I looked for Mark in the gang at the back of the room. But he must have had something better to do that day.

Lana and I got her bicycle and headed off down the highway, taking turns pedalling in front and balancing on the back.

She paid for the ice-creams and got a handful of those new dollar coins in change. 'Hate these things.' Lana passed me a cone with a spiralling mass of ice-cream perched on it. We took a seat on the edge of a picnic table. Neither of us said anything for a while. It looked like a porcupine had met a messy end a few hundred feet up the road.

The dark, plasticky shell on the ice-cream broke as Lana bit into it. 'Come on, cheer up. You'll be out of this town in a few months.'

'You really think it'll be so much better in the city?'

She made a disgusted noise. 'Halifax. Still can't believe you people call that pathetic little garrison town "the city".' And she went on about how four hundred thousand people was barely enough for a village and she was still appalled that I'd chosen it over Toronto, especially because this meant we wouldn't see each other next year.

Green fields all around us, white butterflies weaving through the tall grass. We were both quiet, wrapped in our own thoughts.

'I'm so sick of this, Lana,' I said. 'I'm sick of it and it hasn't even started yet. I mean, is this it? Is this the rest of my life?'

Her head was resting against my shoulder. 'You want to go back to school?'

'Fuck school.'

We took the bicycle back through town, ended up near the railway bridge. That bridge had always freaked me out. Normally I liked heights. I could go up a tree until I was level with the roof of my house and it didn't bother me. But there was something wrong with this thing. Clearly it was pretending to be a solid Canadian railway structure, but in its soul it existed as a rickety collection of slats suspended over an abyss, something from an Indiana Jones movie.

We were walking the bike around the back of the elementary school. It must have been lunchtime because the yard was full of kids. One of them noticed us and smiled and called out, 'Hey, fatso! Hey, faggot!'

'Hey, partial-birth abortion!' Lana shot back.

The boy wandered off to another part of the playground, unconcerned.

'Lana, you're not fat.' It was a reflex.

She had reflexes too. 'And you're not ... well, I'm sure he didn't mean it the way you think he did.'

'It's nothing. I don't care.' I kicked at a squashed juice box. Lana tried to put her arm around my waist, but the bike twisted out of her grasp.

'Look, I don't know why he called you that, Stephen. It could be because you seem sort of ... uncomfortable. In your own skin. I guess a certain type of person would see it and want to go for you.'

'Please stop talking.'

That's what Mark had said. When we were kids. If you act scared, it makes people want to get you. Well, fuck this. Fuck being scared.

I turned and went over the railway bridge.

'Hey, what if a train comes?' Lana yelled from the bank.

'What if it does?'

Okay. Giant steps onto crumbling wooden beams. Sunshine on the water, everything quiet. I tried to remember the words to Mark's hymn. Like I said, I was a bit fixated on it.

'"He who would valiant be 'gainst all disaster."' I was muttering into the stillness. Couldn't stop looking down, holding on to the rusty steel on the side of the bridge.

'"Let him in constancy . . . " Something . . . and something . . .'

Take a step. One step. Okay, good. Still here. A twig drifted down towards the river, all the time in the world to fall.

'"No foe shall stay his might, though he with giants fight …"'

Another step. Then another one. Sun on my back. Someone started up a lawnmower outside one of the houses behind the school.

Cool. I was halfway across this stupid bridge.

And I was happy, suddenly, to be there. Blue sky all around, a light breeze on my face, suspended over the river with its sparkling surface.

'"Then fancies flee away."' Keep going. '"I'll fear not what men say …"'

Then all I could hear was this panicky little voice behind me. 'Shit! Oh, God. Shit! Oh, God.'

No way. Lana, walking the bike across the railway bridge. This girl couldn't go up a stepladder without freaking out. I never would have started across if I thought she'd try to follow me.

'Couldn't stand seeing you out here by yourself,' she said. 'Shit! Oh, God. This is horrible …'

'It's okay. We can do this.'

I moved back the way I'd come until I reached Lana. We took big steps from one railroad tie to the next, trying to keep our eyes off the water, hands clasped under the bike's handlebars.

Then I heard a familiar sound. Too familiar.

A train. Coming straight for us.

'It's not on the bridge yet,' I said. 'Run!'

She tried to turn the bike around. The front wheel twisted and jammed between the beams of the railway ties.

'Not that way. Towards it!' And I picked up the bike and tried to carry it to the other side of the bridge.

'We're gonna die!'

Thanks, Lana. 'We're not. Come on!' We both took hold of the bike and ran with it, towards the train, trusting that our feet would hit one of the railway ties and not plunge into empty space, the bicycle bumping along between us. Keep going, keep going. No time to be scared.

We made it – collapsed on the opposite bank holding on to each other, the bicycle lying in a tangle beside us, one wheel spinning in shock.

The train went roaring past.

Eventually it did, anyway. We'd had a lot more time than we thought. In fact, we could have strolled the rest of the way across the bridge and maybe stopped to take a few photographs. Oh, well. The near-death thrill of it all was what we decided we were going to remember.

And I made a promise to remember the moment before all that, when everything was quiet.

We spent the afternoon at the Kovalenkos' writing terrible songs about trains. I wanted to stay for supper because Lana's mom had made *pyrohy*. But I'd just had a brilliant idea and I needed to set it in motion.

Okay, Mark seemed resigned to fail the year and be a dropout, even though I was sure that deep down he hated the idea. But it didn't have to happen. He had me on his side. I'd got him through big tests before, and I could get him through these finals.

I said goodbye to Lana and headed off for Mark's place. I'd faced down a speeding train and guided a girl and a bicycle safely across the Bridge of Death. Now I was going to save my friend.

But first I had to pass the town hall where the tough kids were hanging out, like they did pretty well year round. Slouching and smoking, draping themselves across the front steps, too cool to let on that they had spinal columns. Today there were about five guys.

Or that was my best guess. Like always, when I came out of the side street and onto the main drag, I made sure to keep my eyes fixed on the pavement, trying to blend into the background with its dusty little stores and sidewalks. But this was Riverside. I was also probably the only moving object for miles.

'Look! It's fucking Jew-le-vitz!'

'Jew-le-vitz! Over here!'

'Hey, Stephanie!'

And on and on. Same old insults I'd been hearing since I came to this town plus some new ones, all the guys pitching in to make each other laugh. I glared into an abandoned shop window, pretended not to hear. Should have just kept walking, but something in me didn't feel like slinking away this time.

Then I recognised one of the voices.

Oh, fuck. I should have known.

There he was. Lazing on the steps between Randy and Phil, smiling through drifts of smoke and tossing his yellow lighter skyward for no reason except maybe to show off that he could catch it again without looking. My best friend.

He wouldn't meet my eyes. Maybe he was waiting for me to disappear.

I stayed, staring stupidly. What now? Go to his place and wait with a pile of textbooks until he decided to come home? March up there and tell the whole pack of them my great idea? *Hey, gang! Let's go study. We can pass our exams and graduate. It'll be keen!*

Phil poured a wet splash of Coke onto Randy's head and then they were all jostling and shoving, battering deflated pop bottles against each other's backs, laughing in a heap together. I made my escape.

I was being an idiot again. Mark didn't want to write the exams. It was possible that he didn't even care if he graduated. He'd given up.

I should do the same. Walk away. Forget him.

But that was the coward's way out of Riverside. And I'd decided that it was time to start being a bit more brave.

Part 3
One long night

Chapter 14

There was a heavy stillness in the house when I woke up, like a storm was coming. But a glance out the window showed nothing was wrong. The sun was throwing long, morning shadows across the backyard and the sky was a perfect innocent blue. A Friday in early June. The kind of day that seemed to be making promises.

It was Stanley's wife's birthday, so I made a quick call to Montreal in the kitchen. I chatted with Sheila and my baby sisters, told them I'd see them in a month for the annual visit, tried to get off the phone before somebody decided to wake my father.

No luck.

'Oh, look who's up!' Sheila said, and the next thing I heard was Stanley mumbling at me, offering his congratulations. Apparently he thought I was graduating. I told him no, that I still had at least a week of classes left, then exams and after that there'd be …

'All right, then.' I could hear the shrug in his voice. 'Looking forward to your visit. As always.' This was clearly a 'please hang up' line, but

Stanley stayed on, making vague noises as if there was more he wanted to say. I could hear my sister Sarah by his feet, singing a song about the letter Q and telling my father to move it. They called him 'Papa', these little girls.

'Of course ...' Stanley was still fumbling towards his next sentence. 'Of course there's a strong possibility I'll have to be away some of the time you're here. Five days, I think?'

I was only going to be there for seven.

'Or it could be close to six with the travelling.'

Stanley started to explain: he'd be attending a conference that first week of July. My week. No, he wasn't presenting a paper. But there were some very good speakers scheduled and he really wanted to go. I twisted the phone cord around the base of my index finger, watched as my skin turned white and then purple.

'You understand, right?' my father said.

Before I could answer, I heard Sheila in the background. 'Stanley, we *discussed* this.' Then she must have snatched the receiver away from him, because her voice was in my ear again.

'Just a mix-up, Stephen. Everything's fine. We'll *all* be very happy to see you in July,' she said. 'We'll *all* be here.'

I wished her a happy birthday, pressed down on the receiver and let the dial tone buzz. The house was still quiet, like an empty stage.

He couldn't give me one week. Not one week out of fifty-two. Never mind that we barely spoke on these visits. He couldn't have me as a face at his dinner table.

There was a blank message pad on the counter next to the phone. The paper was scored with deep black marks – like it'd been freshly savaged by a demented badger. I'd been stabbing a pencil into it, over and over. I also realised that I'd been cursing and swearing in a steady growl for minutes and no one had told me to cut it out. I was alone in the house.

I went to look for Mom and caught sight of her through the back window, sitting on the chopping block by the woodshed having a cigarette. It was still early. I made us tea in blue striped mugs and brought it out. Trying to calm down, shake this evil mood.

My mother smiled up at me. She'd been in a great mood herself the past while, buzzing around the house like she was guarding some happy secret. Her acceptance letter from Acadia had arrived a couple of weeks earlier and I figured that was the reason.

'Just thinking about what I'm going to do next year,' she said. 'When it's only me in this old place. Course, I'll be busy with the books. And maybe ...' She broke off, looking mysteriously pleased and flustered, eyes fixed on a collection of spindly rose bushes leaning by the outside wall. The blooms were dark orange and looked as though they'd recently exploded. 'Maybe I'll try to like gardening.'

I settled myself halfway up a ladder leaning against the shed, and we talked until it was time for me to go to school. About nothing. A guy Mom had met through work – she thought he might have a crush on her. About my plans for the evening. This girl Tracey Hicks' parents were out of town and she was having a party at her place by the lake. Nobody was supposed to know about it, but everybody did. Lana was even bringing Adam, her mythical boyfriend from the city.

But I wasn't that excited. I'd been to a few of these parents-out-of-town festivities over the years. By the end of the night, you'd get girls in crying fits and guys pounding on each other, and people smashing things and throwing up and having sex, though not always at the same time. Or this one New Year's thing I was at. Mark tells some guy that the beam he's leaning on is structurally the support for the whole house, and if it goes we're all fucked. What does the guy do? Starts kicking it as hard as he can, while everybody sits around staring and bored. That's how we partied in Riverside.

My mother asked me if Mark was going. I had to tell her I didn't know.

Lana was waiting when I got to my locker, bubbling over with gossip and news to share. All about this stupid party at Tracey's. And the 'real party' she had planned for later, in the guest room at her house after her parents had gone to bed. The room where her boyfriend from the city would be sleeping. Or 'not sleeping', as she put it, looking very pleased with herself.

'So tomorrow I'll be an ex-virgin.' Lana was arranging an invisible mink stole around her shoulders. 'Don't worry, I'll still talk to you. Probably.'

'Lana, are you sure about all this? What about, you know' – I dropped my voice to a whisper, though the hallway was mostly deserted – 'the schlong malfunction.'

'I told you I took care of *that*. I've been on the pill forever. This time he won't have any excuse.' Lana blushed deeply, let out a stumbling little laugh. 'I mean ...' She broke off and turned away from me, started humming a quavering tune that turned into 'Reel Around the Fountain'.

My rotten mood from this morning was still with me, pulsing like a headache, gathering speed. He was going to make her cry again. Just like the last time they'd tried to do it – and there was nothing I could say that would stop this.

'Don't wait up,' my mother told me.

It was almost eight thirty, still light outside. I paused by the front door with my backpack looped over one shoulder. 'No, Mom. I'm the one who's supposed to say that.'

'Are you sure?'

I asked her what the hell was going on.

'Remember this morning I told you about a ... *certain someone* who has a crush on me?'

I nodded, in slow motion.

'Well,' she said, 'I think I might have misled you just a tiny bit. See ...' She stared at the kitchen table, where she'd been pleating a programme for the movie theatre in Middleton into a squat pink paper fan. 'This crush. It's not exactly unrequited.'

Mom glanced up with a shy smile, waiting for me to say something. I didn't. She told me she had a date with this guy, their first, that they were going to the nine-thirty show at the movies.

'*The Secret of My Success.*' She was close to whispering. 'I think it's a comedy. Oh, and when I told you "don't wait up", you know that was just a joke, right, sweetie? I'm not about to go doing anything—'

'Okay, Mom.' I stumbled for the door. 'You have fun. And ... congratulations.'

There was a quart of vodka in my backpack. I was going to need it.

I stalked off to Lana's place. It was cute, I supposed, that my mom was so excited to be going to see this teenage yuppie movie, that she had a crush on a guy who liked her back. But I knew my mother's taste in men. I hadn't forgotten overhearing that conversation about the married guy. And look who she stayed with for almost ten years – some selfish fucking prick who'd just tried to weasel out of spending seven days with his son, like a kid showing up at a test with a forged sick note.

I hadn't been that interested in Tracey's party. Now I couldn't wait. I wanted to get wasted, completely destroyed – steal a car and drive it into a ditch, beat up Lana's boyfriend, call Stanley and pretend to be his college firing him. Find Mark. Force him to explain why he didn't seem to give a shit about his own life anymore. I wanted to be the one kicking the house down around our heads.

○

At Lana's, Mr Kovalenko answered the door, told me she was upstairs and I could wait in the kitchen. With *the other one*, as he put it, a look on his face like he'd been chewing on old sardines. So I made my way down the hall to the back of the house. Then I saw the boyfriend, and I almost laughed.

I'd been expecting the kid from the photo by Lana's beside, the glum, staring nerd in thick glasses, skin erupting with acne. But Lana was right. He was completely different now. In fact, he was practically a male version of her. Head to toe black – black jeans, black T-shirt with random paint splotches on it, black jacket. He'd done some kind of weird gelled-up thing with his hair too, as if he'd stuck a heap of dead tarantulas up there. A little like Robert Smith from The Cure. He had Robert Smith eyeliner too. I'd never seen a guy wearing eyeliner in real life before.

I stood in the long line of the kitchen's L-shape and watched him. Broad shoulders, pale skin, legs that stretched over the floor as he leaned with one elbow against the sink. A couple zits still stood out redly along his jaw line, along with one very black stubble hair he must have missed with the razor that morning. His eyes were brown, wolfish looking.

He glanced up, caught me staring, stared back. It was the way I was dressed maybe. The Riverside guys' uniform: plaid shirt, T-shirt, blue jeans and sneakers. Total hayseed hick. That's probably what he was thinking.

Mr Kovalenko shuffled into the room and introduced us, muttering and half-hearted.

'Shulevitz, huh?' said the boyfriend. 'Oh, right. Lana's little Jew friend. She told me about you.'

Mr Kovalenko cleared his throat repeatedly.

'Jeez, Andrij, relax,' said Lana's guy. He glanced at me again. 'I'm one too, okay? Or I wouldn't have said anything. Greenberg.' Making some vague gesture towards himself. 'Adam. Hi.'

Seemed for a second like he wanted me to shake his hand, but he was just reaching for a pack of cigarettes. Marlboros. He edged one out and lit it. Lana's father looked as if he was going through some kind of inner torment.

'Listen,' he said. 'I really don't allow people to smoke in my house.'

The boyfriend shrugged and stubbed the cigarette against the side of the sink, angled it back into the pack for later.

What did Lana see in this guy? I felt like breaking a chair over his head. Or asking about the schlong malfunction, how he thought it would affect his performance later, when he'd be deflowering my friend. Mr Kovalenko and the boyfriend got stuck in a strained conversation about the bus ride from Halifax and I was barely listening: wandering around the kitchen full of nervous energy that seemed to have descended from nowhere, bouncing off the furniture like a pinball.

Then the air changed, with a burst of heavy, sweet perfume that clung to my nose hairs. Lana. She was laced into one of her evil princess dresses – dead black with trailing sleeves and a swishy skirt, the usual ample neckline. She glided to the boyfriend, ran her hands along his chest and linked her fingers at the back of his neck.

'Is *Tato* being boring?'

Lana's father cleared his throat again.

'Svetka,' he said. 'Now, darling. I'm driving you to this thing, and I'm going to drive you back too. You call me and I'll get in the car and go. Even if it's four in the morning. If you're drunk, if you're on drugs … whatever. I just want you safe.' She'd ignored most of this. He went on. 'I'll be here all night waiting for your call. Okay, baby girl?'

'Sure, *Tato*.' Rolling her eyes. 'God, he's so irritating,' she said, after her dad had left to move the car.

The boyfriend turned her around and wrapped her in his arms, his hands nearly cupping her substantial boobs. 'Svetka darling, call me,' he said. Had Mr Kovalenko's voice exactly. 'My little baby girl! Even if you're getting fucked by mutants and dwarves …' He leaned in and bit her neck. She threw her head back against him, laughing.

'Yeah, what a tool,' I growled, from a corner of the kitchen. 'Caring about what happens to his daughter.'

This was going to be one fantastic night.

○

Tracey Hicks' house was old, with newly renovated bits stuck to the sides here and there, like it was preying on younger houses and eating them. There was a red barn, a lake glittering behind the house, pastures to either side. The sky still full of June light.

Lana had wanted to make a grand entrance with a guy on each arm, but it turned out we'd mistimed the whole thing. Nobody was around. It was too early. We couldn't even find Tracey. A few nervous knots of people were trying to figure out what to do with themselves, wandering around the back lawn or collecting in sad clumps outside the barn. Down by the lake there was a loud group who'd been drinking since the afternoon, but they'd set up their own tribal society by then and you couldn't get near them.

We explored the house looking for Tracey and ended up in a dusty rec room in the basement that was set up like a bar – but bone dry except for half a bottle of warm cream soda on a shelf. There was a bell hanging from the ceiling, some artefact from a British pub. The boyfriend jumped onto the bar counter, shook the clapper and rang it.

'You're supposed to make an announcement.' Lana gazed up at him raptly.

'Not much to say, is there?'

'Stephen! C'mere!'

I'd managed to get away from Lana and the boyfriend and had drifted upstairs, my backpack over my shoulder weighed down with its full quart of vodka. The rooms were empty, the windows were open and you could just make out thin echoes of music, heavy metal from a boom box down by the lake. And I kept hearing my name – somebody calling me in a strange, hissing whisper.

'C'mere! Stephen! Over here!'

It was Mark, outside a door near the top of a set of stairs leading to the bedrooms. Jesus, he was so glad to see me. As if all the awkwardness over the past while had never happened. I had to glance away for a second.

Then I got closer. Oh. He was drunk. Really drunk. Must have been with the crowd near the lake. Mark was grinning kind of lopsided, face red, hair sticking up, shirt buttoned all bizarre. 'Stephen, man, I totally need a chair.'

I felt like I was dreaming, pictured myself carrying a La-Z-Boy recliner up the staircase on my back. I asked him what the hell he wanted a chair for.

'Under the doorknob. These doors, they got no locks …'

A girl laughed from a room behind him. It didn't sound like Stacey. She called his name, stretching the syllable in a long whiny drawl, asked him why he didn't just get me to stand guard or something.

'I think,' Mark said, looking a bit shamefaced, 'she wants you to keep people out of here. While we—' He broke off, grinning.

The girl called him again and that seemed to make up his mind. 'Okay. I'm real sorry to ask you to do this, man, but … could you? Just, like, hang around? Not right outside the door, but you know …'

I felt myself sinking, wondered which one of them had undone those shirt buttons.

'And if you see Stacey …'

The girl yelled out, 'And Ricky!'

'Right,' said Mark. 'He's Pam's—'

'My fiancé.'

I noticed with reflexive snottiness that she pronounced it as 'feeyoncy'. I knew this girl now. Pam from Arnottville. Stiff hair. Big boobs. Usually only laughed when other people got hurt.

'Mark, you can't just—'

'Thanks, man!' He turned and disappeared into the room, slammed the door. I thought I heard Pam laugh again.

Fuck. They'd both barely remember this after they were done with each other. I was the only one who'd still be thinking about it.

I got halfway down the stairs, smooth shiny blond wood. Then I stopped, lowered myself to the steps and sat blinking into the empty living room. Trying to stop this porn show of despair from haunting me, starring Mark McAllister and Big Boobs Pam from Arnottville. Downstairs there were puffy brown couches with nobody on them, and a huge blank-eyed TV set staring sombrely back at me. I turned my face to the wall. It was a nice pale green.

'Hey, you look sad. Want a Tic-Tac?'

Something bounced off my head. Lana's awful boyfriend was peering up from the foot of the stairs. He had a long glass of something red in one hand, a little plastic box in the other.

'Now, if you'd opened your mouth,' he said, 'that would've actually worked. Wanna try again?' I flinched as another one came at me and felt it land in my hair.

I turned back to the wall.

He emptied the plastic box of white pellets into his mouth and crunched them all up at once. I listened to the sound of candy cracking and grinding into gravel against molars, waited for him to get bored and leave.

'Lana's looking for you,' he said, when he could talk again. 'Thinks you're mad at her, running off like that.'

'Just wanted to give you love birds some space.'

'Don't worry about that.' He swirled his drink and inhaled most of it in one long gulp. Then the boyfriend took a seat on the stairs, two steps under me. He stretched his legs against the wall and blocked my way out.

'So, Lana brings me on a tour of this town, right? And it's like, two streets! I mean, sure there's roads with houses and stuff, but the whole place is maybe one gas station and a bank and a grocery store. That's it.'

Not true. He'd left out the lawyer's office, the bakery, the park and a whole bunch of other stuff. I told him so. He didn't seem to be listening, finished his drink and started chewing on the ice cubes. More liquid crunching and smacking noises.

'Guess you're right. Halifax isn't that great either.' I hadn't said anything like this, but I let it go. He'd pushed himself up two steps and was sitting beside me.

'I mean, you should've seen it. First time I went to school like this' – he gestured at his face, his hair – 'all day it was like, "Hey faggot, where's the clown show?"' He shot me a quick sidelong glance. 'Whole school wanted to beat me up, basically. I looked a hundred times worse than now, though. Black lipstick! Black eye shadow too. And a dog collar – a real one. Used, of course.' He was laughing. 'I went around all day smelling like my fucking dog.'

I wanted to smile but forced myself not to. Couldn't figure this guy out, spilling his guts as if he'd known me forever. Was this what Lana liked about him?

'What'd you do?'

He leaned back, gazed into the ceiling. His arm was stretched over the step just above my shoulders.

'Oh, jeez. I just about cried, man. Went to the bathroom and I was about to wash it all off. Go back to looking like nobody. When I just said, "Fuck it. Fuck these people."' His expression shifted into a cold, superior sneer. Exactly how he'd looked at poor Mr Kovalenko when he'd told him not to smoke in the house.

'So that's my super-villain origin story.' The sneer was gone. He turned and grinned at me. As if he was concentrating the full force of his attention my way, like sunshine.

My head ducked. I could feel my cheeks getting hot. I had no idea what my face was doing.

'Oh, look at that,' he said softly. 'You can smile. I wondered.'

I slid away from him, towards the green wall. 'You … you were really rude. To Mr Kovalenko back there. He's a nice guy, you know. Wants people to like him.'

The boyfriend nudged himself closer to me without seeming to move at all. 'Oh, that. You want the truth?' Our knees were touching. I couldn't move any farther away.

'The truth? Sure.' Barely got the words out.

His head inclined towards me at a lazy angle. 'I was just trying to impress somebody.' He whispered it. He brought his mouth right up to my ear. His breath was on my neck. I closed my eyes. Couldn't keep my legs still all of a sudden.

'Lana.' I felt for my backpack with the quart of vodka, eased it onto my lap. 'You were trying to impress Lana. Right?'

He didn't get to answer because that's when the drunk girl showed up.

The boyfriend jumped out of her way as she came barrelling up the stairs out of nowhere. Rachel Clements, shyest girl in the whole school. Very drunk, pulpy-faced and sobbing. She opened a door at the top of the stairs. Gave a little scream. And Pam gave a little scream. And Mark cursed. Rachel slammed the door, turned around and ploughed through another one. After a few seconds, all you could hear was the sound of this poor girl being noisily sick into the toilet.

Lana's guy was looking up the stairs after Rachel. 'Is she okay? Do you know her?'

I told him she just seemed drunk to me. Business as usual for a Riverside party.

'It's too early to be that drunk. And she was crying.' He went after her. Rachel had locked the bathroom door and the boyfriend tapped on it with one crooked finger. 'Um, Miss?' He seemed overwhelmed. 'Stephen, what's her name?'

I told him, from my post halfway down the stairs. He was making me ashamed. I'd grown up with this person and still only looked at her and registered 'crying drunk girl'. It never hit me that she might need my help or have a good reason to be crying.

The boyfriend knocked again and asked Rachel if she was okay. She should at least unlock the door, he said. Nobody was going to bother her, we just wanted to know that she was safe. I got up and joined him, shaky on my feet. We were right across the hall from Mark and Pam and whatever they were doing to each other.

Then I heard footsteps taking the stairs two and three at a time, and Emily MacBride was pushing the boyfriend aside.

'Not how you do it.' She twisted and shook the round handle expertly. Emily was the younger MacBride girl. Long dark hair and intense eyes. (The one in my class was blonde. It was how you told them apart.)

'Poor Rachel,' Emily said. 'Down by the lake all afternoon with those guys. I think something happened to her, I don't know—'

There was a popping click and the bathroom door swung open. Rachel was sobbing and crouching by the toilet seat. But she seemed okay, at least she hadn't hurt herself or anything. Emily dropped to her knees beside her.

'Guys, you're nice, but we can do without the staring.' She pushed the door shut.

The boyfriend stood rubbing his forehead, his back to the bathroom door. 'Good God. So this is what you country kids do for fun.'

'Well, what do you do in the city that's so great?'

He didn't answer. Instead Lana's guy smiled at me again, slowly, as if he were inviting me to share in some secret joke. My defensive pose melted away and I started to smile back. I couldn't seem to help it, felt suddenly and completely self-conscious, staring into the wood grain of the bathroom door with my face heating up. Rachel was still crying in the bathroom and Emily was cooing reassurances at her. Across the hall Pam gave a little moan. I tried not to connect it with an action.

'Jeez, what is in there?' The boyfriend took a step towards the closed door with Mark and Pam behind it and I moved to block him.

'Nothing. Nobody. Mark. My … my friend. He's with a girl.'

'Your *friend*.'

The scrutiny of that look. I tried to replay what I'd just said, my tone, how much I'd given away.

'Your friend,' he said again. We let the word vibrate in the air. 'Okay. I think I get it now. So … could that *possibly* be the reason you were looking all heartbroken when I came and talked to you?' I didn't answer, tried to will my expression into something blank. His slow smile was back. 'Because your *friend*'s in there banging some girl?'

I told him to shut up.

He took another step towards Mark and Pam's door. 'We should totally go in. Let's see what he looks like, eh?'

I shoved him hard and he stumbled back. We were close to the top of the stairs again, and it was a long, steep way down to the living room.

He grinned. 'Oh, you wanna fight?'

The boyfriend threw a punch at me.

I ducked and shrank away, waited for the impact. But when I looked up from under the crook of my arm, he was laughing. He threw another one, in slow motion this time, his arm sheathed in black drifting past my face. A fake punch. And I'd cowered from it like a girl.

The fucker. Standing with his back to the stairs, heels on the edge of the top step, giggling away. I'd never wanted to hit somebody more.

So I did.

Or I tried to. He dodged me easily, but I'd put all my weight behind the blow, nearly pitched myself down to the living room with the force of it. My left arm jerked backwards. He'd grabbed it to stop me from falling. My legs slipped under me and I crashed down on one of the upper steps, my arm nearly jumping out of its socket. He was still holding on. Holding my wrist and staring at my hand.

My left hand. The one with the scars.

'Oh fuck,' he said. Barely audible.

I snatched my arm away. He sat beside me on the step and grabbed my wrist, forced my hand back towards him. He was stronger than me. Maybe. I didn't want to test it. The boyfriend uncurled my fingers. I felt panicked, like one of those bugs running around in the sudden light when you take their rock off them.

He was glaring at me sternly. 'Okay, what happened?'

'Nothing!'

'This is nothing? Come on, Stephen. Who did this to you?'

'Nobody.' I tried to free my hand again. He wasn't letting go. 'It was a long time ago.'

'Listen. My mother works with abused kids. It doesn't matter if it happened a long time ago. You shouldn't cover up for this person.' Still giving me that accusing stare. 'Now was it a babysitter? A relative? One of your parents?'

'No!' I laughed, but it came out small and broken. 'It wasn't anything like that.' I was staring into his shoes: black with yellow lacing along the edges. 'It was me. I did it.'

He looked shocked, like I'd reached over and slapped him.

I thought at first I could just reel off a few facts, keep it neutral. Then I found I was telling him everything and it was impossible to stop.

I talked about the first time it had happened, the pressure in my head, the way I'd felt so bottled up and horrible and then so relieved when it was over. How I'd been such a miserable kid, poking around my empty house for years, blaming myself because my mother was unhappy and my father was gone and my friend would hate me if he knew who I really was. I told him I'd had some stupid idea the burns might save me too, save me from always wanting.

And as I was talking I started to realise something. Something that should have been thundering obvious, if I hadn't been so good at blocking my thoughts like an obstacle course or letting them slide away like a game of snakes and ladders.

He was beside me, brown eyes soft, just listening. My one scarred-up hand in his two good ones. And it hit me.

Jesus Christ. He's gay. Lana's boyfriend is gay.

I hardly had time to process this before another realisation struck, a shock like a loop on the rollercoaster that leaves your stomach behind.

And so am I.

Yeah, I know. Duh! But the truth was, I'd always squirmed away from looking at it head on. I'd said things to myself like, 'I'm in love with Mark' or 'I'm attracted to men' but I'd never taken out that particular stamp and smacked those three letters onto my head. I was still afraid of it. At the same time, I had this terrific urge to say the words out loud. But I didn't, not then.

'What do you mean?' he said. 'You thought it would save you from always wanting. Wanting what?'

I couldn't stop looking at him, his eyes and his lips.

'Wanting to do … stuff …'

No, no, no. This was Lana's boyfriend. I would hurt my good friend who loved me. I would hurt her more than anything.

'To do what?' the boyfriend said.

'You know.' Our faces were very close. He was still running his fingers along the back of my damaged hand. If I moved my head slightly, we'd be touching noses.

Mark upstairs. Lana going through the house looking for us. Anybody at all ready to wander past and witness this.

Don't do it. Don't do it. Don't do it.

'I don't get you,' he said. A little smile.

My breath was coming deep and shuddery. This was the high-diving board, the fifty-storey building, a leap into nothing.

'Wanting to do what?' Adam said again.

'This.'

I kissed him. He kissed me back.

Yes. Hell, yes. Hallelujah.

Chapter 15

How did it feel? Picture a dark empty house in the winter. Then somebody goes walking through the rooms switching on every single light, basement to attic, one by one, until it's so bright you can hardly stand it. It felt like that.

His lips were very warm and soft. He tasted like Wild Berry Kool-Aid and cigarettes. His arms were around me and one hand was moving under the back of my T-shirt. He couldn't get to anything else because I'd hauled my backpack onto my lap again. It slouched between us like a chastity boulder.

I was twitching my head away from him by degrees, trying to see down the stairs – kept glimpsing shapes on the edge of my vision and imagining it was somebody in the living room staring up at us. Usually it was that big dark void of a TV, or long curtains moving with the breeze, but I'd freeze with fear every time. Why didn't we get up and go to one of the empty bedrooms? I didn't understand it myself. There was some kind of dream logic working here. Or maybe

I was scared that if we moved, he'd get a better look at me and change his mind.

My arms hung by my sides. He had to pull my hands under his T-shirt and settle them on him. I just left them there, palms clammy against his skin.

'C'mon,' he said. 'Stephen. Relax.'

'I am.'

'You're shaking.'

I was.

'Don't worry. There's nobody around. We're fine.' Kissing my neck now. I swallowed back my dry mouth and let myself touch him. His skin was softer than I thought it would be. I ran my hands over his back, his chest, curls of hair under my fingers, brushed his stomach with the backs of my nails. His breathing got faster. He pushed my backpack away from me and I heard the vodka sloshing around.

Somewhere downstairs, a dishwasher chugged into life. I pulled the backpack over my lap again.

'Listen. Thought you said there was nobody here.'

'There isn't.'

A radio switched on. Somebody fumbled through the stations and then Belinda Carlisle was singing 'Mad About You' on FM102.

'Well, what's that?'

He shrugged. 'Mice?'

I started to laugh, even though I wasn't completely sure what was funny. He was giggling too and pulling me towards him. We were lying halfway down the stairs. I felt boneless and drunk all of a sudden, though I hadn't even touched the vodka.

'I didn't make that up.' Adam was whispering breathlessly. 'It's from *Duck Soup*. The Marx Brothers. I totally love the Marx Brothers ...' I told him I liked the Marx Brothers too, almost didn't notice that he'd slid the backpack off me again.

Then we were kind of grappling together – kissing, breathing hard, hands everywhere, steps pressing into my back, into his. My skin felt shivery and exposed, like I was missing a protective covering, and I couldn't get close enough. I braced my sneakers against the steps so we wouldn't fall.

I was glad for the radio – it helped me keep track of how much time was passing. After 'Mad About You', we got to hear about how to get money for nothing and our chicks for free. And Bob's Chainsaw Sales and Services Ltd was the one-stop place to go for all your chainsaw maintenance needs. Take Exit 15.

Adam shoved my shirt up till it was bunched around my armpits and went at me with his lips, his tongue, sometimes his teeth. I gasped and knocked my head back against the steps, bit down hard on my lip. From upstairs, there was a crash as Rachel pushed something over. Emily MacBride said something to her in a low, soothing voice. I couldn't hear a sound from Mark and Pam's room.

I pulled his shoulders back towards me and kissed his mouth. It was all so intense, I imagined I could feel myself bruising under him. He threw his jacket over us. Seconds later he was fumbling with my belt and then he had the zipper open and I held my breath, thinking, *Jesus, if he touches it, I'll die.*

He did. I didn't. But I made some kind of noise. I couldn't help it. He echoed the sound in the back of his throat, mouth against my neck. One hand was moving over me, very slowly. It was torture. It was fantastic.

'Oh, fuck,' he said. 'I really want you.'

'Same … same here.'

191

Saying this out loud made me feel like I'd got away with something. I was nervous and sexed-up and elated all at the same time.

Pressure was building. He wasn't going to stop.

Weather for tomorrow was clear and sunny, chance of showers towards evening. In Hants County a fire had broken out in a poultry slaughterhouse and the chickens were all dead.

I grabbed a hunk of his hair, the fingers of my other hand digging into his back and pushing past the waistband of his jeans. He kissed me again, but I couldn't kiss back, jaw stiff and lips curled back from my teeth, eyes squeezed shut. I turned my face away and pressed my cheek into the step. I felt feverish and I was trembling all over.

Hank's Home Building Centre. Conveniently located on Highway One. Pre-summer bonanza blow out sale on at … somewhere. Good-Time Gardens. Good-Time Gardens Family Farm Market. And Greenhouses.

'You gotta stop, Adam. Oh, God. You gotta …'

There was a squeak of a door above us.

We jumped away from each other. I went frantic, struggling with zippers and buttons and body parts, pushing my shirt back into my jeans, running my hands over my hair to make sure it wasn't all fucked up. There was somebody walking on the landing. Then down the stairs.

I looked up quick. Mark and Pam. Tiny creaks and groans from the wooden steps as they descended together. My backpack was on my lap again. I'd taken the bottle of vodka out, was trying to seem as if I was absorbed in opening it. Like a bit part actor in the background of a high-school play. Stage business.

Mark gave me the smallest little nod of acknowledgement as they passed, and I returned it. I watched them until they were out of sight, let my head fall back against the steps and started to breathe again.

Adam nudged me in the shoulder with his foot.

'So that's the beloved.' I heard him lighting a cigarette. 'Seems a bit dumb for you, doesn't he?'

I was surprised by how angry this made me. But before I could say anything, we got distracted by traffic upstairs. Emily was half-carrying Rachel out of the bathroom and into the bedroom. Adam asked if they needed any help and Emily told him it would be better if he stayed out of it.

He bumped me with his foot again. 'Listen, Stephen. That was fun, huh? But dumb. Very, very risky and dumb.'

I didn't answer. Adam's chin was rubbed and raw-looking from us mashing our faces together for so long and I wondered if mine was too. And the eyeliner was kind of ridiculous, I decided. He was still talking.

'Now the smart thing would be to just pretend this never happened. Keep away from each other for the rest of the night. But, you know …'

'I get it.'

Fun, risky and dumb. Sounded like cousins of the seven dwarves. Obviously we were both there, but we weren't.

He was sitting up straighter, shifting uneasily. 'No. What I mean is …'

Then we both had to stop, because Emily MacBride was clomping down the stairs towards us. She took a seat on the step just above me and rested her feet on my shoulders.

'Hey, Stephen! What are you drinking? Give it here.' Reaching for the bottle. 'Pretty please?' I passed her the vodka, glowering at the empty living room. I felt stupid, like I'd just been dumped.

Emily took a drink. 'God, if you died and went to hell, how would you be able to tell the difference?' We both just gaped at her. 'It's

Rachel. I have a feeling she got fucked down by the lake. And she didn't want it.'

Adam's expression turned serious. 'Well, we should call the police, right?'

Strange how that had never occurred to me, I mean, not even for a second. Guess I was used to this stuff. Too used to it.

'The police?' Emily was saying, 'And tell them what – that I have a feeling? Rachel won't say anything.'

'Yeah, but you can't just …' He messed up his hair with both hands. 'Look, I'm gonna go talk to this girl. Is that okay?' Adam didn't wait for an answer, heading for the bedroom. He paused. 'Hey, Stephen. Don't …'

'I won't. Do anything.'

Adam seemed a bit confused, like he wanted to say more, but he didn't.

'Weird guy,' said Emily. 'Gives you hope, though. I was starting to think all men are like something squirming around in a Petri dish. No offence. Hey, is that a Tic-Tac?' She grabbed at my head. 'Hmm. Minty Dandruff.'

I shoved Emily's feet off my shoulders, went stalking down the stairs and out of the living room. Needed to be alone.

But this was suddenly impossible. The house was filling with people, a trickle and then a flood. Out of nowhere, it had turned into a real party.

In the kitchen, a bunch of girls were mixing drinks, all clustered around this wooden table that seemed to have too many legs. The radio was on. *That* radio. I felt a sudden jolt of fear, asked if anybody'd been out by the stairs in the past while, barely registered relief when the answer was no. Something inside me was crashing down like the side of a cliff into the ocean. I took a slug of my vodka, then another one. Maybe these girls knew, and they were just too polite to say anything. Maybe everybody in the house knew. I was going to have to talk to them all and find out.

Patty Marsh took the bottle away from me. 'You need some mix with that. Want me to make you a Smashola? We just invented it. Vodka and Wild Berry Kool-Aid.'

'Sounds disgusting. Hit me.' And, my God, he was Lana's boyfriend. She trusted me. And I trusted her, with all my secrets. I could have lost my best friend. Because of some jerk who was into doing the smart thing.

'That was quick. You want another one?'

'Yeah. Make it stronger this time. Way stronger.'

○

On my way out of the kitchen, I nearly tripped over Adam, cross-legged on the floor going through the local phone book. He was wearing glasses with thick dark frames. The same nerd glasses from Lana's photo. This sort of fascinated me, but I didn't want to make a fool of myself staring.

Adam smiled and pushed the glasses steady on his nose. 'Stephen, where the hell did you go? The girl won't tell me anything. I'm just getting some numbers for her to call in case—'

'Look, I'm out of here, okay?' I walked away from him. Backwards. Probably a bad idea because my balance was starting to go wonky. 'I'm not trying to follow you around.'

His smile faded into a baffled look as he watched me leave.

I took up my project of talking to every person at the party. Then I forgot why I was doing it. Then I remembered and got paranoid. I had a few more Smasholas. And a couple beers. More straight vodka. I'd started drinking to calm down, but I forgot why I was doing that too. After a while I began to enjoy myself.

●

Later on, stumbling and falling into Patty Marsh's lap.

'Aw, hey, honey,' she said.

I tried to get up, lost my balance and found myself lying across Patty and Eleanor MacBride on the sofa. Eleanor was stroking my hair. 'You see? That's the kind of guy I used to think I was into. You know. Nice. Quiet. Looks like he reads a lot.'

'Of porn! Hi, Eleanor,' I said.

'I still like that type,' said Patty. 'Got "virgin" written all over him.'

'No, I don't.'

'Ya do now!' Eleanor took a lipstick out of her pocket and ran it over my forehead. I couldn't see what colour.

'Is that a *V*?'

She looked down at me, puzzled. 'No, I screwed up. You're upside-down. It's more like an arrow pointing into your hair.'

'Well fix it. I already know where my hair is.' I started giggling, smeared at my forehead. My hand came away looking smashed and deep red.

Patty Marsh was leaning over me. 'Think you made that too soon, Eleanor. Stephen, you got a hickey. Big one on your neck.'

I sat up, almost cracked heads with Patty. 'Oh, shit! What do I do? How do I get rid of it?'

Patty put some kind of concealer make-up on the hickey, told me to wear my collar up. Then they both started getting on my case about who I'd been kissing until I had to get out of there.

'What the hell's that on your forehead?' Evan McDonald said. There was a group of guys outside the kitchen with beers in their hands.

'I was on a motorcycle,' I said. 'Ran into a really big bug.'

'Looks more like lipstick.' That was Doug Sutton. Confused, as usual.

'Maybe it was a bug wearing lipstick.' I thought this was hysterical. Everyone else stared at me blankly. I noticed Adam on the edge of the group, laughing and shaking his head.

'Listen,' I told him. 'I'm not following you. Honest.' My hand was clamped over my neck. He stopped laughing.

I was going to have to try harder to stay out of his way.

○

The rec room had filled up. Everybody seemed happier, clumsier, drunk or getting there. A bunch of us were dancing to music from a squeaky-wheeled tape player set on the fake bar counter. It was The Cure. 'A Night Like This'.

Lana's arms were around me. I leaned down and rested my head against hers. We were slow dancing, which really meant we were just swaying and holding on to each other while I kept getting attacked by horrible, horrible guilt for lying and messing around with her boyfriend. I kissed her forehead to say sorry. I hoped she'd never find out why. I noticed she was wearing a little blur of red from the lipstick cloud on my head.

Adam appeared on the other side of the room, picking his way towards us, tripping and stumbling. I unwound myself from Lana.

'Sorry. Look, I'll go. You guys have fun.' I started away.

'Aw, Stephen,' Lana said. 'You don't have to ...'

I glanced over my shoulder and saw Lana talking to Adam, but he wasn't looking at her. He was glaring after me instead, muttering soundlessly like he was swearing.

Doug Sutton wandered by with a big lipstick V on his forehead.

○

A set of sliding glass doors led off the rec room, and then I was outside. It was dark, finally, though the sky was still half-dusk, daylight struggling on the horizon.

I leaned with my back to the side of the house. Felt like I should hold on to it, as if I was on the edge of the world. The porch light was glowing and moths were hurling themselves towards it in looping patterns. By the glass doors, two flowering plants stood guard in enormous clay urns that reminded me of ancient Egypt.

Adam was on my periphery. Again?

'Okay, sorry. I'll get out of your way,' I said. I tried pushing past him into the house. He stuck his arm across the doorway. Then he took hold of my shoulders and demanded to know what the hell was wrong with me.

I shoved him away and freed myself. Or that's what I tried to do. But I had spots in my eyes from staring at the porch light and no sense of balance because I was drunk. Something happened involving centrifugal force and we ended up smashing into one of those funeral urns for potted plants and knocking the thing over. There was dirt everywhere. I was sitting in it. He looked half-buried.

Adam went mental. 'Oh, fuck my life! Geraniums? You want to plant geraniums, there's, like, five hundred miles of farmland here. You gotta put them in this Satan's asshole of a thing just so I can ...' He chucked a handful of dirt at the doors behind us where it made a soft explosion against the glass. 'Fuck you, Riverside. This is the worst night ever.' Then he scooped up a second handful and let it fly, at me this time.

'Hey!'

'Farm-boy freak. Who do you think you are, treating me like I don't exist?' Another volley of dirt sprayed towards me. Dirt and part of the geranium.

'But you said …' I tried shaking the clods of soil out of my hair. Couldn't get mad. This was too insane. I felt like I was watching a foreign movie with the subtitles mixed up. 'You said it wasn't the smart thing to do. That we should keep away from each other. And you were right.'

He collapsed, lay back staring up at the sky, or possibly the bugs hurtling against the light.

'Oh, for—! I was just going to say it wasn't smart, so we'd have to be more careful next time. God, you're an idiot, Shulevitz.'

Somebody had started a bonfire down by the lake. You could hear that heavy metal off the boom box again – guitars in a lurching pattern, the singer with his hoarse phlegmy voice like a caveman swearing in a stalled truck.

'So, um,' I said. 'You …? You actually …'

'Yes. I like you, Stephen.'

I couldn't look at him, started making patterns with the dirt instead. Why was I so happy? We couldn't possibly get together again. We'd be caught. I'd hurt Lana. In the rec room, people were talking and laughing with no sound, under glass like fish in an aquarium.

'You gave me a hickey,' I said finally.

'Oh, shit. Really?' He was grinning. 'Oops.'

Somebody slid the door open. Lana.

'Hey! It's my song. One of you dopes get in here and dance with me.'

'Me!' I said. Couldn't miss Lana's song. It had already begun – Siouxsie and the Banshees, 'Cities in Dust'.

'No, I'll do it.' Adam stood up, shaking earth from the folds of his jacket. 'Stop trying to steal my woman, Shulevitz.'

We smiled at each other like he'd just said something impossibly witty. I was blushing with potting soil in my hair. He turned away. Inside the house, Lana started up her priestess dance.

Something was bugging me. 'Adam?'

He stopped. 'Mm?'

'How did you know … about me?' I coughed and shook my head. 'I mean, was it my … my voice, or my hands? Or …?'

'Aw, don't think that,' he said. 'You make a really good straight boy, Stephen. You're trying so hard.'

'Then …?'

'It was Lana. She told me.'

I felt like I'd been plunged into ice-water.

'No, she didn't. Lana wouldn't do that. She promised—'

'Look. She talks about you all the time. I was going to use you as an excuse to break up. So she told me.'

Lana called Adam from the rec room. He whispered that he'd see me later and then I was watching them behind the glass. He was dancing goofy on purpose. She threw her head back and laughed, pulled him in for a kiss.

I found my backpack by the remains of the geranium and took a long gulp of vodka.

Lana betraying me. Me, wasting the night drooping with pity and guilt. And who else had she told? Was her dad really smirking behind my back whenever he acted like I was her boyfriend?

The song was over. Lana was leaning against Adam with her head on his shoulder, running one lazy hand up his thigh.

Fuck you, Kovalenko. Fuck you, you Cossack twit. You want another reason to hate Russians? Look no further than your friend Stepan Vladimir.

I took another drink, resting my weight against the house.

I've done so many stupid things tonight.

I was only getting started.

Chapter 16

I couldn't hold on to that fine righteous anger for long, though. Instead I started to get happy. Walking up to people I barely knew, hugging and slapping backs, trying to initiate complicated high-fives. Two shades off obnoxious. That kind of happy.

I even hugged Stacey, threw my arms around her and spun us around. In the hallway off the rec room with its green carpet that smelled like something drowned.

'Hey! Stace, my man! My woman! Isn't this great? Class of '87! It's like, who are we all gonna turn out to be? One of us could be Hitler. Isn't that amazing?'

'Where's Mark?' She extricated herself, pushing at me as if I were a blanket around her shoulders on a hot day.

'I'm fine! How are *you*?'

'Look, do you know where Mark is or what?'

'No clue.' I started walking away, grinning sloppily. 'But good luck!'

'Hey. My friend Tina's here. She likes you.' It sounded like an accusation. I gave her the thumbs-up and kept bouncing down the hall.

I collided with Adam.

'Finally,' he said, and slung his arm around me. He started walking us somewhere, told me Lana was busy with her friends and wouldn't even notice we were gone, not for a while. Then we were outside. I reached for my cigarettes as a reflex. We must have been on the same wavelength by then – he took a pack from his coat pocket, stuck a smoke in my mouth and lit it.

'Filthy habit,' he said, smiling.

'So are you.' I was pleased with myself for coming up with that, even though he told me it was cheesy. We veered in wavering lines all over the back lawn. The lake was a dark shape with its bonfire light glaring against the water.

Adam decided we should check out the hayloft, said it was too good a cliché to pass up. So we were striking out in that direction, but something was screwy. We kept getting pulled back towards the bonfire instead – like it was a sun with its own gravity reeling us in.

Then I heard my name. Sort of.

'Jew-le-vitz! Hey, Jew-le-vitz!' But it sounded almost friendly. I made my way over to the fire.

Adam followed. 'Are you sure we should be—?'

'I'll just figure out what they want.'

A circle of guys were hunched over the blaze. It was too bright against the dark – I could barely make out their faces, or even how many there were. Five? Six? Randy McTavish, Kevin Dickson. Phil Doyle, who'd given Mark fifty cents to beat me up back when we were kids. A couple guys from Arnottville. Everybody seemed to have long hair, baseball caps, black T-shirts decorated with lightning bolts and screaming skulls.

'Jew-le-vitz, my man!'

I high-fived a few of them. Why not?

Adam seemed to shrink into himself. Randy McTavish glanced at him, face screwed up in contempt. 'Who the fuck's this? You wearing make-up, man?'

'It's just … It's nothing,' Adam mumbled.

'It's like Robert Smith,' I said. 'You know. The Cure?'

Phil Doyle smiled, very slowly. 'So … you're dressing up? As Robert Smith?'

'Yeah, it's kind of dumb,' said Adam.

I felt like I had to explain him. 'This is Lana Kovalenko's boyfriend.'

Instant reaction. They looked hungry.

'Lana!'

'Lana Ko-va-len-ko!'

'Amazing tits.'

'Fucking awesome tits, man. I mean she's a bit, like, heavy.'

'Bit on the chubby side.'

'But great tits.'

Adam sighed, miserably. 'Yeah. I've always thought so.'

I wasn't sure how I felt about Lana's boobs being discussed this way, but the mention of them seemed to have spread a wave of contentment around the bonfire.

Phil was nodding, as if in response to a voice only he could hear. 'Jew-le-vitz. Come on and sit with us, man.'

Kevin Dickson backed him up. 'You never talk to us. Come on, man.'

What was I going to say? No? I lowered myself to the ground, not getting too comfortable. Adam stood behind me. He nudged my shoulder and made some movement with his head in the direction of the house. I wanted to tell him I'd get us out of there as soon as I could, but it was impossible to say anything in front of these guys. At this level, they looked bigger. The way the light from the flames would bring some faces into focus and blaze and dazzle at your eyes so the rest were left in darkness. A boy at the end was listing to one side, nodding sickly with the music from the boom box. I couldn't see his hands. He might easily be chewing on a skull. Somebody started passing a joint around.

'Jew-le-vitz! Oh, yeah! Give it to Jew-le-vitz!'

I took a mouthful of acrid smoke, handed it to Adam.

'Shit,' he said. 'Think I dropped it.'

The guys made disgusted noises at him, but before things could get too scary someone started another one. Didn't seem to make much of a difference. Phil took a stick out of the fire, blew on the end until it turned glowing red-orange. 'Looks like you're in a good mood, Jew-le-vitz.'

I told them I'd met a girl. That she was from out of town and her name was Anna. Adam kicked me in the back, told me in an undertone that I was a complete moron.

'You met a girl!' said Randy McTavish.

'Now that's just fucking adorable.'

'Gonna take her to the prom?'

'Where is she, man? Gotta meet this woman. Jew-le-vitz's woman!'

Phil smiled again, leaned in close. 'Cause we all thought you was some kind of faggot, man.' He poked me in the chest, hard. Still had the piece of wood with the glowing end in his hand.

'Oh.' I looked at the fire. Something more needed to be said. Obviously. I couldn't see everyone's faces, but I knew they were all watching. I tried to keep my voice level. 'Why would you think that?'

This made everybody laugh. Adam pulled at my collar and tried to get me to stand up. *Bad idea, Adam. Can't just leave like that. They'll come after us.*

Kevin was actually making some attempt to answer my question. 'Just the way you ...'

'Don't play sports,' someone else said. Marty from Arnottville? How would he know?

'Don't do, like, anything.'

'Always hanging off McAllister.'

'McAllister.'

'Gotta wonder about McAllister.'

'But ... Mark always has a girlfriend,' I said.

'Yeah – you.' Phil Doyle was laughing. 'You know how you can't beat on Jew-le-vitz or McAllister will be right there.'

'Oh, yes. First thing you learn. You don't fuck with McAllister's boyfriend.' Randy leaned back and poked a skinny blond guy sitting beside him in the head. 'That right, dick-breath? McAllister gets a bit unreasonable if you mess with his boyfriend.'

The blond guy snarled at Randy to shut up. I recognised him. Sean Flynn. He'd started school at Riverside in Grade Eight, tried to beat me up on his first day to prove he was tough. Mark had broken his nose and humiliated him in front of everybody.

Randy went on, gesturing as if he had an invisible cigar in his hand. 'You might wanna beat on that fucking skinny little stuck-up Jew prick ...'

'Oh, yes. Sitting up at the front there ...'

'Sitting up at the front just licking the teacher's ass. But you can't.'

That was when I took a better look around the fire and realised that just about everybody here hated me, had probably hated me for years. How was I going to get out of this? And I was terrified they'd do something to Adam. I'd asked for whatever I was going to get when I sat down with these trolls. He was innocent.

There was a gust of smoke in my face as the wind changed, making me gasp and blink. The centre of the fire was white. Branches and twigs crumbled and twisted. Kevin poked at the blaze and a few sticks of wood fell in on themselves, sent a shower of sparks against the darkness.

'Yeah, can't fuck with McAllister's little honey,' he said. 'Of course, now that you're with this make-up guy here ...'

Phil was looking around, grinning. 'No, guys! He's got a woman. Didn't you hear him?'

Adam tried to haul me to my feet again. What would I do if they went after him? Start a fight with the alpha male, maybe. Distract them. Tell Adam to run for it. I tensed up, tried to figure out which guy was the boss.

'So tell us about this woman!'

'Did you fuck her yet?' They were all leaning towards me. The circle seemed to be closing.

'Did you go down on her?'

'Yeah, did you eat her out?'

'Did you get your face down in there, Jew-le-vitz? Did you get all messy?'

I didn't know what to say, panic blanking everything. 'Uh ...' I remembered the baseball cap from that guy Mark had beaten up outside the bar on my birthday. Something about girls being made of sugar and spice and not tasting like ... you know. At the time it'd taken me at least a minute to figure out what it meant. 'Uh ... tastes like tuna!'

Silence for a second. Then the guys were all laughing. 'Jew-le-vitz! My man!' Everybody slapping me on the back, hard.

Adam kicked me again. 'Hey, Jew-le-vitz. I hear Anna is worried about you. Maybe she thinks you're some kind of witless, self-destructive idiot.'

I stood up. 'Yeah, we should go back.'

'And I gotta see my girlfriend,' Adam said into the circle. 'The one with the amazing tits. Tell her how happy they make everyone.'

They all smiled and nodded, and for some reason this unnerved me. We turned around and started walking.

'We gotta run,' Adam said in my ear.

'No, you don't run. You never run.'

'Suit yourself.'

He sprinted off in the direction of the house, and I had to follow. Was there anybody behind us? I didn't look, thought probably not. Even if this was a bunch of guys who'd always hated me, it was also a contented bunch of guys getting stoned in front of a fire, and they probably didn't want to break a sweat chasing after us and tearing my head off and throwing it into a tree or whatever they had planned.

We ended up at the barn instead. It was locked, but we got in anyway. Then we fumbled up to the hayloft in the dark, making the horses nervous, feeling for the next rung on the ladder and hoping it would be there. Adam got all claustrophobic and I sat on a barn cat by mistake, so we opened the big creaky window in the front where you throw down the hay – got some air and moonlight into the place. We had to stack a couple bales in front so the good old boys at the fire wouldn't be able to see us.

I sat with my back to a bristling rectangle of hay, sweating and trying to convince myself that I had not just escaped from certain death. Beside me, Adam took a rolled-up joint out of his jacket.

'Stealed it offa them fellers,' he said, in a hick Valley accent so perfect it almost made me nervous. 'You wanna smoke this with me, Cousin Luke? Stay out here for a spell? With me?'

For a spell. I surely would.

○

But how long was a spell supposed to last? Forty minutes? Four hours? A week?

'Gotta be the dumbest thing I've ever done in my life,' Adam said, pulling my T-shirt over my head and pushing me to the floor. 'Imagine if those freaks find us.'

True, but at the same time, I was so sure we could get away with it. And we did, sort of.

Everything passed in a haze as we sneezed up crumbs of dried grass and animal fluff, splinters shoved under our skin from the rough wooden boards. At times we'd be crazy and panicked, wrestling and bruising at each other. Then lying thick and slow with our hands drifting, trying not to fall asleep, stuck in inane circular conversations while random twitches ran through us like electrical blips. A couple barn cats sat on bales watching everything. We'd chuck handfuls of hay at them and they'd flick their little conical ears and keep right on staring.

I asked Adam if we were going to do it for real, and he told me no, that he wasn't about to try boffing a virgin in the dark with the cast of *Ron's Redneck Revival Hour* massing outside. And besides, he said, we didn't have any of the stuff we needed. I knew he probably meant condoms and whatever, but for some reason I thought of party hats. Then I couldn't get the image out of my head – both of us earnestly humping away with elastic strings under our chins, paper cones in birthday colours nodding forwards and falling over our eyes. Adam was propping himself on an elbow and trying to lecture me about safe sex, and I couldn't stop laughing, holding on to him and giggling until my stomach hurt. He called me an idiot and a weirdo, but he was holding on too.

'Not even gonna tell me what's funny, right? See, I know you by now, Shulevitz.'

He did. The laughter trailed off into shuddering hitches like at the end of a good cry. We were sweaty and gross and covered with stray bits of dried meadow, arms tight around each other. I couldn't remember when I'd been this happy.

But a few minutes later we heard voices. Tracey Hicks and her boyfriend, trying to figure out why the barn door was open, stepping inside. We stuffed ourselves into clothes and jumped out the front window. The spell was over.

Back to the party. It had to be done. Pop songs on different stereos bashed up against each other, people leaned over banisters and screamed – could have been from happiness or horror, I wasn't sure. In the rec room, a crowd of kids were belting out the chorus to a Duran Duran song from Junior High. I wandered around trying to make sense of it all. My skin was still vibrating with the memory of being touched, like ocean waves washing over me. There was no sign of Mark anywhere.

Then it was late and I was alone. A lot of people had left at that point, and the ones who remained were pooled in areas of concentrated activity like the rec room and the back lawn, or siphoned off into private spaces in pairs. I was huddled on the floor with my back to the fridge, clutching a handful of souvenir magnets that had come skidding down after me. 'Visit glorious Maine,' they advised me. 'Alberta is wild rose country.' 'I coasted up Magnetic Hill.'

So unfair. Where was Tokyo? New York? Paris? Who would want to remember Magnetic Fucking Hill in New Brunswick? Pity and exhaustion settled over me like a physical weight. By the time Adam found me, I could barely lift my head.

We could never leave each other alone for long. Since we'd got back from the barn, Adam and I had spent most of the party stuck together – wedged on a couch or stumbling through the halls, wrapped in some private joke, ignoring everybody and avoiding Lana. Every once in a while, we'd decide we had to split up because we were making a spectacle of ourselves. But then we'd get lonely and seek each other out again. So it must have been his turn to be lonely.

Adam settled in beside me on the linoleum. I let my head loll forwards till it thumped against his chest, took a handful of his plaid shirt and hid my face with it. It was my shirt. He was in the Riverside guy's uniform, the sleeves looking like they'd split if he bent his arms. I was in his black T-shirt and jacket. A mix-up from when we'd had to get out of the hayloft so fast. He'd told Lana I was just helping him blend in with the locals.

'You okay, Stephen?'

'Yeah.' A small voice mumbling into him. 'No.'

He pushed my head up so he could see my face. I felt like I was on a hinge. I tried to tell Adam how much I was going to miss him. He didn't answer, seemed preoccupied with an empty beer bottle that was stuck to his finger. Maybe it had attacked him. The whole kitchen was bristling with empties, hollow green and brown glass crowding the counters, the table, the stove, the sink.

'Makes me sick,' I said. 'You. Going home with Lana. You don't want her. It's … it's cruel, that's what it is.'

He tapped the bottle against the floor like a cat twitching its tail.

'Stephen, don't be an asshole. *Cruel.* Jeez. You should've seen my parents' faces when I introduced them to Lana. They were so fucking happy. So … *relieved.* Made me want to cry. Or … or kick them, or something.' He wrenched the bottle from his finger and it came away with a deep musical pop. 'Anyway, she's got no reason to complain. I'm gonna do it with her later. I guess. And I mean, let's face it. A girl like that's lucky to get a boyfriend at all.'

'But Lana's beautiful.'

'Are you kidding? Total lard-ass.'

'Oh, fuck off, Adam! Why are you such a pig?'

He put his hands on my shoulders and told me to calm down. It was late, he said, and any minute Lana might decide to call her dad to come drive us home. Then before you knew it, we'd be in the car saying goodbye forever in front of Mr Kovalenko, and did that sound like fun to me? I had to admit it didn't.

Adam started to kiss me. Soft and lazy at first, and then more intense. We stayed like that, sliding around on the floor, gripping each other's backs and hair for leverage, sloppy and drunk. I wondered if this was the last time I'd be kissing Adam, or anybody. Maybe Lana really was about to call her dad. And where was Lana anyway? I opened my eyes and glanced sideways to check the clock above the doorframe. *Oh, there she is. Standing in the doorway watching us.*

What?

I shoved Adam away. He looked sulky and confused for a second. Then he saw what I saw.

Her face. Like a child who'd just been slapped in the middle of a laugh. Lana who had a smart answer for everything. Saying nothing at all. In the party dress she'd worn to impress him.

Adam was babbling away at top speed. Some stupid explanation or excuse. I wasn't listening and neither was Lana.

I closed my eyes. I could still see her.

She never would have hurt me like this.

Adam scrambled to his feet, trying to approach her, still rambling on and on. I stayed in a miserable heap by the fridge in my borrowed black clothes, digging my fingers into my scalp. She left. He went after her.

She'd sat beside me and held my hand the day I found out Stanley wanted me to be an abortion. Gave me her father's guitar. Kissed me when I was sad. This morning by the lockers, nervous and hopeful, trying to cover it up. I'd been so scared that Adam was going to make her cry.

I took a few shaky steps around the kitchen, looked at my reflection in the window over the sink and called myself every name I could think of. But it was stupid – they were just words. I'd ruined everything.

Then Adam was back. I saw his shape in the window behind me.

'I don't know where she went.'

He swore. I swore. We paced around, bumping into counters and tables, knocking over empty bottles. Adrenaline was giving me a second wind and I couldn't believe I'd just been moping and whining on the floor over this guy.

'Looks like I'll be bunking at your place,' he said. I realised I didn't care.

'She's my best friend. Goddammit, why am I so stupid!' I kicked at the cupboards behind me. 'I mean, I don't even *know* you!'

He was standing with his back to the stove, huddled into himself. 'You think she'll start telling people?'

I stared at Adam, greenly. 'Oh, *fuck*! She wouldn't. Would she?'

'Looked pretty mad. Might've heard me saying she was lucky to have a boyfriend cause she's fat.'

'Yeah, thanks for that. Oh, *Jesus*. What are we gonna do?'

He mumbled that he didn't know and I was stressing him out, kept picking empty beer bottles off the table until he found one that was more than half full. He took a long drink. I stuck my head under the cold water tap. No effect. Adam shoved me out of the way so he could spit into the sink.

'There was a butt in there.' We faced each other. I turned off the tap.

'We're screwed. Adam? We're screwed.'

'No.' Hands on my shoulders again. 'No, we're not. Don't say that.'

'We are.'

'Stop it.'

He turned away from me, messed up his hair, closed his eyes. Then he was walking in circles around the kitchen, snapping his fingers distractedly and mumbling to himself. At first I thought he might be praying. Then I recognised the words 'fear', and 'mind killer', and realised this was the Bene Gesserit 'Litany Against Fear' from *Dune*. I wished I could remember how it went. It seemed to be calming him.

He stopped. Stood up straighter. 'I got it.'

I waited.

'Lana's not going to tell everybody.'

'How do you figure that?'

'Because you are.'

'Are you mental?'

He tried to explain, said it would be so much better for me this way, that I wouldn't have to wonder who knew because I'd be telling them myself. Lana would turn it into a nasty rumour, he went on, but I could say it plain and simple – just another fact. School was almost over anyway, and I was going to have to be an adult and own up to myself, not some kid with a sock drawer full of secrets.

'Trust me. You act like nothing's wrong and nobody else will.' Adam was smiling, his eyes bright. He seemed evangelical, or insane. And he went further. We could make this a pact, he said. If I went first, he'd tell his parents the truth as well. As soon as he got home. He'd tell his whole school. I watched him building momentum as he spoke, gaining confidence, getting taller. Convincing himself instead of me.

'No more fake girlfriends, huh? You're right. It's a shitty thing to do to somebody.' That unsettling smile. 'You'll never regret this, Stephen.'

I pictured it. A big announcement, here at this party. Then nothing but silence. Faces staring back. Some shocked, some repulsed, some smirking. And afterwards. An invisible label hanging over my house. Mom hassled at the grocery store. Me getting the shit kicked out of me every day. Mark. Oh, God. Mark.

'It won't work. I can't do it, Adam. I can't.'

'I know,' he said. 'I'm gonna do it for you.'

He clasped my hand, like a fighter pilot off on his last mission. Then he turned and strode out of the kitchen. I blinked and watched his plaid back receding.

Was this a dream? Was I still in the hayloft, asleep?

I stood in the kitchen doorway. The lights were off in the rooms outside it and I stumbled as my eyes adjusted to the dark. I trailed after Adam. Where was he going in such a hurry? Past the stairs leading up to the bedrooms. Through the living room.

Oh, Jesus.

Just then everything around me slowed down to nothing, like we were all stuck in syrup, because I'd figured it out.

He was heading for the basement.

Down those stairs was a room, more than likely still full of people. There was a fake bar in that room, with a very loud bell hanging over the counter. The type you'd ring if you were going to make some kind of announcement.

He wouldn't.

Would he?

No. Fuck, no. Run. Stop him.

Chapter 17

Oh, God, no. No, no, no.

Adam was already at the foot of the stairs to the basement. I threw myself down the steps after him, hands skidding over the railing. There was a crash behind me. I ignored it.

The hallway, green carpet with its heavy mildew smell. Door to the rec room coming up. I could hear music. The Pogues. Accordions, fiddles, Irish grumbling. It sounded bigger than it should have, echoing. *Please stop, Adam.*

The possibilities crowded into my head. Mark finds out. My mother finds out – and from somebody on the street, not me. Give it a couple days and the teachers know. The janitor knows. The milkman fucking knows. In Riverside gossip travels in nanoseconds. My life wouldn't be worth living.

I caught up, grabbed his shirt – my shirt, looking stretched and unfamiliar in my hands. 'Adam,' I said, terrified and out of breath, 'this is such a bad idea—'

He shoved me away. 'Quit it, will ya? I'll never be able to go through with this if you keep—'

'Good. Don't go through with it. Don't!'

Adam thought he was helping. That was the crazy part. But he'd never have to see these people again. I would. Nine o'clock in homeroom on Monday morning and every day after that until the summer wore down or I died of embarrassment.

'Look, you're gonna wreck everything!' I was pacing backwards in front of him now. 'I finally got people here to like me. I mean, for years I didn't have any friends except Lana and Mark. Now they'll all go back to hating my guts again.'

'Well, if they do, fuck 'em. They're not worth it.'

What was I going to have to do – punch him? Would that even work? I wasn't what you'd call competent at punching people. And how could I hit somebody I'd spent most of the night making out with?

Hesitated too long. He was already pushing past me and into the rec room.

I followed. 'Fuck's sake, Adam, why do you want to do this to me?'

'It's for your own good.'

'No, it isn't!'

People were watching us. I took in the room, panic making me hyper-aware of every detail. The low, white ceiling in whorls of plaster. The fake-wood-panelled walls, the calendar by the bookshelves, a tractor on a brown furrowed field for June. Empty bottles were shored up around the bar counter like they'd arrived with the tide.

There were maybe twenty left out of the crowds I'd seen earlier, most of them girls from my class. Everybody seemed to be in a great mood – jumping around to The Pogues, flush-faced and grinning, loving the hell out of being wasted and pretending to be Irish. Patty Marsh was luxuriantly drunk, bright red cheeks and brighter eyes, bouncing with her arm thrown around Evan McDonald. And there were the MacBride sisters leaning against the bar – Eleanor smirking at a private joke, Emily laughing and lazy with her head thrown back. Was Lana part of this group? I couldn't see her.

My stomach had dissolved. Walking into a nightmare, everybody smiling. Except me.

Adam had turned his back again. I grabbed a handful of plaid fabric at his elbow. 'Adam, please.' Trying to keep my voice down. 'I really like you. Don't fuck everything up for me.'

He ignored this and swung himself up on the bar counter, pushing Emily to one side. She looked quizzical, annoyed, took a swig from her bottle of beer and pinched his ass. He turned and smiled down at her. All happening in slow motion.

Adam leaned forward and hit the pause button on the tape player. The music stopped.

'Hey!'

'Fuck off!'

'Turn that back on!'

Well, he had their attention all right. There was no need for him to ring that stupid bell next, but that's what he did. It almost made my teeth hurt, the sound of it.

I'd crossed around to the front of the bar, clinging to the edge and staring up at Adam, trying to will him into silence.

'Just gotta ... just gotta say something, guys.' Adam's face had gone deep red, but his voice carried to every corner of the room. 'You all know Stephen Shulevitz here, right?'

Somebody in the crowd went, 'Duh!' Someone else went, 'Who?' There was a splash of giggling.

I couldn't look at any of them, digging my fingers into the back of my neck, whispering, 'No, no, no, no, no …'

'Well, Stephen and me … that's to say, I mean, the two of us …'

Oh, Jesus. Here it comes.

Adam glanced at the floor. 'Both of us are …'

It was very quiet. He closed his eyes.

'We're both a couple of fucking Jews, man! Anybody got a problem with that?'

Relief. Like somebody knocking the wind out of me. That asshole. I was grinning. That complete tool. Fucking Adam. I risked a glance over my shoulder. People were looking at each other, shrugging and mystified. Somebody was saying we should turn the music back on.

'Yay! Jews!' It was Emily MacBride. She started clapping idiotically from behind the bar, and there was a bit of half-hearted applause from the group in return. Emily was nuts, but people liked her, usually followed where she led.

Adam looked down at me sorrowfully. 'I couldn't do it, Stephen. I'm so sorry. I'm a gutless *fucking* failure …'

'Don't be sorry. That's fine. That's great!'

'No, it isn't. It's not good enough.' He held up a palm for attention. 'Hey! Everybody! There's one more thing.'

And he leaned down, grabbed my head and gave me a big horny kiss right on the lips.

The fucker, the fucker, the fucker.

He was above me. I couldn't push him away, couldn't get the leverage to break it off. I closed my eyes, out of embarrassment, confusion. Maybe I kissed him back, just for a second. Maybe I didn't know what else to do.

I could hear the room going nuts.

'Oh, my God …'

'Gross!'

'What the fuck!'

'Stephen?'

It built. General noise of shock and repulsion. I felt a shuffle through the crowd of somebody leaving, more than one. Maybe a lot more.

'Yay! Gay Jews!' Emily MacBride, in exactly the same tone of voice as before. The same demented clapping. Then nothing.

Adam let me go and I stumbled backwards, found myself facing the group. Every eye in the place was on me. They were all waiting. Waiting for me to explain myself.

I was going to throw up. I was sure of it.

I started babbling instead, like a moron.

'Well … you know it goes through the mother. And I was never educated in it or anything. So. So, I don't … I don't really think I am … I don't consider myself to be … Jewish, really.'

Still no one had said a word. I wanted to sink quietly into the carpet, to die.

I heard my own voice again, as if it was coming from across the room.

'But the other thing …' Squeezed my eyes shut. *Am I really going to say this?* It all seemed to be happening without me.

'The other thing. That one's true. I actually am … you know.' Glanced up at the crowd, too quick to register anything, then stared back down at my feet. 'Gay.' An almost physical shock, the word coming out of my mouth. Floating above our heads like skywriting.

I was squirming, felt my face burning up.

So quiet.

For the first time, I understood how heavy silence can be. The air felt practically solid, molecules of oxygen suddenly hard-edged things, impossible to draw into my lungs. I kept staring downwards. The carpet fibres were a light nicotine brown, rough and packed together, like carved-up bits of brain pressed stiffly into the floor. There were splotches and spills, stray bits of hair. A lonely crescent of toenail.

Somebody took me by the shoulders. Emily MacBride. I concentrated on her face. Collapsing into myself in slow motion, terrified to look anywhere else.

'Stephen.' I knew everybody was watching, like we were people on a stage. 'Stephen, why didn't you tell us?'

I wanted to say that it was nobody's business and I'd never trusted any of them in the first place, but that's not what came out.

'I … I didn't really know myself for sure. Until maybe a couple months ago. And … I thought you'd all hate me. Think I was gross and stuff.'

Some girl in the crowd went, 'Aw!' This frustrated me, but I couldn't lose focus on Emily.

'Oh, Stephen,' she said. 'None of us would ever think that.'

I tried not to laugh. Hadn't she seen these people getting collectively grossed out by that kiss, just a few minutes ago? Yet I could sense the room realigning itself to agree with Emily – a wall of certainty. Even a few girls murmuring 'Yeah,' along with her. I felt like asking what was the matter with them that they didn't remember the last ten minutes of their lives. But, no. Couldn't say that.

'Everybody's listening to us, huh?' I half-whispered this. Emily laughed. There was some rustling from the crowd then, and a few people tried to put together a conversation. But it subsided like tree branches rattling in the wind. Of course they were listening. They wanted to see what would happen next. I was clutching Emily's hand. She was holding a half-empty bottle of Labatt's in the other.

Emily looked around, smiling broadly, a game-show hostess all of a sudden. 'Well! You know what I think?' She raised her bottle of beer. A toast?

She smiled at me again, lit from within, pulled me towards her. Then she held the bottle higher, above our heads.

Turned it upside-down and dumped it all over me.

Shock of the cold, chemical water, shock of the smell. I swiped it away from my eyes, felt it running down my neck and soaking my back.

Behind me I heard, 'What the fuck?' and 'Emily!' and 'Emily, what the fuck?'

I couldn't move. Wanted to ask her what I'd done to make her mad, if she was crazy, if we both were. Emily was grinning like she'd just heard the best news in the world and couldn't wait to share it with me. She ran her hands through my hair, messing it up. Little flecks and droplets of beer went flying off my head.

She kissed me on the forehead. Kissed me on the cheek, just under my eye. Kissed the other side of my face too. It felt so light – like getting a goodnight peck from your baby sister.

I said, 'Emily …,' without being aware that I was saying anything. She kissed me on the mouth then – a quick smack, then pulled me into a hug. A real one, close and solid, hands moving in reassurance across my back. I started to laugh, hanging on to her. What else was I going to do?

'Congratulations.' She breathed this, over my shoulder. 'It must be great to know who you are. I wish I did.' My eyes were closed. No idea how the rest of the room was taking this.

Then I heard somebody clapping. Was it Adam? Or Emily's sister? Another person joined in. Then more. This wasn't like the muddled slapping of hands that Adam got when he told everybody we were Jews.

This was an actual round of applause. Something that built on itself, that grew and grew. So we were on a stage after all.

Emily let go. She turned me around, pushed me at her sister Eleanor.

'Your turn,' she said.

Eleanor had a bottle in her hand too. I heard Patty Marsh yelling, 'Beer him, Eleanor!' Another girl took it up.

'Beer him!'

'Come on, Eleanor.'

'Go for it!'

Eleanor looked around, shrugged. She pulled me close and upended her beer over my head. There was a swelling of applause as it hit, stinging my eyes, and somebody saying, 'All right!'

Then Eleanor did the same thing as her sister: kissed my forehead, both sides of my face, a quick one on the mouth, and wrapped me in a hug so tight I could barely breathe. I just hung on.

'Me next!' Patty Marsh was shouting from the group in front of the bar. But she had to wait. Somebody – Adam, maybe – put The Pogues back on and everybody went back to jumping up and down and pretending to be Irish. Except now they were also passing me through the crowd – not much of a crowd now, only twelve or fifteen people left. I was grinning helplessly, my head spinning, hardly able to stand up. Got pushed into the arms of a jock girl named Cynthia.

'Look at you,' she said. 'What a waste!' My head was splattered with beer again as she poured the dregs of her bottle over me, then reached up and kissed me quickly – same as the MacBride sisters: the head, twice on the face, once on the mouth, then pulled me into a fierce hug and told me congratulations. So it was a ritual now.

The Pogues on the tape player joined in with a sing-along chorus fit for a rainy night in the pub, something about beer and whiskey and saying goodbye. The girls were pressing in, pushing me from one to the other – everybody wanting to be part of this game, this collective insanity.

'Give him here!'

'My turn.'

'Stephen! Over here now. I'm doing it next.'

Patty Marsh was facing me, quivering with laughter, and half a bottle of Miller went glugging down my back. 'So that's who gave you the hickey. Too funny.' She kissed me, held on tight. The sound of accordions, tin whistles and drunken farewells at a train station flowed from the tape player.

Evan McDonald splashed beer on my head. 'I'm not gonna fucking kiss you,' he said, 'but, yeah. Congratulations. I think.' He shook my hand, clapped me on the back. Passed me on to the next one.

I was laughing so hard I was almost hysterical, shoved through the crush of my fake Irish friends. Then I was at the end of the room, embracing a shaky Rachel Clements. Was that everybody? No. One left.

Adam poured a couple ounces of Budweiser onto my hair. Then he took my face in his hands and kissed me: light on the hormones, heavy on the romance, Prince Charming and Prince Nerdly. Probably he was laying it on for the girls, who rewarded him with a smattering of applause, some of them crooning 'Aw!'

I heard Evan McDonald. 'You don't have to keep doing that, you know.'

And Patty saying, 'Shut up. I think it's sweet.'

The same people who'd been so shocked and grossed out, here in this room, not twenty minutes ago. This was insane.

Then he let me go and I was back to where I'd started. Facing a room full of people – everybody waiting for me to say something. I could barely stand, holding on to Adam for balance.

'You guys …' I started, choking. 'You guys are so nice.'

I couldn't say anything more because I was breaking down in tears. I didn't even know why. I pressed myself into Adam's shoulder, his arm around me keeping me steady. When I looked up, I saw some of the girls were getting teary-eyed as well.

Then a voice by the door behind us.

'Hi, kids! Hate to interrupt, but has anybody seen my daughter?'

Mr Kovalenko ambled into the light. We all froze. An adult in the middle of this. It was like having water thrown in your face when you were deep in a particularly involving dream.

'She's …' I stammered, 'she's around, Mr Kovalenko.'

'Well, you guys can help me find her. We're all going home now.' He looked around the small group of stunned faces. 'Anyone else here need a lift?' Nobody answered. 'Okay, then.'

Lana's dad rolled down the hallway with his easy, sauntering gait. 'Y'know, this isn't half as bad as I thought. Should have seen the parties I went to when I was a kid. This generation doesn't have, I don't know, the same spirit.'

Adam and I followed, so slowly we were lagging a good twenty feet behind. Near the end of the hall he was met by a small figure – eyes dark with blurred make-up, pretty black princess dress hidden by an old grey cardigan.

'*Tato!*' she said and collapsed into her father's arms. Mr Kovalenko looked over his shoulder at us, raising his eyebrows.

The elation of the past few minutes drained away. I was starting to feel like something squirming and hairless, a newborn rat cowering at the end of the hall with another newborn rat. I hung on to Adam's elbow. We could talk about this later, I thought. How to make it up to her.

Adam shook his head. 'I better go make my peace. Or I'll have nowhere to sleep tonight.'

'Oh.' I hardly wanted to mention it, felt so stupid suddenly. 'I thought you said you might want to, you know ...' Voice dying in my throat. 'Remember? My place?'

He wouldn't meet my eyes, started spieling off excuses. Went on about his contact lenses, which were at the Kovalenkos'. His *Sandman* comics.

Something inside me was refusing to process this.

'So you really have to go?'

No answer.

Adam turned and started off to the end of the hall where Lana and her dad were huddled together. I followed, numb with guilt. But I had to face her sometime. And how else was I going to get home?

Lana broke away from her father, stood glaring at Adam as he paced towards her.

'You piece of shit,' she said. In a quiet, controlled voice, her hands in fists. 'You worthless, lying fuckhole. Parading me around your school, making sure everybody saw us together. What a joke.'

'I know,' he said. 'I know, Lana.'

'And you let me think it was my fault. Remember? At your place, when I was crying all afternoon because I could tell you didn't want me? Remember what you said?'

'Oh, God. Yeah. I remember. I'm a total asshole ...'

They were standing very close now. She smiled coldly. '"Maybe if you lost some weight." That's what you said to me.' Lana started to laugh. 'Yeah! If I lost some weight and grew a dick! Isn't that right?'

'I don't get this.' Mr Kovalenko had edged a few feet away and was whispering to me. I just shrugged.

Then Lana started pounding on Adam, cursing and telling him how much she hated him, every word accented with a thumping blow. They were staggering back down the hall towards the rec room. I couldn't watch, got in between the two of them and grabbed her arm.

She slammed me against the wall. 'You!' she said. Was she going to start walloping me next? Shit. I couldn't hit back. She was a girl. Besides, she'd probably kick my ass. And I deserved it.

But what happened was worse. My friend broke down in painful sobs, said she never wanted to see me again.

'Aw, Lana, no,' I said. 'Don't talk like that. I'm sorry. I was a selfish jerk, I know, but just let me tell you my side of this …'

She wrapped her arms around her father's shoulders, told him it was time to go. There was no need to drive me home, she said. I was catching a ride with somebody else, someone I hadn't treated like garbage. I realised the hallway was empty except for the three of us. Adam had probably left a couple of minutes ago.

'Lana, please just listen.' I followed along, tried to get her to look at me. We were at the stairs and Mr Kovalenko was rubbing his head and mumbling something in Ukrainian.

'*Tse kinets' svitu*,' he said. Then they were gone.

I felt heavy, drowned. Turned around, staring at the doorway down the end of the hall. The crazy scene in the rec room was like something I'd seen on TV, broadcast from another planet. I had no idea what to do or where I was supposed to go now.

Somebody touched me on the shoulder. Adam.

'You came back!' I said. 'Listen, I don't know how we're gonna get to my place, but …'

'Um … Kind of need my jacket? Sorry.'

'Right, right.' I was still wearing his stupid jacket. It was soaked with beer, didn't smell too great. But I guess he thought it was worth running back for.

'You can keep the T-shirt if you want.' He still couldn't look me in the eye. 'Listen, you're gonna be okay, huh? I feel bad leaving you stuck here with all those rednecks.'

'They're not rednecks. These are my friends.' I handed over the damp black mass of fabric. 'Here's your jacket.'

Adam stood twisting the jacket in his hands, seemed on the verge of telling me something important. Then he kissed me on the forehead. 'Bye, Stephen!' He took off up the stairs.

'Adam, wait!'

But then I had no idea what I wanted to say. I hovered at the foot of the steps, feeling helpless and stupid, then came out with, 'You're gonna call me, right?'

'Sure. Absolutely.'

I wanted to laugh. 'You don't have my number.'

'I'll get it off Lana.' He turned away.

That was it. Up the stairs, out the front door. Gone.

And all I got was this lousy T-shirt.

I wandered outside. I'd pretty well given up on getting home – think I was just looking for a quiet place to pass out. This guy Jason Brent walked by, one of Mark's new friends. Chucked a lit cigarette at my face and called me a faggot. I wasn't sure how to react. So I ignored him, kept going. Where? I wasn't sure.

The lake. I could see the bonfire a hundred feet away, looking more like a handful of charred sticks by now. A couple of caveman shapes were still hunched in front of it. Have fun, assholes.

I took a seat on a bumpy, stubbled rock that scratched at my jeans. The sky was magnificent. We were deep in the countryside, and it seemed like there were more stars than dark.

Images, faces, pop songs, a moment in the hayloft. All buzzing through me. Some of it made me so happy, elated, and at the same time full of strange little flickers of sadness and fear. Tomorrow I was going to hurt, and not just from the hangover that was waiting. But I was also pretty sure that I'd still be there, that I'd be okay.

The breeze off the lake. The stars. This crazy, incredible night. I remembered when I'd been at the river making lists – razors, pills, ropes, rigging up a car to feed me carbon monoxide. I'd actually wanted to be dead. It seemed so strange now.

How could I have thought about killing myself, even for one second? I would have missed all this.

Just hold on to it, I told myself. It's such an easy thing to forget.

Chapter 18

I woke up suddenly. I was shivering.

It was June, but deep into the night, with a wind off the lake. I only had Adam's black T-shirt on over my jeans, and that was mostly soaked with beer. I looked back towards the house. Every window was still screaming with light. Had to find somebody with a car and get home.

I pulled myself up and started shambling back to the party. There was dew on the grass already; when I walked I made trails I could see from the porch light, like a slug. Other kids were milling around me – zombies looking for a grave to rest in. The air was dense and clammy.

An elf was trundling along with a load of pumpkins in a wheelbarrow.

I looked closer. No, of course it wasn't an elf. It was a girl, tiny and slender. And she had a wheelbarrow, but it wasn't full of pumpkins. It was full of Stacey, wrapped in somebody's orange hunting jacket. Her head was hanging off the edge of the barrow as she bumped and lurched along. The elf girl was smiling.

'Hey, Stephen!'

Did I know her? Yes. I suppose I did. My birthday last year. At the end of the night we'd met up with two girls. This one had been my girl. Tina from Arnottville. Lots of bushy brown hair, wide blue eyes and a sweet smile, some kind of permanent acne condition. She'd liked me. Maybe she still did.

She stopped the wheelbarrow to wait. When I got closer, I realised Stacey wasn't out cold after all, or maybe she was one of those people who could smoke in her sleep.

'She's kind of fucked up,' Tina said cheerfully.

Stacey kept her eyes closed, growled something about how her boyfriend just banged some slut practically right in front of her, so what were we expecting?

'Aw, come on, Stace.' I tried to sound convincing. 'Mark wouldn't do that. I'm sure this is some kind of misunderstanding.'

'Misunderstanding. Right. You'll say anything he wants.' Her eyes were open now, and she'd lifted her head for a better look at me. 'You'll do anything he wants. I been watching you. The two of you.'

I started feeling a bit nervous, asked Tina if they'd been anywhere near the rec room in the past while. But no. Stacey had been busy puking up and having crying fits, and Tina had been busy taking care of her.

They didn't know a thing.

We stood around awkwardly for a moment. Then I remembered my manners and offered to push the wheelbarrow.

'Aw, that's real nice!' Tina was beaming at me. 'Careful over bumps, huh? Gonna take her to my truck.'

Tina's truck was a monster blue pickup, hulking in the driveway next to the garage. She said she'd been waiting for all the other cars blocking her to drive off so she could leave. Told me she'd take me back to my place – just as soon as we got Stacey home safe.

The truck was coated with a thick layer of road dust. I played a quick game of tic-tac-toe against myself on the side door while Tina tried to explain to Stacey that she had to stand up now, that it was time to go home. In the end, we were forced to lift and load her ourselves. Stacey was not exactly co-operative – she kept accusing me of trying to grab her tit – but eventually we were able to haul this heavy body into the cab of the truck and get a seatbelt strapped over her. She lolled against the dashboard muttering a steady stream of curses.

I climbed into the cab of the pickup between the two girls and Tina gunned the motor. We roared off into the dark.

Stacey's place was down a long dirt road on the outskirts of Arnottville, a red wooden farmhouse with sharp corners and narrow windows. A light was on in the kitchen. We were waiting for it to go out.

'He'll kill her,' Tina had explained to me. 'Stacey's dad. If he sees her coming in this late, all liquored up.' Tina's plan was to sit in the truck until the light went out, and then she'd sneak Stacey up to her room. So we sat, the three of us, cold and bored and waiting. I concentrated on that light in the window for so long that I could still see it when I closed my eyes. Sometimes I'd fall asleep without knowing and my dreams were mixed up with that endless dirt road, that red shingled house that seemed to be looking back at us.

Stacey was sprawled over most of the pickup cab, with her head against the window and her feet jutting to the accelerator. She was breathing deep and rhythmically, a soft buzz of a snore. I was nestled by the steering wheel with little Tina. Tina told me she remembered meeting up last summer on my birthday, that she'd seen me around since, thought I was real sweet.

'You know what?' she said. 'I never met anybody like you, Stephen.'

Then Tina stretched herself up, pulled my neck down, and kissed me.

We started making out – I had no idea what I was doing, but she didn't seem to mind. I suppose I was curious. After all, I'd been trying to train my imagination to go in this direction for years. And maybe, I thought, there was a chance I was bi. Wouldn't that be great? *Like Bowie.*

But at the same time I wasn't comfortable with it all. So at first I tried to keep things above the neck. That didn't last too long. Then I decided I'd settle for above the waist, which didn't really work either. In fact it hardly mattered what I did. This was one determined girl.

'I don't know, Tina,' I said, when it was clear to me what was going to happen. 'Stacey's right there.'

'She won't wake up.' And I still must have seemed kind of unenthusiastic because she asked me what the matter was.

'I guess I'm nervous.'

'Aw, it's your first time!'

'No, I've been nervous lots of times.'

She thought this was the funniest thing she'd ever heard. Didn't have the heart to tell her I'd stolen it from *Airplane!*

Tina said I had no reason to be worried, that she'd done this with a million guys and it was no big deal.

'Yeah,' said a voice beside us. 'Just remember you gotta move it in and out.' The shape that was Stacey stirred, gave a low, rasping chuckle.

'Oh, jeez, Stacey!' I tried to fix myself up so she wouldn't see anything.

Tina was mad too. 'You shoulda told us you was awake!'

'Didn't want to ruin the moment.' Stacey smirked at us. 'Good to know you're not some kind of queer, Stephen. I was never sure.'

Tina clambered over my knees and walloped her. 'Hey, you know, that's totally rude!'

A violent argument began. By some miracle I found myself drifting off to sleep, the girls' voices fading as I slumped against the door by the driver's side, my head fusing itself to the cold window.

When I opened my eyes, I was alone. I had a scary moment when I wasn't sure where I was. Then Tina was opening the truck door. Mission accomplished, she said. Stacey was safe in her bed.

Night air in my face. The house was a silent blank, the light gone. I slid over to the passenger side and Tina drove us to Riverside. She kept looking at me and smiling, like we had a secret together, which I suppose we did.

We got to the outskirts of town and I asked her to stop and let me out. Didn't want that truck driving up to my house in the dead of night and waking my mother. I opened the creaking door on the passenger side. Tina sidled over, put her small, cold hand on the back of my neck.

'I really like you.'

I kissed her on the forehead so I wouldn't have to say anything.

She smiled. 'You'll call me, right?'

'Sure. Absolutely.' I got out of the truck, slammed the door. 'I can get your number from Mark. He can get it from Stacey.'

Tina gave me that secret smile again, pressed her little foot to the accelerator, and then she was gone.

Even though I was exhausted, I found myself taking the long way back to my house. Too much had happened. I had to walk it out, be alone for a while.

Past the town hall, back of the high school, edge of the graveyard. I seemed to be heading for the usual spot: the drop-off over the river. Our place, Mark's and mine.

Then I was there. Pine needles thick on the ground. The river below, moving slow and grey.

Mark.

I stopped short, stood very still. No, I wasn't imagining it. His head was nestled in the roots of a pine, a bottle of beer beside him.

His body. His face. Eyes closed. Eyes opening. I shivered with a brief flush of everything at once: love and wanting and sadness and guilt. I felt like I'd cheated on him.

'You look wrecked,' Mark told me.

'Very good, retardo.' It was something we used to say when we were kids. Made me laugh. I sat heavily and felt my head hit the ground before I knew I was falling. He was lying beside me.

Mark asked about the party – he'd left early with Pam. So he'd been miles away from that rec room. Relief made me dizzy, but I kept it out of my voice and continued talking, telling him nothing special had happened, going into the story of the drive home with Tina and Stacey, how we had to sneak Stacey into her house.

'Her dad. Yeah, I forgot.' He sounded guilty.

I couldn't think of anything to say to this, so I told him about making out with Tina in the truck. Thought it was something he'd want to know.

Mark laughed. He was sitting up now. 'No way! You finally got a girlfriend.'

'She's not my girlfriend.' I pulled myself upright, sitting beside him.

'No, but she'll probably fuck you.'

'I'll get it on video since you're so interested.'

'Ew.'

Mark made me promise I'd at least ask Tina out again. I asked him where I should take her, if I should bother going to a movie or whether we could just drive around. I realised I'd never actually taken a girl out before, and that I was only considering doing this because of him.

'So, any advice for me?' I said. '*Sensei?*'

He shook his head, serious and tired. 'I got nothing to say to anybody, Stephen.'

'Shut up. You're the best person I know.'

'Stupid kid.' He ran his knuckles over my head.

We didn't say much for a while. The night was gone and the light was pale and unreal – a strange, in-between feeling, like we were in another world.

'Almost over, huh?' Mark's voice sounded softer, as if he were alone.

'You mean high school? I know. Isn't it great? I'm really …' I stopped. Couldn't say out loud that I was happy. I was afraid of jinxing it.

There were weeds by the edge of the drop-off, wildflowers. You could see them more clearly with each passing minute. Alien-headed clover, dandelions, a daisy leaning drunkenly. Mark frowned into the river.

'Guess it's different for you,' he said. 'You're gonna get out of here. That's kind of the reason I stopped hanging around so much. We're going in different directions, right? Time to let you be with the smart kids for a change.'

'Is that it? Jeez, I thought you just couldn't stand me all of a sudden.'

'Been in my face almost ten years. Think if I suddenly decided I couldn't stand you, it would've happened before now, huh?'

I smiled, picked up an old pinecone and rolled it along the ground. It looked dried and skeletal, seed pods like teeth in an animal's skull reaching out.

'Think I was kind of ashamed of myself too,' Mark said. 'That day at the town hall. When those guys were all calling you names. Shoulda stood up for you.'

'Don't worry about it.' Why should he? It was a thousand years ago.

'No, I was acting like a dick. Just got really tired. You know? Always defending you when you won't do anything yourself. And part of me was thinking: *Well, at least these assholes are gonna be around next year. Stephen's gone.*'

'Not yet.'

'Hey, listen. Can I tell some of my friends? About you and Tina?'

I asked him why he'd want to do something like that.

''Cause people say shit about you, man.' Mark dug his fingers into the ground. 'Okay, not everybody. Just a few guys I hang out with. They … they think you don't like girls or something.' He mumbled this at the pine needles. 'Listen, I don't know where they'd get that crap. Maybe it's cause you're not into sports, or you're shy—'

'Or because I'm gay.'

Mark choked, sat up stiffly and stared at me.

Then I grinned, and I could see relief washing over him. 'Aw, don't even joke about that!' Laughing. Was it just my imagination or did this sound forced? 'Jeez, thank God I never met one. Think I'd puke right up looking at him. *It.*'

'Wouldn't want you to do that.'

I'd heard him say stuff like this before. I don't know why I felt like he'd just leaned over and slapped me. Slapped me awake.

I dragged myself to my feet, using a branch for leverage, and held out my hand to him. He took it. We were exhausted, swaying. He slumped against me. We staggered home as the sun travelled upwards.

The in-between light was gone. We were on the wrong side of a new day.

Part 4
The last days of Riverside

Chapter 19

My mother told me she'd had 'a very nice time last night'. But that was all she'd say. She threw open the front door and let in a bright blast of June sunshine, humming a chipper little tune that turned out to be Steve Winwood, 'Higher Love'. The kitchen cupboards squeaked and whined. The drawers slid back and forth, went thud-bang.

'Mom.' This zombie drawl coming out of me. I'd been sitting at the table for what felt like days. Staring into a glass of soda water, still in Adam's black T-shirt, reeking of beer. My hair was sticking straight up and my eyes were dark blasted tunnels. I felt like a stain drying on the carpet, a skunk smeared across the highway.

All the stupid things I'd done last night. That one incredibly stupid thing.

Telling everybody. *Oh, God.*

I imagined the news travelling from person to person, moving through the town's bloodstream to its heart. There were another ten days of classes left. Then exams, prom night, graduation. How could I face them all?

'Mom,' I said again. She stood waiting, a dishtowel in her hands. 'I made a big giant idiot of myself last night.'

'Oh, honey, I know the feeling.' My mother dragged a squat kitchen chair over beside me, reached her arms around my shoulders.

'Quit it.' But I was lonely and sick and sinking into something that would have felt like despair if I'd had the energy for it. So I let myself lean back against her, closed my eyes.

'Sweetheart,' she said, 'what happened?'

'Nothing.'

I felt itchy, uncomfortable. Pushed my chair away and staggered to my feet. My mother looked up at me, squinting and baffled.

'But, Stephen, you just told me …'

'Nothing, Mom. I said nothing happened.'

'Honey, please.'

'Look, if you keep asking I'm just gonna make something up. I don't want to lie anymore. Don't you get that?'

I forced myself out the front door. Sunlight was flooding over me. Too much. I stood, a musty pharaoh waiting to disintegrate. But I survived and somehow ended up in the backyard, where I sat on the chopping block by the woodshed and gazed miserably up at the house. She was at a window, staring back at me, pretending not to.

What the hell was I going to do about my mother?

I wondered how long it would be before somebody told her. Then again, she worked in another town, didn't have many close friends here. Who'd take the first step and let this bomb blow up in her face?

Me, I supposed. It would have to be me. But not yet.

I let my head slump forwards, found myself thinking about Lana.

Again. Maybe I'd die of this hangover and then she might forgive me, toss a plastic daisy on my grave. Or just use the stone to park her gum while she stomped all over my miserable bones. It would be a relief.

○

On Monday, I sneaked past the classroom door where everybody was gathered for homeroom. Lana's locker was next to mine. I got out my books and waited for her.

I said hi. She said nothing. I told her I was a worthless jerk. She ignored me. I touched her shoulder. She shrugged me off like a bug, walked away.

Time for English class. I was aware of every step I took, the faces I was passing. Most of the kids were staring at me. Others were trying not to look in my direction at all.

Could be this was all just my imagination.

But then, the first time somebody kicked me, I didn't know what was going on. I actually said sorry. Thought it was an accident, like when you're walking in front of people too slowly and they have to step on your heel. Knew I was wrong when I looked up to see Randy McTavish mouthing some insult over his shoulder as he passed. I should have thought of a snappy comeback. Instead I just felt choked and stiff.

That was the first time. There were a lot of other times.

It was the same five or six guys. Mark's friends from his remedial classes, the ones who'd got me so terrified back at the bonfire. I figured they'd probably always wanted to do this stuff – kick me and spit on me, slam me against the lockers. Now they had an excuse. But I could handle it. They had faces and names, these guys. They were just people.

It freaked me out more when it was anonymous. I didn't like it when

I'd come back to my locker and find insults painted in liquid paper or scrawled with marker. Or once I got up to go to the bathroom in Math. I took my seat again and my notebook was open to a blank page. Or not completely blank. There was a message: 'Kill yourself faggett.'

I flicked the page aside, stared at the blue lines on the graph paper until they merged into one big square.

Fucker couldn't even be bothered to spell it right. Whoever it was.

Those were the times I'd stop thinking I could handle this just fine on my own.

I needed Lana, but she still hated my guts. I'd have to improvise.

On Thursday, I forced myself to push through the cafeteria doors at lunchtime. For the past few days, I'd been scarfing back sandwiches in little out-of-the-way corners around the school, the same spots where I used to grab a smoke and some time alone when I was skipping gym class. But today I'd decided I was going to claim a place at one of these tables and start talking to people. I took a look around. A bunch of girls I knew were gathered in a corner. Patty Marsh. Cynthia the jock. The MacBride sisters, Eleanor and Emily.

I banged up to their table, made Emily shove over so I could sit. The girls stopped talking and stared at me. I stared back. We all remembered the party, of course, and the rec room. But I felt weird mentioning it.

'People are being assholes,' I said finally.

Patty Marsh put a hand on my arm. 'Well, you got friends, right?'

I felt irritated with myself, being so grateful.

But the girls had their limits. Their conversation could be difficult to follow – you'd need a stack of footnotes to understand the significance of Darla lying about going to Tammy's bridal shower. And when they talked about men, I didn't know where to look. Or sometimes I tried to take part, which was even worse.

'Okay,' I said once, breaking into the middle of a debate. 'Suppose somebody says they're going to call you. Only they don't.' The girls went quiet. I stared down at the cafeteria table, trying to keep my tone casual. 'How long should you wait before you call … that person yourself?'

'Forever.' Eleanor smiled. 'Hold on to your dignity, man.'

But Patty had put down her nail file and was gazing at me with liquid sympathy. 'Aw! Was it that guy from the party?'

Then they all started.

'He didn't call you?'

'Aw! That's a sin.'

'That was so sweet, wasn't it, guys?'

'I mean, I was a little grossed out at first.'

'Me too.'

'Just a little.'

'But then …'

'Aw!'

I felt like poking myself in the eye with a fork. Where was Lana when I needed her? I missed her so much it was like a phantom limb. I missed Adam too. And I did call him. That night. I went through the city phone book and dialled each Greenberg till I found his house. He ate an apple at me and made excuses to get off the phone fast. I sat on the kitchen floor for an hour afterwards, head in my hands.

So I'd ruined my friendship with Lana, over somebody who was treating me like a telemarketer. And the girls at school were no substitute.

Still, it did make me feel safer, being in a group. Maybe I was being paranoid. Maybe not.

Tuesday, the second last day ever at this school. I was in the guys' bathroom looking at an ink mark I'd made on the side of my face, when I got nervous. Felt like I was being filmed or watched. I was suddenly conscious of every sound. Water in the sink. Tiny squeak of the taps. I saw a movement in the corner of my eye, reflected in the mirror. Something was behind me. Somebody.

Then three guys started coming out of the stalls all at once.

I couldn't yell. There was a hand over my mouth. Another guy held my arms. More of them appeared out of nowhere. I didn't know who they were, or even how many. They forced my head down. I could only see legs. Sneakers. I twisted my arms, tried to kick them. No use. It felt like I was in a straitjacket. They were whispering at me, laughing.

'You're gonna die.'

'You fuckin' cocksucker.'

'Gonna die, Jew-le-vitz.'

A stall door banged open. Somebody's sneakered foot kicked up the seat of the toilet.

Fuck, no, fuck no. I threw myself backwards, tried to squirm out of the grasp of whoever had my arms. Didn't work. I was getting pounded and kicked on all sides. It hurt. Jesus Christ, it hurt. One guy took hold of my hair, shoved my head in the bowl, and my skull banged against the edge, hard. I choked, water rushing in all around me. They were laughing in that soft, colourless way, talking to each other, low voices. Somebody pushed my head down and kept his hand there, hit the flush again. I was thrashing around like crazy but nothing would help, and they were still all punching at me. Panic. I breathed in. Had to. Breathed in water.

What a stupid way to die. Please, God, no.

Then the hand on my head was gone. Sudden movement all around me. They were leaving, in a big hurry. I could lift myself out of there.

Breathing. Oh, my God. I sat by the toilet in a heap. Gasping, spitting water back into the bowl. Spots in front of my eyes. Everything hurt. It took me a second to realise I wasn't alone. Someone had come in – had come back in, wheezing and mumbling to himself about how he just wasn't fast enough anymore.

'You all right, son?' A hand was pulling me to my feet. Mr Richardson from gym class. I'd been afraid of this guy for years. He dragged a bundle of paper towels out of the dispenser and pressed them into my arms. I stood and held on to them. Moving was painful. Moving my arms, moving anything.

Mr Richardson was scratching the back of his neck, frowning at the water on the floor. 'Hm. Unusual for the Grade Twelves. Even that bunch.' Then he got a better look at me. 'Oh, right. Stephen Shulevitz.'

What was that supposed to mean? Did he know? Mr Richardson thumped a hand on my shoulder. I wasn't sure if he was attacking me or trying to be fatherly. 'Listen. Anybody gives you more trouble, you come to me, okay? Come straight to me. I'll deal with them.' He moved towards the door. Sunlight was filtering past cobwebs and crud in a little window above our heads.

'Mr Richardson.' He turned around, faced me. There was too much to say. How did he find out about me? Did all the other teachers know? Was anything going to happen to those guys? But I couldn't talk, couldn't make sense.

He was nodding away to himself, like there was a motor in his head keeping it in motion. Standing uncomfortably close now. 'Don't let this bother you, son,' he said. 'Don't you even give it a second thought.' He gave me a slap on the back that nearly knocked me off my feet. 'You're a good kid, Stephen.'

The last bell rang. I got my stuff out of my locker, tried to sneak off before anybody else, out the side door and into town. My hair was still wet. I was walking carefully, feeling bruised and mangled.

A beautiful afternoon in early summer. Green lawns with yellow dots of dandelions. Kids running through a sprinkler. A big fat Golden Labrador ambled up to me wagging its tail.

Fuck off, dog. Fuck off, kids. Fuck off, all of you.

I'd been lucky, Mr Richardson showing up when he did. And the bathroom was a pretty small space, so I was guessing those guys didn't have room to work me over like they'd wanted, especially when they had me in the stall. This could've been something I didn't walk away from.

Yeah, I was lucky. What a great fucking day.

I was almost at my house when I noticed Mark signalling from the other side of the street. I couldn't figure him out. It was impossible that no one had told him about the rec room. This was Riverside. But he hadn't said a word about it, at least not to me. I was guessing Mark knew about all the rumours and was choosing not to believe them. He was loyal that way.

He came running over. 'Stephen! You okay?'

I asked him what he meant by that. He shrugged. 'Looks like you've been through some shit.'

If I said anything, I'd have to tell him why they did it, what they were calling me the whole time.

'Don't want to get into it.' I hoped I sounded blank and manly.

Mark was weaving around, trying to get me to look him in the eye. 'But you *are* okay. Right?'

I nodded. He lit a cigarette, offered me one. 'So, you wanna come by tonight? Watch TV or something?'

I couldn't think of the last time I'd been to Mark's place. But it was nice of him. I said I'd be there after supper.

'Cool. See you then.' A little punch on the shoulder, same as always. I stood watching him go.

The bathroom. How did those guys know where I'd be? They hadn't been waiting in the stalls all day, obviously. But I guess I was predictable. I'd never go during the breaks. Always while class was on, usually about twenty minutes into Math. You could practically get out a stopwatch and time it. If you knew me really well.

He didn't ask why my hair was wet.

Don't even think it.

I turned, kept walking. Didn't want to talk to Mark. Or Patty or Eleanor or my mom or anybody.

I wanted to talk to Lana.

I'd call her and she'd hang up. I'd walk next to her and she'd cross to the other side of the street. I wrote her letters, made her a mix tape. Nothing.

Now I'd had enough. This was going to end today. I marched to the Kovalenko house, jumped the steps on the veranda, banged on the door. I waited. Somebody's wind chimes were clunking random notes in the distance.

The door opened a crack. It was her. 'Lana, I—'

She slammed it shut. I could see her through the pebbled glass on the window, walking away.

I kept thumping on the door, ringing the bell. Even kicked it a couple of times. Then Lana's dad was ambling towards me, a roundish blue blur. He pushed open the door and squinted into the sunlight.

'Stepan, listen. I'm trying to relax here.' He was in a T-shirt and sweatpants, bare feet. I'd probably interrupted him at yoga. 'She won't talk to you, okay? Just go home, please.'

'I'm sorry, Mr Kovalenko. I need to see her.' He was shorter than me, so I slumped down. Didn't want to seem rude. I wondered if there was a bruise on my head from the toilet bowl, if I looked like I'd been in a fight.

'Hey, what's this all about, anyway?' he said. 'Can I ask? I've never seen Svetlana like this.'

'Um …' Something was bubbling away in the kitchen, probably potatoes. 'Well, Mr Kovalenko, I …' Oh, fuck it. Maybe if I made this sacrifice, she'd come back.

'I was … I was kind of …' I stared over his shoulder at a piece of Ukrainian folk art in the hall. 'I was sort of messing around.' Happy peasants dancing in a circle. 'With her boyfriend.'

Horrible silence. Mr Kovalenko's eyes crinkled. 'You mean you were fighting? Like, you hit the guy?'

I became aware of Lana's mother standing behind him. 'Sweetheart, you really should go home. She doesn't want to see you. Just respect that. Huh?'

'Can't make any sense out of this kid,' Mr Kovalenko told her.

'Well, I meant …' I felt dizzy. 'We were … fooling around. Messing around. Me and Adam.' They stared at me. A big, heavy fly coasted through the door over Mr Kovalenko's head.

'Making out. We were making out.'

Mrs Kovalenko's eyes were getting bigger. She got it. 'Stephen! You don't mean you did something sexual with this boy?'

Mr Kovalenko grinned. 'Course he doesn't mean that, Larissa.'

I swallowed. 'Yeah, I do.'

He clapped his hand over his mouth. 'Holy shit!' Burst into shocked laughter.

Lana's mother took a step backwards. 'Oh, my God—'

'Mrs Kovalenko, please don't tell my mom!'

'Don't worry,' she said. 'I am not *touching* this one.' She turned and headed back into the dark house.

I was left alone with Mr Kovalenko. 'Ah, Stepan. Guess it was too good to be true, huh? The boy next door. Even part Ukrainian.' Big sigh. '*Tse kinets' svitu. Tse kinets' svitu.*'

Behind him, I could see Lana and her mother arguing in the hall. Lana looked up.

'Stephen,' she said. 'You *told* them?'

First words she'd said to me since the party. I couldn't help smiling.

Lana's mother ordered her to go back upstairs, said she'd get rid of me. Lana made a snorting noise at her. She turned and left her mother in the hallway, swept past her father at the door, took my arm and escorted me down the front walk. Her mother stayed on the veranda and told her husband that their daughter was crazy and wouldn't listen.

We found ourselves in the park by the river. Somebody had mowed the whole expanse of it down to a buzz cut of green, but on the edge near the water there was tall grass, Queen Anne's Lace, clusters of daisies. A set of steps led to a tiny pier – a platform of wooden boards suspended on the water. We headed down without saying a word.

This was probably the most private place in town. There was the steep wall of the riverbank on one side, shielding us from the rest of the park. On the other side, only water, green fields and cows grazing on the opposite shore, the railway station standing quiet and empty. I could feel the sun warming the back of my neck. My hair was nearly dry. We sat facing each other.

Lana was in black again, a big black skirt and black tank top. She took off her clunky sandals, seemed extremely interested in scraping thick purple lacquer off this one toenail. Then she glanced up at me.

'So, Mark tells me you had sex with a girl.'

I started to laugh. 'He *said* that?'

She was smiling in a hesitant way, like she didn't really see the joke.

'No. Lana, no. That never happened. I mean, I got kind of close for a minute, but ...' And I told her the whole story of Tina in the truck and Stacey listening, making it sound even worse than it was. 'Trust me,' I said, 'I am *never* doing that again.'

Lana looked out over the water. 'It's funny. Or maybe it isn't. You sneaking off with Adam was humiliating, all right ...' I told her again that I was sorry. She shook her head. 'But, it was the girl, Stephen. Thinking about you and that girl just made me crazy.'

I lit a cigarette. 'That's weird.' Something was bugging me. 'Hey, what were you doing talking to Mark anyway? You guys never hang out.'

'Oh, you know. Went over to his place to fuck him.'

I sat bolt upright, felt like I was being smothered.

'I thought it would make us even,' she said. 'You stole my boyfriend.'

'That is *not* the same! And I didn't—' Jesus Christ, the two of them together. I threw my cigarette in the river.

'Calm down, Stephen. His little sister came home before anything could happen. Thank God. I mean, he's not even that attractive. And all I could think of was how he'd talk about it later to those other troglodytes.'

'And me.'

'And you.'

I'd had enough of this stupid fight. I slid myself closer. 'Listen. I am really, really sorry. I was a selfish tool. But I think you should forgive me now.' I took both her hands in mine. 'I love you. You know I do.'

'Yeah, I know, Stephen. You love me. Like I'm your sister. And I—' Her eyes were shut, her head bowed.

'Are you okay? What's wrong?'

'I love you,' Lana said. 'Like …'

She couldn't finish. I didn't want her to. I realised I'd moved away – just a few centimetres, but it was enough. Lana was looking into my face now.

'You're so stupid. You're so smart, Stephen, but you're so fucking dumb. What I mean is …' Still clutching my hands. 'I'm yours. You're mine. We're supposed to be together. Why don't you get that?'

'But—'

'I knew it from the first night I met you. You remember? When my parents had that lame party. I was watching at the window when you were walking home with your mom. And I thought, *That's it. There's my boyfriend …*'

Her voice failed and she turned away. I never wanted to see her like this. Rejected, getting her heart broken. And I was the one who was hurting her. I moved closer.

'Don't, Lana. Don't. It's okay.' I put my arms around her shoulders, smoothed her spiky hair.

She reached up and kissed me.

I kissed her back. My first impulse was to pull away, but I wouldn't let myself. I was so tired of disappointing people.

We sat locked together on the platform, mouths and tongues working against each other. Sunlight was bouncing off the water, little waves jostling us. It was like the trampoline, that day at her place. But we knew who we were now. No more confessions.

She broke away from me so she could peel off her tank top. There was a black lace bra underneath and she unhooked it and slid the straps over her shoulders. Red marks were branded into her skin from the elastic. It didn't seem fair that I should see this.

So whitely naked. I wanted to cover her.

She lay back, pulled me down to the platform. We kissed. She guided my hands where she wanted them. I kept my eyes closed, tried to concentrate on supporting my weight so I wasn't squishing her. There were sharp bolts of pain whenever I'd bump against something and set off one of the sore spots where I'd been hit. She pulled up her skirt until it bunched in a wide band around her waist. Somewhere above us a crow gave a rasping caw and flew off over the water. You could hear its wings slicing the air.

Lana undid the front of my jeans, started touching me. My whole body sort of backed away. I couldn't help it.

'I can't. I can't do this, Lana.'

'But you can. That girl. You said you were really close ...'

'No. Not with you.'

She shut her eyes. It looked like the tears were coming.

Fucking agony. How could I leave her like that, half her clothes off in a public park? How could I do anything else?

So we did it. We had sex.

She kissed me and told me she loved me. She guided me in and I pushed against her. And I felt so ashamed. I didn't even know why.

I wasn't moving very easily. Those bruises from the bathroom were making everything painful and my knees were burning as they scraped the platform. Her head started to knock against the boards. I tried to reach my hand around to cushion her. Stopped for a second, breathing hard.

'Lana, are you okay? Does it hurt?'

'Shh. Course not.'

She ran her hands along my back and kissed me again, but I couldn't really concentrate on two things at once, still pushing into her and wondering how long it would take to finish. I noticed we were edging forward along the platform, and if I didn't watch it we'd both be in the water. Lana made a soft moaning noise. Was she into this? Or just trying to encourage me?

I thought about Adam. I thought about Mark. I watched the shadow of my head moving back and forth. Closed my eyes so I wouldn't see it. Or her.

Then I was very close. It happened so suddenly – overwhelming and impossible to stop, like a sneeze. And at the last second, I remembered: this is how babies are made. She wouldn't be taking those pills anymore. I panicked and wrenched myself away. Then I lay gasping and expiring on the platform as the sun poured down on us.

So embarrassing. *Please look at something else, Lana.*

I blushed deeply, crawled away and tried to clean myself up. Beside me my friend lay sprawled like a road accident. There was blood, on both of us. Of course. Her first time. I was shaking and I couldn't look at her. My back was against the riverbank, my knees pulled up to my chest and my arms around my knees.

'Stephen, I'm so …' A small, defeated voice. 'I thought … I thought you'd like it with me.' She was crouching with her arms crossed over her chest. Her top and bra were in a black tangle by my feet. I slid them over. She turned away and starting squirming back into her things.

'A bunch of guys stuck my head in the toilet today.'

Lana was dressed again, sitting up close. 'So you waited to tell me until after I kissed you.'

That made me smile. She brushed the side of my neck with her fingertips. I flinched away without meaning to.

Then I felt terrible. The look on her face.

'Lana ...' I wrapped my arms tight around her. We sank to the boards of the platform and stretched out, let the sun warm us.

'I just wanted you to be my friend again,' I said.

'I'll always be your friend, Stephen.' The tears came back, she was shuddering against my collarbone. I wished she'd stop because she was setting me off too. Waves slapped the side of the platform.

'Jesus Christ,' I whispered. 'Couple of losers, huh?'

She laughed softly. A freight train hurtled past the railway station across the river. The cows didn't even look up.

'Hey,' I said, 'want to go to the prom with me?'

She didn't answer for a minute. Maybe she thought I was joking. Then she asked me if I was sure I wanted to be there, with everything that had happened and all the awful stuff that was going on at school. But I did. Even more.

'It's my prom too,' I told her. 'And yours. Come on.'

'Oh, God.' Tracing my jawline with one finger. 'This is not how I pictured this moment at all. But yes. I'd love to.'

So I had my friend back. And I had a prom date. Although there were moments of weirdness between us that never quite went away, not for months. If I saw Lana turning her eyes on me, kind of sad and wistful, I'd make cross-eyed faces at her, or we'd just sit with our arms around each other and wait it out. And I had my moments too, when something would trigger the memory of that afternoon in the park and I'd be barely able to look at her. But I was determined this whole mess wasn't going to force us apart.

Classes finished the next day. Exams came and went. I could have written them in my sleep. Maybe I did. A few days afterwards, Lana and my mother took me out to a tux rental place and got me suited up for the prom. I really wanted this polyester blue thing with a ruffled shirt that made me look like a sleazy game-show host – I was going to draw on a fake moustache and everything – but the women wouldn't allow it. So I went home with the standard black and white number instead.

Lana came to my place to pick me up on the night. Traditionally, I should have been doing this, but her mother still wasn't thrilled about having me at the house. And anyway, as Lana said, 'It's not like we're a traditional couple, right?'

My mom took pictures as we stood in the doorway, all dressed up.

'God, you're beautiful. You're both so beautiful!'

'We sure are!' said Lana. She looked like the Queen of the Underworld, corseted in dark red satin and black lace, boobs pushed up to magnificent heights. I couldn't wait to step into the gym with this girl and watch every guy who'd ever called her 'fatso' collapsing in a stupor of sexual frustration. Lana grabbed me by the lapels. 'Look at you! The girls are gonna go nuts. And all the boys are going to turn.' She glanced back at my mother. 'Turn envious.'

Mom kept snapping photos, oblivious. We did look pretty damn gorgeous. I was trying to think of professions where I'd get to wear a tux every day.

The gym was draped with paper streamers and balloons, an enormous disco ball sending squares of white light spinning around us. Everybody I'd been to school with since Grade Three was there, dressed up like they were on *Dynasty*: tuxes and satin and shoulder pads, big stiff waves of hair.

Of course some people said lame stuff – insulting me, insulting her for being there with me. But they were just a couple of stupid losers who didn't know any better.

Lana and I hit the dance floor, improvised a demented tango to 'The Sun Always Shines on TV'. And for a while I didn't give a fuck what anybody thought of me.

Chapter 20

The book slid from my lap and hit me on the foot. I blinked, knocked out of a bad dream. Sunlight was glaring off the side of the wing. Miles below you could see a layer of drifting cloud, green land gone blue with distance.

The annual visit had rolled around: a week in Montreal with Stanley, his wife Sheila, and my two baby sisters. This was my fourth journey to the Shulevitz house – possibly the last. We'd never discussed what would happen when I was in college. And of course if I got my revenge, I'd never be going back again.

I was always full of resolve, every time I got on the plane, every year since I was fourteen. Biting my nails and looking out the round window at tiny fields, forests and towns, rehearsing all the terrible things I was going to say. Oh, I would make him sorry. For everything he'd done to me, to my mother. This year I'd do it.

Stupid kid.

My little fold-up tray was open and covered with garbage. I could see my book under the seat in front – *The Brothers Karamazov*, all nine hundred pages of it. I squirmed and angled myself so I could get my fingertips around the spine, just ended up knocking it farther away.

It was July. I wasn't a high-school student anymore. I was a graduate. The ceremony had been fun, although we didn't get those platform hats to throw in the air like on TV. Lana was valedictorian. They'd offered it to me, but I chickened out. Speeches weren't my thing. Winning prizes was. I got them all, except Physics and Math. Money in the bank. Had to stop myself from swaggering up to the podium and waving at the audience when I collected the last few.

It was weird not to see Mark there. I wasn't even sure if he'd shown up for his exams.

My father called on the night with congratulations – at least he'd got the date right this time. I made excuses to get off the phone. This is what I usually did, when I was left clutching a plastic receiver, confronted with the fact of Stanley.

Being around him was like watching something slip out of my hands and shatter against the floor, over and over again. Stan Shulevitz. 'Spider' to his friends. I wasn't a friend.

I was nine, wearing *Star Wars* pyjamas. I woke up because my mother was screaming.

'Stanley, don't. Stanley, don't!'

I could hear him on the stairs.

Then he was in my room with me, my old child-sized room with the high narrow bed in the corner. The light was on and I couldn't stop

260

blinking. Stan closed my door, used a straight-backed chair to force it shut behind him.

'Up here, Maryna!' He was smiling. 'I'm up here with your little half-kike son.'

'Jesus, Stanley!' It sounded like she was just outside. 'You're not telling him that. I said I didn't mean it!' The doorknob twisted. Stan held it steady and blocked the door with his body. I sat hugging my knees into my chest, covers bunched around me.

'Yeah, your mother just called me a kike,' Stanley said. His voice was loud. He was talking to both of us. 'It's an insult. Just thought I'd warn you, buddy. In case she calls you one.'

The doorknob rattled again. 'Oh, God, Stanley, I told you I'm sorry. You made me so mad and I wanted to hurt you. And nothing I said made a difference. Nothing I ever say makes any difference!'

My father tested the chair to see if it was secure and then took himself for a walk around my room. He peered at my books on the set of shelves Mom had built for me, seemed fascinated by my nightlight.

'I can't believe she lets you keep that thing. People need darkness, you know.'

In the hallway behind the door, my mother was crying. 'It's not my word,' she said, muffled and echoing. 'It's not even my father's word. I don't know why I ...'

Stanley sat on the edge of my bed and started flipping through my old copy of *Stuart Little*. 'Look at that. The mouse has hands. Actual hands. He can hold a knife and make a boat. Now that is weird.' He turned to me. 'Do you like this book, buddy?'

His eyes were red and he had that smell on him. I asked my father if he was high and he said yes, he was.

'Stanley,' I said, 'can I open the door? Please?'

He lay back on my bed, holding the book above him.

'I'd rather you didn't.'

I stayed put. The chair was still wedging the door in place. I hoped it wasn't dark in the hallway.

Stanley rested the book face-down on his chest. 'The people she's from. You have no idea. I didn't listen to anybody. Not my family, not my friends. I wanted Maryna Solovyov.' The way he said my mother's name made her sound like a different person.

She was knocking softly. 'Please. Can't we forget this ever happened?'

I must have made a move towards the door, some twitch. My father shook his head at me, frowning.

'Stan? Stephen?'

I curled up in a corner of the bed by his shoulder and hid my face, grabbed a handful of his scratchy wool sweater and squeezed it. Stanley was talking about a party, some party he'd gone to in college when he was still living with his parents in Toronto.

'She was getting sick on a rose bush,' he said, in a dreamy half-asleep voice. *Who was? Oh. Mom.* 'I was watching her most of the night. Very, very pretty, but she didn't know what to say to anyone. On the outside of every group.' *Stuart Little* went sliding off his chest and smacked onto the floor.

'She drank too much and then somebody got her high, so she was in the backyard throwing up. There was a person standing over her. A man. She wouldn't know what she was doing. And I thought: *I will not let that happen. Not to that beautiful girl.* So I helped her up, and I took her upstairs, and do you know what I did?'

I whispered that I didn't know. I did. I'd heard this story before, although the details shifted around depending on his mood, and he never said what happened after they left the party.

'I made her brush her teeth. Stomach acid. Very bad for the tooth enamel.' He stretched himself out. 'Everything I said made her laugh. Everything I said made her smile. Beautiful girl. Before she went home, she had to change back into these awful clothes her parents made her wear. All covered up, skirts down to the floor. She went behind the shower curtain. I wanted to look, but I didn't. She stumbled and I caught her. Touched her through the plastic.' He smiled. It made him look younger.

'Then we walked home. I mean I walked her home, but I had to stay by the gate. Actually hid behind a tree in case her father saw me. He was waiting. Filling the doorway. Big guy, Stepan Solovyov. You're named for him.' I was still curled up by his shoulder, trying not to move. This was the part of the story I'd never heard.

'She was walking up to the house alone. Taking these careful steps towards him. Neither of them said a word. No other noise from the street. She must have been so scared. It was close to two in the morning and she wasn't supposed to be out past ten.' Stanley went quiet for a moment. I thought he'd fallen asleep. Then his voice came again, softer, sad.

'He hit her, buddy. Right across the face. Maryna. I did nothing. Just stood there. But I thought to myself: *Now, I am going to save that girl.*'

Then his arm was around me. 'Buddy? What's wrong?'

I'd started crying as soon as he got to the part about Mom's father hitting her.

'Did he really do that?'

'Yes, but …'

Couldn't stop. 'She just wanted to go home. And he was waiting?'

'Emotional boy,' he said. 'What am I going to do with this emotional boy?' Stanley ruffled my hair. 'Hey. It was a long time ago. That was your grandfather. He's dead now.'

'Good.'

My father relaxed into the bed, gave a low chuckle. 'Oh, I'll miss you, Stephen,' he said, and I was suddenly terrified.

I remember walking home from school with Mark in our lumpy winter coats, a few months after my parents had had that fight. Snow banks were still skulking on the edges of the roads, low clouds shutting out the sky.

A few doors from my house, I'd started to run. Something was wrong. The car. Mom was supposed to have it today. Some days Stan would need it to get to the university, and then he'd bring her home from her office job two towns away. But this wasn't one of those days.

I got closer. Mark was behind me. Our old green Volvo was backing out of the driveway, Stanley behind the wheel. I didn't have to look in the windows to know it was all there. The guitar, the typewriter, everything.

I ran to the side of the car. He hit the brakes and the noise of the engine died. We glared at each other. Stanley told me something through the window that sounded like 'get out of the way' and rolled down the glass.

'Look. You weren't supposed to be home. I should have been out of here by now.'

'Where are you going?' I grabbed the door handle and pulled. He'd locked it. I hung on.

'Stephen, don't … don't make this …' He reached out the window and tried to pry my fingers away. I held tighter, fusing myself to the car.

'We'll see each other again,' he said. 'Don't worry.' Seemed like he was making a move to touch my head but I dodged him. 'Aw, come on, buddy. Just wave me goodbye. Huh?'

I didn't answer. I wasn't going to let him go. He could drive off and my arm would still be there, stuck to the handle.

'Stephen,' my father said. The voice he used for giving orders. 'I need you to go to the house. I need you to … get me something.' He closed his eyes. 'It's in the kitchen. Third drawer down from the left. You understand?'

'What is it?'

'It's … you'll know when you see it.'

'Promise you won't go anywhere?'

He sighed. 'I … yeah, I promise.'

I was breathing quick and shallow, felt nauseated. I wanted him to stay. But he wanted to go, and he was stronger. The only way to end this was if I went into the kitchen like he wanted. If I decided to believe him. I relaxed my grip on the door, fingers coming away red and stiff. Took a few steps towards the house. Mark was in the front yard. He'd been there the whole time. I'd forgotten all about him.

'Mark,' I said. 'Stan promised he wouldn't …' Mark nodded at me, folded his arms and kept his eyes fixed on the car. I opened the front door.

Couldn't remember which drawer. I opened them all. Placemats. Birthday candles. Casserole dishes. A box of matches. Knives and forks and spoons. I kept looking. Even when I heard the car start up, sound of the motor getting softer in the distance.

I stayed in the kitchen, turning around in circles, bouncing from one corner to the next. Tried not to think about my mother coming home. *Don't be mad, Mom.* I wanted to go down in the basement and hide, but Mark was calling my name. There was a brass bottle opener in the top drawer next to the spoons. I decided this was what my father had asked for.

I opened the front door. The car was gone.

Now it was real. I didn't have to imagine it anymore. I wondered if I'd still need a nightlight in my room.

'He lied to you!' I'd never seen Mark like this. He was practically shaking. 'He lied to you, Stephen. I threw a rock at his car, but it didn't hit.' Mark stared down the road. 'Fuck!'

I echoed him, gazing down that empty street. I wasn't supposed to use that word, but it felt right.

We stayed in the front yard all afternoon. Usually Mark and I would play some variation on soldiers pretending to kill each other, but I couldn't focus, kept wandering into the line of fire. Then it was almost supper time. No sign of my mom.

'Please don't go home, Mark.'

'Okay.' Mark chucked rocks against the fence while I went ranging up and down keeping an eye on the street. He stayed with me till my mother arrived, in a car I'd never seen before. She didn't even have her feet on the ground before she was asking about Stanley. I told her everything I could. Mom said he'd taken our car for the day and promised he'd pick her up after work. But she'd waited and waited, called the house a dozen times. We were outside, so we didn't hear.

The next day at school everybody was lining up by the classroom doors like always. I sat at my desk and stared at the other kids. Poking each other in the backs with their rulers, passing notes, sneaking bites of their lunch, sometimes smirking and calling me 'Jew-le-vitz'. Mark was the only one who understood.

I never knew what to expect when I came home. Mom might forget to eat, or to cook, and then I just made myself cereal. Cereal at night.

266

This is what happened at the end of the world. And sometimes she'd come to my room after I'd fallen asleep, climb in beside me and curl up close, clutch at my shoulders. Smelling like cigarettes, all her clothes on, even her shoes. She'd cry. She'd say, 'I don't want to be alone.' I'd roll over and tell her she should go to sleep. And I'd be thinking she should go to her own bed because there really wasn't room for the two of us in mine, but I didn't want to sound mean. Maybe I didn't want to be alone either.

There were no more fights. Just the two of us, and the clock ticking.

A couple of weeks later we got a TV.

○

Five years went by. Summer 1984, on a plane for the first time in my life. Cranking up my Walkman over the noise of the engine, waiting. He'd left me as a stupid little kid who couldn't see what a bastard he was. Now I could think for myself. I could get back at him.

I was barely able to look him in the eye.

Instead I helped Stan's wife with the babies – washing dishes, wiping spills, getting up early every day and making myself useful. I even changed diapers.

'Two babies in two years!' Sheila said, as we unpacked bags of groceries. She explained that her plan had been to have them close together so she could get the girls in school sooner and be able to concentrate on her career. I was amazed. I'd never thought of a life as something you planned before.

'Yeah,' she said. 'Look at me now. Some plan!'

Sheila and I went to movies, took in some of the Jazz Festival, got to be pals. 'You're such good company,' she told me one night when we were hurtling off home on the Metro. 'Like your father.' And she laughed. 'When he wants to be.'

I was there because of her, as I figured out over time. Sheila liked projects. The house was always full of workmen going in and out, drop sheets and paint, power tools whizzing away. Stanley and his family in Toronto were an impossible mess, she'd told me once. But maybe she thought she could fix Stanley and me.

Mom would have been so mad if she'd seen this. All the effort I was putting in at my father's place, after slouching around our house mumbling monosyllables at her half the time. But I needed Sheila and the girls to like me.

It was part of my revenge.

Look how great I am, I was really saying. Funny and interesting and helpful and kind. Good company. Now why would Stan Shulevitz leave a nice kid like me?

Because he's a shit, that's why. And he could leave you too, the three of you. At any time, and for any reason. Don't trust him and don't love him. That's what I wanted Stan's new family to understand.

○

We were descending. I'd rescued my book. Karamazov and his sons were having an argument about God over a glass of brandy. There were empty plastic glasses crunching by my feet and my ears were popping. Here I was again. The annual visit, off to destroy my father. This could be the last time.

Better make it count.

Chapter 21

I was knocking around the basement of my father's house, escaping the summer heat and watching my sister Becky as she jumped on the fold-up couch in the TV room. Four years old. Talking away. Advice about my girlfriend.

I'd invented this person to cover a bad mood on the drive from the airport. Stanley hadn't bothered to come with the rest of the family to meet me. He was at a launch. For a book, not a boat. I'd stared out the passenger-seat window, drifting into mopey silences. Sheila had asked me what was wrong and I told her I was having romantic difficulties. Well, it was true, in a way.

'Oh, honey,' Sheila had said. 'She'd have to be blind. What's her name?'

'Marcie. Marcie McAllister.'

The little girls had loved this. 'Is she pretty?' Becky piped up from her child seat in the back.

'She's the best person I know.'

Becky had started telling a long story I couldn't follow, something about true love and an enchanted strawberry. Beside her my other sister Sarah smiled and waved, a lazy parade wave. Three years old. My favourite.

Now Sarah was sitting on the floor in front of the TV, with her Ken doll and her Spiderman doll, touching their heads together and making kissy noises. Ken's teeth were bared in a thin white smear of a smile. Sarah was chortling to herself. She'd told me the dolls were in love and were going to have a baby 'any minute'.

Her sister Becky soared upwards, higher with each bounce off the couch, her hair spread out around her. 'You should give Marcie a lion! And the lion has a rose. And then the rose opens and there's a ring. And when she puts on the ring, she can't stop dancing. She can't even stop to go to the bathroom, so she has to poop and pee everywhere. And then …'

I hovered close by, ready to catch her. How could anybody be this bright and happy and confident? A home with two parents. Money for anything she wanted. Living in a city, not some village full of inbred bigots. Nobody was ever going to stick this girl's head in a toilet.

I was jealous of this nice little child who loved me. Snap out of it. 'Let's go upstairs and make popsicles,' I said.

On the floor, Sarah had thrown Ken and Spiderman in a shoe box together and was shaking it violently. 'Carry me!'

'Okay.' I scooped Sarah into my arms. She wiped her nose on my shoulder.

Becky made a thudding landing off the couch. 'Carry me too!'

'Sorry. Can't do that, Becky. I'm too cool.' It was what I always said when I was pretending not to do what they wanted.

I was pretty sure I loved these girls. And I loved being in Montreal.

Even if I was in a basement with the children, I knew that just outside the door, there was a network of people and streets and cars, a galaxy. I couldn't take my eyes off it. You'd go walking and you'd pass a church. And then a strip club. An art gallery. A tattoo parlour. Delis with slabs of pebbly smoked meat in the window. Kids sweating in black clothes waiting for tickets to a heavy-metal concert. There were people everywhere you looked and everywhere you looked it wasn't Riverside. It wasn't even Halifax.

Once on St Catherine Street I actually saw two guys with their arms around each other moving in for a kiss – one with a hand on his friend's butt, no less – and I was so stunned I just about walked into a lamppost. The blond sneered at me over his shoulder. 'Fuck are you looking at? Dumb hick.' Was it the way I was dressed? I got out of there fast. But I did think it was pretty cool.

There was just one problem with these visits to Montreal – the person I was supposed to be there to see. At night I'd lie awake, having one-sided conversations with him in my head. In the light of day it all disappeared. The clock kept ticking, the days drifted by, and I realised that once again I was going back to Riverside with everything unsaid.

Then it was my last night at the Shulevitz house. The heat was making me crazy. Nova Scotia had the cold Atlantic slapping up against us, but here we were stuck in the middle of a continent, cooking in the summer sun. In July, the air turned heavy and still. Bugs moved through it in slow motion, like they were swimming. Sleep was impossible and all food was gross.

I was in my guest room, three in the morning. Still awake, with a dry mouth and eyes that felt like they'd been rolled in sand. I had to be up in a few hours to catch my plane, but sleep wasn't going to come, so I was back to *The Brothers Karamazov*.

Couldn't concentrate. This airless little room was killing me.

I stumbled downstairs and planted myself against the wall at the kitchen table, in a T-shirt and boxers, my cigarette hand out the window just beside me. Turning on the electric light seemed wrong somehow – like I'd be pretending it was day. So I lit a white candle in a silver holder I'd taken from the dining room instead. I leaned close to the little flame, hunched over my book. Wanted to find out what was going to happen to Mitya.

I glanced up to take a drag off my cigarette. The table was a circle of glass. Light refracted through it onto the floor. There was a bowl of fruit, awkward shapes resting against each other. A round-faced silver clock on the wall. Stanley. Sitting across from me.

I jumped to my feet in a stumbling hurry, almost knocked over the candle.

'Oh,' I said. 'Hi.' I hid the cigarette behind my back. Should have just chucked it out the window, but my reflexes were scrambled. He was fully dressed, jeans and a white linen shirt. I was standing there in my underwear.

Stan reached out and plucked the book off the table. 'Hm. Dostoyevsky. *The Brothers*. I envy you.' He flipped through the pages. 'Reading this for the first time. And the perfect age to encounter it.'

'I'm gonna …' I gestured lamely at the hallway, the stairs.

'Sit down. I know you're smoking. It doesn't matter to me.'

I sat, stubbed the cigarette against the edge of the fruit bowl and crunched the end into a sad little accordion.

Should have realised he'd still be up. In the summer, Stanley was nocturnal. It was part of how I'd been able to avoid him so well on these annual visits. You'd stumble over his body in that little study just off the kitchen where he'd be tangled in a sheet on the futon mattress, sleeping off another late night. I'd walked in there more than once looking for a book and nearly stepped on his head.

Stan stood up abruptly and started banging around in the cupboards. He unhooked a child-proof lock on a little door over the fridge and came out with a small squat bottle, poured a measure and set it in front of me. Then he opened *The Brothers Karamazov* to the table of contents, pointed at the title of one of the chapters. 'Over the Brandy'. *A joke?*

'The famous chapter,' he said. 'Well, come on, Stephen. I'm sure you drink. And you're legal age here, right? Eighteen.'

'I'm seventeen.'

'Okay, you're seventeen.'

'My birthday's in …'

'I was there.' He sat down again and I looked at the glass he'd poured for me, candlelight reflecting off the sides. Nothing for himself. 'A very difficult birth. Maryna was hardly more than a child herself.'

'You're up late.'

He didn't answer this. I watched him for a while. My father tipped back his head, gazed at the ceiling. In this warm light, he looked younger. Like I remembered him.

'Got a little home movie playing in my head about now.' Stan's voice was soft, distant. 'See, I'm outside the dome house. Back when we lived on the side of the mountain. Smoking something. Moonlight so strong you've got these sharp black shadows behind you. And I see somebody walking down the dirt road. I'm scared half to death at first, cause I think it's a ghost. But it's my son. My kid.' He was smiling at me. 'In your pyjamas and that blue sweater with the snowflake. Said you couldn't sleep. The moon was too bright in your window. So you were taking a walk.'

'Yeah, I used to do that.'

He went on talking. 'I told you to go back inside and lie down. And then I said I'd shut it off for you. The moon. And the thing was' – shaking his head – 'you did. Nodded at me so seriously, went off into the house. And I thought, *My God, he believed that.* Believed me. It was … terrifying.'

'You could have just got me some decent curtains.'

'Not really the point.'

I pushed my chair back. 'Anyway, I should get some sleep.'

'Sit.' He was running his thumb along the edge of the fruit bowl. 'You're angry.'

'No.' Not ready to start this now. The brandy was still in front of me. I hadn't touched it. 'Don't you want any, Stanley?'

'I don't like drinking. That bottle's for guests.'

I wasn't going to chug this stuff alone while he sat and watched. So I got up and took a glass out of the cupboard, poured a couple of fingers and set it in front of him. We were facing each other across the table again. He frowned to himself. I drained my glass in one go. Made me gasp, but I could handle it.

He shifted the dark amber liquid around.

'It was a good idea. Overall. Making contact with you again. Very good for the girls. We never wanted them to grow up not knowing they had a brother. And they love you.'

'Well, it's nice to have sisters.' I felt hypnotised, like I was staring at a cobra with its dance of a head.

'It's nice for Sheila too. She's always said what good company you are. Compared to me.' Stan gave a little shrug, drank the brandy down. He shuddered. 'It was her idea, you know, bringing you here in the first place. She had to work at me for a while before I said yes. I think …' He looked at the ceiling again. 'I think I was actually afraid of you. See, I left this sweet little kid. I was getting back an angry adolescent.'

'Why do you keep saying I'm angry, Stanley?'

'All teenagers are angry. You've got more cause than most.'

'But I'm *not*—' My voice was raised. Stop. I poured myself more brandy, filled his glass too. 'I'm not angry.' I poked at the candle flame.

'Course not,' he breathed. 'Maybe we shouldn't attempt this conversation till you're twenty-five.' My father linked his hands behind his head. 'But I suppose it would be better to get it over with. Okay, go on, Stephen. Stepan Vladimir Shulevitz. You're telling me you're *not* angry. Fine. Why don't you tell me why?' Stanley tilted backwards in his chair. 'You have the floor, Stephen. What's on your mind?'

I looked down at my glass, at the stupid book, stared into the candle. Unfair. It wasn't meant to be like this. I was supposed to surprise him – when I was ready. I tried to think of some of my favourite lines, all those imaginary conversations.

'You …' I choked, my voice echoing. Hopeless. It was as if the words were curling away in the candle flame and disappearing. I had nothing to say to this man.

But at the same time, so much was crowding in. Mom crying on the stairs as he made me choose between them. Mom in a daze for months after he left, forgetting to eat or brush her hair. Mom alone. Hanging on to me like I was the only person left in the world. Which I was.

'You ruined my mother's life.'

He blinked slowly. 'Odd. I don't remember doing that.'

'Why'd you drag her down there to the middle of nowhere? You could've stayed in Toronto. Or what's wrong with Montreal?'

Stanley's folded hands made shadow-puppet shapes against the wall. 'We didn't stay in Toronto, Stephen, because our families hated the thought of us together. We had friends in Nova Scotia who said there was land going cheap and it was paradise. And they were right. Beautiful place to be young.'

'But … that stupid little town. Why couldn't I grow up in a city? Some place people would *get* me. I wouldn't be treated like a freak for …'

He raised his eyebrows at me. 'I thought this was about your mother.'

'It is.' I stared over his head at the kitchen counter. Boxes of cereal were lined up ready for the next day. Cornflakes and Cheerios. Rice Krispies, little elves gazing in awe at a bowl of bloated, blond rice grains. I was losing this.

Stan ran his fingers along his moustache. It reminded me of a cat's whiskers.

'Ruined her life. Is that really fair, Stephen? I mean, it's true I got Maryna pregnant, and we were very young. But she was the one who insisted on keeping it.'

I laughed. Came out sounding brittle, cracked. 'It.'

'You, then. You.'

Sitting up straight. 'Yeah, what a mistake, huh? Too bad she decided to keep *it*. Would have been better if you'd just flushed *it*. Then you wouldn't be wasting your time talking to *it*. Like you are. Right now.' I could see my knees through the table top, my feet with their craggy toenails looking back at me.

He tilted his head, eyes narrowed. 'Teenagers are so great at judgement, aren't they? Especially if they've never actually done anything except go to school. I mean, what would you do, Stephen, if you got some poor girl "in trouble"? Run out and get married?'

'I'd … I'd take responsibility. I think it would be nice to have kids.'

I regretted saying this right away. He was leaning forward now. 'It would be *nice*. To be responsible for another human being for the rest of your life. So I suppose when you and your girlfriends are having sex, you're hoping the result will be a child.'

'That's not an issue.'

'Issue.' The corner of his mouth twitched.

'I wasn't trying to make some kind of pun.'

'No, I didn't think you were.'

'I mean I don't ...' Getting closer to it. But part of me wanted to.

'You don't have sex. Right.'

'Not ...' I looked him in the eye. 'Not with girls.' I drained my glass of brandy, tried to keep the reflexive shudder down.

Take that, asshole. Come on, disown me. Let's go.

It was quiet, and I listened to the noises of the night outside. Footsteps on gravel, a couple of kids walking home drunk and talking too loud, a car whooshing past like a tired sigh.

There was a measuring look in his eyes.

'Okay. So you're gay. Or you think you are. Interesting.' He picked up his glass, which was empty. Put it down again. 'Well, so much for my name.'

I felt like kicking the table over. He was going to shrug this off too. Well, what *would* get a reaction? I realised I was rolling a sullen, bruised strawberry across the table, pocked with hard little seeds like face stubble.

'Hm.' He was rubbing his own chin stubble, collected around that pubic scrub of a beard. 'So are you going to be one of those angry gays? Some kind of activist with a chip on your shoulder?'

I wanted to laugh, but my throat felt stiff and painful. 'I haven't decided yet.'

Stan acted as if I hadn't said anything. 'I've always found that sort of thinking so limited. So shrill. Taking the whole experience of being human and reducing it to sexuality. Language itself turns into some kind of political grid …' He stopped talking. I felt like I was sitting in a classroom in front of him.

'Actually,' he said. 'This could be very helpful. I'm … I'm in a bit of trouble. No, that's too strong a word. Inconvenience. Some of my more … *vocal* students have accused me of … I mean, "homophobia" is such a stupid term, isn't it? But if I tell them that my own son is gay—'

'Sure, Stan. You do what you want.'

I placed my palm on the strawberry and pressed down, watched it bleed against the glass.

'Thank you.'

Another shot for Stanley, then one for myself. I stared at him hard and knocked the brandy back. Yuck. Really starting to feel it.

My father moved his glass in meaningless little circles, watching the liquid cling to the sides. 'So now I guess I gotta drink too. Again. Is this a contest? See who's the man here?'

'What kind of a contest would that be, Stanley?'

'Oh, I don't go by stereotypes.' He looked pitying. 'After all, there was Alexander the Great, right? There was—'

I leaned in towards him, one elbow on the squashed strawberry. Say it slow and careful. Make this one count.

'I wouldn't leave my wife and child. I wouldn't leave them all alone with no clue where to find me.'

I was playing with the candle, breaking off bits of wax and touching them to the blackened wick. The flame flared up and then down again.

'So how long have you been waiting to say that?'

I didn't answer, didn't look at him.

'Bit much,' he went on. 'All this self-righteousness. Considering it's not likely you're ever going to have children of your own.'

'Yeah, well that's too bad.' I filled Stan's glass higher. He hadn't touched it. 'Cause I'd be a fuck of a lot better at it than you.'

My father shook his head. 'I'm not drinking this, buddy.'

'Don't. Call. Me. That.'

Our faces were reflected in the dark window. We did look similar, like people said. He had my book again, running his finger along the edge and flipping the pages together, a soft creaking sound repeating itself.

'Yes, I suppose I wasn't a great father to my only son. It's different with the girls. I'm older. With you there was always so much pressure. Waiting for me to shut off the moon.'

'You know, I don't even remember that.'

'But I did give you one thing, Stephen. Very, very valuable.' I looked up at him. Couldn't imagine what he was going to say.

'Somebody to blame. For everything. I suppose you'll blame me for your being gay too.'

'Course not.' A layer of cold remove was settling over me. I felt like him. 'But if I end up going through a bunch of older guys who like to smoke a lot of dope and ignore me ...' I smiled. 'I think I can lay that at your door, all right.'

He laughed, a real laugh, low-voiced and delighted. 'Okay. There's a sense of humour down there. Under all that ... addiction to melodrama.' He stood up. 'But listen, I'm tired. I think this conversation has run its course. Maybe we'll continue next year. Yes?'

He siphoned his brandy back into the bottle, took our glasses to the sink and ran the tap over them. Then my father was shuffling out of the kitchen. Probably heading for his little study. To sleep. Or read. Do something more interesting than talk to me.

'Stanley.' He stopped. Almost at the doorway. I was facing him on the kitchen chair, huddled by the window. Fragments of candle wax and a murdered strawberry lay littered on the table glass next to my book. I tried to keep my voice steady. 'Did you ever want me?'

He smiled at the floor. 'Not really.' He glanced up at me. 'Not really a fair question. Is it, buddy?'

And then he was gone.

The candle was sputtering. I had a sudden urge to hold my finger against the flame until the skin blistered and broke. There was so much poison inside. I didn't know how else it would leave.

I forced myself to stand, breathed hard on the candle until the kitchen was in darkness again. I went outside and sat on the back steps, grabbed handfuls of my hair and pulled. *Fuck him, fuck him, fuck him.*

I marched back into the house, to my father's little study. The shape of him was tumbled on the mattress. The dark made me whisper.

'Stanley? You're an asshole. You're a total fucker. You screw with people's heads, and when they react, you call them emotional. You think you're brilliant because nobody ever knows what the hell you're talking about. You're not. You're boring. You broke my mother's heart and you broke my heart and' – finished lamely, my voice failing – 'and … I want you to die.'

I was talking to a pile of blankets and sheets. He was upstairs with Sheila. I was alone in an empty room. And so tired.

I lay down on the stupid little futon. It smelled like him. I fell asleep.

The light woke me a couple of hours later. Had to get going or I'd miss my flight. I ran up to my room, threw some clothes on and dragged a razor across my face.

Downstairs, Sheila and the girls were waiting to say goodbye. I picked up little Becky and she kissed me and wrapped her arms around my head, told me to come back soon, bring Marcie and all our babies. I said okay. Sarah wouldn't even look my way. She'd decided she was mad at me for leaving. I sneaked a kiss on the top of her head, and she brushed me off with an angry gesture, went stomping into the next room, making a lot of noise, her hands in fists.

Sheila gave me money for the taxi to the airport. She lifted my suitcase to test it for heaviness. 'Oh, I don't know why you can't just go to school here,' she said. 'It would be wonderful to see you all the time. So good for the girls.'

'I want to live in Montreal,' I told her. 'I do. But, you know, there's my mom. It's a twenty-hour train ride away. She'd be all alone.' This was the real reason I'd never applied for anything out-of-province. I'd never admitted it before.

'I understand, sweetheart. You're a good son.' Sheila pulled me into a hug. 'Listen, you take care, huh? I hope things work out with Marcie.'

Guilt was making me queasy. 'Sheila.' I whispered it into her ear. 'I'm really sorry. There's no such person.'

She pulled away, smiling like she didn't quite get the joke. 'So why would you—?'

'His name is Mark.'

'Oh,' she said, and then, 'Oh!' Eyes full of shock. But a second later she was all compassion. 'Honey, you didn't have to keep it a secret!' She went on to tell me she wished she'd known sooner, that she could have fixed me up with Ruthie Smolash's son down the street. Another project. I got the sense that nothing would throw this woman for long. 'He's a few years older,' she went on, 'but such an attractive person. Clever too. And good company. Just like you.'

I smiled. At the same time, I could feel Riverside descending over me, even in this Montreal kitchen. I had the rest of the summer to get through. Another month of keeping my head down, looking over my shoulder. It had been such a relief, I only realised then. To get away from it. Be somebody else for a while.

'Thanks,' I said. 'Thank you, Sheila.'

Chapter 22

There were brilliant days, hazy with sunshine. Orchards flanked the highway. Lawnmowers revved up and droned through afternoons. You could see kids in swimsuits jumping from the railway bridge, distant screams as they hit the river together. I continued to chip my way through the reading list for college. I finished *The Brothers Karamazov*. I started *The Divine Comedy*. I stood perfectly still and watched it all.

My mother seemed to spend the summer flying around in a state of near giddiness, buying textbooks and new clothes for college in September, out several nights a week with the new guy. Mr Secret of My Success. She hadn't introduced me. Not yet. But you could tell she was planning to. Once I overheard her on the phone with him and it was like listening to a different person – someone confident and flirty, who expected attention.

'Well, I guess I should thank him,' she was saying. 'Got enough for three Psych papers if anybody would believe me. I swear, that kid has done *nothing* but complain about this town since he was eight, and now I can't get him to throw some clothes in a suitcase. Or open a newspaper so we can find him an apartment – do you know he won't even consider living at the boys' dormitory? Isn't that strange?' And then collapsing into a helpless giggle. 'Oh, Fred, you're so *funny* …'

I left the house quietly. She was right. I was being very weird about this move. I wanted to leave Riverside – more than anything. But at the same time, something in me couldn't face it. Packing up my childhood, saying goodbye. Dealing with unfinished business. I suppose deep down I was hoping I could just close my eyes and have it all disappear.

I read Plato's *Republic*. I started *The Iliad*. I borrowed Mom's car so I could drive to the gravelly beach over the mountain, spent a long time staring out at the water melting off into the sun. Keeping watch over my six-year-old friend Kyle Healey as we walked up and down looking for shells and funny rocks.

That was my summer job, babysitting this nervous child. Usually it was during the day when Mrs Healey was at work, but sometimes I'd be there at night too. Once I found Kyle sitting up in bed hugging his knees – all freaked out because there was a bag in his closet that looked like a chicken. I picked it up and showed it to him, proved it was just dead plastic.

'But,' he said, 'what if you turn the lights off and it turns into a chicken again?' Well, he had a point. I said I could take it outside.

'No! Then it'll be out there. Trying to get in!'

I had to think about this.

'Want me to shoot it?' I said.

'Yes, I do! I do!'

Kyle and I got along pretty well.

One night I was walking home from Lana's place, when I saw a familiar blue pickup truck hulking in front of my house. Tina Thomson. Tina from the party in June. I didn't ask how she knew where I lived. This was Riverside. She invited me out for a drive. I said okay. A few hours later, we were parked on the side of a dirt road, having a long argument about why I didn't want to do it with her.

I remembered when we met on my birthday she'd been really impressed because I said it was better to be friends first, so I tried that again. She told me we were already friends. I claimed we hadn't spent enough time together. There was a debate on the nature of friendship. There was a lot of making out, starting and stopping and starting again, sliding all over the pickup cab. By the time I got back, it was three in the morning.

Safe to say my big news never quite hit Arnottville. Or if it had, Tina had felt pretty free to ignore it.

Usually I'd see her around ten or eleven when she was finished her shift at Tim Horton's. We'd stay out till early morning and I'd get home exhausted, grab a few hours' sleep before dragging myself off to the Healeys' around nine. I was scared Lana would hear some rumour and get the wrong idea, so I kept her informed of everything.

'Stephen?' she'd say. 'It's two o'clock in the morning. Why do you think I'd want to hear about this *now*?'

After that first 'date' with Tina, I had to come up with more and better excuses for avoiding the obvious. I faked being too tired. I faked being too drunk. I faked being sick. I got creative.

'Tina, I don't think God wants us to do this,' I told her one night.

'But aren't you Jewish?'

Well, at least she let me drive the truck sometimes.

Why didn't I just break up with this girl? It all came down to Mark. Suppose I ended it, dumped her. Suppose he found out why. Who could stay in denial after that?

○

I continued to keep still, watching the summer as it creaked along. There were cloudy days, cold and foggy. Mist came rolling off the mountain and the air tasted like salt. I read *La Princesse de Clèves*. I read *Utopia*. I tried reading the Heidegger we'd been assigned and felt stupid for weeks.

Then it was late August.

We were in the pickup. Again. Tina was gazing at me, little hands on the wheel, face lit up with a sweet smile. I smiled back, forcing the corners of my mouth into position. Gauges and dials glowed on the dashboard. The truck was filled with the sounds of Jefferson Starship singing 'Sara'.

'I wish I was dead.'

'What's that, sweetie?'

'Nothing.'

We parked down another dirt road somewhere on the ocean side of the mountain, close to where I grew up. The wind was lashing the branches of the pines with their sharp, green smell. Tina sidled up close. I moved away. She held my head steady, kissed me. I clenched my teeth so she couldn't get that muscular tongue of hers into my mouth.

'Jeez,' she said, 'what's up with you tonight?'

She was sitting on my lap now, kneeling with one leg on either side of me. *Just say it*, I thought. *You don't have to tell her why.*

'Tina, I can't do this. I don't want to go out with you anymore.'

'Aw, Stephen, you don't mean that. What's going on? Feeling bad cause you're leaving?'

'No. I told you …'

'Don't feel bad. It's only for a few months. Then you're gonna come home.' She smiled tenderly. 'And everything'll be just the same.' Tina started talking about visiting me in the city in September. The bars we'd go to. The people from Arnottville and Riverside we could hang out with. It would be like I never left, she said.

I reached up and snapped her bra strap.

'What is your problem?' She was balancing on her knees now, making herself taller than me.

'My problem? I'm breaking up with you and you're not even listening!'

'Silly. You're just in a bad mood.' Her voice turned breathy. 'I can fix that.' She trailed her fingers across my crotch.

'Oh, for—!' I tried to push her off.

'Stephen!' Still smiling, like a mother with a fussy child. 'Are you sick or something?' Her hard little knees were pressing into me. Tina on all sides. 'Or maybe you're worried I'm gonna fool around on you when you're gone.'

'No. I don't care about that. I mean—' I tried to squirm out from under her. So frustrated I couldn't think straight. 'Fuck's sake! I'm gay, all right?'

Well, too late now. I couldn't unsay it.

Tina stared at me for one stunned second. Then she started to laugh. 'Quit messing around.'

I should have been relieved. But this was making me even more irritated. 'It's not a joke,' I heard myself saying. 'I'm gay. I'm a homo. I'm into guys.'

'No, you're not.'

'Yes, I fucking well am!'

Start again. I shut my eyes. 'Look. I was never attracted to you. We shouldn't have gone out in the first place. I'm really sorry, Tina.'

'Hey, I know what's going on.' A high, sneering tone crept into her voice. 'It's that fat girl, isn't it?'

'You mean Lana?'

'I'm so gonna give that bitch a pounding when I—' She was staring over my shoulder, mouth moving furiously.

'Hey! Tina! Remember the first time I kissed you? Well, just before that I was making out with a guy. Like, for hours.' That got her attention. So I told Tina the story of me and Adam. Or I started to. She slapped her hand over my mouth before I got past the part about kissing on the stairs.

'Oh, *fuck*! You're telling me that stuff was true? What Marty and them were saying?'

'Jesus, so you heard? And you still …'

'I thought they were making it up just to piss me off. You mean you actually … with a *man*? That is gross! That is plain disgusting!'

I was laughing now. 'And kind of fun, if you want the truth.'

'All right, that's it.' She clambered off me, back to the driver's side. 'You get out of my truck.'

'Fine.' I popped the door open and was about to jump, when I realised I had no idea where I was. I slid back into the seat. 'No.'

Tina pivoted so she was facing me feet first, then started kicking me towards the open door, using the steering wheel for leverage. I held on to the doorframe, twisted around and tried to dodge her flailing sneakers.

'Get! The fuck! Out!'

'No! You're not leaving me here. I don't know where the hell I am!'

I grabbed her ankles and shoved her back to the driver's side. She slammed into me with her shoulders. I slammed back. She went at me again, all nails and elbows, gouging and pushing. I anchored myself to the truck with the seatbelt. We stared each other down, the sound of our breath filling this metal canister.

'Drive me back to town,' I said.

'You fucker. You gross, disgusting, creepy—'

'I know you are, but what am I?'

She didn't think it was funny.

Tina turned the key in the ignition and we started back the way we'd come. She kept glancing over at me, not smiling this time. Sometimes I'd make faces or give her the finger. Near the top of the mountain, I recognised a sign for a campground. We were still a long way from home. At least I had some idea where I was, though. 'You can stop here.'

She slowed down, but wouldn't hit the brakes. I opened the door and jumped, landed with a scrambling thud on the shoulder of the highway.

Tina was yelling at me. 'Hope you get AIDS!'

'Yeah? I hope you get bowel cancer, you cross-eyed slut! You stupid, fucking hick!'

I watched the brake lights of the truck receding. The quiet of the night came back. I felt great. Better than great. Alive on top of a mountain. I walked along the highway. Then I ran. The moon was right over my head and I wanted to howl at it. I felt like shaking somebody, kissing somebody.

There was a clearing by the side of the road. I could see the valley below: tiny pools of light against a dark patchwork of fields and forests, just visible in the moonlight.

There it was. My life, spread out at my feet. I laughed. I'd always had this murky idea that my life was an object, something awkward and breakable. And I'd be constantly telling myself, 'You'll drop it. You'll ruin it. You'll fuck everything up.'

'But that's bullshit,' I said. I looked out over the valley, feeling light and solid. It was all going to be fine. It was going to be incredible.

When I hit the valley floor, I began to shut down. My legs were buckling under me, I had a blister on my heel and I wouldn't be home for hours. Reality trickled back.

It was Thursday night, turning into Friday. I had babysitting at nine o'clock. Then later on there was a party on the edge of town. I wasn't invited, but then neither was anyone else. It was the kind of thing where you didn't need to be asked – more like setting up a lantern in the middle of the forest to see what nocturnal creatures flocked to it. Everybody was going. We'd almost reached the end of the summer and a lot of us would never see each other again. A celebration and a wake.

I couldn't go to this thing now, could I? Tina would be there. And Mark. She'd tell him. A first-hand report from my girlfriend – impossible for even Mark to ignore. I'd kicked something when I started this fight with her. The first stone of a landslide.

Of course I shouldn't go. But I felt like I had no choice. I was moving through squares on a board game, and somebody else was rolling the dice.

Cold now, wrapping my arms around myself, teeth chattering. Why was I so sure I needed to be there, at this stupid party?

'Because,' the answer came back, 'that is where you will die.'

I stopped short. *Why would I think that?*

But once it was there, I couldn't get rid of it. And with every step I took back to town, I was more and more certain it was true. On the top of the mountain I'd been so confident that everything was going to be fine. Now I was in the valley, and I was just as convinced that it would all be over, and soon.

I'd been standing still these past two months. Everything else was racing towards me.

Chapter 23

I got home around four in the morning. One of my socks was stuck to my heel with dried blood from the blister that had burst a couple miles out of town. I sat on the bathtub's edge and poured peroxide over it, watched the cut foaming and bubbling as I waited for the chemical sting to calm. I was so tired that nothing would register except objects that were right in front of me, as if my brain were a colouring book with pictures and labels. (A foot. A bathtub. Some Band-Aids.)

Then when I got to my room, I tripped and nearly smacked my head open on the corner of the bedstead. A box. A big cardboard box in the middle of the floor. I turned on the light. It was all boxes in here. Boxes and bags. Nothing on my shelves, in my desk drawers, the closet. There was a note on my pillow. Mom.

Looked like she'd decided I was moving to the city sooner than I'd thought. The note said we'd leave Saturday morning to find me an apartment. I could move in right away, my mother's note added, have a week alone to get settled before classes. She was sorry to have to do this, but since I'd refused to even discuss moving, much less get my things in any kind of order, I'd left her no choice. This last part was underlined several times.

Jeez, Mom going through my stuff. I did a quick check of my current hiding places. Untouched, thank God. Well, there was no sense getting mad. One of us had finally done something to get my new life started.

Wait a minute. Wasn't I going to die before we'd even make this trip? I didn't know what to think about it anymore, that bizarre idea that had settled on me as I limped along the highway. It already felt embarrassing.

It was Friday morning. One more day in Riverside and then I'd be free. I hit the bed with my clothes on. Seemed like seconds later my alarm was ringing for work.

○

'Today's your last day, huh?'

Mrs Healey slung her purse over her shoulder. Mom had called her and explained everything. 'Don't get me wrong,' she said, 'I understand where your mother's coming from. It'll be just about impossible finding a place to live in Halifax at this date. But still.' She turned to me with folded arms. 'You could have given more notice. Kyle is very upset.'

I mumbled apologies. Everything was coming at me from a scratchy-eyed distance. I'd had maybe two hours' sleep.

○

My mother was still at work when I got home. I had soup for supper, ate it cold out of the can as I leaned against the counter listening to the sounds of the empty house: the clock, the shifting hum of the fridge, my spoon scraping patiently against metal. The stairs gave off their signature squeaks and groans as my feet hit them, the same responses to the same pressure all the years I'd lived here. In my room, I packed away the stash from my hiding places so it could go to the city with me.

There was a quart of vodka wedged into the box-spring under the mattress. I loaded it into my backpack, left a long note for Mom about the party tonight, and headed off to say goodbye to Riverside.

Later I was ambling along the shoulder of the road, on my way to this gathering. Guess I should have called somebody to give me a lift. But I was already a little drunk – didn't want to go home to use the phone and face my mom. It was in between night and day, headlights glaring on the cars but no lights in the houses, the sky's blue draining into colourless dusk. Beside me a car slowed and I heard somebody yelling out the window. I got a bit nervous. Usually when people yelled at me out of cars, it didn't mean anything good.

But these were my friends. The girls from the rec room, piled in a station wagon together. We were going in the same direction. Pilgrims.

I squeezed into the back between the MacBride sisters. Evan McDonald sat rigidly in the passenger seat, the only guy besides me. And, I saw in a hurry, the only halfway sober person in the car. Patty Marsh was driving. Eyes too bright, grin too wide.

'You gonna make another announcement at this one, Stephen?' She twisted around to look at me and the wheels of the car gave a sideways jolt.

Emily MacBride lolled against the opposite door.

'Oh, wasn't that a great time? I'm not Jewish … but I *am* gay!' She was laughing with her mouth open. A twist of green gum reclined on her tongue.

'It wasn't that funny,' Evan mumbled at the window. 'Seemed more like he didn't want to say it.'

'Great night. Tracey's party,' Emily said again, as I opened my backpack and took a swig of vodka, then passed it to her sister beside me. A window was open a crack and whistling wind tore through the car and blew the girls' hair around. The radio scratched out a metal ballad.

Evan handed the bottle to Patty without drinking. 'Guys, come on,' he said. 'I'm not sure that was such a good time. Or a good idea, telling everybody.'

The car was full of disapproving noise. Evan made a shushing gesture. 'Well, remember, Stephen got beat up pretty bad after that.' He looked over his shoulder at me. 'Or that's what I heard, man. Last week of school, just before exams, right?'

I took my bottle back from Patty. 'Yeah. The bathroom. Wasn't as bad as it could've been.'

Evan nodded. 'Mark McAllister and those guys.'

Patty was holding a cigarette against the dashboard lighter. Eleanor MacBride was leaning into me, red-faced and crooning, 'Awww …' Outside the car, fence posts ticked past like railway ties.

'No,' I said to Evan. 'No, Mark wouldn't do anything like that. We're friends.'

'Right. Guess I got it wrong.'

'Guess you did.' I stared out the window past Eleanor's hair, at the fields as the dark settled over them. 'Anybody here cold? Besides me?'

The final party was at a neglected, grey house on the edge of town. Somebody's friend's cousin lived there a few days out of the week, but tonight it was ours. We stumbled out of cars in the near-dark, shouldering cases of beer, a procession winding up the narrow driveway with its spine of spongy grass. The door was open and all the lights were on. Inside, the rooms seemed empty of everything except people: drunk and loosed-limbed, with small suspicious eyes. Something was going to happen.

I avoided Lana as she floated past. Didn't feel like starting a conversation with her. Or anybody. I stuck to the walls, wedged myself into corners, tried to be invisible. Some people noticed me anyway and sang out, 'Hey, Stephen!' Some snarled, 'Fuckin' AIDS-bag. Don't let him touch you, man.' And I'd get a shove that would send me spinning off into a wall or a doorway or another person.

I caught sight of Stacey on her own, leaning with her butt on a window ledge, the night in a dark square behind her. She noticed me staring and threw me a knowing smirk. Obviously she'd been talking to Tina. I loped over.

'I always knew it.' Her voice barely crawled out of her throat to meet me. She was clutching a bottle of beer and her cigarette hand trailed smoke.

'Guess you're some kind of genius, Stace.' We watched the party, side by side with our backs to the window. The walls were white, the floors rough and wooden with clumps of hairy dust in the corners, and everybody was milling around clinging to brown or green bottles as if they needed them to breathe. A set of shelves that looked like it had once held books was now crowded with empties, glass reflecting the light from a bare electric bulb. AC/DC was cranking out of a tape player in the next room. I tipped back my own bottle and let the liquid roll into my throat and burn.

'Hey, Stacey.' She ignored me. I kept talking. 'Stace, does Mark believe in God?'

'What the fuck are you on?'

I told her she'd know the answer to that, if Mark talked to her at all, but obviously he didn't. Stacey laughed, a dry rattling sound.

'You make me puke,' she said.

'Mutual.' I threw my arm around her. Stacey tried to duck out from under me, but I hung on, grabbed one of her intimidating boobs. She shrieked and thrust an elbow at my gut. I dodged it. People around us were grinning, pretending to continue their conversations as they shifted around for a better view. Maybe they were waiting for us to start pulling each other's hair.

'Stace. You remember Mark's birthday last year?' I was smiling pleasantly, as if nothing unusual had happened. 'When he kept going on about "this is my little brother ..."'

'Yeah. "This is my little brother. He's a virgin."' She gave a snort. 'He shoulda said he's a—'

'Know what he wasn't saying? "This is my beautiful girlfriend."'

'So what?'

'So? Mark doesn't give a fuck about you, Stacey.'

She took a deep drag off her cigarette and blew the smoke into my eyes. It's hard to put a word on what I felt then. Evil, I guess. Lit up with malice like a jack o'lantern.

I was still smiling blandly. 'He cheats on you all the time. Never even thinks about it.' Then I told her what Mark had really been up to at Tracey's party, him and Pam in that room upstairs. Stacey's face stayed expressionless. But her breathing got faster and she took a step away from me. Half the room was orbiting us and listening. I didn't care.

'Want me to tell you about all the other times?'

No answer. I moved closer.

'Or just when he fucked your friends?'

'I'm gonna kill you.' Her voice was surprisingly calm. I leaned close and whispered in her ear, like a boyfriend.

'There was your cousin Darla. There was some girl in a car down by the Fitzgerald farm. There was—'

'I said I'm gonna fucking kill you, you stupid little faggot!'

She slammed me into the wall. Then she was thumping her fists on my back, kicking me, cursing. I sank to the floor and curled my arms over my head, tried to roll away from her. A second later, I felt myself bump into something that wobbled, and a heavy object came crashing down and seemed to explode beside me.

It was a bottle. I'd knocked against the shelves piled with empties. My fingers curled around glass and a jagged shard cut into my palm. I wouldn't let go. The cut went deeper. Stacey was still kicking at me. The shelves shook as I collided with them again. More bottles fell to the floor and smashed into fragments, raining down. I found I was laughing.

I wasn't the only one. I peeked out from under the crook of my arm and saw that we had the whole room's attention. Some people were wincing, most just giggling away. Red splotches from my cut hand made snowflake explosions on the floor.

Somebody grabbed Stacey's arm and dragged her off me. Mark.

'Jesus, Stephen, what'd you say to her?'

She turned and pushed at him blindly. 'You fucker! You asshole!' Stacey started to break down in tears. Not like I'd seen her do sometimes to get her way. This was real. 'Mark!' she said helplessly.

'Aw, Stace. Stacey …' His arms were around her, one hand stroking her hair. I faced the wall. Heard Stacey blundering out of the room, still crying, and the creak of a staircase. She was racing up to the bedrooms. When I turned around, I saw Mark was gone too. The audience was still watching it all. I waited for applause.

I'm not sure what happened next.

There was a strong smell of mould and I was in the basement – a dark place with concrete floors, walls that were made of stone and wept trickles of water. I was standing over a white double sink. Somebody turned on the tap and shoved my head under. Lana.

I started to calm down. Then I noticed ribbons of red in the porcelain, fading to rust as they swirled down the drain. Blood from my hand. I was dissolving. Lana hauled me up by the hair, held my palm under the thundering cold water. I watched the blood welling up and disappearing.

'Don't touch that, Lana.' She ignored me, jerked my arm towards her and dabbed at my hand with a battered fragment of Kleenex. It bloomed into red as the blood soaked it. 'Don't,' I said again. 'It's contaminated.'

'Didn't know stupidity was blood communicable.' She took a flat pink square from her purse and ripped off the plastic wrapping. It unfolded into a rectangle of white. She pressed it against my palm.

'Not what I meant.'

'I know. You don't have AIDS, you moron.'

'No, that's okay. I don't need any,' I said, as if she were selling it door to door. 'Mark's gonna kill me.' I went rambling on. 'He beat me up with a bunch of guys in June. Now he's gonna kill me. And then I'll die.'

There was a roll of duct tape on a dusty ledge by the sink. Lana grabbed it and tore off a length with her teeth. 'In that case you should go home, right? Like, now. And stop making such an almighty ass of yourself.' She wound the tape around my hand in a tight bandage.

Just then I realised where she got the white rectangle she'd used for gauze. 'Aw, Lana! Is that a maxi pad? Get it off!'

'Come on. Not like it's used.' She was laughing up at me. 'Besides, it'll keep you safe. In case you fall.'

'Why?'

'It has wings, dummy!' Lana gave me a smacking kiss on the cheek. 'Now I think you've done enough damage for one night. Time to go home.'

'Nah. I'll be fine.' I was backing towards the stairs. They were steep and wooden, with nail heads craning out. I stumbled against them and had to sit down.

I wouldn't let Lana take me home. Mark was still here. We had unfinished business. I clambered up the steps. Then I was barging through rooms and hallways, tripping over people's feet, looking over my shoulder for Lana coming after me, or for Mark. Every time I bumped into a girl, I'd apologise, then grab her ass or her boobs. Most of them went 'Hey!' And I'd get shoved and smacked. Some grabbed me back. I laughed.

I dragged myself to the second floor. It was dark and all the doors were closed. No, not all of them. There was one at the end of the corridor, ajar with a crack of light spilling out. I heard voices. Mark and Stacey. Thick orange shag carpet muffled each footfall.

'Look, Stace,' Mark was saying, 'I told you I don't want to hear it. There's enough rumours in this stupid little town. Bunch of dickheads were saying I molested my sister just cause I drive her to ballet class …'

I was outside the door now, trying not to breathe too loudly. I couldn't hear what Stacey was saying. Mark was getting irritated.

300

'Okay. He's weird. He's a nervous person. But what can you expect? His father left and I think both the parents were disowned or something, cause there's no grandparents, no cousins. Just his mom. And me. That's all he's got.' Her voice in reply was low and full of contempt. He answered.

'Yeah, well, I'm not gonna believe it if I hear it from Phil or Randy. Or Tina. Or you either. I'll believe it when I hear it from him.' Then the subject shifted to Pam, and he was calling himself all kinds of names, telling Stacey he was going to be a different person from now on.

I turned and inched my way back to the stairs, crippled with shame. Maybe Evan had it all wrong, about Mark being one of those guys in the bathroom. Mark was right. You couldn't believe every stupid rumour you heard. I should have trusted my friend.

Downstairs, flying, nearly falling on my face. I got lost in a haze of people. Couples in corners were kissing in this aggressive, down-the-throat way. A girl shrieked, 'Don't! No, don't!' In the kitchen the drawers hung open, and somebody was taking all the food out of the fridge. Somebody else picked up a bottle and smashed it against the wall.

That was me.

Then Lana was apologising to everybody, gripping my elbow and pulling me towards the door. I tried to squirm out of her grasp.

'No, Lana. You don't want to go home yet. Robin Fitzgerald's here. You've always wanted to fuck him, right?' Oops. Robin was behind us, drawing a dartboard on the wall with lipstick. He turned and leered at Lana in an encouraging way.

She walloped me on the back. My feet skidded and I almost fell. But I didn't hit the floor. Somebody else was holding my other arm, pulling me upright. Not Lana this time. Mark.

'Don't worry. I got experience with this,' he was saying. 'Stephen, you're fucked up. Come on home.'

'I don't know if that's such a great idea.' Lana was staring into my eyes like she was trying to tell me something. 'Remember in the basement? When you said … somebody was going to kill you? I mean, was that a joke or—'

'Aw, c'mon.' I took a reeling step towards Lana, threw myself around her and held on tight. 'I was kidding back there,' I mumbled into her hair. 'I was full of it.' I shifted back and planted a smeary kiss on her forehead. 'I love you, okay? Just remember I loved you.'

'I don't like the sound of that …'

'Come on, asshole.' Mark hauled me forwards. I let go of Lana, watched her receding as I moved away.

'Bye!' Held up my bandaged silver hand in a wave.

'You drive me insane,' Lana said quietly. 'Utterly insane. Please be careful.'

I left my girl standing in the hallway. Stumbled off with my guy. Mark was talking to Stacey over his shoulder, saying he'd meet up with her later.

Yeah, later. But first you're gonna deal with me, McAllister. Finish this one way or another. Tonight.

Chapter 24

Trucks hurdled by and blasted through the silence. I was sitting on the bench slats of a picnic table, its wooden surface coated with industrial brown paint, slumping forwards with my head between my knees.

'I'm gonna puke.'

'No, you're not.' Something was bumping against my lip. The edge of a paper cup, scratchy lid with its torn-off tab of plastic, steam rising and making me confused about where the liquid ended and the air began. Black coffee. Mark tipped some into my mouth and I had to drink.

I raised my head. It was the parking lot outside Tim Horton's. We were at the town limits. 'What am I doing here?'

'You …' He was beside me on the picnic table, holding the coffee cup, trying not to laugh. 'You sat right down a couple minutes ago and I couldn't get you to move. Kept saying how you were gonna puke.'

'I *am* gonna puke.'

'Drink your coffee.' He pressed the cup into my hand. I didn't drop it.

Neither of us said anything for a while. I counted the customers in the windows, huddled at their tables lit with stern fluorescent-white like subjects in an experiment. Then I had to stop counting and concentrate all my energy on not throwing up.

Mark's voice in the semi-dark, orange firefly glow of his cigarette. 'Tina was saying a lot of shit about you, man. Stacey too. I told them I didn't believe it.'

'Stacey kicked my ass.' I muttered this into the cornfields where the parking lot ended.

'You deserved it. I can't believe you told her about Pam. And Darla too? What the fuck were you thinking?'

I pretended to drink out of my cup. It was empty now. 'Just came out.'

'Is that right.'

He was waiting for an apology. Well, of course. Guys don't tell on guys, not for stuff like that. Guys don't get in cat fights with each other's girlfriends either. I dug my fingers into the back of my neck, eyes on the ground. Told him I was sorry.

'Damage is done now.' Mark took a pint bottle from his jean jacket. It looked like whiskey. 'You really shouldn't push her like that. Stacey's under a lot of stress. Her body's under a lot of stress.'

'Seemed strong enough to me.'

Mark took a swig. I watched his throat moving. He wiped his mouth with the back of his hand, gazed off into the rustling fields.

'Stephen,' he said, 'she's pregnant. Stacey's pregnant.'

Like something smacking into the side of my head. Was I supposed to congratulate him? The hand with the duct tape bandage was sticking to me.

'Jesus Christ, Mark. You're only seventeen.'

'I'm eighteen. Birthday last month. Remember?'

My throat felt like part of a machine, metal plates shifting and sparking off each other as I tried to swallow.

'Are you gonna marry her?'

'In a couple years.' He was swinging his feet against the side of the picnic table. 'That's okay, isn't it?' Looking at me sidelong. 'I mean, you don't think of yourself as a bastard, or illegitimate or whatever, cause your parents waited till after you were born, right? You don't blame them.'

'No. That stuff doesn't matter.'

His sneakers scuffed against mine. 'Do you want to be my best man? I know you'll be busy with college and stuff by then ...'

I asked him if he was sure, considering we hadn't been hanging around a lot. He told me he knew who his real friends were.

'Course.' My voice was shaky. 'Of course I will.' I pictured myself standing next to Mark in a church. He'd be squirming and uncomfortable in his tuxedo. She'd be pacing up the aisle wearing white, on her father's arm, a child toddling along beside them. And this would be Mark's whole life. Living in Riverside, working all day at Home Hardware. To support his family.

'This is so wrong. Mark, you don't have to do this. You don't have to keep it.'

His face shut down. 'Are you telling me,' he said slowly, 'to abort my kid?'

'It's not a kid yet. Just a bunch of cells. And she was smoking and drinking back there. It's gonna have, like, nine heads.'

He frowned. 'She told me it's fine to do that for the first couple months.'

'She's an idiot!' I was on my feet pacing around, too much energy all of a sudden. 'She's stupid! She's a stupid, boring person.'

'Stephen—'

305

'And she doesn't even know you. You're just another guy to her.'

'Stephen, shut up.' He was standing now, facing me.

'I asked her if you believe in God and she didn't have a clue.'

'So do I?'

'You …' I stopped. 'You want to.'

'That's correct.' Gold liquid in the little bottle sloshed as he took another drink. 'Guess I should marry you instead, huh?'

My chest felt tight. The people at Tim Horton's seemed like they were starting to notice us, out here circling each other in the parking lot. I wanted to put both hands on his shoulders and shove him, start this for real.

'Bet it's not even yours.'

He chucked his cigarette away. 'I am so close to kicking your ass right now.'

'Oh, go ahead, McAllister. Too bad you don't have your friends here to help you this time.'

The tension went out of him. Our eyes met for a second. He knew exactly what I was talking about. I was running my hands through my hair, trying to keep from tearing it out by the handful. I didn't want to hear him say it. I had to.

'Were you one of those guys, Mark? In the bathroom at school?'

He exhaled slowly. 'Yes.'

'Did you hit me?'

'I kicked you. And I hit you a couple times. Tried not to make it hurt.'

I stared at our feet. Our sneakers, in various stages of coming apart, laces thick and frayed, the ends soggy with mud.

'Hey,' he said. 'You think I'm proud of myself here? Five guys jumping a skinny fuck like you? Watching my little brother get—'

'Yeah, well, you're a fucking coward!' I realised I was still holding the stupid coffee cup, and I crunched it into a twist of cardboard and plastic. 'Somebody tells you to do something and you do it. You're gonna be a great father, Mark. Wonderful example for little … five-headed Jimmy-Joe-Bob or whoever.'

'That's right. You're a snob. I keep forgetting.'

'Of course I am. These people are animals!' I threw the cup away from me, waited for it to smack against the window of the coffee shop. It sailed through the air and landed with a useless clatter two feet away from Mark.

'I am "these people".' He took one step sideways and kicked the remains of the cup past me and clear onto the highway where it skittered and bumped along.

'Right. That's where you take your orders from anyway.'

'Orders?' Mark leaned back, hands in his pockets. Looked me straight in the eye. 'The whole thing was my idea.'

'Oh, *fuck*!' I was stumbling backwards, dizzy. Had to get away from there. Away from Mark. Middle of the highway, I didn't care.

The blister on my heel was firing up again. He came after me and I couldn't go fast enough. Felt like the sky was tearing itself in two, the road wobbling and warping under my feet.

'Stephen, listen.' Mark grabbed at my shoulder.

'Don't talk to me! Don't fucking talk to …'

Wooden houses were lining the highway as it morphed into the main street. We were in town. I imagined lights flickering in the windows, people listening. Mark kept saying my name. My eyes were fixed on the road ahead. We passed the used-car dealership. Then the high school, towering brick building in the dark.

He was walking backwards in front of me. 'I'm not gonna apologise. Okay? Far as I'm concerned, I saved your life.'

'Hey, thanks!'

We were behind the high school. I turned and started off down the middle of the soccer field, hunching forward, lopsided from my bad foot.

'What are you doing? That's not the way home.' Mark had hold of my arm.

I shook him off. 'I know. I don't wanna go home. I don't ... I don't know what I want.'

He gave me a little shove. I pushed back and missed him, reeled sideways. It seemed like he was holding back a laugh. He strode along beside me.

'Look. You were never gonna get hurt. I mean, not seriously. It was the middle of the afternoon. Lots of teachers around. I even knew it would be Mr Richardson out there in the hall and not Miss Phinney or somebody.'

'Jesus, you really did plan it.' I was taking a path through the stretch of long grass on the edge of the field.

Mark slowed his steps to match my limp. He kept going on about the scene in the bathroom. Something about Mr Richardson, and didn't I think it was weird, him suddenly showing up like that. Mark told me that was because he'd got some first year to go and find him, that he'd ducked out for a second to do it while the other guys had me in the stall.

'The whole thing only lasted a few minutes,' Mark said. 'Then you were safe.'

'Wow, you're right. I should call Randy and Phil so I can thank them too. Fucker.' We were skirting the edge of the graveyard. I knew where I was going. I wasn't sure why I wanted to be there.

Twigs snapped under my sneakers, then the soft crunch of evergreen needles. We were at the usual place. I couldn't see the river, but I could hear it. Clusters of scrubby trees gave way like a curtain parting on the water, on our lair, this place we'd made together.

He was gripping my arms. 'Look, you retard. I had to do it. I know the toilet was gross and humiliating and you got banged up pretty bad. But my idea was the only one I could see you walking away from. The stuff those guys wanted to do …'

I squirmed out of his grasp. 'So why didn't you just warn me?'

'Because I know you, Stephen. You would've got so freaked out that you'd be hiding in your house for, like, a year. And it wouldn't stop them. They wanted you.' He glanced around the clearing, frowning, like he thought he'd see Randy and Phil under the lower branches somewhere. 'It was weird. I mean, I hate fags too, but I wouldn't actually plan to go fuck somebody up just because of that.' Mark ran a hand through his hair, looked out over the black river with its stuttering stripe of moonlight. 'Maybe it's some kind of power thing. Like you can do whatever you want to them cause they're not real people.'

He was turned away from me. So quiet now.

'Holy fuck.' I whispered it. 'Mark. You really believe that?'

'Course not. Those guys, the way they were going on about you, about somebody they grew up with. Like they were talking about killing an animal.'

Sudden panic made me want to laugh. 'What do you mean, "killing"?'

The river was right in front of us, thirty feet down. It sounded stronger, faster than usual.

'You would've died.' He glanced back at me. 'Some of the stuff they were coming out with.' And he told me what the guys in the bathroom had really wanted to do to me, or at least talked about doing. Knives.

Baseball bats. My arms fractured, chucked off the railway bridge. Something horrible with a broken bottle. I felt a wave of nausea sweeping up.

'I don't want to hear this shit. I don't want to hear it.' I lurched forward. Nearly banged into a tree. I pushed ahead, cursing. Then Mark had his arms around me and was hauling me back.

'Fucking moron!' he said. I looked at the ground in front of my feet. There wasn't any. I'd nearly charged off the edge of the drop-off. A couple rocks and clods of dirt went tumbling into the black river. Mark walked us away from the edge until we were safe.

I'd been half-convinced that this was the night I was going to die. Was it because of this? We stood slumped together, our weight against a tree with a wide, smooth trunk. Bodies at rest warming each other. He'd let his arms drop, but I was still clutching his elbow, denim bunching under my fingers. My chin grazed his shoulder. I could smell him. If I let my head fall forward, my lips would be touching his neck.

'Jeez, Stephen. You just about killed yourself.'

'Mark.' Hardly able to find my voice. 'I'm leaving tomorrow. I'm going to the city. Mom says we need to find me an apartment.' My breath was coming fast. I was still freaked out over nearly going over the drop-off. And terrified. Of what I was about to do.

'That's great, man. You'll have your own place.' He started to shift away from me. I wouldn't let him go.

'I'm leaving tomorrow.'

'Yeah, you said. That's cool. I'll come by and visit. Give me a place to stay in the city.'

I just nodded. Sharp-edged and far away, even when he was right in front of me. I leaned in closer. One hand was still ringed around his arm. *Please don't freak out, Mark.* I reached up, fingers brushing the back of his neck. Slightest bit of pressure as I tried to bring his head to meet mine. *Please just go with it.* My face moved towards his. I was shivering. It had turned cold, and I was scared, so scared.

Mark's eyes widened. He understood.

He understood, and he was stone cold horrified.

Oh, God.

Mark threw me off, jumped back. My teeth started to knock together. I was sweating. Panic. *Say something. Save this.*

'Mark, what the fuck, man.' It came out weird. My throat had closed up. I couldn't look at him. Twisted grey ghosts of leaves were lying with the cigarette butts in the roots of the trees. I glanced at Mark, forced myself to. His whole body was tensed, eyes huge. Staring at me.

'No.' My voice was small and distorted. 'You … you got it all wrong.' As if I were answering him, though he hadn't made a sound. 'I was … joking. It was just a joke.' The look on his face. Shock. Revulsion. Fear. My shoulders started to shake, a steady throb like a pulse. I realised I was crying. I hadn't even felt it start. I listened to the river. I wanted to die.

'Jesus,' Mark said. I wasn't sure if this was a curse or a prayer. He shut his eyes for a moment. Then he held out one hand, like he was trying to regain his balance.

'Okay! Okay. Just calm down.' Mark's tone was weirdly familiar. It was how my mother used to sound just after my father left. When she was trying to put it all back together, go on like nothing was wrong. 'You … you said you were joking. I believe you. It was a stupid joke, but now it's over. Tomorrow you're gonna go to the city. Find somewhere nice to live. Everything's okay.'

I was still crying. 'I shou— I should've …' Words chopped up between gulps of air. It was a minute before I was steady enough to make sense. 'I should've told you,' I said. 'You're the first person I should've told.'

'Look. I don't know what you're talking about.' He came back into focus. We were facing each other. I had my back against the tree. He was two steps away, the river behind him.

'I've known you since we were kids,' he was saying. 'Okay, you act a bit weird sometimes. But basically you're a normal person. You're like me.'

'I'm also gay.' Sound of the word like a sour joke, out here in the dark. That playground insult.

'But you're not, Stephen.' As if he were explaining something I was too worked up to absorb. 'It doesn't make sense. You were going out with Tina all summer.'

'I hated it.'

'Come on. That's not true.'

'And there was this guy. Tracey's party.'

Mark flinched. 'Okay, I heard about that. But you were drunk. You were really drunk that night—'

'I'm in love with you.'

'What?' For a second he smiled uncertainly. Like he really did believe I was joking and was waiting for me to say so, to release him. He shook his head in a quick little movement. 'No. No, you're not.'

'I am. I love you, Mark.'

'Stop. Stop saying that.' Mark's jaw clenched, his eyes welling.

'So much. Ever since I can remember—'

'Man, don't fuck with my head!' He kicked at a rock, sent it flying over the edge of the drop-off. I didn't hear it hit the river.

'Just listen,' I said. Took a step towards him.

'You stay right there.'

'Mark, I—'

'I said don't fucking come near me!' Near the edge now. I started babbling, telling him he was everything to me, the best person I knew, that it tore me apart thinking he'd be stuck in this rotten little town for life, how much I wanted to save him. I said he could come to the city with me. Bring his sister. Bring the baby too. We'd all live together.

He was on the crumbling lip of the drop-off. The dark was fading and the horizon was starting to colour – grey light, a stripe of orange.

'Watch out,' I said. 'You're gonna fall.' I moved closer.

Mark lashed out quick, lunged at me. Then there were flares of pain just under my eyes. My face was smashed against the trunk of a tree, the same one we'd been leaning on. He'd taken me by the neck and slammed me into it. I gripped the bridge of my nose and it was like glass shards stabbing into my brain.

'You,' he was saying. 'You made me do that.'

'Mark.' I couldn't even see him. 'That fucking … hurt …'

I took a couple steps backwards. Heard him yelling my name, fear in his voice. Then there wasn't any ground under me. I was gone.

Chapter 25

There was a jolt all through my elbow, like my arm was getting ripped out of its socket. A rock? No time to register anything. I was plunging into thick, cold water. And then I was sinking.

I kicked downwards. Treading water like they told us in school, craning my head. The right arm was useless. I pushed at the water with my left. I was numb all over, then pain took hold, throbbing redly and tearing at me every time I moved. But I had to move. My clothes were soaked. I couldn't get my shoes off. I didn't know where I was, didn't know where the shore was, which direction I should go if I wanted to try to swim for it. Black water kept rolling towards me, slapping at my nose, my mouth. Everything seemed to be pulling me down. I went under, gagged, forced my head to the surface. Gulping air, kicking harder.

How long can I keep this up? My legs were stiff and heavy, machine parts I couldn't control. Not allowed to stop, not for a second. I'd sink. And then float. The sky was turning grey with dawn. Somebody was talking, a small desperate voice. It was me. I was telling someone that

I didn't want to die. I was saying 'please' over and over. I heard myself calling for my mother, begging her to help. I called for Stanley too. And Mark.

A sharp tug jolted my throat – like a dog's chain pulling. I kicked against it and my head plunged under water. Then my T-shirt was making a tight band around my neck as someone hauled me up to the air. It was Mark. He dropped the shirt collar and grabbed hold of my arm. The wrong one. Pain blocked everything and I thrashed away from him. Mark called me a stupid moron. His elbow closed over my neck and then he was swimming us to land.

We heaved forward. I still couldn't see anything. I tried to help but only made it worse, fucking with the direction. Mark gave my throat a wrench and told me to quit it. There was a moment when water surged over both our heads. I panicked and swallowed a cold gulp that choked me.

Then the riverbank came into view. He let me go and I scrambled for him, felt myself drifting down. But it was okay. My feet could touch the bottom. I could stand.

I splashed towards the shore. Almost on dry land when my ankle caught a bramble root and I lurched forwards, hit the ground and lay sprawled with my face pressed into mud, gasping and coughing, pulling air into my lungs.

Everything was washed in a ghostly half light. Behind me the drop-off stretched upwards – a sheer wall of crumbling dirt with hairy tree roots peeping out like reaching fingers. The riverbank was mucky and crowded in bushes, brambles and garbage, shocks of tall green cattails coated in grey river dust. I'd crushed a few of them falling.

After a while, I forced myself into a sitting position. My nose was probably broken. My right arm hung at a demented angle from my shoulder, hand still wrapped in ribbons of silver duct tape. I couldn't move it or touch it. I sat very still and concentrated on being alive. Birds were starting to wake up all along the river, chirping and whistling. I remembered reading somewhere that songbirds actually make those noises to mark their territory and warn other birds away. So we think they're trilling sweetly for joy, but they're really just saying, 'Fuck off, everybody! Fuck off.'

I laughed, thinking about this. The sound was a rattling croak and it echoed weirdly in the stillness. I was pretty sure I'd gone crazy.

Where was Mark?

I heard him before I saw him, the slow trickling splash of his legs pushing through mud and sludgy water. His sneakers were in a tangle at the foot of a bramble bush and he shook the wet out and struggled into them. When he glanced over, I pretended to be examining my arm. I wanted to thank him for saving my life, but nothing would come out. My face was frozen and my voice didn't belong to me.

He started stumbling forward. Dripping hair. Clothes solid with water. Red raw face staring down. His expression was impossible to read.

Mark spat, then was hit with another coughing fit. He waited it out, head lowered and breath coming in waves that seemed to hurt him. Finally, he looked me in the eye. He spoke.

'Your mother's always been real nice to me.'

I started laughing again. A nice little chat about my mom. After we'd both nearly died. *Well, okay. Whatever you want, Mark.*

'You think this is funny?'

I didn't anymore, but I couldn't stop. Wheezing and creaking, shaking with it.

'Your mother,' Mark said grimly, 'would just lose it if something happened to you. Maryna's a good person. She doesn't deserve that.'

I closed my eyes and shut everything out, waited for it all to slow down. After a minute, something cleared in my head and I could talk.

'Mark. You … you saved my life.' The broken nose made me sound like I had a cold. I tried to pull myself up, stand and face him. Didn't like Mark looming over me like that.

He made a sudden movement and there was a wrench of pain like light. My chest was caving in. I couldn't move or think.

Kicked me. He kicked me. Why? What did I do? Smiled maybe, when I told him he'd saved my life. Or it could be that when I was trying to stand, I'd held out my hand to him. Because normally he'd be there to help me up.

I felt myself sinking back, swiping at my chest with my good arm. I wanted to ask him why, but I couldn't form words. I made a low sound, panting for air. He came at me again with another kick. *Jesus, no.* I tried to move out of range, bring my legs up, make myself into a ball, fold up or roll away. It was useless. His foot slammed into me again. My stomach and my ribs. There was nowhere I could go. I told him to stop. I told him he was acting like a psycho, that he was going to kill me. Then I realised I wasn't saying any of this out loud because I couldn't talk.

He grabbed hold of my hair and I was hauled upwards. I glimpsed his face for a second, then his knuckles were smashing into me, just under my eye. I couldn't see straight. My ears were ringing. Was there blood? He took a handful of my hair again, yanked my head towards him at an angle. My stomach heaved.

'Listen to me,' Mark said. His threatening voice. 'You …'

I pitched myself forward and threw up into the mud. I heard Mark go, 'Oh, jeez,' saw his sneakers hopping out of range of the splash. Every time my chest moved, the pain in my ribs came back, pressure bearing down and inwards. I threw up again. Mostly liquid and the dregs of that soup I'd spooned out of the can a hundred years ago. Then blood. I spat. I had tears in my eyes. I stared down at muck and meal remains blurring together. My face was turned away from Mark, but I knew he was there, standing over me.

He waited until he could tell I was finished. Then from the corner of my eye, I saw him come at me again. I shrank back, tried to bring my good arm over my face and shield myself, told him to leave me alone. I'd meant it as a yell, but it came out more like a whimper. He grabbed the collar of my shirt and pulled it tight around my neck, leaned in close.

'You. Don't talk to me, ever again. Do not fucking look at me. I don't even want to see you on the same side of the street. Got that?'

I nodded. My head felt heavy. His mouth was next to my ear. Everything was too loud. I wanted to throw up again.

'I pulled you out of there because of your mom. If it wasn't for her, I woulda let you drown. And if I see you again, I will fucking kill you.'

'But … you don't get it …'

Suddenly I was plunging downwards and I couldn't breathe. He'd shoved my face into the mud. I could feel his hands pushing on my head, one knee pressed into my back. Silent explosions, pressure. I kicked. I pounded my fist on the ground and tried to pull him off me. I was making high, panicking sounds and low growls in the back of my throat.

Then the weight was gone. I lay spitting up mud and gasping for air and I found I was swearing at him.

I was also crying, but I didn't connect it with any emotion. It was a reflex, like the vomiting. I sobbed and choked back strips of snot, trying to keep my mouth clear of the mud. My hand hovered over my head in case I had to fend him off again.

But he wasn't moving. He was a shape hunched on the mud beside me, sitting with his knees folded under him and his head bowed. He seemed to be chuckling. Laughing away, his shoulders trembling, hands gripping each other tightly.

I lay still. The laughing noise kept bubbling out of him. He couldn't seem to shut it off.

Then I blinked my eyes open and his face came into focus. Oh. I'd got it wrong. Mark wasn't laughing at all. He was crying.

'Oh, God.' He was rocking. 'Oh, Jesus. Jesus.'

There was an unnatural clarity to everything, like it was all cut-outs pasted on paper. The tall clusters of grey-green weeds on the bank, the sky the colour of skim milk, the river behind us.

'Mark.' My voice was barely a sound at all. It made me think of sand in my throat. 'Mark, I'm not dead.'

'But, you are,' he said, without looking up. 'You are, Stephen.'

Did I dream it? I was never sure.

A second later, I was closing my eyes – as the dead are expected to do. When I opened them he was gone. There were footprints in the mud and I was alone.

I lay there for a long time. The sun climbed up. The mud on my clothes started to dry. I felt hollow and strangely calm. It was just like after my father had left, when I came out of the house and saw that his car had gone. All real now. I didn't have to imagine it anymore.

I listened to the birds in the trees telling each other to fuck off. The world had ended again. I was in a new one.

But I had to live in it. I grabbed hold of a tree root poking out of the side of the drop-off and pulled myself to my feet. My joints were cemented together. My chest seemed to be crushing in further with each movement. My arm was a dull throb. I'd been raised from the grave too soon. There was nothing else to do but go home.

Two steps inside the house and my mother was pushing me back against the doorframe, crying and clinging, demanding to know what had happened. I couldn't answer. Couldn't drag those words into the light and make it real. Mom, he despises me. He broke my bones. No. Instead I begged her to give me some time. Twelve hours, I said, pulling a number out of the air. Twelve hours and I'd tell her everything.

I held her eyes and made her promise. She kept her word, even though I know it must have been killing her. We drove to the hospital in Middleton to get me fixed up and I told the doctors what they needed to know, but I wouldn't say anything when she was there.

Later we were home, loading my stuff into the car. Mom thought we should stay in town another few days so I could rest, but I insisted. I didn't care if I was a torso in a box, I told her. We had to leave.

'You remember what day it is, sweetie?' She pushed a garbage bag full of pillows and blankets into the back seat.

'No, and I don't care.'

I didn't say much while we were packing. I said nothing at all for the first hour we were stuck together, driver and passenger, on the way into the city.

Instead I glowered out the car window at the shoulder of the highway rolling past. Everything felt flat and distant. My arm was broken. My nose was broken. Two of my ribs were cracked and I had a big puffy bruise on my face and a deep cut on my palm. I kept spinning the dial on the radio, fumbling with my left hand. Couldn't settle on a station.

When the news cut in, I took a sharp breath. I looked at Mom. The date. I'd completely forgotten.

I was eighteen. Today was my birthday.

Part 5
The new world

Chapter 26

There wasn't much of a crowd at the old Gag 'n' Spew. I pushed open the door, felt that strange delayed reaction that comes with doing everything left-handed. My mother followed.

The Gag 'n' Spew was really The Garden View, an elderly Chinese restaurant in downtown Halifax. It was all red – fuzzy red patterned wallpaper, red vinyl booths, red carpeted floors faded pink with time. If you sat at the back away from the windows it was like hanging out in somebody's mouth. When I was a kid, I'd been enchanted with the place. Probably why I'd agreed to come here with my mother, to celebrate eighteen years of me.

I was moving slowly and stiffly, everything bruised and pressing inwards, my right eye half-closed and my right arm hanging in a blunt plaster sock that knocked painfully against my chest. We slid into a booth that gave us a view of the place. Mom's head bobbed down every thirty seconds to look at her watch. Maybe she'd ordered me a singing telegram and was waiting for it to arrive. I decided I hated birthdays.

But I suppose we'd accomplished everything we'd set out to do. I had a place to live in the city. My new home was a bachelor apartment with fire damage, a stinky little box with black-streaked walls and a kitchenette shoved into a corner. It wasn't fit for anybody to live in now, the landlady had told us, but we could have it if we agreed to paint the place ourselves. Mom had got all excited at the prospect of making my home look less like a jail cell, so the next stop on our itinerary had been Colour My World, where she pored over handfuls of sample strips, trying to assemble the perfect combinations that would open up my awful little room. I picked up a vat of blue that had been slashed to half price and told her we were getting that.

'Are you sure, dear?' She was still clutching her rows of coloured squares: fern green and birch white, buttercup yellow. 'It looks like the bottom of a swimming pool, doesn't it?'

'I love it,' I said, in the same dull tone I'd used to tell her I loved the apartment. Then it was time for this birthday dinner.

A waitress bustled up to our table. She was only a few years older than me, with frizzy blonde hair in French braids and feverish slashes of red on her cheeks. I ordered the Double Happiness Combo without even thinking. Then I realised it was mostly stuff my mother didn't like. I apologised and she said she didn't care.

'It's only food. This is your birthday.'

'Let's pretend it isn't.'

She ignored this, tried to fill the table with bright chatter. Telling me and anyone within hearing distance that her little baby was all grown up and legal voting age now, and wasn't it wonderful? My present from her, she announced, was going to be a futon. From IKEA. She lingered on the vowels of these foreign words like they were something miraculous. The waitress sailed by with the first courses and then the table was crowded with chrome dishes leaking steam. My mother glanced at her watch again.

'What?' I said. 'Is it the parking meter? Why do you keep—?'

'It's seven fifteen.'

'So?'

She was sitting up with her hands folded. 'You said to give you twelve hours. And then you'd tell me everything.'

Oh, Mom. So careful to keep to our little agreement. I wanted to cry. Instead I scooped a soggy heap of bean sprouts onto my plate and tried to work out what I was going to say next.

'I was drunk. Okay? Really drunk. I went to that party I told you about, and I was walking home and I went off the edge of the drop-off. Fell in the river.'

'You were ... you were drunk and you fell in the river.' She was gripping her fork tightly. 'How did you get ... out of the river?'

'Mark.'

'Thank God for that boy.' Then she looked at me, considering. 'So wait a minute, what about your arm?'

'A rock. Hit it on the way down.'

'How did you break your nose?'

'That was ... that was Mark too. We ...' I half-heartedly mimed a punch.

'He *hit* you?' My mother reached for her cigarettes. 'Why, honey? Why on earth—?'

I stared down at the dishes with their clattering lids and thumbprint smears.

'Well. He hit me because ... I mean, he thought—'

My throat jammed. I'd gone clammy and nauseated and my skin under the cast was itching. Mom hunched forward like she wanted to grab my shoulders and shake the words out.

I sat up taller – careful that I was making eye contact. Here we go.

'He thought I was a homo. That I wanted to kiss him. Put the moves on him. And stuff.'

She froze with a cigarette peeping out of its red cardboard pack. 'Good Lord. Was it acid? Were you guys on acid? I mean, where would he get that idea?'

'Because it's true?'

I'd wanted my voice to come out strong and clear. It had dropped to a phlegmy little croak instead.

She just stared at me.

'It's true, Mom.'

I tore a long strip off my paper placemat. My hand was trembling. Our waitress paced past, counting tables, watching the door. I ducked my head so she wouldn't think I was signalling her.

'So,' my mother said. 'So, you're telling me …'

'I'm …'

'Gay. You're gay.'

Mom lit the cigarette she'd been clutching for the past few minutes. I hadn't had one since the party and it was driving me nuts. She exhaled smoke in a steam blast at a mural of cascading Chinese mountain streams.

'Is this one of those times you say something shocking and it's like, "Ha, ha, Mom, you believed me"?'

'No. I'm serious.' My head was still lowered. I was running my good hand through my hair and pulling at it. My mother stubbed out the cigarette in a tiny tin ashtray. I thought things might go back to normal if I ate something, but I couldn't make myself move. Above us, the restaurant's sound system struggled into life. Janet Jackson was telling us to wait a while, before it was too late, before we went too far. They used to play Chinese music in here when I was a kid.

'Oh, God,' my mother said, in a whimper of a voice. 'I can't do this.'

Then she was pulling herself to her feet.

'Mom?'

She picked up her purse and slung it over her shoulder. Her coat was gathered in the crook of her arm.

I lunged across the table, grabbed at her wrist.

'No. Please.' I felt my fingers closing around her. Her bones, the links of her bracelet watch. 'Mom, you can't.'

'Look, I need to be alone. Just for a minute.' She tried to shake herself free. I wasn't letting go.

Alone. I pictured myself in this long, red funeral parlour of a restaurant – a guy on his own in a plastic booth surrounded by food. Watching the clock, staring at the door, poking at tortured masses of chicken in a Day-Glo orange sauce. Wondering if she was ever coming back.

Mom surged out of the booth and I felt myself getting hauled along after her, off balance with this one heavy plaster arm.

'For God's sake,' she said. 'I just need some air!'

'What are you talking about? There's air in here.'

'I have to think.'

'No, you don't. Please. Please don't leave.'

My mother tried to wrench herself away again. I held on. It must have looked like we were breaking up. Our waitress came sauntering up to the table with her notepad ready, and I turned and said the first thing that came into my head.

'Listen, I just told her I'm gay. Can you give us a minute?'

'Okay, no problem. Take your time.' The girl twirled on her heel and I watched her bobbing off to another table, as if this kind of thing happened to her every day.

Mom looked around warily. It was like she was only just becoming aware of the other people in the restaurant. She massaged her wrist, slowly lowered herself into the booth again and gazed at the mural on the wall. I picked up a brown blistered egg roll and took a bite out of it.

'Didn't think you'd get so mad.'

'I'm not mad. It's just … Stephen, are you certain about this? Are you sure?'

'Yes.'

'God.'

She looked at me, so long and so compassionately that I felt like opening my mouth to show her the wad of chewed-up food on my tongue.

'I knew I'd damaged you in some way,' she said.

'Mom, come off it.' I was talking through bites of egg roll. 'You didn't have anything to do with this. Unless you were showing me movies in my sleep or something.' I shook my head. 'And I'm not damaged.'

'But Stephen, what if you get AIDS?' Her face was tense and horrified. 'Oh, honey, to think of you lying all alone in some hospital ward, everybody afraid to touch you—'

'Could we not talk about that?'

Mom seemed to bite down on whatever she was going to say next. I could see a parade of expressions twitching across her face. Probably imagining my funeral. I wanted to ask her who did the eulogy and whether Stanley showed up.

Instead I turned my attention back to the sad little clumps of food in front of me: slimy vegetables in watery brown, grains of rice that seemed to want to dribble off everywhere. Mom wasn't eating. All she did was stare down into her lap, pressing her lips together.

'This isn't the life I wanted for you.' My mother's voice was low and soft. 'You were supposed to get married. Start a family. Be surrounded by people who love you. A father to your children. I wanted you to have a real home.' Her eyes were welling. 'You're so lonely, sweetheart. You've always been lonely. It hurts me to see it.'

My fork slipped away from me with a clatter. I closed my eyes. Was that what I wanted too? There had to be a reason I was feeling this heavy and sad.

It was painful, moving all this stuff around in my throat. After a while I sensed she was looking at me again.

'No. Stephen, listen to me. I shouldn't have said that. You already have a family. You always will. Always. No matter what.'

'I know.'

But something was itching at the back of my mind. That line of hers. It reminded me of the stuff she used to come out with when I was thirteen or so. We'd be watching TV and there'd be a heroin fiend on some cop show, and she'd turn to me and say, 'You know I'd still love you if you got addicted to drugs, right? You wouldn't have to hide it from me. I'll love you no matter what.'

And I'd answer with something really disgusting, like, 'Yeah? So you'd love me if my head was made of solidified vomit?'

'Would you stop it!'

But this wasn't being addicted to drugs. Or having a head made of solid barf, or putting dead people in her bed, or any of those scenes I used to invent to shut her up whenever she'd get all sloppy-devoted on me. This was not a 'no matter what'.

I leaned back in the booth. When I spoke, my voice sounded like Stanley's.

'No matter what. Well, aren't you the heroine, Maryna. Continuing to love me even though I'm a total pervert. Sorry I don't have a medal for you.'

'That's not what I meant at all!'

'There's nothing wrong with me, Mom.'

'I know that! I just ….' Her face crumpled, eyes twisted shut. She dropped her head and her shoulders started to quiver.

I'd made my mother cry. Again.

'Aw, Mom. Mom, I'm sorry.'

I tried to take her hand, but she pulled away from me, shrank into a corner of the booth and turned her face to the wall. I watched her. Pressure was building behind my eyes and I couldn't breathe right. The expression on Mark's face as he kicked me. Leaving my home to go live in a smelly little box. My mother, all alone in that empty house, that empty town. Mom weeping in the booth in front of me. Because of the rotten things I'd said.

My arm was folded on the table and my head was on my arm. I was so tired, so sick of trying to hold myself upright.

After a minute, I felt her patting my hair. Then my mother got up and slid into my side of the booth, wrapped me in her arms. She was crushing my cast against my cracked ribs, but I didn't say anything. My nose was pressed into her neck. I reached my left arm around her shoulders. We both held on tight, telling each other how sorry we were, over and over.

The older waitress trundled over to our table, a solid, motherly woman who wore little wire frame glasses like an apple doll. She quietly placed a jumbo box of Kleenex on the lid of a chrome dish in front of us.

'Now!' she said. 'Thought you two might want these. Anything else? Drinks? Coffee? Dessert?'

'Double whiskey,' my mother said dully. 'Stephen?'

'Just so you know, I can't serve him.'

My mother let go of me, pulled herself up to her full sitting height. 'And I'd like to know why not!'

'Mom, she's talking about alcohol. I'm eighteen. You were telling everybody, remember?' I was still leaning against her shoulder.

'Oh, right. Right. Sorry.'

I glanced at the menu, asked the waitress if they had cherry-vanilla. She told me she'd see what she could do.

'So. One ice-cream and one double whiskey.'

'Two straws,' my mother muttered under her breath. She ripped a Kleenex from the box in front of us and blew her nose.

Back at the hotel exhaustion made us go all normal. We talked in dull voices about painting my new apartment. We made a list of the furniture I'd need. It was weird to be sharing a room with her – thrown together in these strange neutral surroundings like we were exhibits in an alien zoo. I changed in the bathroom and made sure my shorts didn't have holes in them.

Outside there were lights glimmering from tall buildings and houses, and the black water of the harbour beyond. I read for a while. She watched TV. I got into one bed and she got into the other.

I lay in the dark sinking into starched white sheets. It was impossible to sleep. I could feel my mother tossing around in the next bed, then weeping to herself in that almost soundless way she had. I thought maybe I should pretend to be unconscious to give her some privacy. I couldn't.

'Hey. I'm gonna be okay. You didn't do anything wrong.'

Her quavering voice coming back at me. 'But you're so miserable! I can't leave you here like this.'

'Mom, I was in love with him.' I could say this with the lights off.

'Oh, sweetheart.'

Her arm was reaching out whitely between the beds. I manoeuvred around so I could stretch my left hand to meet her. I brushed her fingers with mine.

'Do you want to watch TV?' she said.

I did. We went zapping through all the channels from the States. Then they ran out of shows and we were down to infomercials. The Psychic Friends Network. A miraculous food processor. She drifted off to sleep and so did I. We left the TV on, flickering and murmuring into the night. We woke up to sunny American voices telling us good morning.

Chapter 27

Three o'clock and already you could feel the sunset waiting. I was on a concrete platform at the train station in Halifax, huddled into a black overcoat I'd bought second-hand. I thought it made me look older, sophisticated, maybe even French. My friend Janine said the effect was more like a Semitic vampire. Janine was there with me, clinging to Eleanor MacBride, both of them saying goodbye. It was Christmas and Eleanor and I were heading home – two weeks of winter boredom before our real lives could start up again.

One more hug. Eleanor lifted Janine off the floor. I paced around with my hands in my pockets, thinking: *Oh, just kiss already and get it over with.* Behind us people were angling themselves and their suitcases full of Christmas presents up the steps and through the narrow doors of the train.

I decided to give the girls a few minutes alone, waved goodbye to Janine over Eleanor's shoulder and staggered after the Christmas travellers, loaded down with my suitcase and Eleanor's too. I was even thinner than when I'd arrived here four months ago. Came from eating nothing but Mr Noodles and leftover pizza. I wasn't great at cooking and liked to save my grocery money for the important stuff – caffeine and cigarettes, alcohol, cover charges, clothes from second-hand junk shops, books, prophylactics, weed.

I found a couple of seats in the smoking car and Eleanor joined me as we started pulling away from the station. We were packed in close together; it was one of those very full holiday trains. Eleanor turned her face to the window for a while. The sun was on the horizon when I realised she was talking. I pressed the stop button on my Walkman.

'Stephen,' Eleanor was saying, 'how did it all change so fast?'

I didn't know. It was a blur. But she was right. Everything was different now.

I remembered the first day of classes. How the chatter had died away as we filed into the lecture hall, everybody hushed and excited like Christmas morning. What did Santa bring us? This wide, sunny room full of yellow wooden chairs. These windows that stretched to the ceiling, twists of leathery ivy framing the September sky, edges of the leaves just starting to singe with red.

I'd taken a seat behind a pillar. I was nervous thinking everybody was staring at me and also a little scared that nobody was – dressed like a Riverside farm boy and looking like I'd lost a fight with a pig on my way to the slaughtering shed. I'd breathed in perfume and hair gel and floor cleaner, and waited for the lecture to start. When it did, I'd realised I was screwed; there was no way I could take notes with my left hand. My pen slid uselessly as words like 'Gilgamesh' and 'Mesopotamia' went flying past. My binder bumped along towards the edge of my knees, getting ready to belly-flop onto the floor and embarrass me.

Then somebody poked me in the shoulder. A girl, tall and oddly regal looking, with short blonde hair and icy blue eyes, wearing a man's undershirt, cut-off shorts and cowboy boots. She said I could photocopy her notes after class. Her name was Janine. A few days later she was my best friend.

Well, Lana was in Toronto. Mark hated me. I needed a new one.

Friday night we sneaked into this long tavern downtown, all wooden tables with scummy surfaces, white walls darkened to nicotine yellow, packed with college kids and a few rough-looking locals. A drunk girl careened into me while Janine was at the bar. We went through the usual – where was I from, what school did I go to, what was my major and did I like it – then, of course, the inevitable. 'How'd you get the arm?'

I'd been telling everybody I was really wasted and fell in a river, which was more or less true, and it usually made people laugh. So I got ready to churn out this story again, but something was jamming in my head and it wouldn't come to me.

The girl took a sip from her beer and smiled. The noise of other people's conversations surrounded us, waves of sound rising and falling. There was a line of red lipstick on her teeth and I wondered if I should mention it.

Instead I heard myself telling her about my friend who'd broken my nose and then kicked the shit out of me on a riverbank as the sun came up, all because I was in love with him and he couldn't handle it. 'Sucks, huh?' I finished. The girl stared at me. I went to rub the red stain off her tooth and she jerked backwards, then stammered out some neutral reaction and pushed herself through the crowd. She found a friend.

Shock and laughter, quick glances in my direction. I pretended I saw somebody I knew on the other side of the room so I'd have an excuse to turn my back.

Janine was standing behind me. I could tell by her face that she'd heard everything.

She handed me a beer. Big, clunky mug of amber liquid with a scud of dishwater foam on the top. I took a long drink and tried to figure out what to say.

Janine leaned in close. The strap of her top looped off one bare shoulder and I sensed tiny head movements as the guys milling around us all zeroed in on it. She asked me if what I'd said to the girl was true. I said it was. Then she asked me if it was a secret. I surprised myself.

'No,' I said. 'Course not. Tell whoever you want. Tell everybody.' I gulped down mouthfuls of terrible beer. I felt like I'd just escaped from an exam room. Realised I was smiling. So was Janine. Then she was hugging me. Beer swilled over the side of her mug and splashed the back of my neck.

'I just don't know why you didn't tell me sooner,' she said. 'We're friends, right?'

○

Then it was a low, grey Tuesday afternoon in the second week of classes, and I was alone in my apartment with a boy who'd walked me home from the meeting.

What meeting? Campus gay and lesbian society. Janine had made me go, even marched in there and sat beside me holding my hand to make sure I wouldn't chicken out and leave. I don't know why I'd been so nervous. It was just a bunch of nice kids making plans for social events. Or something. I couldn't take much in because I was busy watching this guy Christopher. Very beautiful, just about angelic, with soft brown hair that curled around his ears and blue eyes he kept half shut behind little John Lennon glasses. So I stared. I looked away and blushed. I realised he was staring back. I grinned at the floor and didn't know what to do.

Later he was in my blue box of an apartment listening to me trying to hold a normal conversation, stammering and tripping over my words and mixing up details about my own life until it must have seemed like I was lying or insane. I decided I'd try to make us tea. He kissed me in my kitchenette as I fumbled in cupboards looking for spoons. I tasted vending-machine coffee from the Student Union Building on his tongue, felt my arm getting nudged out of its sling and thumping against the counter, and I wanted to touch him so much but could only swipe clumsily with my left hand – half a bound-up plaster mummy in his arms. He laughed and said I should calm down. He wasn't going anywhere.

That's when I realised we were probably going to end up doing it. For real this time, not just messing around in a hayloft. I wished I'd done more research.

Christopher eased my shirt off and it hung in a heap around my broken arm and I was just about shaking.

'Holy cow,' he said softly, when he saw the bruises left over from Mark.

We met up again the next day, and the day after, and on and off and on again through the fall. I missed three lectures on *The Iliad*, but it was worth it.

Late September with Janine, lying stretched on a sunny patch of grass in the quad, two sets of headphones plugged into her Walkman. Working our way through readings for the next lecture or going over scenes from *The Duchess of Malfi*. I'd auditioned on a dare and got the part, so until December I was Antonio, Janine's steward and secret husband.

I hung out with actors now, and with guys and girls from the meetings, and sometimes the serious kids in class, who were all demanding to know why I kept getting *A*s on my papers when I skipped so many lectures. (By working like mad, of course, though this was a secret. It took a lot more effort to be smart here than it did in Riverside.) On Fridays we'd go to the campus pub and jump up and down in the little sweaty dance area to New Order and REM, the whole group leaning into each other and yelling the words to 'Bizarre Love Triangle' in a drunken slur.

My mother phoned almost every day. Lana would call too on weekends, and even Adam checked in once in a while. I'd run into him just before he moved to Toronto and he was actually really nice to me – seemed sorry about how mangled I looked and brought me an ivy plant he'd stolen from his mother.

And there were times when the phone would ring and there'd be nothing but silence on the other end, and I'd have to hang up. Was it a wrong number? A burglar hoping to break in and steal my mould-encrusted dishes? Someone who wanted to talk, but didn't know what the hell to say? Mark?

It couldn't be.

October rolled around. The plaster cast and most of the bruises were gone. I started wearing black and getting a reputation for sarcasm.

One Thursday afternoon, I was at the head of a table in the tavern, telling my Mark story, playing it for laughs. Mark was dumber than a brick in this version, a cross-eyed redneck Neanderthal who spoke mostly in grunts, and I was a lovesick little twerp who just had to keep saying exactly the wrong thing. When I got to the part where he punched me and I threw up on his shoes, the whole table went nuts. (Except Christopher, who was drawing on a beer mat and handing it to someone farther down the table. He'd heard this one before.)

I kept my eyes moving from face to face. Wanted to make sure I had the right reactions, laughs at the right lines. And I found my attention constantly going back to a bizarre-looking guy at the outer edge of the group. He had dry, frizzy, red hair, light-coloured eyes and a beaky nose, a beat-up trench coat like Columbo. Staring at everybody, at me, unsettling and intense.

I finished my story on a down note and got the usual nods and smiles and, 'That's rough, Stephen.'

Then the weird kid pulled himself to his feet.

'Well, I think you're all shallow,' he said after a strange pause. 'Utterly superficial.' Looked right at me. 'Especially this jerk.' He turned and swept out.

Everybody started talking at once. We were trying to decide whether the 'shallow' comment was some kind of slur because most of us at the table were gay, but then we couldn't figure out if he was as well. Nobody could even remember who'd invited the scary redhead along in the first place.

I lit a cigarette. 'Great guy. Kind of looks like Eric Stoltz fucked a chicken, no? And that's the love-child.' I got a couple laughs.

The next day the same guy bought me a coffee and decided to explain why he thought I was a superficial jerk, which I suppose was nice of him.

'It was that story,' the weirdo said. We were at one of the outdoor tables at the Student Union coffee shop. He'd flagged me down as I was daydreaming my way along the sidewalk, waving his arms. 'Stephen! Hey!' I wasn't even sure how he knew my name. His name was Ryan.

He unfolded his legs and the table wobbled dangerously. 'I mean, if it was true, then that's some pretty harsh stuff. But you were using the whole thing as a joke. To get attention. Doesn't that seem wrong to you?'

His accent sounded slightly off, vowels that lingered a hair's breadth too long. Turned out he was American.

A cold breeze numbed the end of my nose. I could have said something mean, but instead I told him it was just a way of keeping it all distant.

'You know what I'm talking about, right?' I said. 'Turn something painful into another dumb story. It's human.'

Ryan looked at me as if to say that he'd heard of these humans of which I spoke. Then he asked me how long I'd known Mark. And which bands Mark liked, and what we used to do on his birthday, and on and on. I told him way more than I should have. Ryan started tearing napkins out of a chrome dispenser chained to the table and throwing them at me.

'I'm not going to touch you. Obviously. But I'm sorry you're upset.'

Afterwards we stopped by a second-hand bookshop so I could buy him the *Hitchhiker's Guide* trilogy. I'd said something about that night with Mark being like going through the Total Perspective Vortex and I knew he wouldn't be able to understand that without the second book. I still wasn't sure if Ryan was gay, straight, or some asexual being from outer space. Over the next few weeks, he turned into best friend number two.

I liked him for his weirdness. Most people didn't – Ryan was mercilessly excluded just about everywhere he went. But I think he sensed that I wouldn't hurt him, because after that coffee he was stuck to me like a barnacle.

Midnight and spitting flecks of rain. I was outside a club, exposed on a hill away from the rest of the bars, shivering and getting carded, watching my friends filing in without me. I launched into this stupid explanation of how I'd left my liquor ID and my passport and my driver's licence at home – not really listening to myself, drifting in and out of an English accent, hoping I'd bore the enormous heavy-lidded bouncer into waving me in. No luck. I told him I had a student card and he said he wouldn't take it. I handed it to him anyway. He ran his thumb along the plastic and smeared off the little bump of marker where I'd tried to turn 1969 into 1968.

'Nice try … Stephen,' he said, reading off the card. Somebody looked up at the sound of my name. It was Christopher, stumbling out of the club with his arms around a boy I'd never seen before. Beautiful like him. Christopher nodded at me.

'Hey, how's it going?'

I just stood and stared.

Christopher's friend lost his balance and lolled back against him, glanced at me and then back to Christopher.

'Is there, like, weirdness here?'

341

'Course not,' Christopher said. 'We're cool, right, Stephen?'

I stammered out something stupid. I think I told him that of course we were cool, nothing was weird, and I hoped they'd have a great night. 'Just gonna go home,' I finished, smiling vacantly, 'drink some arsenic.' Christopher said that sounded nice. I watched them swaying down the sidewalk together. He mumbled something into his friend's hair.

'The Valley!' the guy said. 'That's so cute. Did he grow up on a farm?'

At the end of the night, I was down by the waterfront, sitting on a wooden pier with my feet knocking over the edge. The air smelled like gas stations and old fish. Ryan was gazing into the horizon and babbling on about string theory. I'd dragged him out of his room at the guys' dorm so he could join me on this hellish walking tour of misery. Now I couldn't keep my eyes open.

Ryan poked me in the head. 'Stephen, you're missing it.' Missing what? Oh. Sunrise over the harbour.

'Think I got dumped tonight.' My voice was like something crushed under a tyre.

I was expecting him to say something dismissive. Instead he reached up and very tentatively stroked my shoulder blade through my coat, like a small child trying to make friends with some large and dangerous animal.

'Poor little muffin,' Ryan said gravely.

I was strangely moved, but at the same time couldn't help laughing. He shrugged in his twitchy way. 'My grandmother says that.'

'Nice grandmother.'

I closed my eyes against the cold wind off the water, sound of seagulls fighting over food scraps. Wondered how I was going to find the strength to drag myself home.

Then it was Saturday morning about a week after Halloween and I was shuffling aimlessly along the shore. There was no sand for a beach, just slabs of stone and some wind-blasted pines; across the harbour you could see hills thick with coloured leaves and a clutter of houses and office buildings that was Dartmouth, the purgatorial twin city. Ryan was with me. His turn to haul me out of bed so I could keep him company on a long and pointless walk around the city.

Ryan was looking especially awful that day: acid wash jeans and a yellow polo shirt with his own musty sneaker footprint across the front. Like he'd picked the closest thing off the floor and pulled it over himself. This is exactly what he'd done, of course – I'd seen Ryan getting dressed before, fresh out of the shower in his dorm room, so wrapped up in explaining his lecturer's inadequate methods that he didn't seem to notice he wasn't wearing anything.

Pale and smooth and graceful like a marble Jesus. It had surprised me, that body.

Then he'd realised and thrown a towel over my head, made me sit blinded on the edge of his bed like a damp terrycloth ghost until he was decent.

Light was glaring off the rocks. I kept my sunglasses on. Ryan had left the trench coat at home and the wind was making him shiver. I was painfully hung over, kept bumping into him as I walked, a sick swayback horse. He accused me of putting the moves on him.

'I'm just tired, you idiot,' I said.

'Probably because you were fucking that Chinese guy all night.'

I had to stop. 'He's not Chinese,' was all I could think of to say. 'And how …?'

A look of utter disgust, as if a bug had just flown into his mouth. 'Bunch of my friends saw you. All over each other at the bus stop. It was gross.'

'What friends are these, Ryan?'

He kicked at a wine bottle with an inch of red sludge still rolling sickly inside. It went spinning for a moment, then wobbled off down the side of a length of rock.

'You know, you really disappoint me, Stephen. I don't know if I should be around somebody with such low moral standards.'

'Okay, great. See ya.' I turned and headed off over an incline of sun-bleached stone, gave him the finger over my shoulder so he wouldn't follow me.

The next morning he appeared outside my apartment building with a box of Timbits.

'I don't take back what I said, of course. You really do have shockingly low moral standards.' He was looking up from my doorstep where I'd nearly tripped over him on my way out. 'But it's possible this is none of my business.'

'Gee, really?'

Ryan was around a lot that cold November. His roommate at the dorm got a girlfriend and they wanted their privacy – in fact, they wanted privacy day and night, which meant Ry ended up crashing at the blue box on a regular basis. It was cosy and companionable. Or it would have been, if he wasn't warning me every five minutes not to 'try anything'. He kept all his clothes on when he was sharing the futon with me, even that filthy trench coat. Took me a while to get used to the smell.

One night I woke up to a small choked voice from the other side of the mattress.

'People back home actually like me, you know.'

I knew what this was about. We'd been to a party that night and, as usual, Ryan could not seem to stop pissing people off. After about an hour the whole building was united against him: the girls sneering, the boys ready to put him in the hospital. He'd sneered and threatened back, but I could tell he'd had enough.

'Nobody has a problem with me where I'm from. Must be hard to believe, huh?' He sounded like he was about to cry. 'I miss them all so much. I miss my mom and dad. I miss my stupid brothers. I miss my dog. I really, really miss my dog.'

'Aw, Ry.'

He was quiet for a minute.

'Stephen, will you hug me? I mean, don't act too gay about it, but—'

'C'mere.'

We lay on our sides with our arms around each other, him in his Columbo get-up, me in a T-shirt and boxers. Ryan had shoved a pillow over his crotch, said it was in case I got a boner being this close to him, that at least he didn't want to feel it. I just laughed. He talked for a long time about the sadness of being Ryan Darby, alone in this cold country with only one friend. I stroked his frizzy hair; it crunched under my fingers like fine polyester lace.

'Ryan. Poor little muffin,' I said. We fell asleep.

Ryan avoided me after that. I tried not to take it personally.

○

November turned into December. I'd just finished an exam and was outside the Science Building wrapped in my big black overcoat, smoking and waiting for Janine. I was on an incline at the top of a set of steps.

Made me feel like I was surveying my kingdom – the Arts Building opposite with its immense historical pillars, the girls' and guys' dorms in grey stone closing the square, light reflecting off a fresh snowfall in the quad.

Then I noticed somebody marching across the square. Ryan. He was bundled into an enormous parka, the kind of thing jumpy American parents would buy their son bound for study in the frozen wastes. I watched his footprints making a dotted line through the snow. Then he was an arm's-length away – snuffling with a red-nosed cold, frowning as if I were the one who'd gone running after him. I mumbled a 'hi'.

'Here.' He shoved something into my hands. It was small, with hard corners. A box. 'It's your Christmas present.'

'I'm Jewish.' It was what I always said whenever people would get Christmassy at me. Ryan ignored this.

I turned the box over in my hands. A perfect little entity, set with careful patterns of stained wood. There was no hinge, no lid, no way into this thing.

'You gave me a cube. Hey, thanks.'

'You have to open it.' Same intense stare as the day I'd met him. He slapped his arms against his sides in the cold. I was reminded of a chicken again. Ryan started down the steps backwards, eyes fixed on my face. 'Don't be stupid, Stephen. Just open it.'

He turned and scurried off following his own tracks, so fast I wondered if the box was rigged with plastic explosives.

Janine strode out of the exam hall lighting a cigarette, in a tight red winter coat that was all black piping and buttons. She told me Ryan's gift was one of those Japanese puzzle boxes. I gave it to her so she could open it, but she just pushed the thing back at me.

'Afraid of what's in there,' she said.

We were both at a low point. *The Duchess of Malfi* was over, exams were nearly finished and the dark was slamming down earlier every day. This city seemed to be closing its doors, getting ready to kick us out.

Janine looked over my shoulder as I fooled around with the box. I shook it next to my ear. There was nothing in it. I could tell. Not even a piece of paper. Nothing but Ryan Darby craziness.

'Maybe it's a condom with a red ribbon on it,' Janine said. 'Maybe it's a cheque for a thousand bucks if you do him.'

'I'd take it. Really broke lately.'

'Bet he's got red pubes.'

He did, actually. I remembered that day in his dorm when he'd thrown the towel over my head for modesty. And, um, yeah. Like a Clydesdale. But I wasn't about to tell Janine this.

The snow made our footsteps crunch. Eleanor MacBride came out of the girls' dorm on the other side of the quad. I watched Janine's smile turn into something genuine.

I stuffed the box in a pocket of my overcoat and forgot about it.

A week later, I was on a train heading back to Riverside for Christmas break, and Eleanor was facing me with the sunset behind her head and asking how everything had changed so fast. I didn't have an answer for her.

We talked about other stuff instead. Classes. Bands. Which bars were easy to get into and which of our profs were the laziest at marking. My favourite guy would just write 'Adequate as far as you go' on everyone's papers. I said I wanted it carved on my tombstone. As we got closer to our destination, I turned quiet.

'You look like you're going to faint,' Eleanor said.

Sick dread and longing to be home were churning together inside me. I sank into my seat. 'Thought I got away.'

Eleanor reached over and squeezed my hand. I think she understood.

Chapter 28

December. Short days, long sunsets, quiet dark nights. It was three in the morning, and I was at Lana's place looking at the mirror over the bureau in her room. Our guitars were on the floor; we'd tried to have a band reunion of The Wretched Noise, but couldn't remember the words to any of the old songs.

I drew a line through the dust on the mirror glass. Photos were wedged in peeling shingles around the frame. There was a picture of Lana, a bright jolly three-year-old poised over a birthday cake. Another of her grandparents. Florence the dog as a puppy. The two of us at the prom. And one I'd never seen before.

Me and Mark. On the steps of my house in the summer. We were dressed practically the same, loose plaid shirts and jeans. I had my Walkman headphones around my neck and it looked like I was just coming out of a laugh. We were sixteen.

I sat on Lana's purple bedspread holding this picture in a little pool of light from a reading lamp. She was beside me, her arm curled around my waist. Lana eased the picture out of my hand and slid it into the pocket of my shirt.

'I don't know what you ever saw in that boy,' she said.

Eventually we made our way downstairs to the TV room, where Florence the dog lay sprawled like a rug across the floor, lightly rumbling in her sleep. Through the glass sliding doors we could see the cold white yard and black sky, a birdbath holding up an awkward wedding cake of snow. Lana was falling asleep. We lay back and were swallowed by the Kovalenkos' enormous couch with its smears of Florence hair. I shielded Lana from the glare of the TV. *A Charlie Brown Christmas* was on.

'Still in love with somebody too,' she mumbled, her eyes closed. 'Sometimes.'

'Ouch. Don't know what you see in him either.' I stretched out. 'Lana.' Traced the edges of her face. 'Too bad. Too bad we can't stay together. You and me, huh? Live somewhere nice. With our kids. And. Our ...' Drifting off.

'Boyfriends,' she said. It made me smile. I was nearly asleep, the scene assembling itself in my head. Lana and me in a white kitchen with lots of windows, long wooden tables, children setting places for each other. And boyfriends. One in charge of each kid. I supposed we'd feed them all cinnamon toast. Somewhere near our feet I could hear Florence giving off a steady current of twitches and growls – sounded like a really good dream. I opened my eyes and found somebody had thrown a blanket over us. There was light in the sky and it was a new day.

○

A few nights later, I headed out for Taggart's Cross, population 893, three towns down the highway from Riverside. Off to spend the holidays. I'd always been comfortable more or less ignoring Christmas, a tradition Mom and I had kept up from the time Stanley was still around. But this year was going to be different. My mother had a boyfriend now, and he had a family, and we were invited to stay until January.

I'd finally been introduced to Mom's movie date from the summer – she'd even dragged him down to Halifax to watch me get stabbed to death in *The Duchess of Malfi*. His name was Fred Dowd. Fred was a little older than my mother, balding and round-shouldered, with glasses and a grey cardigan that seemed permanently Velcroed to his body. If he touched Mom's elbow to guide her somewhere, it was like he was handling fine china. I was relieved at how much I actually liked the guy. Enough to follow him into my first real family Christmas.

So there we were, crammed with the whole Dowd family in an old blue and white farmhouse just off the highway. A woodstove in the kitchen devoured logs and blasted heat. The thermostats were cranked up. Dowd bodies wrapped in wool expelled warmth and breath and sounds. Windows were never allowed to open.

At dinner, we ploughed through piles of meat and potatoes, canned fruit under glops of Cool Whip for dessert. We made lame small talk with our mouths full. We listened to the Dowd men holding forth on immigration and free trade and Mulroney and the rest of it, while a dusty cuckoo clock on the dining room wall kept up a steady creaking rhythm, permanently stuck at a quarter past one. Below the clock was a picture of Christ with liquid brown eyes and folded hands, gazing up. If I was in a silly mood, I'd imagine the cuckoo bird suddenly appearing, and Jesus catching it on a long sticky tongue that unrolled like a frog's. Then I'd have to bite the inside of my cheek to keep from laughing. I'd decided to help my mother by acting as normal as possible – even went back to the Riverside guys' uniform. As far as anyone knew, I was just a regular boring kid who read a lot.

Several times a day I got my coat and escaped on my own to smoke. Nothing but pastures and woodland from the house to the horizon.

But Mom seemed happy enough, and I could just about stand it for her sake, though I don't know how thrilled the Dowds were to have me there. The adults prodded me with the same questions over and over, forgetting that they'd already asked and I'd already answered. I'd step into the TV room and the Dowd children would turn and silently stare at me until I left. If I talked too much in front of Granny Dowd, she stared as well, her mouth moving like she was chewing on gristle.

This was the first granny I'd ever met, and she was a major disappointment.

I think she was actually one of the granddad's aunts. Dusty crypt old. And nuts. She'd go skulking around the place in crocheted slippers with pom-poms on the toes, forever tied up in some piece of behind-the-scenes family resentment, hissing at one of the Dowd daughters in the upstairs hallway. I overheard her once, as I was plodding off to my little guest room to grab some time alone. She was going on about an old buried conflict, somebody's kid she didn't approve of, or possibly she was talking about a dog.

'I suppose she's proud of herself,' Granny was whispering. 'Raising *that*. I'd hang my head in shame. I certainly wouldn't sit it at the dinner table. With children. With *married* couples!'

Embarrassing overhearing these family conflicts, even if I had no idea who they were talking about. It was like the Dowds were parading around in front of me in their underwear.

Which they did, eventually. Or their pyjamas, which seemed about the same thing.

Christmas morning. My mother and I exchanged gifts in the hallway at the head of the stairs before anyone else was awake. We were fully dressed. Not into this communal pyjamas thing. I gave her a nice scarf and a gift certificate for the bookstore where Christopher worked. She got me a subscription to some kind of gay magazine. I thanked her.

'Well,' she said, blushing deeply, 'I actually thought you might prefer something a bit more … uh … raunchy. But—'

'Jeez, Mom!' I put my hand over her mouth. 'That's okay. That's fine. I don't want you looking at gay porn.'

We were whispering, glancing down the hallway. My mother started getting the giggles.

'I really hate Christmas,' I mumbled into her ear.

People emerged from their rooms, and then it was time to file downstairs with our adopted family. The gift-giving was a bit unnerving – tearing off the paper and displaying your winnings to the rest of the tribe. Fred Dowd got my mother an expensive necklace and his sisters all glanced at each other. He gave me a thesaurus, which I thought was sweet.

A few hours later, we all sat down and started passing hot dishes of meat and mush around the table. Our glasses were full of wine or grape juice. We raised them and clinked hollowly. My mother got brave after a glass of wine and starting telling the story of the Riverside elves.

'I'll get home from work and somebody's mowed the lawn. Or the leaves are swept in piles. Even the snow cleared out of the driveway. No note, no bill, no nothing.' She shrugged, smiling. 'Elves!'

'She's not kidding,' said Fred, although no one had contested my mother's story. 'I went over there once with a leaf-blower to help her clear the yard. Course that was really just an excuse to get some time alone with Maryna.' He blushed and covered her hand with his, and she giggled at him like a teenager. The rest of the table ignored this. Fred recovered. 'Anyway, I get there and – poof! It's all done.'

The Dowds nodded blandly and several people said that it was a strange thing all right. Then the brother-in-law with the beard changed the subject so he could go off on one of his rants. This time it was AIDS.

'If you ask me, anybody who's got it deserves it.' He was leaning forwards with his mouth full of winter squash. 'Kind of lifestyle that pretty well encourages disease. Thousands of, you know, *partners*. Sexual partners,' he said, dropping his voice and glancing guiltily at the children at the far end of the table. 'And now it's getting so that good, decent people can't—' I switched him off. Heard a lot worse than that.

Thousands of partners. I started smiling into my mashed potatoes. Could you fill an auditorium with them? A convention centre? Jeez, mine could all hang out with the coats in the hall closet and they'd still be comfortable. Of course, if I included all the people I'd only thought about sleeping with. Now that would be a party. The underwear guys from the Sears catalogue trooping into this banquet hall, filling up tables. It was Christmas, so I put them all in Santa hats.

Then beside me I heard my mother whisper the man's name, fiercely. 'Joe!' His wife nudged him. Her eyes darted to my side of the table. Joe glanced at me, startled, caught. So did the guy next to him. And his wife. And Granny Dowd. And … oh, no.

The whole table was looking in my direction. The whole room. I felt cold, suddenly aware of the food in my mouth, this pulpy mass.

Joe cleared his throat. 'Although I probably don't have … all the facts and … uh …' He changed the subject, started talking about Oliver North, but you could tell his heart wasn't in it.

I moved the mush on my plate around. Didn't dare look up.

They knew. They all knew. Mom must have told them before we'd even come here, probably to stop Mr World Policy from mouthing off like this. And of course somebody had shared the news with Granny. Sneering at me when I talked, getting freaked out if I brushed past her. 'If I'd raised *that* ...' *That. It.* All made sense now.

Flat scraps of turkey seething in brown gravy, red gore of cranberry sauce still bearing the imprint of the can it had slid from. We were staying past New Year's. Another week to go.

Then something occurred to me. Like a message from an angel, clarity descending from a cold, perfect place.

You don't have to do this.

That's right. Walk away. This is a crazy old lady who hasn't actually met that many people in her life. This is a family under strain, suddenly coping with two potential grown-up members. Nothing to do with you. Leave now.

'Mom,' I said. It was quiet at the table. I still hadn't taken my eyes off my plate. 'I think I forgot some stuff back at the house. I'm gonna borrow your car and go, okay?' I stood up. 'I'm gonna go now.'

There was a flurry of protests behind me. I didn't listen, went upstairs for my suitcase and coat. Got to the front door before I realised I didn't have the keys to the car. Shit. My clear sense of purpose was getting muddy. I stared through the gloom at the dining room doorway, lit up with its long table full of Dowds, its cuckoo clock and Jesus.

Then someone was bustling towards me in the dark.

'Just let me get my coat.'

'Mom!' She had her purse clamped under her arm, a ring of keys in her fist.

'Well, I'm not staying if you're leaving.'

'Don't …' I couldn't take my eyes off those keys. 'I want to be by myself. And what about Fred? He really likes you.'

'Oh, honey. He doesn't know me. Not really.'

'Well, maybe, but …' I felt so sorry for Fred. 'Give him a chance. You got a good thing going with this guy.' I reached down and took my mother's hand. The hand with the ring of keys. 'Mom, can I?' I shifted the car keys off the little chrome circle and closed my fingers around them. She looked wounded. I gave her hand a squeeze. Turned to go.

'No.' My mother grabbed my arm. 'I'm sorry,' she said helplessly. 'I know I'm being clingy.'

Hadn't we done this before? Weren't we always doing this? Back and forth. Round and round. Please go. Don't leave. Please. Don't.

'We never see each other anymore.' She took hold of my wrist.

'Course we do. You're up to visit all the time.' I tried to break away. She was still holding me. 'And nobody else I know calls their mother practically every day. Look, I'm not complaining. But … oh fuck.'

'No need to swear.'

'Please let me go.'

'I'm not stopping you.' My wrist was still in her grip. Attached to the hand with the car keys. We stood not moving, eyes locked on each other.

'Mom, please. I'm not even gonna stay in Halifax forever. There's so many other places I want to see. I might end up in Toronto or Montreal. Or the States. Maybe even London. Paris. Who knows?' I shut my eyes, but kept talking. 'Now I just want to drive to Riverside.'

I heard the closet doors behind us sliding open and the hangers jangling. Then Fred Dowd was beside my mother, stuffed into his winter coat.

'Listen, Stephen, you're obviously not comfortable here. Why don't we all go somewhere together? Your house in Riverside? Or is there another place?'

I grinned at him. 'Jeez, Fred, you're so nice!'

He put a hand on his glasses. 'Oh, well ...'

'You are,' my mother said, and she reached over and traced the edge of Fred's ear. I looked away. He was smiling at her shyly, like a boy.

'Guys,' I said. 'I'm gonna go now. By myself. Okay? Just want to be alone. No big deal.'

Fred stood with his arm around my mother. 'Now, I'm sure we can all ...'

But she was nodding bravely. 'Okay, sweetheart. Okay.' She threw her arms around me. 'Oh, God, I—'

'I know. I love you too, Maryna.' I kissed her, just under her eye.

'So much,' she said.

I kissed the other side of her face. Then I unwound myself, stumbled out the door past piles of Dowd boots drooling old snow on a mat. I hugged my mother again, shook hands with Fred, told them I'd be back soon. I wouldn't.

The cold hit me as soon as I opened the door. A few white flakes were starting to fall, twisting and looping in the wind. Behind me my mother and Fred stood framed in the doorway, a plastic wreath behind their heads, all the windows of the house lit up with orange electric candles. Mom and Fred waved as I drove away and I watched their figures get smaller and then disappear.

The roads were quiet. Houses were glowing with colour on the still, white fields. Soft blue and green, crazy whorehouse red, flashing lights, twinkling lights, lights blinking from under a cover of snow.

Our own house was dark, and very cold. We'd left the heat on just high enough so the pipes wouldn't freeze. I liked it that way. I read until

I fell asleep in my own bed. My dreams were so vivid, there were times I was sure I was awake.

A funny mix-up of the daydream about the banquet with all the people you'd slept with, or wanted to, and that vision I'd had of Lana and me feeding a room full of people. It was the same kitchen with wooden tables. Lana was there, and a man who loved her. Mom was at a table with Fred and Sheila and my two sisters, Becky and Sarah. They were college age in this dream, beautiful women. Stanley was there too. And the underwear guys. The girls from the rec room at Tracey's party sharing a table with Janine and Christopher and Adam. Everybody talking, passing plates. The people kept coming and the tables kept multiplying, but nobody was crowded and there was enough for everyone.

Where was I in this dream? Standing at the stove. I was old, maybe thirty. A little girl was perched on a high stool beside me. I was shadowing her hands with mine because I didn't want her to burn herself, but she didn't need me. She wasn't going to make the same mistakes I did.

'I can do it myself, Daddy,' she said.

When I woke up I was almost laughing and it wasn't Christmas anymore.

Chapter 29

It was quiet and cold. There'd been a snowfall during the night and the town had that stillness over it – like a new planet. I wanted to get out there. I made myself a coffee and took it with me. Tree branches were outlined in feathery white. The only tracks were mine. I walked to the riverbank behind the elementary school and had a smoke, making sure I pushed the ashes deep into the snow. I didn't want to spoil anything.

The dream was still with me, like an extra layer of warmth. Who was the little girl's mother? Lana? Or was the kid some kind of metaphor? I closed my eyes and tried to get the sense of it back – the room, the tables, the people. It was a good sign, having a dream like that.

The river was crusted over with a slushy layer of ice. I had another cigarette. My coffee was cold, but I pretended it wasn't.

I decided to take a walk around town, maybe go bother the Kovalenkos later. Turned for a sentimental look back at the river and the mountain. There was somebody on the sidewalk about a block away. Ruining it. Big winter coat, tractor boots, hands shoved into his pockets. He never remembered to bring gloves.

Mark.

I froze. 'If I see you again, I'm gonna fucking kill you.' That's what he'd said.

Mark was walking with his head lowered, his shoulders hunched. Then he slowed down. He stopped. Two hundred feet of sidewalk between us.

'Hey!' he said. 'Hey, Stephen!' He broke into a jog.

I was about to get my head kicked in. *Run, you idiot. Move. Go now.*

I turned and started pounding down the street. Didn't even know where I was going. I could hear him, behind me, gaining. Everything was coated in snow – sometimes it stayed packed under my feet, at other times it seemed to want to make me slide. I jumped over a snow bank, pelted up another block past quiet houses, holding the coffee mug close. Back at the elementary school again. I'd done a loop. My breath was tearing at me, I had a pain in my side and I was sweating into my overcoat. *Keep running.* The playground, where I'd got beaten up as a kid so many times. Mark was yelling. I couldn't make out words. *Go.* Past the old jungle gym. The swings.

One leg went sprawling out from under me as I skidded on a patch of ice. I fell, still clutching the mug, felt a splash of cold coffee as the last drops hit my face. He was practically on top of me now. I crawled backwards like a crab.

'It was an accident.' I didn't even know what I'd meant by that.

'Fucking relax.' He was breathing so hard it sounded like dry heaves. 'I'm not gonna hurt you.'

I grabbed hold of one of the metal poles supporting the swing set and pulled myself upright. Mark was shaking with a smoker's hack, the vapour of his breath hitting the cold morning air. He spat a wad of yellowish phlegm into the snow.

Then he paced around, taking deep drags off a cigarette. 'Not allowed to do this in the house anymore,' he said. 'The baby's coming in a couple months. We don't know what kind yet.' He stopped for another round of coughing, then straightened up, swiping at his nose with the back of his hand. 'Oh. Stacey's living with us now. At my place. With me and Mom and Krystal.'

'Congratulations.' I kept the bars of the metal frame that anchored the swing set between us. His face was fuller. What was she feeding him, bacon grease? I probably looked like something skeletal and alien in my big, dark overcoat.

Mark was holding his pack of cigarettes towards me at arm's length, shaking it. I stayed where I was. He shrugged and tossed me the box. I took one and slid it back towards him over the snow. Beyond the playground, I could see rows of wooden and brick houses lined up together, smoke unrolling from the chimneys. Then, the highway, the north mountain in the distance closing us off.

Mark watched me light up. 'So,' he said.

I waited.

He clasped his reddened hands together. 'My minister told me I should forgive you.'

I sputtered, gulped down cold air. 'What? He …' Mark was staring at me. He looked intent, serious. I started to laugh, but it was like reeling from a punch. 'He told you to *forgive* me. Oh, fuck. Oh, Jesus *Christ*.'

'You think this is funny.'

'No. No, I think it's fucked up.'

'So you don't see anything wrong.' His arms were folded now. 'With what you did.'

'I did … I did a lot that was *stupid*. But …' I'd started pacing as well, disoriented, too much energy. 'I mean, did you hurt your foot on my ribcage or something? Cause, yeah, I'm real sorry about that.'

'Don't forget who got you out of the fucking river.'

'How did I get in there in the first place? You hit me with a tree!'

He looked at the ground, his face cloudy, ignoring me.

I risked a step towards him. 'I was supposed to be starting a new life. You know, college. The city. A chance with people who didn't know me. I looked like some little victim …'

'So I ruined your first day of school, huh.' A quick jerk of his neck, as if he was spitting. 'I ruined your class picture.'

'Fuck you, McAllister.'

'Sorry, man. Bet you wanted to look pretty. For all the other faggots.'

'No, the arm was a total dick magnet. *Man.*'

We were walking around each other in circles now, stiff-legged, like dogs about to jump into a snarling fight. Our boot tracks had beaten down the fresh snow and left brown smears of gravel from the road, trails of cigarette ash.

'Tell your minister to go fuck himself, Mark. I had to take painkillers. I couldn't sleep …'

He made a violent dismissive gesture. 'I asked you to be my best man. You remember that? Then, like, an hour later you got your faggot hands all over me.'

I glanced down at my hands reflexively. Wondered when Mark would get tired of his new word.

'That's not how it was.'

But then I realised I didn't know how it was. Not for him. I felt a rush of heat to my face. That night, the way I must have been talking and acting – slow and drunk with sudden clumsy movements, slurring and pawing at him.

Mark threw his cigarette into the snow. He took a step towards me and I took a step back.

'Touch me and it's assault.'

He gave no sign that he'd heard. I shrank against the swing set and he kept coming closer.

Then he had the collar of my overcoat in his fists, half-choking me.

'It's assault. I'm serious, McAllister,' I said, quick and breathless. 'You're too old for Juvie now. You'll go to jail. Do you get that?' His eyes went very cold. My head was pressed against the swing-set's beam. I wondered if he'd crack our skulls together. I'd seen him do that once.

I kept talking, couldn't stop. 'You'll be in jail when your fucking baby's born. You redneck piece of shit. You should be in jail now, for what you did to me. Only reason you're not is cause—'

'Yeah? Why?' He gripped my collar tighter.

'Cause it was bad enough the first time. Didn't want to keep reliving it.'

Mark's lip curled over his teeth in a snarl. When he spoke his voice was quiet and deliberate. 'You were lying to me. For years.'

I didn't say anything. I was sweating.

'Everybody knew,' he said. 'The whole town. The whole Valley. Oh, that McAllister, he's so stupid. So. Unbelievably. Stupid.' He knocked my head back against the swing set frame in time to his words. 'Doesn't even know his best friend's an ass-fucking faggot.'

Mark let go of my collar and I braced myself against the rail. He was still leaning into me.

'I defended you so many times. I said you were just shy. I said you were weird. I said you had a girlfriend.' He shook his head. 'Bet they were all laughing at me, huh? Bet you were laughing worse than anybody.'

My hands went to my collar, my neck. 'Laughing at you? Jesus ...'

He took a step back. 'Your friend the big, stupid moron. Takes care of bullies for you. Believes whatever you tell him. I guess I was useful, huh?'

Mark pulled the sleeves of his coat down to cover his raw fingers. The same thing he used to do when he was a little kid.

'Mark, you don't really think that, do you?'

'Fuck. I don't know. I don't know what was going on here.' He gestured from me to him and back again.

I told him I didn't know either, but that I'd thought we were friends. He stared at me for a minute. Coldly, up and down.

'Know what?' Mark said. 'When I was a kid. If I had to draw a picture of my family, or write a composition or something for school, I'd always put you in there. Me, my mom and dad, Krystal, and my friend Stephen.' Such contempt, the way he said my name. His head dropped lower. 'You used to lend me those books. I'd lie and say I read them. I didn't. But I kept them perfect. Not even fingerprints. Cause they were yours.' He glanced up at me. 'And now ... I mean, what was all that about? Were you, like, watching me? When I was changing and stuff? Were you just waiting for a chance to—?'

'Aw, no, man. Don't think that. Makes it sound so ...'

Something was gripping me, across my chest. It hurt.

He scratched at the back of his neck. I watched Mark's hands, the knuckles and finger joints white in this frigid air. He'd never wear gloves. I'd seen him out clearing his driveway at twenty below, clutching the handle of the snow shovel with raw, frost-bitten fingers. Then I remembered my mother's story about the Riverside elves, and something clicked into place.

'Mark? Have you been doing yard work? For my mother? And not telling her?'

'Yeah.' He shrugged. 'Just wanted to make it up to her somehow. I went to your place to apologise and she wouldn't let me in the house.'

'I don't get it. You wanted to apologise to my mother? For what?'

'What do you think, dummy?' he said softly. 'I nearly killed her son.'

Snow crystals caught the sunlight on the top ridge of the playground fence. Mark turned away. 'I lied to you too, Stephen.' His voice sounded distant in the quiet. 'When I told you I only got you out of the river because of your mom. I mean, you think I really had time to have a little debate with myself up there?' He glanced back at me and twisted away again. 'I didn't think at all. Just panicked. Saw you go into the water and … I would've done anything. And I got this idea maybe that meant I was queer too. So I freaked out. I lost it.'

'That's your excuse?'

'No. No, man. There's no excuse.'

An engine muttered in the distance. On the street beyond, a snow plough was rolling along, leaving twin heaps of chewed-up gravel and lumpy white shapes lined against the pavement.

'Okay,' Mark said. 'Okay, here's what's really been bugging me. Here's what I don't get.'

I watched him. He'd backed away from the swings and was standing with the sky behind him, shuffling in place.

'You were drunk off your ass. Saying all kinds of shit. I don't know what to believe.'

'What … What did I …?'

'Stephen. This is serious. I mean … are you … do you really …' Mark squeezed his eyes shut. Then he seemed to gain control over himself. 'Do you actually love me?'

Both of us sober. Morning in a playground, hazy sunshine on the snow. I swallowed, couldn't find my voice for a second.

'Do I? Yes.'

He ran his hands through his hair, staring into the trampled white ground. I clutched at the swing set frame again. Needed to hold on to something.

'See, I believe you.' Mark was squirming into himself. 'Stacey tells me that all the time. And I say it to her too. But I don't know. I get the feeling it's because we think we're supposed to. We're together more than a year, and there's this baby. But you. I mean, who knows me better?'

He'd moved towards me, very close, brought his hand up, careful and hesitant. I thought for a second he was going to touch my face, but instead Mark gave me a little punch on the arm, same as always. It barely connected.

'What a joke.' He sounded so lost. 'What a joke on both of us, man.'

I just nodded. His hand had drifted down to my elbow and I felt the pressure of his fingers through my coat as he held on.

He closed his eyes, tightened his grasp.

'It's impossible. You know that, right? Makes me sick. Physically sick. To think of you … like that. Even for a second.' Mark's head bobbed as if someone were pressing on it. 'It's not because of you,' he added, talking fast. 'It's not you as, like, a person. I mean, I do kind of … love you. In … in a way.'

'I know.'

Mark leaned in close and rested his forehead against mine. Maybe it was so he wouldn't have to look me in the eye.

'There were times, past few months … I thought I could actually make myself do it. Force myself. It'd be the perfect punishment.'

'Punishment? Jesus, Mark.'

'But, I can't. I just can't.'

We were gripping each other's arms now, shuffling like dancing bears.

'Mark. Don't worry. That's not what I want. It wouldn't work.'

He'd lifted his head from mine and was trying to force a smile. 'It's cause I like Bon Jovi, huh?'

'No,' I said. 'It's because I don't forgive you.' Talking like I was in a trance. I didn't know it was true until I'd said it.

Mark nodded. He let his hands drop and moved back, away from me.

'Do you think …?' He cleared his throat. 'Do you think you ever will? Forgive me? I mean, someday?'

'I don't know.'

He rocked on his heels, avoiding my eyes. 'Hope you do. I want you to meet my kid. Think you'd be a good influence. All the stuff you read.' He seemed so shy. 'Even thought maybe, if we ever got to be friends again, I could ask you to be godfather.'

I felt myself smiling into the snow. Buying books for Mark's child, watching this person grow up. I was flattered. But I was also pretty sure it was against the rules.

'Don't think that'll work, Mark. I'm not exactly a Christian.'

The corner of his mouth twitched. 'A fairy godfather, then.'

I leaned back, knocking my skull against the swing set railing. '*Jeez*, man …'

'Sorry.' He laughed to himself, lamely. Then a little movement of his head, a long breath outwards.

'Aw, Stephen. Listen. For what it's worth, I hope you do find somebody who's gonna love you back. *He'd* …' Mark paused. The word seemed to taste bad in his mouth. '… he'd be a lucky guy.'

I realised Mark was walking away, stepping backwards, his eyes on me.

'I gotta go home,' he said. 'I'm needed.' He held up his hand. A wave, or a salute. 'February. The baby's due in February. You have to meet my kid. Please.'

'Course. Course I will, Mark.'

'Cool. I'll see ya then.' He stopped. 'Goodbye, Stephen.'

'Goodbye.' I wasn't sure if I'd said this out loud. He turned to go, striding away, same as when he'd first come into view by the river: head lowered, hands thrust into his pockets. I settled onto one of the swings. The only other thing moving was a black dog at the edge of the playground, stepping carefully over the snow. I felt like I was getting squeezed to death by something I couldn't see.

I'm not sure how I got back to my house. I remember calling the Dowds and leaving a message that I was holding on to Mom's car for another day. After that, I just sat at the kitchen table, watching the shadows get longer and the sun fade in the windows.

The flashing light from the answering machine on the counter seemed to be getting brighter as the kitchen sank into darkness. Who would want to talk to us that badly? I forced myself out of the chair, stiff and creaky like an old man, rewound the tape and pushed the play button.

Ryan Darby's voice filled the room – nerved-up, nasally, ready to pick a fight with the whole world. It made me laugh.

'It's me.' An angry sigh. 'It's Christmas. It's Christmas and I'm not home with my family. I'm at a lousy stupid youth hostel. Because … oh, forget it.' That was the first message. How many more? At least five. Inertia made me listen to them all. Ryan was having a one-sided argument with me, with himself, his voice thicker and more slurred after each brisk little beep. He was at the Harbour Front Youth Hostel, he said. The college wouldn't let him stay at the dorm over the holidays. And he couldn't go home to his family in the States because he was having emotional problems. I was the cause of his emotional problems, he told me.

'Goddammit, Stephen.' Second last message. I could barely make him out. 'You're so stupid. I don't know how anybody could be as stupid as you and still be alive. Why didn't you open that box? Did you just throw it away or something?'

He sounded like he was on the verge of tears. Another beep, and he was wishing me a merry Christmas and happy Hanukkah, even though he said he knew I didn't celebrate either one. He finished by telling me he hoped I'd have a good life. And that I was still stupid. There were a couple of other messages. Sheila and the girls calling from Montreal. Lana. Then nothing.

So Ryan Darby was having a meltdown in some Halifax hostel and he'd apparently spent Christmas Day harassing me about it. What was the deal with that stupid box? I couldn't even remember what I'd done with it.

No, wait. It was here, in a pocket of my overcoat. I took it out. Still perfectly seamless, lidless, covered in tiny intricate patterns. I found I was squeezing and pushing at the edges with my fingernails. Then something started to move. A side of the box slid downwards a few millimetres. I fooled around with it for a while, nudging little tiles of wood around until the top of the box glided off. Easy. So what was in the damn thing?

Nothing. It was empty.

Or maybe not. There was some kind of pattern on the bottom. Letters? I held the box up to the window, caught the last of the afternoon light.

Oh, shit. Written on the bottom, in felt marker. Very messy, very crude. Almost illegible.

'I love you.'

On the inner sides of the box, scrawled in even messier letters: 'Ryan loves Stephen.' There wasn't a little heart, was there? Yes, of course there was. And a smiley face.

Fuck. It wasn't fair. I didn't want to hurt this freak. I was pacing around the kitchen, bouncing from corner to corner, the box still in my hand, saying 'I love you' every time I looked at it. Something a twelve-year-old girl would put together and give to a boy, who would show all his friends and laugh at her.

Outside now, locking the front door, heading for the car. The city was a two-hour drive away. I could be there by six, ask Ryan what the hell he'd meant by this box myself.

I pulled out of the driveway. Packed snow groaned under the tyres. Out to the main road, past houses I'd trudged by a thousand times on my way to school. Then I hit the highway. Goodbye, Riverside! Goodbye.

It was almost dark. There was nothing on the radio but Christmas carols and country songs. Mom's terrible music lay in a clutter of cassettes shoved into the glove compartment. Phil Collins, Steve Winwood. No thanks. But there was an old Big Country tape near the back that she'd borrowed off me way back when. I eased it into the cassette player. Sing-along tunes from the bad old days. When the tape went quiet, I kept singing. Long, white fields gave way to scrubby pines, miles and miles of nothing. The road to the city.

So what was I going to say to this poor dork? Sorry, Ry. It makes me sick to think of you like that. Even for a second. You know how it is, man. He'd probably still be in his pjs. I'd seen him knocking around his dorm room like that at four in the afternoon. Blue flannel with a pattern of comets, moons and stars. They were actually girls' pyjamas, but he got extremely prickly and defensive when I'd tried to tell him this.

The puzzle box lay on the passenger seat with its lid off, still telling me that it loved me. Well, box, I like you too. And I also liked my space alien friend Ryan. I remembered the time he'd helped me clean up the apartment before my mom came to visit. We'd decided the dishes were too far gone to save, so we'd lugged all these plates and bowls and saucers across town and chucked them off the top of the ferry terminal building and into the harbour at three in the morning. I'd miss times like that. I'd miss him.

That day when we were walking along the shore and he was driving me crazy, going on about my moral standards or whatever. I think I'd known then that he was really just feeling jealous and left out.

And what was I feeling?

Ryan Darby, shivering into the wind in his awful yellow polo shirt, pale like uncooked poultry, squinting and twitching his head as if he were expecting the whole world to come up and attack him. I'd looked at the blue veins on the undersides of his elbows and felt something unbearably tender sweeping over me. 'Don't kick sand in his face,' I'd wanted to say, though there was no sand, only slabs of white rock. 'Everybody, please just try to understand. Don't hurt him. He's with me.'

No, no, no. Imagine if I ended up with Ryan. We'd be arguing half the time, just like we did now, but I wouldn't be able to walk away from it and go, 'Jeez, what a weirdo.' Because he'd be my weirdo.

And goddammit, he still looked like Eric Stoltz fucked a chicken.

A nice chicken. A strangely graceful bird. I could see why Eric had stopped and picked her out from the flock, said hello.

Such a temptation, to start something. Normal life would seem exciting and precious for a while. Maybe I'd bring him back to Riverside. Even Taggart's Cross. Go into a big Hollywood smooch on the front steps of the Dowd house, give Granny a good old heart attack.

Or I might just sit beside him on his hostel bed and hold his hand, let him talk until I understood everything. Would that be better? The smart thing to do? Which would make Ryan happier, being loved or understood? Imagine if you could have both.

But there was another option, lurking alongside these. I could be cruel. Cruel to him, like so many people had been cruel to me. It was possible. It might even be likely. Maybe I'd been banged around too much. Maybe I was rotten now.

I'd made good time. Only five thirty and I was already nearing the city. But I realised I'd had nothing to eat all day and my head felt like it was suspended above me on a string. I pulled into one of those gas stations with a truck stop restaurant attached, filled up the car and paid with a credit card. It was so cool, being an adult. In the restaurant I flipped the menu open and closed, spun around on a stool by the counter, too jumpy to settle down and eat real food. I convinced the waitress to bring me cinnamon toast instead. It was nice. Tasted like home. But home had its limits and I needed to be somewhere else.

I floated back to the car, feeling light and new born. The sky was a deep royal blue, with a thin crescent of yellow moon, stars just beginning to show.

Of course I didn't drive all the way out here to be cruel and give Ryan the talk. Getting dropped on your head doesn't make you rotten. Bruised, yes; addled, maybe. But bruises come from outside, and rottenness is yours alone. Something different was going to happen. I wasn't sure what.

I lit a cigarette and leaned with my elbows on the top of the car, looking down. There was the highway, a swathe of grey with its broken line curving past a blue hill layered in trees and snow. After that the sweep of the land opening up into the distance, with the dark water just beyond. I could see the lights of the city nestled in the harbour's curve, softly glowing white and yellow and orange. I lived there now.

In a few days, it would be 1988. Twelve years left before Armageddon, in case you believe that sort of thing.

If the end of the world came, would we all be like that, just a bunch of little coloured lights swept into the water and the dark, everything mixed together and dissolving?

Or maybe it wouldn't be cold and dark. We'd be sitting at the same table in a room that kept expanding to fit us all.

I swung myself into the car and pulled onto the highway, blasting 'Fields of Fire' out the windows. Guitars that sounded like bagpipes. After a few seconds, I started singing along again. I coasted around the curve of the hill, moving into the horizon, out of sight of anyone who might be watching from the parking lot above. Twin red and white beams on the back of the car, another set of lights heading into the city.

I could say more, but I won't.

Acknowledgements

It would be impossible to thank everyone who contributed to this book's development, but I'll see what I can do. Firstly, the brilliant Brendan Richardson was with me every step of the way for over two years, sharing feedback, editing suggestions, encouragement, and his vast knowledge of all things eighties – I can't thank him enough. Thanks also to Ben Fergusson, who read early drafts of the first chapters and provided detailed feedback, Maryna Pilkiw for help with Ukrainian phrases, and Lee Sutton of Sixteen Labs for his (unpaid) work setting up my website. My agent Jonathan Williams saw the book's potential early on and promoted it tirelessly, and I owe a major debt of gratitude to Ciara Doorley for her insightful editing, and of course to everyone else at Hachette Ireland. I would also like to thank Carrie King, June Caldwell, and all the lovely people at the Irish Writers' Centre for their support during the Novel Fair 2012 and afterwards. I'm grateful as well to Gerald Dawe, Carlo Gébler and the gang at the Oscar Wilde Centre at Trinity College Dublin, especially the magnificent Workshop B 2011, and to

Helen Bovaird Ryan and the gang at Pen to Paper, Mount Merrion. Big thanks as well to those who read the manuscript and commented: Peter Sheridan, Eibhear Walshe, Patrick Brownlee, Mikael Dam, Marni Amirault, Steve Parks, Rose Merrill, Miriam Gormally, Lisan Jutras, Alice Blondel, Edel Corrigan, Marianne O'Rourke, Sandra Furlong, Bernice Barrington, Sheena Lambert, David Vaughan, Richard Barnes, and Fiona Cameron. Most importantly, I owe everything and more to my patient husband Aodhan, without whose loving support I would not have been able to either begin or complete this book. Finally, love and thanks to my family and friends (Leigha Worth, I want a signed copy of your next book; Alice Brown, the same goes for you), as well as the infamous Library Bar group, and anybody who danced at my wedding. Thanks all.

Reading is so much more than the act of moving from page to page. It's the exploration of new worlds; the pursuit of adventure; the forging of friendships; the breaking of hearts; and the chance to begin to live through a new story each time the first sentence is devoured.

We at Hachette Ireland are very passionate about what we read and what we publish. And we'd love to hear what you think about our books. If you'd like to let us know, or to find out more about us and our titles, please visit www.hachette.ie or our Facebook page www.facebook.com/hachetteireland or follow us on Twitter @HachetteIre.